# Fires in Their Wake

## Faye Perez

*T*o a new generation of unsung heroes. May you burn too bright for
this world.

# FOREWORD

All good fiction has its roots in reality. While I am aware that many use books as a means to escape this reality, the stories we read also have the power to shape this world. I, as an author, have a responsibility to my readers to represent them and the issues they face in respectful ways. That being said, this novel contains various sensitive topics including: domestic violence, sexual assault, sex and labor trafficking, slavery, pedophilia, bigotry, medical trauma, gun/weapon use, death, and violence. None of these topics are intentionally depicted in a graphic or crude manner. Many of these topics are only briefly and vaguely mentioned. However, I would be remiss if I did not give some warning beforehand. Given these topics, I would recommend this book for readers sixteen and older. A chapter by chapter breakdown of content warnings can be found on my website www.fayeperez.com for those interested.

Please take care of yourself.

Happy reading,

Faye Perez

THE WORLD OF
ODNECUS

INANIS

KOLASI

LABEZ

SOLVANA

TYRIA

GERECAE

SVLANA

LUCERAN

VOLNI

MILLAVIA

KRAYTHA

ELESKAAV

Inanis
Summer of 2484

## One

# ANGER IS THE BEST FUEL FOR A WOMAN...WELL, THAT AND HUMAN FLESH

## CW: Sexual harassment

A severed head rolled past Perrianna's lacquered toes. The cherry red polish was stained a darker shade of crimson as blood splattered onto the cement beneath her bare feet. Perri felt bile rise in her throat as the stench of the place hit her. It had been little over a week since she had fed, and the scent, in all of its gruesome glory, was tantalizing. She swallowed hard in an attempt to ignore the emptiness of her stomach.

A scrawny Hunan man scooped up the head into a wooden box, full to the brim with body parts. Perri knew that this place could afford the robotic janitors that cleaned the streets of every city, but she suspected that the higher ups enjoyed watching the Humans struggle. As the man bent down, his fingers shook, threatening to spill the contents of the box onto the floor. Blood was caked into every crevice of his scarred hands. He tried to avert his eyes away from Perri, but even shackled she was a forest fire: disorientingly hypnotic in her deadly beauty.

As she was shoved past him, she bared her fangs, tracing her tongue over her lips. The man jerked backwards and stumbled into the wall behind him. A smirk flitted over Perri's face and her bright blue eyes flashed in amusement. Her blue curls bounced. The guard charged with monitoring Perri hardly found the exchange laughable however. A ring at the base of his hairline, in front of his left ear flashed blue. His fingers danced in front of him as he pulled up a screen only visible to him and typed in a command.

The golden bracers that clashed with the gray on her body tightened around Perri's wrists, delivering a shock. She hissed as her muscles spasmed. A metallic tang sat on her tongue, reminding her of the time she took too many pills with her friends in Sanctus. She whipped around to snarl at the guard for daring to shock her, but a command was already leaving his chapped lips.

"Save it for the Pit," he growled.

*If he knew who I truly were under this shitty makeup, he wouldn't dare to be so disrespectful. He would fear for his fucking life.*

Nevertheless, she bit her tongue and kept her thoughts to herself.

Above them, the ceiling shuddered. The lights flickered as each body hit the dirt floor above. As they wound around the labyrinth of halls, she suddenly found herself wishing she had paid more attention years ago. In her best dress, a date had the audacity to bring her here, to the Pit, the arena where the worst of the worst criminals fought for the enjoyment of wealthy patrons. She had paid little attention to the "Human Gauntlet" which was supposedly nothing more than an appetizer meant to kill off some of the most unappetizing Humans crowding the traditional prisons. Instead, she had been trying to find herself a drink and a way out of the date without alerting her security that she had snuck out. When she defeatedly returned, she was oh so pleasantly informed that the boy had bet nearly every credit he owned on his favored Demon Champion. Credits that he had promised to use later that night on drugs. As the air filled with the scent of sweat and sweets, the main event began. And while killing blows were strictly prohibited, the spear of ice that the Vitare produced did seem to accidentally pierce that Demon at the right angle. It is hard to tell with Vitares they'd argue, given that they're just genetically modified Humans. Regardless, watching the meltdown her date had after learning he lost all his credits was enough to make her leave early. If only she had known back then that she would end up back here she might have forced herself to watch the rest of the matches.

The faint sounds of dying rang through the air. Their whimpers and groans echoed down the empty hall. As Perri was shoved around the corner, the unanswered cries for help grew louder. Along the edges of the hallway Humans lay, fading in and out of consciousness. Some of the lucky ones were already dead. Perri could smell it. This is where the Pit Masters dumped both those who awaited the horrors of the Pit and the few who survived it. Regardless, they all would meet the kiss of death soon. After all, there was no point in wasting resources on Humans.

More blood coated the soles of Perri's feet as the hunger throbbed in her veins. Yet, she couldn't let that distract her. In moments the shackles would be taken off of her wrists and she would be tossed into the Pit to fight and then, the Pit Masters would place their bids on her. If she didn't get a bid, she risked execution. Not that that would happen.

A Human woman reached from the shadows to grasp Perri's ankle. Frail, dirty fingers tried to cling to the flawless brown skin that shone like old copper money, but Perri kicked the hand away with a huff. A hoarse cry fell from the lips of the woman. Perri paid no mind.

As she was forced further down the slight incline of the hall, the people in the shadows vanished and the throbbing hunger in her veins subsided slightly. At the end of the corridor, a set of double doors were propped open. Even from here the crowd could be heard over the blaring rock music. The stage was set for her entrance.

Perri held her head high and puffed out her chest. Her gait changed and grew more confident with each step that she took. Even in her dirty, days old jumpsuit, she looked less like she was about to fight and more like she was about to step foot onto the familiar territory of a fashion runway.

As she stepped through the doors into the Pit, the crowd jeered. The patrons all stood high above the arena, leaning in to see the newest competitor. Cameras floated around in the air, broadcasting Perri's figure onto large screens around the edges of the Pit. A smooth male voice called out over the arena.

"Introducing, in the west corner, Arianla Stillman!"

She grimaced at the alias. It was ugly. Too Human sounding. She shouldn't have been surprised that they were trying to hide her true identity. Still, it would have been amusing if she could see the looks on everyone's faces if they knew she was the President's daughter.

"Now I know you're wondering what this lovely little Siren did to get here. Look at her. Isn't she a charmer?" Anyone could hear the sickening sweetness in his voice, so Perri returned a smile to match.

The announcer continued on. "Well, ladies and gentlemen, first up on the sheet is attempted *ass*assination, although looking at her I'd say she can at least successfully fill out those pants. Oh, and look at that! Unsurprisingly, she's got theft on here too, probably from trying to steal a couple of hearts."

Perri took a breath to steady her rising anger. She had already mapped out three different ways to murder the man in the commentator's box. But she knew enough about what the people in those damn chairs wanted. She knew what the audience expected to see.

So she held out her wrists expectantly, shifted all of her weight to one hip, and batted her eyelashes. She'd behave-for now. She huffed as the guard used his screen to unlock the golden bracers and yanked them from her arms. Instantly, she felt warmth rush over her, as if she had just stepped into the sun's rays. All of the power returning at once would have been too much for a weaker Siren, but it only took her a breath to readjust. She ran a tongue across her fangs as she stared up to the crowd of bejeweled faces. If she looked hard enough, there was no doubt in her mind that she'd find one of her father's associates. She beamed a wicked smile up to the patrons, who were already sizing her up.

She'd play their game, if only to please one man in the crowd. She'd done her research. Careful eavesdropping during her time in the holding cell had earned her the knowledge she desired. She knew which Pit Master she had to win over in order to get to the woman that got her tossed in here.

As the guard hurried away and slammed the doors behind him, Perri glanced once more up to the crowd. She could barely make out the shimmer of the safety dome that kept her powers from touching the patrons while still giving them an uninterrupted view of the chaos below. As she scanned the many men above, her eyes fell on the Master's booth. It was a lavish suite positioned much higher above the general crowd. An untouched buffet table laid in the back of the room and a few beautiful women stood against the red wall, waiting to serve.

Five men sat in front of the glass window on plush thrones, many with glasses of liquor in hand. They were familiar in the way that her childhood toys were. Blurry around the edges but somewhat recognizable, only seen a few times before being lost to the hands of someone in the too large house. The men would recognize her even with the makeup, no doubt, if they weren't previously told of her arrival. Three of the five Masters were Sirens, their bright blue eyes a dead giveaway. One was a Demon, complete with horns and tail. His black veined wings extended behind him as he perched on the arm of his chair. Their names hardly mattered, their voices all the same fraudulent jovial loudness in her memory. The man in the center, however, with golden tattoos decorating his body, was Artemis, a Vitare. The man with a scar across his face, the one who had given her a doll on their first meeting. His golden eyes raked up and down Perri's body, a small smirk on his handsome dark face. That man, that was the one she needed to impress.

Perri tore her eyes from the booth as the doors on the other side of the Pit flew open. Perhaps she should have been afraid, given her lack of training and the being staring her down, but her lips curled into a smile. As the guards took the bracers off her competitor, the same male voice as before rang out over the arena.

"On the east side is Odastron's favored Halfling Champion, Cambrie! While this half Demon is also half Angel, you wouldn't know it from the way they fight. They may be repulsive to look at but you're in for a show. Remember to place your bets gentlemen, this will be one hell of a match."

Perri felt her adrenaline begin to kick in. The Halfling before her cracked their jaw and shook out their wrists. The single horn on the left side of their head and their tail had obviously been mutilated by some kind of blade. Short black hair that hadn't seen proper care in months fell from behind their ear but they didn't seem to mind. The Siren had heard of Halflings in passing but had thought them more of a myth than reality. Her curiosity was only amplified by the scars and burns on every last visible centimeter of their brown skin. Normally, competitors would take care of their appearances to possibly give themselves another alternative at the end of this road. But this one seemed to have other priorities.

The Siren tore her eyes from Cambrie and took note of her surroundings. There were only two exits, the one behind her and the one behind the Halfling. Both would be bolted shut during the match to ensure the fight remained in the Pit. A few freestanding cement barriers that stood chest high were scattered around the arena, providing little cover. A rather flimsy looking knife was discarded in the dirt behind one of the barriers, and a wooden baseball bat was far to Perri's left. The air was stifling and sticky against her flesh as she scoffed at the provided weaponry. Another glance at her competition told her man made weapons wouldn't be in the cards tonight.

As all of the guards backed away through the doors, the announcer spoke up once more.

"Remember competitors, a kill would mean an automatic fifty point deduction in your scores with the possibility of the death penalty from your Master. Anything else besides deadly blows goes. The match will begin on the count of one. Ten, nine...."

Perri dug her feet into the dirt, feeling the power flow in her veins. She rolled her shoulders forward as she stared down Cambrie.

"Eight, seven, six...."

Cambrie held out their palms and let the roar of the crowd fade away. Their heart beat slowed as they slipped into a deadly calm.

"Five, four, three, two...."

Perri and Cambrie met each other's eyes. Bright blue met silver and crimson as each tried to detect the slightest movement, the tiniest tell. Anything to give themselves an edge.

"One!"

Perri darted to the right, launching herself behind a barrier. A fire-ball kissed the hairs on her forearm as the attack narrowly missed and crashed into the wall behind her. Perri's chest heaved as she caught her breath. She squatted down, her back against the barrier, and tried to steady her startled heart. Blood pounded in her head, masking the sounds of her competitor's footsteps.

With each breath she took, the power in her veins thrummed. She had to give the Masters a show. So she gave herself over to the ancient energy. Her muscles throbbed, her bones elongated, her face contorting into a silent scream. Familiar pain seared through her body. It took every ounce of self control she had not to cry out.

She bit down on her tongue as dark feathered wings tore through her shoulder blades. Blood filled her mouth. Silent tears fell from her eyes as the bones in her feet shattered. Sharp talons instead dug into the dirt. Ebony feathers sprouted from her legs and gathered into a group of tail feathers. Her torso and face were the only reminder of her Humanesque appearance. The pain dissipated, replaced by straight adrenaline.

Perri shot up into the air. She flapped her wings, propelling herself higher and higher until she reached the top of the dome. The air was hot and abuzz with the cheers of the crowd. Her feathers glistened under the lights. She could see herself on the screens, a deadly representation of what power she held.

As she craned her neck to scan the ground below, the dirt stood still. To the naked eye, Cambrie was nowhere to be found. Perri sniffed, taking in the sweat and fear that lingered in the air from previous competitors. It took mere seconds to find the scent that belonged to the Champion. The Halfling still remained on the ground, invisible.

With the scent still in her nose, Perri tucked in her wings and dove. The wind kissed her cheeks as she plummeted. She extended her talons and reached out, hoping to catch Cambrie. They easily sidestepped the attempt.

Cambrie grinned as they palmed the dagger they had found. The Siren was predictable, clumsy, slow. Plus, she had completely disregarded the valuable weapons laying in the dirt. So it took nothing for Cambrie to slash at her arm, her torso, her cheek, and sprint away before she knew what happened. They made it to the other side of the arena before revealing themselves, their powers slipping off them. They twirled the dagger in the palm of their hand.

Fury danced on Perri's face as she reached up to touch her cheek. As she pulled away bloodied fingers, she snarled.

"You cut my face."

She launched herself at Cambrie. Any thought of a show was discarded in exchange for revenge. She began attacking the mental walls Cambrie had put up around her mind. Tendrils of Perri's own mind pounded against the Halfling's. Desperate, Perri searched for a weak point. If she could get into Cambrie's mind she could see their memories, see their weaknesses with her perception. But years of training had caused Cambrie's mind to have walls of steel.

Cambrie launched a fireball towards Perri, but the Siren ducked the attack. Perri's body trembled with rage as sweat poured down her face. She stalked towards the Halfling. She dodged every fireball thrown. Cambrie slipped behind the cement barriers in between attacks. They knew better than to let the Siren get too close. Perri chased after the Halfling but each step put her two steps further back.

The roar of the crowd only fueled her rage. She was supposed to be winning this thing. She couldn't lose. She didn't spare a glance at the timer above but she knew time was running out.

Perri flung herself into the air, sick of the game of tag. Without hesitation she dove for her prey. Cambrie ran. But they were just a hair too slow. Perri scooped up the Champion with her talons. The sharp claws dug into Cambrie's torso. The dagger in their hands clattered to the ground. They tried to conjure up another attack, but it was too late. Perri already had her grip on them. The pair hovered a few feet off the ground, Perri's wings flapped slowly.

Perri began singing in an ancient tongue, a rich hypnotic sound that echoed throughout the dome. Somewhere interwoven into the melody was an order for her opponent to stop resisting.

But despite the enchanting tune, Cambrie still tried to pry Perri's talons from their body. Perri bit back a scream of frustration. She should have known better. Of course Cambrie's mental walls would hold, preventing Perri from using her persuasion to convince the Halfling to give up. So she flew higher, heart pounding.

Cambrie however, realized Perri's plan. The Siren was out of weapons and was resorting to whatever dirty tactic she could manage. The mental walls Cambrie had spent years fortifying weren't going to be penetrated by the enchantress's perception or persuasion, the two main weapons in a Siren's arsenal. But, no doubt the woman had seen Cambrie's shredded wing and noticed the Halfling's inability to fly; dropping them from a high height would be a surefire win for her. Perri was inexperienced however, and used to living in a mansion with every need attended to. Cambrie wouldn't lose to her.

Cambrie nearly grinned, but then let the power overtake them. It was a blinding, agonizing experience that they were all too familiar with, one that made seconds feel like days. Screaming wasn't an option, the pain blacking out every sense. But as their bones shrunk and their skin melted, Cambrie slipped through the Siren's talons. They plummeted. Then, as Cambrie fully realized their form, their wings shot out and they caught themselves from colliding with the ground.

Perri realized too late that the Halfling had inherited shapeshifting from their Angel parent. She let out an audible shriek as she dove for Cambrie. They had transformed into a raven. Perri was sure it was to mock her bigger, bulkier form.

Cambrie however, sensed the limitations of their form and was quick to fly behind a barrier and endure the shifting process again. It took seconds to return to their true body, but those seconds gave Perri the ability to shift as well. Perri was faster, more agile in her Humanesque body, something she'd need for the end of this fight. She scooped up a jagged knife by her feet and stared down Cambrie.

Cambrie lashed out with a whip of fire. Perri side-stepped the attack, but the flames still managed to kiss her shoulder. She didn't give the pain any attention, adrenaline still pulsing in her veins. She rushed towards the Halfling.

Cambrie was surprised by her speed and stamina. Exhaustion was weighing heavy on the Halfling, their limbs heavy, their reactions just a second too slow. Perhaps that's how Perri closed the gap between them before they had a chance to attack again.

She lashed out with the knife. The blade sliced the Halfling's chest and sent them stumbling backwards. They fell to the ground. Dust rose around them as they scrambled to stand, but Perri was faster. She stepped on Cambrie's chest before dropping to straddle them.

Any training Cambrie had received went out the window. They knew how to get out of this, it was ingrained in the very fiber of their being. Yet, they froze as Perri sat on their chest and wrapped one hand around their throat. Paralysis gripped them as Perri gripped the knife. The blade pierced their skin, tracing a line from cheekbone to jaw. A cut identical to the one they had given Perri. Cambrie wanted to fight back, to spit at the woman, but already reality was blurring with memory. Was it the beep of medical equipment or the countdown of the timer overhead? The roar of an overzealous crowd or irate scientists? Their breath stuck in their chest. No amount of desperate gasps could bring air into their aching lungs. Then, Perri brought the hilt of the knife down on their head.

Perri rose, dropping the knife into the dirt. She brushed the dirt from her legs. As the bell sounded, the crowd gave their thunderous applause as guards rushed through the doors. They hauled an unconscious Cambrie off after slapping bracers onto their limp wrists.

The same guard from earlier wordlessly replaced the restraints onto Perri's arms. Music intermingled with the leftover adrenaline pounding in her chest. As she had expected, she found a few familiar faces from her father's meetings and her mother's parties as she stared up into the crowd. If only they knew who she truly was.

Blood, dirt, and debris mixed together on her flesh. She glanced around, trying to wipe the mess from her face as she searched for any sign of the Masters. She needed to get this over with. Then she needed a shower. Dirt and sweat hardly made a good face mask.

The Master's box was devoid of the men she sought after. The only sign of life was a young Human girl. The girl dropped a shard of glass onto the floor, missing the disposal chute in the wall. She quickly scooped it up as she glanced over her shoulder as if searching for an invisible hand to strike. Then she set about to clean up the rest of the furniture that had been thrown around. Her bare feet danced around the remnants of wasted food she wouldn't dare to taste and shattered liquor glasses she knew better than to complain about when they pierced her skin.

Someone grazed their hand across Perri's lower back, causing her to whip around. Of course, the commentator, Aarlin, had descended from his box to announce the winner. She should have expected as much. His face was plastered on screens all around the arena. His

dyed black and white hair always styled so that it was curled in a
horrifying loop-di-loop was trademarked and had its own ten step hair
care line in the gift shop here. His glittering purple suit shone under
the lights, nearly blinding Perri. As much as the Masters owned the
Champions and the Pit, Aarlin sold the experience. Without a word
to her, he gripped her arm and held it in the air as he shouted her
name. The crowd was on their feet in seconds as he announced her
the winner. His other words were drowned out by the raucous crowd.
The patrons, some victorious, others having lost great sums of credits,
all shouted Perri's alias.

Aarlin's pearly white teeth grinned a powerful grin as his eyes raked
over Perri's beaten body. She yanked back her arm and crossed her
arms over her chest.

"Congratulations darling!" he crooned. "I heard you got a few bids
tonight. Although, I wouldn't be surprised if some of the Masters
didn't just want you on top of them like you were with that *thing*."

Aarlin didn't know who he was messing with. She wanted to spit in
his face, to knee him in the chest, to delve into his memory and spill
his dirtiest secrets. Now that he was here, there were another forty-two
ways she could think of to murder him before she'd get hauled away.
What would they do with her? Take her to prison? Yet she forced a
blinding smile. She'd play the woman he wanted.

"You're hilarious!" Perri went to place her fingers on the man's
shoulder but the guard yanked her back. She rolled her eyes so hard
she could practically see her own brain. "Buzzkill. It's not like I could
do anything."

Aarlin placed a hand on the guard's arm, dropping his smile and
lowering his voice. "Careful with that one. I want to see her here
again."

The knot in Perri's stomach that she had been refusing to acknowledge grew to an irrepressible size as those words echoed in her brain.
Her bones shook as the guard guided her towards the door, her feet
like cement. That's when she saw him. Pit Master Artemis was waiting
for her.

## Two

# There's Too Many Stupid Rules in Life and Chess

"Your performance was terrible." Pit Master Artemis leaned back in his chair and sighed. "Where was the intrigue, the drama? You only won because Odastron's thing froze up. If it weren't for my curiosity, I wouldn't have taken a risk on you."

Perri's gaze stayed unwavering on the pristine chessboard sitting on a table alongside the wall. On any other day it would have struck her as odd and out of place. Board games belonged in museums these days, not in an office. However, she was only vaguely aware of the fact that the shower she had been permitted to take hadn't washed away the blood from beneath her fake nails. She had spent her precious minutes beneath the lukewarm water ferociously scrubbing away until she no longer felt like herself. A tendril of hair slipped from its place in her ponytail, causing a water droplet to drip down her neck. Yet, she didn't move to wipe it away.

"Do you remember when we first met?" Artemis asked, taking a sip from his glass. When he was only met with a blank stare, he continued on. "It was your birthday. I brought Cain over for your party. Before, he hadn't wanted to come, so I picked out your present for you. What was it?"

"A doll. She had a golden dress." Perri stared out the window, the words pouring from her lips as if she wasn't fully aware she was saying them. She shook her head as if that would make the wood beneath her fingertips feel real.

"That's right, he was so intimidated by you that he made me give it to you. But he fell head over heels for you, I swear. He talked about you for days afterwards. I knew you'd remember. You were both so young then." Artemis placed the drink down on his desk to pull up a picture of his son. "This is him now. He's headed to Evilin University in the fall."

Perri raised her brows and nodded, barely glancing at the picture. What was his angle? Was this a fucked up prison or a nightmarish reality dating show? Either way, she wanted no part of it.

"Congratulations to him, I guess," she said with no lack of incertitude. For a moment the silence that followed was welcome as it let her breathe and him drink.

"I have to admit, this ordeal has had me lying awake for nights on end," Artemis crooned, tilting his head to try to get Perri to look him in the eyes. "We never did get an answer as to why you're really here."

"You saw the trial." The words had the consistency of chocolate mousse, airy but foreign in this place. They soaked into the golden velvet wallpaper that was desperately trying to masquerade this place as something like a royal hall.

Artemis stood from his desk as he noticed where Perri's eyes lay. Moonlight cast shadows across the countless artifacts he had spent his time curating. Shelves filled with books in languages lost long ago covered one wall. Curves of metals and flashing plastic things adorned the shelves of another. A ginormous golden M nearly blocked the door as its ominous glow warmed the room.

The man brought the chessboard from the table to the desk with ease, his smooth, tattooed hands pushing aside a now empty glass.

"Do you know how to play?" When Perri nodded, he surveyed the pieces and gestured for her to scooch forward.

Perri tried to oblige. Chains were now attached to her bracers which anchored her to the floor, limiting her motion. The chains clinked on the desk as the chair scraped along the tile floor. She shifted her jaw and flicked her tongue across a fang as the cloud fell away from her mind. The sounds that had been dulled banged on her eardrums, the colors filling her retinas like fireworks. That's when she really looked at the board. Shit.

"Tell me the truth about what happened. Why are you here?" Artemis asked as he moved his white pawn forward.

"What does it matter? You bid on me." Perri met the man's golden eyes. Past him the lights of a ship could be seen in the distance. They were up so high that Perri wouldn't have been surprised if the building touched the stars. She took a breath, then jumped the black queen over her pawn.

"You owe me the truth," Artemis sighed as he shook his head, placing Perri's queen back on the starting square. "It's part of why I bought you. You know just as well as I do that you're not made for this," he said as he gestured around him. "So I have to believe some of the alternative theories out there."

Perri bit her cheek to keep her face neutral. Another piece of her plan fell into place. And as an unbearable silence wrapped around the room, he broke down, and brought a fist down onto the desk.

"What is going on with your father? As an investor here he-" Artemis shook his head, regaining his composure. "Look, if you cooperate I can make your life easier. The other Masters can and will make your life unbearable. I can provide you protection from them. But I promise you, what they have up their sleeves, that's nothing compared to what I'll do if you don't behave."

"Yeah, sure. Do you really think I'm going to be intimidated?" Perri held a hand to her cheek, the cut from earlier already healing nicely. She gestured to the dark facial hair on Artemis' jawbone which had been groomed to resemble flames, copying his golden tattoos. "I mean, you're obviously compensating for something. We both know you're nowhere near as powerful as me. I bet that's why Dinah left-"

The words died along with every ounce of false confidence Perri had managed to conjure up as the chess board went flying towards her head. Wood splintered behind her as it hit the wall. Artemis pushed back his chair and strode around the desk so he stood in front of Perri, bracing his palms against the desk. For a moment, she considered telling him everything she knew. But she couldn't, not when she had gotten this far.

Artemis pushed himself forward. He leaned in close, his breath tickled her nose, his fingers tucked a stray lock of hair behind her ear. Perri refused to flinch away, keeping her eyes locked on his.

"Don't ever bring up my wife again if you know what's good for you, Nextulus. I'd hate to have to tell your dear mother that there was an accident. So here's a tip: Actually learn my rules and play my game."

Perri stood. The chains clanged against the edge of the chair. She stared down at the man, her fists clenched.

"I'm not some pawn for you to manipulate," she hissed. "I'm not some stupid, naive, little girl anymore."

"Oh, sweetheart," he chuckled before pushing himself off the desk and standing to his full height. With a careless shove, she went stumbling back into the chair. The force sent the chair toppling over. The chains did little to stop her from falling with it. Her back hit the floor with a thud, the tile knocking the wind from her lungs. Chess pieces lay scattered all around her. He towered over her wheezing body. "That's exactly what you are."

He turned away from her and strode to the window. The ring on his jawline shone blue as his fingers danced across his invisible screen. A guard rushed in seconds later. The Master didn't bother to glance their way as the guard hauled Perri to her feet, unlocked the chains, and drug her away. Just before the door shut, he called:

"Training starts at seven. You might wanna sleep with one eye open though. Take her to room 7."

As the door shut behind them, Perri whipped around to face the guard, yanking her arm free from his grip.

"If you want to keep that hand, I suggest you keep it to yourself," she hissed.

The ring in his head flashed blue as she said that, his fingers on the invisible screen. Another shock pulsed through Perri's body, her heart racing. She grit her teeth, fangs bared as he led her down the hall and into the waiting elevator.

A gentle tune played as the elevator shot up a dozen floors, causing Perri's already nauseated stomach to lurch. The doors opened to a common room reminiscent of a medical waiting room. Moonlight poured through the single glass wall, causing the other stark white walls to be blinding. Chairs encased in faux white leather that would cling to sweaty skin were arranged around the room. Off to one side sat an arrangement of tables and chairs, all varying sizes and shapes in horrendous beige. A dining area lay, awaiting for the morning. On the other side of the room, a set of double doors led off to the Champion's living quarters. Above the door, a large golden sigil resembling a flame stood guard. The sigil of Pit Master Artemis. Her new keeper.

Perri stepped from the elevator, her body still tense with anger. The guard hurried her across the room, through the double doors, and into a hall full of bedrooms. A few guards stood watch along the walls and Perri took note of the small cameras hanging along the ceiling. Numbers hung on the wall outside each doorway. They stopped at the seventh room, the guard not bothering to knock before he tossed open the door.

As Perri crossed the threshold, an all too familiar scent lodged itself in her nostrils. She knew who took up the top bunk of this cramped room even before the woman bolted from the bed, landed on her feet, and had her hands poised to attack.

A smirk creeped onto Perri's face as the door shut behind her. She shifted her weight to one hip, crossed her arms over her chest and cocked an eyebrow.

"Paranoid much?" She said as the woman's eyes widened.

"Fuck me, they did not make *you* my roommate." The woman turned her back to Perri, calloused fingers interlocking and resting on the back of her head. The golden tattoos on her limbs shimmered, reminiscent of stars in the black depths of space. Her infinite curls coiled in on themselves like sprawling ivy to match the vines along her body.

The woman paced the narrow walkway between the beds and the tiny table with trained deftness, avoiding Perri each time she swung her arms about to untangle her bedsheets.

"Some assassin you are, turning your back on me," Perri grimaced as she set about putting stained sheets on the bottom bunk. "World renowned assassin, The Duchess, Najah Irozi, killed because she turned her back on a little old Siren."

"Like you could kill me. You couldn't even kill your own father." Najah stopped her pacing to stare at the struggling Siren. "Hell, you can't even put on sheets apparently. You're only here because I saved your ass."

"And we're *here*," Perri said as she gestured to the room around them, whacking her arm on the bedpost, "Fuck–because you got us caught."

Najah scoffed. "Fine. Next time I'll let you die, then I'll kill the bastard after he eats your fileted body." She leaned against the edge of the dirt-encrusted table, crossing her arms.

"Sirens don't eat other Sirens." Perri slumped down onto a knot of sheets and plastic mattress. A yawn forced its way past her lips.

"How did you even survive? You had to have paid someone, or at least sucked them off," Najah scoffed. "I thought for sure you'd die before you got here."

"Don't patronize me." There was no more bite in her voice as Perri avoided the assassin's gaze. "We can't all be government trained, genetically modified killers."

A silence fell between them. Minutes creeped by, each woman in their own thoughts. Najah's heart slowly returned to a normal pace as she tried to sort through this new wave of emotions. A strange mix of irritation, frustration, and yet, relief. It made her skin warm, her head heavy. Would she ever get used to this, the freedom of feeling again?

Something clung to the worn stitches in Perri's patchwork heart, ripping at the thinning threads. Those pieces of her heart that belonged to her mother and boyfriend left her with gaping holes and too many thoughts to process until she saw them once more. Then there was Anna. The bloody memory of her would forever be scarred into Perri's corneas, her ghostly presence in every corner of the Siren's mind. Some may have called this sensation grief, others anguish. But years of practiced poise had forced the remaining pieces of her heart back into tattered places before it could overtake her.

Perhaps another day would bring the capacity to deal with the sensations felt so deeply, but for now, she struggled to lose the death-grip exhaustion had on her tongue. She had fought to get bid on by Artemis, to get to Najah for one purpose, and yet, any words she had prepared felt inadequate.

"Just tell me whatever you're going to tell me," Najah said. "You obviously pulled all kinds of strings to get in here with me. They wouldn't have made you my roommate otherwise."

"You seem to forget that I don't have that kind of power anymore," Perri grumbled as she pulled at the mess of sheets. "I guess I don't have any powers anymore."

Najah rubbed her temple and stared at the Siren, eyebrows raised. "Well then this is all one hell of a coincidence don't you think? And I don't tend to believe in coincidences." Then she shook her head and gestured for Perri to stand. "This is the saddest thing I've ever seen. Get up."

"I did want Artemis' bid so that I could get to you," Perri admitted as she watched Najah untangle her sheets. "I wasn't sure how the whole rooming thing worked, but I guess Artemis thought you were actually trying to kill me."

"Why would he think that?" The assassin handed back the sheets to Perri. "Fitted one goes on the mattress. Blanket goes on top. Why would Artemis think we were anything but allies? Everyone saw the trial."

"He doesn't believe the whole story everyone's been saying, and I wasn't about to tell him the truth." Perri finally began to properly make her bed. "Apparently, he heard some conspiracy theories about the whole thing and hoped you'd deal with me since I pissed him off." There was no need to mention that she had helped to spread those false theories using burner accounts on her smuggled communicator just days ago. She laid on her bed, picking at her flaking mascara.

"Well, you seem to be really good at that." Najah stared at the woman who had seemed so put together on all of those screens. Now the Siren lay before her with running makeup stained under her exhausted eyes, dark roots growing in, bruises along her arms.

"What?"

"Pissing people off. I didn't even get a thank you for saving your ass." When she received no response, she continued. "Look, if this is some weird attempt to try and get close to me to kill me for, I don't know, ruining your life or something, then this is pathetic. It's not gonna work."

Perri snorted. "Goddess no. You think I want to kill you? Are you really that paranoid? Of course you are, what am I saying? Look, as much as you might think otherwise, I was raised with manners. I came here to thank you, and my thanks comes with a gift. A life debt in exchange for saving my life. So, Najah Irozi, I pledge myself to you. Although, if you're insufferable, I'll see just how easy it would be to kill you."

"Wait, what?"

Najah would have found it more believable if a talking tree burst into the room. A life debt was antiquated legend, a rarity, especially from this woman. That much she knew from the little bit of history they had taught her at the Egg.

"What if I don't want you to be... indebted to me?" Najah huffed. "What does that even mean?"

"It means that I'm committed to you. Wherever you go, I follow. I have to work in your best interests, to protect you from harm, and to serve you. And since I already committed myself to you, well, you have no choice in that." A yawn interrupted Perri's spiel. The full force of her words hit Najah like a truck. "Until I fulfill that debt, or die, I'm going to stay at your side." Perri lay on her side, facing the wall, back towards Najah.

"No, no, I don't want you." Najah felt sick to her stomach. "I don't need you. You got us in here. What use could you possibly be to me?"

"If you truly don't want me, you can just kill me yourself." Perri's tone was smug.

Silence fell over the room. Najah's brain was whirling. Surely, the Siren had some reason for this plan. Perri would never willingly bind herself to someone like her, regardless of whatever bullshit tradition she claimed.

"So if you're not going to kill me, for my first act, I plan on getting us out of here."

The words were so soft that a Human would have missed them, but Najah's Vitare hearing heard them clear as day. Najah blinked rapidly as the meaning of the words hit her with full force. No, the girl must be delusional. No one escaped from the Pit. Najah opened her lips to tell her as much, but she was already fast asleep.

The assassin pulled herself into her bed, head whirling. This was why Perri had done this. Maybe it was some last ditch effort to save her own skin, to distract Najah enough to let her rise above the assassin in the ranks. Or maybe she thought Najah would protect her once more. No matter the reason, Najah was right. This was all a self serving ploy.

Just a few days ago she had seen the Siren, with her sharpened fangs and enchantress tongue, in shackles awaiting sentencing, just the same as Najah. When they hadn't arrived together, The Duchess had assumed that she had pulled some last minute deal, or maybe died along the way. The woman was a model, a celebrity, the President's daughter, royalty in her own right. There was no way she would make it here. Yet, here she was.

As Najah lay there in the dim, she stared at Perri's sleeping body. Stupid. That's what the Siren was. So unfathomably stupid to think that she could kill her father, and even more so, falling asleep with an assassin above her.

Months ago, Najah might have killed her just to make her life easier. Taking her life would be incredibly easy, no matter what pomp the Siren claimed. Fewer Champions made it easier to move up in rank here. Not to mention that she was the reason that Najah was here in the first place. Yet, as Najah pulled her blankets to her throat, noting that Perri didn't stir, she couldn't help but feel nauseated at the thought of killing her. The numbing cloud had lifted on her emotions only a few days ago, leaving her to sort out the mess of emotion for the first time in years. There had been very little before, only a sliver of humanity she had managed to hold onto beneath force-fed drugs, feelings which she buried for her handlers. So, often, there was no remorse, no empathy, no sadness, joy, or rage in her kills. Even here where money flowed instead of government ink and they didn't want the taint of death on date night, the wounds she gave were purely survival.

She pulled the blanket tighter around her and shook her head. No, she wouldn't kill the Siren. Not yet, at least. Besides, the words still bounced around in her head. "I'm going to get us out of here." It was stupid. Najah had already cased the place, and had notes on every inch of the prison. She had stored away information on every guard, their rotations, their tells, their marital status. She had spent every waking moment dedicated to thinking about potential escape plans, and in every one, the outcome was ugly. There was no way that this woman could get them out of here, not with her naivety and lack of training. And yet, for just a second, Najah let herself hope.

## Three

# BREAKFAST IS THE MOST IMPORTANT MEAL OF THE DAY

Cambrie stared out across the training room. The dark cement walls were stained with Goddess knows what. Muscles tangled upon muscles into undistinguishable forms upon the grappling floor. The stale musk of sweat hung in the air, the grunts of other Champions seeming to grow louder by the minute. Above them was a balcony for the Pit Masters to play Goddess at their leisure, although they never sought to leave their cushioned luxury to see the ugliness they created. They would leave that work to those below them.

The guards that stood sentry around the room let their fingers stab the air in front of them, each one's rings blue. They were too preoccupied with their Alcoriums to pay attention to their charges. For a moment, Cambrie let their mind wander back to the memories of that powerful device. From the second it had been in their head to the second it had been yanked out there were shimmering jewels left in their footprints and clouds of glitter in their breath. Stolen paintings and stolen smiles in the corridors of pulsing light. Every kiss was a firework, every touch neon. If ever there was euphoria, it was in those moments between the capsules and the green of the ring and him. But it was never meant to last for them.

The gym reverberated with the wild and bright ghosts of yesterday's news, unruly tongues filling every ear in the place. Her name itself was an enchantment. She had arrived late last night and had been disguised during the round. Upon seeing her now, everyone recognized the face that had graced the side of President Nextulus and the screens of their social media platforms. But as Champions took in the Goddess-like form of Perrianna Nextulus, Cambrie's gaze fell on The Duchess.

The assassin had only arrived two days ago, and Cambrie could hardly believe the rumors that floated around her arrest. Her and Perrianna Nextulus tried to take down Triton Nextulus together? Had Najah really turned her back on the government she had so dutifully served for years, only to attempt to assassinate the President of Inanis, his daughter at her side? The story was incredible, incredulous even. Yet, everyone seemed to believe it. And the story only raised more questions than it answered.

Even still, it had been years since Cambrie had seen her, had trained with her in the Egg, and even though they were separated by an invisible barrier and different Pit Masters, Cambrie couldn't help but admire the finesse with which she wielded her power. To anyone else, the power of controlling roses would have been an insult, a slap in the face in comparison to the powers other Vitares were given. But it fit Najah like a glove.

Even without access to her powers, she was a force to be reckoned with. In a gray tank top and shorts, her muscles were on full display. As she sparred with a fellow Demon Champion, she landed each punch with precision, even her lightest blows causing the Demon to grimace.

In a fluid movement she kicked his legs out from under him and had him flat on his stomach. She stepped on his back, her hand on the fake dagger in the waistband of her pants.

Cambrie's cheeks flushed as they noticed the assassin's thighs clench. Those thighs that could easily wrap around an attacker's neck and choke them out, Cambrie settled on. That was definitely their reason for staring. And as if she could feel the eyes on her, Najah met Cambrie's eyes, her lips curled in a smirk. Cambrie hastily tried to put any kind of emotion on their face other than adoration. But their cheeks only burned brighter at the realization they had been caught staring. Before they could revel in their embarrassment too much, an arm slipped around their waist. They whipped around, pulse racing.

"Chill babe, it's just me," a young Human woman said, her voice defensive. She held up her calloused hands as she feigned innocence, nails jagged. Scars were carved into her skin like craters on the brown undertones of a faint blood moon. Over a dozen lopsided inked hearts given by strangers dotted her upper arm. Now without thoughts of The Duchess in their mind, Cambrie could smell the familiar combination of rust, sea salt caramel chapstick, and adrenaline that made up Zennebelle Everard.

"That's Perrianna right? She got a bid with Artemis?" Zennebelle gestured towards the Siren. "You fought her?"

"Yeah, apparently. I didn't know it was her when-"

"I would've thought you could take the damn Human eater."

As Zennebelle cut the Halfling off, Cambrie rolled their eyes, staring out over the room. There was no point in explaining last night's fight. Belle wouldn't understand.

As more Champions poured into the room, sweat crawled up the walls into a choking musk. One of the sole Angel Champions to ever exist here flew up to the ceiling. His pure white wings contrasted the black paint. He glanced down to the Halfling, disgust lining his gaze. Cambrie in return just stuck out their pinky and ring finger in order to flip him off.

When he had first arrived here, he thought that perhaps they could form an alliance. After all, an Angel here? He should have been desecrated. Despite the end of the Hundred Year War between Angels and Demons, the feud between the two groups still ran strong and the Pit was primarily Demon territory. He thought that Cambrie's outsider status could offer him allyship and protection. Given the large tattoo of three interlocking circles symbolizing the three Goddesses he believed created both him and the world adorning his upper arm–a symbol of his devotion to Theralaan, the old major religion of Inanis–he would need all the allies he could get. Unfortunately for him, Cambrie wasn't one for allies. At least, they tried not to be.

"Where's Ella?" Cambrie asked as they turned back to Belle. The smaller Human's familiar scent didn't cling to the air nor did her animated frame bring much needed life to the room.

"Still eating breakfast," Belle sighed. "She knows she needs to be training harder since the agreement is almost up, but you've seen her. I don't think I'm going to be able to get an exemption this time, especially since my score is down." She rubbed her eyes as if that would wipe away the nightmare she had found herself in.

Zennebelle's younger sister, Ella, had been pardoned each month under Pit Master's Odastron's agreement with his only Human Champion, Belle. With each win in the Pit, Champions were awarded points, which earned them rewards of their choosing–within reason. Subsequent losses, or loss of patron interest, resulted in those rewards being taken away. And when those losses became too great to recoup, death was imminent–unless one had earned enough favor to keep patron interest in other ways.

In Belle's case, every month she exchanged her points for the safety of her sister instead of cashing in her points for a better room or the drug of her choice. So Ella was exempt from fighting, as long as Belle kept people's attention and kept winning.

"Hey!" The voice sounded like puppies frolicking on a summer day and the girl who approached looked as though she should be among them in a field of flowers. Ella, with eyes as bright as supernovas, beamed at the pair, her dimples crooked. "They made blueberry pancakes for someone and snuck extras down for me!"

The girl bounced up and down on her toes. Her skin shimmered as if she were filled with microscopic cracks leaking sunlight around her. Rainbow braids formed a crown atop her head, albeit, a crooked one that looked as if it belonged to a rambunctious princess rather than a supposed terrorist.

"What are you up to? Did I miss anything?" She asked, the bubblegum words falling out of her lips. But when Belle didn't respond, Ella simply continued. "Do you wanna spar Cambrie? I've been practicing my roundhouse kick, like Belle showed me!" She struck the air in a decidedly ungraceful motion before losing her balance and stumbling backwards. She backed into a Vitare, nearly knocking him over. He let out a low snarl to get out of his way but she was already backing away, blushing. "Sorry!" She returned to her group, letting the blood fade from her cheeks before speaking up again. "Anyways, I think I could take you, Cam."

Cambrie smiled and nodded. "Maybe you can! Let's see what you've got."

"Don't go easy on her," Belle muttered just loud enough for Cambrie to hear. "She has to hold her own."

The grey plastic of the empty sparring mat squeaked under their feet as Cambrie and Ella entered the ring. They assumed their positions as Belle stood on the side, arms crossed over her chest. For now, the warm frustration and anxiety she felt rising within was unfounded. She would have to hold herself together.

The ring scanned the pair, closed around them, and began a short countdown. As it reached one, Belle's breath caught in her throat. Goosebumps teased at her arms, reminding her of how very real this all was. Not that she ever needed the reminder.

Cambrie, with their Halfling reflexes, could have been on Ella in half a heartbeat, but waited two seconds before moving. Ella threw out a kick to try and knock Cambrie's legs out from under them, but Cambrie easily sidestepped and brought a knee up to Ella's stomach. Ella doubled over, which gave Cambrie an opening to bring an elbow down on her back. They did so with just enough strength to drop her to the mat, but the air was knocked out of her. She wheezed as she desperately tried to pull air back into her lungs. An automated voice only added another blow to Ella's gut as it added up the points for the round, giving a bonus to Cambrie for showmanship and speed.

Cambrie paused, letting the girl catch her breath. Out of the corner of their eye, they could have sworn they saw Najah watching the fight. They returned their attention to Ella, who was still on the ground, clutching her chest.

Belle and Cambrie exchanged a glance before Belle stepped forward, looking down on her sister. "What was that? Did you even try?"

"Belle," Cambrie reached out to grab Belle, but was shaken off.

"No, she needs to quit relying on me. I can't always be there to save her. I can't keep getting her exemptions."

Ella blinked rapidly. "I'm trying," she wheezed. She bit her lip and wrapped her arms around herself. As she slowly gained her breath back, she kept her eyes downturned towards the mat. "I'm here, aren't I?" Belle huffed and turned away. Cambrie reached a hand down to

Ella, but the Human stood on her own, crossing her arms over her chest. Her eyes glistened slightly as she swallowed hard. "I'm tired of you treating me like a kid. I went through the same things you did." Her voice rose, but the guards along the wall paid little notice.

Champions were pausing their workouts to watch the unfolding events. "I helped enslaved Saybrim escape from Galivantus, just like you. I ran from the cops, just like you. I watched as everyone we knew turned against us when we were branded terrorists, just like you. So stop acting like you're so high and mighty."

Belle let out a chuckle as she approached her sister, adjusting her jaw and jamming a finger into the girl's chest. Her voice was low and dangerous. "First of all, you're sixteen. You're still a child. And if I remember correctly, all of those things we did? I had to keep saving your ass then too. Because guess who failed S.P.A.C.E training? Oh right, you did. But if you insist on being an adult, go ahead. Go into the Pit and get yourself killed."

Bringing up Ella's failed S.P.A.C.E training was a low blow and Belle regretted it as soon as the words left her lips. Both of them had always wanted to enlist in the military because it was one of the few Human occupations that would pay them well enough to hopefully bring their family out of poverty. And despite her prodigal beginnings, the training had been too tough for Ella.

Hurt flashed across Ella's face. She opened her mouth to retort, then closed it. Just then, balcony doors above swung open and a Vitare sauntered in.

"What the hell is going on down there?" She shouted as her golden eyes roamed over the inactive Champions. "Twenty laps, all of you!"

From the other side of the barrier, Perri watched the Humans bicker with amusement. Despite sound being unable to pass through the barrier, the scent of them still hung in the air. She could still smell their frustration, their anger, their pain. Perri breathed in the sweat and the sweet pulse of the blood in their veins. She had been given a Human to feed on during breakfast, but he had been ill for some time and his blood was sour. Nothing like the ones on the other side of the wall. And yet, beside them, stood the Halfling from yesterday.

"Hey, Najah, what's up with the Humans? Are they motivation for the best Siren or something? And what's the Halfling doing with them?" She asked over her shoulder.

Najah paused from where she sat on the floor, doing sit-ups. She glanced across to the Odastron Champions, her eyes lingering on Cambrie. Far too many complicated memories lay in those hands and mouth of theirs though and she shut them out.

"Can you leave me alone? I'm trying to train." Najah rolled her eyes as she continued with her rep. "And you should at least try to look busy since everyone here is going to be taking bets on who can take you out first."

Neither had slept well last night. Nightmares had plagued Perri's sleep and when she woke at an unholy hour, she hadn't been able to get her mind to stop playing scenes of loved ones' horrific deaths. Try as she might to calm herself, her nightmares only transformed into anxiety-fueled scenarios.

Najah, on the other hand, had never gotten out of the habit of sleeping with one eye open. Growing up sleeping beside dozens of assassins made her learn how to function for days on end without rest. But that didn't mean she appreciated having adrenaline pulse through her veins all night all because she had to share a room.

"So you can't tell me while we train? I need to know what we're up against, and I know you've already gathered all the details." Perri stared down at Najah. "Or I could ask you a dozen other questions and follow you around for the rest of gym time."

"Aren't you supposed to follow my orders?"

"No, that was never part of the agreement. Besides, it's in your best interest to tell me everything you know."

"If I tell you, will you leave me alone? I don't need you in my space," Najah grumbled. She rolled her shoulders as she noticed the tension building up, her palms sweaty. Irritation bubbled up under her skin for the first time in forever. Some part of her loved it. She stood and walked over towards the water fountain. Perri, to no one's surprise, followed.

"Sure. Tell me about them."

"The tall one, her name is Zennebelle. That's the only Human to ever fight her way up to Champion status in the history of the Pit. I heard she's an ex S.P.A.C.E cadet. She exchanges her points so that her sister Ella doesn't have to fight." Najah took a sip of water and put her hands on her hips.

"So the short one is, what? A waste of space? That doesn't seem like something a Master would put up with. You think if I were to feed from her, super carefully, they would care? I don't *have* to kill Humans, you know. It's just more of a convenience thing for me and it doesn't hurt them as much."

Najah made a disgusted noise and wrinkled her nose as she stood. "You're repulsive. I'm still Human, you know. It'd be nice if you didn't rub that feeding shit in my face."

Perri shrugged before bending her arm behind her head and pulling on her elbow. "What, that grosses you out? Why? You kill people too. Besides, it's not like you're really Human."

Sweat prickled on Najah's neck. Similar words had echoed among leaders in the Egg, an unspoken hierarchy branded into the minds of every soldier. A challenging tongue there would have resulted in unending punishment, but here she was free to speak her mind. "I get you're new to the big scary outside world, but your racism ain't gonna fly with me. Work on it. I have no issues beating the hell out of you if you make another comment like that."

Perri rolled her eyes. "Fine. You sound like my manager. So what did they do to get in here?"

That only pissed Najah off more. She took a breath, then another to settle her emotions. The anger was a rush, a thrill, but she had to calm herself. There was no point in letting Perri rile her up. Besides, if there was a sliver of a chance that the Siren was truly going to get them out of here, the assassin wouldn't risk that over some stupid fight.

"I heard that both of them hijacked a ship full of enslaved Saybrim, ya know, the same people from the trade your father actively participates in." She gave Perri a pointed look before continuing, picking up a weight from the rack. "They freed them. And, they worked with the Resistance for a while."

"So they're the ones I heard about," Perri muttered. "Interesting."

"You know about them?" Najah asked. "How? I thought Alcoriums censored stuff like that unless you actively look. You don't seem like you're the Resistance type."

"Uh, excuse me, first of all, I'm all for freedom and shit. Didn't you see my picture on Mirror supporting Saybrim gaining the right to a bed?"

"I must've missed it in between the 6am toxicology lesson and the 10am murder, sorry," Najah rolled her eyes. "How did you know?"

"I had a fake Alcorium. It was nothing more than a piece of plastic and unlimited internet access. So, yeah, a lot of other people don't know anything about the Saybrim Resistance, they don't know Saybrim are even enslaved, but I'm not dumb. Even the people who reflected my post just did it for a bit of dopamine."

"You had a fake Alcorium?" Najah tilted her head, surprise in her eyes.

Perri held her gaze with the assassin, eyes narrowed. "You think I'd have tried to confront Triton if I were still under his control? Really, it's not that interesting. Now, answer my question about the Halfling. Why are they here?"

"No, no, it really is that interesting. Way more than any of your questions." Najah snapped. Anger came fast and hard, almost like a suckerpunch to the gut. She shifted her jaw, balling her fists up at her side. It wasn't even a feeling completely her own. She was used to being talked to far worse than anything Perri could dream of and yet-

She took another breath. This Siren was going to make her do something she regretted. "I don't know exactly what they did to get in here. I just know they were some low level thief in Sanctus. They probably fucked up a job. I think they're dating Zennebelle though and that's why they're hanging around." Najah shrugged and began to walk away.

"Wait! So they escaped the Egg then?" Perri rushed to catch up to her and grabbed her arm.

Najah brushed her off. "I answered your questions, so leave me alone."

But Perri was on a roll and didn't stop her questioning. "Did you know them? What was the Egg like? That's where they made and trained you, right? What was that like? Have you ever seen Cambrie experimented on? Did they ever experiment on you like that?"

Najah whirled around and shoved Perri to the ground, snarling. "I don't know who you think you are but you don't get to ask me questions like that, ever. Do you fucking understand me?"

"They were just questions, Goddess," Perri said defensively. She glanced at the guards along the wall, suddenly feeling small. Help, however, didn't bother to look at her.

"You don't care about me, and your questions? They're to satiate some morbid fascination you have with the people below you. If I told you what they did to any of us there you'd have nightmares for weeks. I don't need to put my pain on display for anyone, especially not for the daughter of the man who maintains that torture for his own gain."

"I didn't...I'm not..." Perri stammered.

Najah left the Siren on the ground. She rolled her eyes. She should have let Perri die.

# Four

# Monsters Aren't Always Hiding in the Dark

## CW: Sexual assault, insinuation of rape

Cambrie sat on their king sized bed, fingers gripping the faux fur blankets beneath them. They wanted to offer up the luxuries in some desperate plea, or to destroy them all in a fiery blaze. But they remained rooted to their spot, the bracers on their wrists were a heavy reminder of their contract with the man they so despised. Blood pounded in their ears as they watched Belle pace, expletives pouring from her lips as she narrated the events from her private meeting with Master Odastron.

"He said the damn audience is tired of me, that the novelty of a Human champion has worn off. Then the bastard dared to say that I'd do a better job as one of his girls. He won't put me to death, or to the public." She flopped onto the bed face first and let her voice contort into a gross version of his. "'You've got such a pretty face. I should've just put you and your sister there to begin with.' I should've just tried to kill him," Belle groaned, her voice returning to normal. "It would've been better than this."

Cambrie tentatively reached out and stroked her hair. Their brain was lit with threats, each one more creative than the next. However, it wouldn't have been helpful, and the usual words of comfort always fell flat. So the silence spoke for them like nails on a chalkboard.

"If I don't do it, Ella's going to die," Belle breathed as she looked up at her partner. She was pleading with the stillness but found the noise behind their eyes unbearable. She laid her head in the Halfling's lap. "I can't let her lose the exemption, I can't let her fight. They'll desecrate her."

"I know," Cambrie finally agreed, their voice soft. Their muscles tensed under Belle's head. "But you shouldn't have to do that. We'll find another way. We can figure this out together. You know how he treats those women."

While every Master had their own vices, Odastron had a strong reputation for favoring Humans in particular for their fragility. It was no secret how rough he was with his "attendants." The silent women who attended to his every need were often seen adorned with dark bruises along their bodies. Some of the outspoken ones had been silenced permanently, their tongues ripped from their mouths. Others simply went missing and never returned.

"You know just as well as I do there's not another way. I got her into this. I messed up. I drug her into the Saybrim resistance. She should've stayed at home. She should've gotten to be a kid." Her voice broke as a sob racked her body. She trembled on Cambrie's lap. Tears soaked into the Halfling's pants as panic coursed through their body.

Cambrie's heart raced as they focused on steadying their own trembling hands. Perhaps it could have been masked as rage, but deep inside they knew the growing tightness in their chest wasn't explained by it. Each tear that fell from Belle's cheek burned an acidic hole into the facade that they had managed to put up. The sobs were too reminiscent of the ones from the children in the Egg. They clawed at the edges of their consciousness to try and regain the control they were rapidly losing, with little success.

"If only we could escape this fucking place. Then we could all actually live a normal life." Belle murmured through her tears. They were hot and ugly on her face. She clawed at them, trying to will the dam back up. But it had already burst and here she was, twenty-one, and feeling like a child curled on her mother's lap. She clutched Cambrie's leg as if she hung on hard enough, they would prove to be her savior.

Cambrie choked as bile burned at their stomach lining and hands crushed their trachea. The air was as thick as quicksand. It was all too wet and familiar as the sobs morphed into the voices of a dozen children and tear drops turned into blood. Memories and reality wrestled for dominance in their mind as Belle sobbed. They hadn't even realized that words fell from their lips despite knowing the history of this place:

"We can escape. We can do it."

"What?" Belle gasped, wiping at her puffy face. She sat up, sniffling, letting the cool air hit her raw throat.

*Stupid.* A wave of paranoia rolled over Cambrie. *I shouldn't have said anything. The eyes are everywhere. Anyone could be listening.* Those words could cost them, could kill them. No one had escaped the Pit. It was a simple fact.

Belle wiped her nose on the back of her hand and nodded. "How? I've thought about it. Do you-"

"Not here," Cambrie cut her off, frantically gesturing around. "Not now." They scanned the screen on the wall, as if they would find a pair of eyes peeking in on them. The sterile lights bore down as if to force their mind open. It wrapped around their heart and poured into the unstitched wounds. Pure alcohol drained down the back of their nasal cavities and into their throat, burning and raw. The weights that collapsed their chest couldn't be pried off, wouldn't let them scream. Instead it all came out in a desperate whisper: "They're going to find us. They're going to find us! They're going to kill us!"

"What are you talking about? What's going on with you?" Belle asked. She tried to grab her partner's hand but stumbled backwards as they pushed her off. She saved herself against the dresser, but scraped her arm. Various trophies went clattering to the floor. "Cam, please! You're scaring me! It's okay! We're okay!"

But the words went unnoticed. They were sucked into the whirlwind that surrounded Cambrie. A beast feasted on their blood, leaving only anxiety and terror in return. They muttered about searching the place, stripping the bed of its blankets. They tore through the pile of white sheets and felt between the bedframe and the headboard. After feeling nothing out of place, they turned their attention to the seams of the mattress.

Despite their hypervigilance, they failed to notice that Belle had made her way to the door. Her hand shook as she touched the handle. Tears streamed down her face.

"I'm leaving," her voice shook. "I can't do this."

"Wait-" But Cambrie was too late. The door slammed shut, causing them to jump.

So they sat for a moment on their adrenaline sweat-soaked mattress. Wetness stained their cheeks. Perhaps it was guilt that knotted in their stomach, though it wasn't clear amongst the nausea. But nothing could stop the pulse of paranoia.

Their eyes were frenzied as they examined the television screen set into the wall. A few rough attempts to pry it from the brick left them breathless, but unsuccessful. Without a second thought, they drove their fist into the screen. It cracked in an elaborate spider web of glass.

They ignored the pain as blood dripped down their fingertips. Cambrie, after tearing apart the cushions, hauled an armchair up against the door. The tiny shards of glass embedded in their knuckles were overlooked as they heaved their mattress up against the wall. Their breath was frantic as they ran their hands along the edge of the bed frame. They dropped to the ground, peering under the bed. A few candy wrappers and a pair of boots were the only monsters lurking there, but Cambrie could have sworn a pair of eyes stared back.

They swiped a hand at the murky face, their fingers feeling nothing. A muffled cry left their lips. They jumped back, whacking their head on the metal bed frame. They couldn't feel the pain over their racing heart. It wasn't real, it couldn't be real. Yet, they shoved their blankets beneath the bed to block out the piercing eyes.

Anywhere bugging devices or cameras could be hidden had to be searched. The plush rug was upturned. Fingers were run along the floorboards in search of secret compartments. Dresser drawers were thrown onto the floor. Folded shirts were bloodied and strewn across the room. The dresser itself was yanked from against the wall. Posters advertising past matches were shredded. Cambrie drug their fingers against the divets on the walls. They knocked various belongings strewn across the desk to the floor and drug the desk to the center of the room. Their heart beat in their throat as they climbed atop the furniture. With shaking hands they unscrewed the lightbulbs from the chandelier. After running their fingers along the fixture, they jumped from the desk, tossing the bulbs to the floor.

When the search was over, Cambrie collapsed to the floor. Amongst the messy darkness, they struggled to catch their breath. They pulled their knees to their chest, thoroughly exhausted as they trembled on the cool hardwood. A glance around the room showed months worth of incentives won desecrated. No doubt there would be a punishment for the destruction. But as Cambrie pulled out the shards of glass from their knuckles–their flesh already knitting itself together thanks to their Angel DNA–they couldn't think about that. They just knew that they wouldn't be trapped again.

Belle stood outside the door for a moment, cringing as the sound of glass hit the floor. She should have stayed.

"Cam, it's me, babe, let me in," she cried.

There was only another large crash in response. Belle bit the inside of her cheek as she rushed to the nearest guard. He stood against the wall, unresponsive to the crashes echoing through the hall. The Alcorium ring in his head flashed green, signaling that he was receiving CareFree. The corners of his lips were forced upward into a stupidly wide smile, as if a child were crafting him from dough. His eyes were wide and glassy.

"Hey! Go help Cambrie!" Belle shouted as she yanked on the Demon guard's arm. He showed her the same interest as a horse showed a fly. "Get off your damn Alcorium and do your job!"

She waved her fingers between where she knew his screen would be and his line of sight. That was a mistake. The bracers around her wrists felt much tighter despite the fact he hadn't done a thing to them. Yet. His head snapped towards her, his movement like some twisted sleep paralysis demon. His breath was hot on her face and smelled of something absolutely rank that Belle couldn't quite place.

"Go help Cambrie before they hurt themself," she spat.

"You're not the one in charge here!" He shoved her to the ground just as the doors to the hallway flew open.

A tiny Demon woman stormed into the hall, her face a fragmented mask of fury. The ring in her head glowed yellow, a color Belle knew well from her time here. The woman was in work mode through and through, only using her Alcorium to control her staff.

"What's going on here?" Her voice boomed throughout the hall.

"Commander! It's not what you think!"

"It's exactly what I think! Don't try and lie to me Kurtz! That's the third time this week. This is your last damn warning before you're off fighting in the Pit yourself! Get away from her! What's happening in room thirteen? I heard there was a disturbance."

"I–" Hesitation lined his voice. "--Don't know."

"You don't know? I pay you to know! This is your damned job! I don't pay you to stand there on your Alcorium and shove Champions around all day!"

"They're having some kind of mental freak out! Please, go help them," Belle begged.

"You heard her," the woman said, gesturing towards Cambrie's room. "And be gentle. If I find out that you've roughed them up in any way, there'll be hell to pay, you understand?"

The woman turned towards Belle and crossed her arms over her chest as if to hug herself. "Have you made your decision?" There was something akin to pity lining her voice. "If you haven't, I don't mind waiting. We can go when you want."

She bit her tongue as she looked away from the woman, a sinking feeling in the pit of her stomach. She had known her choice the moment Odastron had offered it to her. There had never been another option. There were no other paths here, not for her. Everything was for her sister. So she nodded. Her feet were heavy as she marched down the hall to the elevator and the doors closed behind her.

The walk was too short to Odastron's office, the Demon too far behind her. She could've sworn she could smell his expensive cologne before she even opened the door. It was too heavy in her nose, the faint taste of it on her tongue. It gagged her, made her stomach churn. And when that door opened, her fingers craved the familiar feeling of a dagger or gun, if only for some semblance of control as she walked into the lion's den.

"I was beginning to think that I would have to drag you in here. It took you long enough," the Master sighed as he kicked his feet up on the desk. With a wave of his hand, the Demon took her leave and shut the door behind her. Belle walked across the room, the white wallpaper caving in on her. She pulled out the chair and began to sit.

"Did I say you get to sit?" Upon her hesitation, he clicked his tongue and waved his hand. "No. Kneel." He brought a small handheld device, an atomizer, up to his lips and took a hit, blowing a puff of smoke into the air. The haze smelled of peppermint as it clung to the air.

Belle looked up at the man from the rug, calculating the probability of managing to get ahold of the cable beneath his desk and strangling him with it. Or perhaps the antique rifle on the wall could act as a bat.

Odastron stood and moved to the other side of his desk, leaning on the tabletop. He gestured to Belle's puffy eyes and still running nose. "I can hardly stand to look at you. I thought you'd be better than a sniveling, snotty, little Human." He used his boot to lift her chin, his face contorted into sick glee. "I thought maybe you'd go and cause a little trouble, and I'd have a little excitement around here. But all you did was go and cry. Absolutely pathetic. I almost want to revoke our deal and just throw Ella into the Pit."

It was all a ploy. She knew that. She refused to feed into what he wanted. But with his diamond knuckles, iron eyes, and barbed wire tongue, all she could imagine were her hands wrapping around his throat. He leaned forward and took another puff from his atomizer, blowing the smoke into Belle's face. The vapors swirled in her nostrils and gagged her.

"Say something girl. What would-"

"I accept your deal as long as you keep Ella alive." She refused to look up, instead focusing on the fish tank that took up the majority of the wall to her left. The swirls of colors moved about as the desk creaked in front of her.

Odastron smirked. There was no mistaking the look in his eye as he raked her body up and down. He rolled his shoulders, cocking his head to one side. He clicked his tongue, as if trying to decide whether or not to let his temper get the better of him.

"So you do speak. I have a feeling I'll have fun with you."

"Say you'll keep Ella alive." Belle grit her teeth, trying to keep her breathing steady.

"Watch your mouth," he spat, spittle landing on Belle's cheek. "I'm the one who gives orders around here, not you. Got it?" After Belle nodded, he continued. "Great. Look me in the eyes, doll. Now, I need to make sure you understand something. I don't need you to agree to anything, but hearing you say yes is part of the fun. So, do you agree to our compromise?"

There was a single moment's pause as she silently said a prayer, then met his gaze.

"Yes."

# Five

## The Best Laid Plans Involve Bloodshed and Shapeshifting

**CW: Brief mention of slavery**

The decrepit man couldn't even scream before Perri's fangs tore through his bruised throat. He slumped, dead, against the wall, his chains and shackles clanking against the floor. They hadn't even given him the decency of clothing to cover his battered body, but Perri hardly noticed as she fed. His blood was bitter against the Siren's tongue. Her eyes crinkled as she pursed her lips. She could smell the disease on him before she feasted, but it wasn't as if she had many options. Her win against Cambrie had won her the privilege of Human flesh, though only the sickest of Humans they could manage to drag up from the halls surrounding the Pit. And while she could technically survive without feeding, she wasn't about to risk Mosines' Hunger Curse-an illness so unspeakably awful it only lived etched in the lines of forbidden textbooks. Perri sighed before returning her concentration to her meal, longing for the clean Human flesh of her home.

When she finished, she rose from the floor, wiping blood from her lips with the back of her palm. She flicked her tongue across her fangs before flinging open the door to the small holding cell, leaving the pile of bones behind her. She stepped into the common room, causing a few Demon Champions to pause their conversation as she passed. Deadly gazes and sneers splashed across her back. She could feel them in every unspoken word, as they pulled at the threads and began to untangle them from a massive web of shimmering lies. In between the doses of the drugs her fellow Champions received, they clawed at half-baked truths in order to figure out how life had gone so wrong, how the world seemed so much darker, and how the President's daughter had really ended up here. And in so many conclusions, all of it pointed to her.

So she watched her back as she glided along the marble floor, appearing unbothered. The common room was packed with early morning breakfast goers. They milled about, the scent of fresh fruit and eggs wafting in the air. The tang of citrus puckered her lips. But Perri wanted none of it.

Instead, she turned her attention to the enslaved Saybrim woman clearing away trays. The woman counted the silverware to make sure no one had smuggled away a knife. Her long webbed fingers should have struggled to pick up the small utensil, but instead she wielded it with ease. Bruises traced up and down her limbs, track marks along her veins. All three large eyes were downturned, unblinking. She didn't dare to glance around, but the crinkles around her eyes told careful observers that she had already seen enough.

The woman was an unswaying rock in the wind, a wise and steady constant in this world. She would remember this place long after the rest were gone. The coarse tendrils that sprouted from her head were a darker gray, tied up with a fraying ribbon. She had no nostrils, instead breathing through her rough, textured, light gray skin. Her lips were thin and if she were to open her mouth, four rows of flat molars would be staring back. A single piece of yellow cloth was tied around her stomach, allowing some semblance of modesty for her otherwise bare body.

Seeing her here clearly, without the haze of substances, the lines of Perri's textbooks continued to unravel. Within the confines of society Saybrim were hardly Humanoids, their intellect laughable. But the growing whispers of her father's Council and the way this woman observed her told otherwise.

Najah was sitting at one of the high top tables littered about, letting her feet bounce off the bar of her chair. Perri slid beside the assassin as she shoveled a bite of cereal into her mouth.

"So are you ready for today?" Perri asked as she brushed her bangs to the side. She leaned across the table for the apple sitting on Najah's tray. She sank her teeth into the skin. Sweetness flooded her taste buds.

Najah rolled her eyes. "I was gonna eat that," she grumbled, then let a small smile spread across her face. "Of course I am. You saw who they put me up against. If you could take Cambrie, then I definitely can."

Perri glanced over the room before casting a pointed look to Najah. She hadn't been asking about the match. She was asking about her life debt to the assassin, the escape plan she had formulated and conveyed with careful whispers last night. It had taken some groveling, promises, and half-hearted apologies to the assassin in order to get her attention, but eventually she had broken through. They had spent hours tweaking the plan together until they felt confident enough to employ the plan tonight. After all, why wait and risk the potential for death? Perri took another bite of her apple in the hopes that chewing could take away the butterflies in her stomach.

"Like I said, I'm ready," Najah replied. She had to give Perri credit. That first night she had doubted the Siren. And while she still had her issues with Perri, the plan she had come up with was brilliant.

She finished her last spoonful of cereal before standing and piling the garbage on her tray, wincing as familiar sharpness shot through her knee. She took a breath and let the pain settle into her joints, leaning back on the table.

"Are you ready?" Najah asked, looking for a hint that Perri noticed anything amiss. But the Siren wasn't even looking at her, eyes glued instead at the Saybrim woman across the room.

"Duh. What I'm not ready for are the laps that Contessa is gonna make us run today." She said the name of the trainer with contempt and took another bite of her apple then let it fall from her hand onto the floor. She made no move to pick it up. "At least my trainer never made me run. I don't understand why people run for fun."

"You gonna pick that up?" Najah asked, gesturing to the half eaten fruit on the floor.

"What?" Perri blinked before turning her attention to the apple. "Why do you care? They have cleaners for a reason."

"Because it's fucking rude," Najah said, rolling her eyes. "You're ridiculous."

Perri huffed as she bent down. "It's not like it's your house." She picked up the apple and deposited it onto the tray. "Happy?"

"You aren't at the Manor anymore," Najah said simply. "You gotta stop acting like it."

Perri ignored her, instead glancing at the clock on the wall. "C'mon, we have to get to training."

Cambrie hadn't seen Belle since their episode. Guilt acted as the stones in their pockets and they were left feeling as though they were continuously choking on the waters of remorse and regret. That night, Ella had come around in tears saying Belle's belongings had been removed from their shared room. From what they could gather, she had been taken to another floor to reside with the other Masters' personal attendants. It was from there that she would live out the rest of her life.

As Cambrie sat in their barren room awaiting the escort to the Pit, their stomach knotted. They ran over hundreds of different escape plans. They had to figure out how to get Belle and Ella out. Cambrie couldn't waste more precious time here while everything was falling apart.

Maybe they could smuggle some utensils from the kitchen. Or maybe they could somehow smuggle a weapon from the Pit. Maybe sneak out through the loading docks? Cambrie shook their head. The weapons, the utensils, and themself were all loaded with tracking devices. If they could find a way to get the bracers off, or overload the security system....

The door swung open, the familiar guard Gavin, sent to retrieve them.

"Time to go," he grumbled as he leaned in the doorway. Cambrie made a show of slowly climbing off the bed and meandering towards him. *Sometime today.*

Cambrie considered the tools along his belt. A pair of spare bracers, a collapsable club, a flashlight. Any of them could be useful, and so easy to slip from under his nose, but without a solid plan, taking anything now was begging to be caught.

He patted Cambrie down, searching for anything that could be considered a weapon before turning on his heel and leading them out of the room.

So the Halfling followed Gavin along dutifully. Down the hall, into the elevator, into the winding cement halls, they cased the place for the hundredth time, looking for anything they had missed. But everything remained the same, still as impenetrable as ever. Although, they had said the Egg was impenetrable too, and they had escaped from there.

As they reached the familiar doors, Gavin patted them down once more before turning to the other guards milling around. He looked around at the other Human competitors that were getting lined up, guards watching over them carefully. Human hands were always quick and anxious at the prospect of escape. There had been more than a few shankings during the Human line up before. But Gavin, almost imperceptibly, tilted his head. Something other than concern had settled in his mind.

"Has the girl been brought down yet?"

"You're here early. They're bringing her down now," a woman said, fingers moving on her Alcorium screen. "Why?"

"I think we should keep them away from each other," Gavin gestured towards Cambrie, reaching for their arm. "They know each other."

"Who's coming down? What?" Cambrie asked, whipping their head around for any clue. There were only two people that the guards could be talking about, and neither should be here.

But before they could beg for more answers, Ella rounded the corner.

# Six

# GIVE A SIREN POWER AND WHAT HAPPENS NEXT WILL SHOCK YOU!

She could practically feel his trachea crush beneath her fingers. She wanted to bathe in the warmth of his blood, to floss her teeth with the marrow from his bones. As soon as she got out of here and repaid her debt to Najah, Perri would go and end her father. But she had to sit on this damned plastic bed and focus. She wouldn't let her thoughts trail to Anna.

But her childhood friend was so interwoven in everything she had done. Anna's voice-not her own-was the one coaching the Siren through this plan. She had always been the mastermind. Together they had spent countless nights learning the ins and outs of Alcoriums in the secrecy of Anna's attic. She had been the one to originally reprogram them and create the fake Alcoriums they had worn while Perri played the innocent daughter for months, learning all of Triton's secrets. And Anna had died for it. So while most people might have been nervous, it wasn't butterflies that filled her chest. She bawled her fists and waited, the burning in her throat threatening to choke her.

Years of suppressing emotions served Najah well. She was numb, emotionless, as she counted down the minutes. She stared at the brick wall beside the bed, her eyes blurring. There was no point in letting anxiety or excitement plague her and dull her senses. It would only make her sloppy. She had learned that much from her training at The Egg.

Time seemed to slow as the door to their room swung open. Perri's heart jumped as she stared up at the guard who stood in the doorway. His eyes were dull as he cased the room without much care. His scent was all too ordinary, the Care-Free in his system cloaking his emotions.

"Get up Najah," he said, his voice tired. "You have to go."

"I don't feel good," she responded, continuing to stare at the wall.

"Does it look like I care?" His feet slid past the red line painted onto the floor just as he had every time he had come by. The arrogance curled up the walls like an overbearing cologne and smothered them with its presence. Such a stupid man.

Perri flicked an eye towards the hall. There weren't any other guards in her line of vision. Typical. Any other day this would have been an insult, a bruise to her ego that they didn't find her challenge enough to be worth their time. However, today she would gladly bare it.

"I have food poisoning. I'm not going." Najah clutched at her stomach as she lay in the fetal position. She stared at the shadow of the man approaching on the wall.

Perri shrugged, looking at her bare nails in distaste. "Might wanna get her some meds, it won't be a fair fight otherwise."

"That's not how this works and you know it. Now quit being dramatic and get up Najah." The guard reached for the assassin, but she was quicker.

She rolled over, letting her Vitare reflexes take over. She grabbed his head and drove it downwards, his head crashing against the metal bed frame. He slumped to the ground, the thud jolting Perri's heart.

"That was it? That wasn't all that impressive," Perri mumbled. She stood from the bed. There still weren't any guards here yet, but there would be soon if the cameras didn't see the guard come out of the room.

"It's not always about being flashy. It got the job done, didn't it?" Najah said as she slid off the bed.

"Don't they have a gift shop here? What are the chances they'd have nail polish?" Perri tried to ignore the adrenaline making her dizzy, her gaze on the doorway. Closing the door would be too suspicious. Red coated her bare soles as she tried to find oxygen in the stifling room.

"That's what you're concerned about right now?"

Najah had already flipped him to his side, perhaps a small mercy to the Siren's twisting stomach. Perri rushed to find no pulse, her cheeks flushed with an inexplicable heat. Blood pooled around her knees as she knelt beside the man. But as she knelt, she felt the tinge of familiarity. It was a position she had found herself in too often in nightmares. The Siren was as familiar with death as the sunrise. All Sirens had to be in order to survive. But this settled into her bones differently. Her fingers traced over his Alcorium as she tried to steady her shaking hands. She tapped the Alcorium ring six times in rapid succession before holding her finger on the device.

"Activate emergency protocol," she said, her voice soft. "Release Alcorium."

The ring flashed purple, then stopped. It popped up, no longer flush with the skin. Perri daintily pulled the device from his head, the wires having retracted into the ring. She swallowed hard. The first part of her plan was working, as she knew it would. Those late nights of experimentation had paid off. Without hesitation, she brushed her hair back behind her ear and held the ring to her own head in the space slightly in front of and above the ear. With her other hand she repeated the tapping rhythm and held her finger to the ring.

"Install Alcorium with restored settings."

The ring carved out a small hole and released the wires into her head. She let out a hiss, but welcomed the pain as it steadied her nerves. A few drops of blood dripped down the side of her cheek but she swiped them away without a care, letting the residue stain her skin. She blinked a few times as the Alcorium settled in before pressing the ring again. The all too familiar screen popped in front of her, an array of colorful apps along the sides of the transparent screen. Before she could continue however, a large notification popped up on the screen and a cheery voice echoed in her ear:

"Unauthorized transfer found. Please enter the emergency passcode before continuing." Perri rolled her eyes but entered the standard emergency passcode. "Thank you," the voice said. "CareFree distribution will be suspended at this time."

The notification disappeared and left the home screen for Perri to explore. Some of the apps were new to her given that guards had custom technology for their jobs, but many were standard on everyones' Alcoriums. After a few seconds, she found the app she was looking for. Every prisoner's name was listed beside a few symbols: a lightning bolt, an arrow, and a lock.

"Hurry up, we don't need another guard coming in here wondering what's up," Najah hissed as she crossed her arms across her chest, tapping her foot against the tiled floor.

"Don't rush me," Perri spit. She stopped at Najah's name and pressed the lightning bolt, but not before lowering the intensity. Najah jolted as electricity coursed through her. She gave Perri a deadly glare as she shook out her wrists. "Oops, sorry," Perri feigned innocence as she looked up at the assassin through her lashes. Perri pushed the lock and heard the unmistakable sound of Najah's bracers unlocking.

Instantly Najah felt her powers return. They coursed through her veins and warmed her body. She kept the bracers around her wrists however. Perri rose from the ground as she scrolled through the list again and found her name. She shook off her shackles, kicking them beneath the bed as she closed the Alcorium. Her own powers burst into her veins reminiscent of the birth of a star. In those moments, the coursing in her body served as a reminder of who she truly was.

"Ready?" She asked, taking a breath to steady herself. When Najah nodded, Perri began channeling her energy into her shift. Her bones elongated and stubble coated her cheeks as she transformed into the guard on the floor, the pain a welcome familiarity. Her eyes teared up and her knees buckled as her skin stretched to create the guard's figure.

"Holy shit, that's really good," Najah said, eyebrows raised.

"I should hope so. All those years with the best trainers in Arayvia had better have taught me something." Perri said, her voice significantly deeper and more masculine. "Let's go."

Perri shoved the door away from the door and made a show of roughly gripping Najah's arm and shoving her through the doorway. No one in the hall cast a second look as the two of them emerged from their room.

"Get moving," Perri barked. "You already took up way too much time with your whining."

"Don't let this go to your head," Najah muttered under her breath as Perri pushed her forward.

They continued down the hall, their footsteps echoing off the tile. As they pushed through the double doors and entered into the common room, Najah canvassed every centimeter of the place. The couches that sat in one corner remained untouched, the dining area waiting for the next morning, the bare walls silent witnesses. Four guards stood against the walls. Two didn't bother to look up from their Alcoriums as the pair entered, while the other two muttered acknowledgements towards Perri, then returned to their screens. But both knew as the setting sun cast a subtle glow across the room that even if some of the guards were negligent, a dozen cameras watched with careful eyes. The thought made the Siren's heart skip a beat. These weren't the eyes of the press or adoring fans, not anymore.

The pair entered the elevator and Perri chose the bottom floor. They continued their descent in silence. Anything Najah could think to say to the Siren was far too risky to say aloud, and Perri was fixated on the Alcorium screen. Her fingers were a blur across the screen as she typed in strings of code, already busy hacking into the Alcorium's many apps. She barely blinked as she bypassed their systems. The programmers had been lazy, and none of them had anticipated her.

By the time the elevator opened to the dark catacombs surrounding the Pit, Perri was finished. With just the press of a button, chaos would rain down on the arena and they would make their escape. As they stepped into the halls, the overwhelming scent of Humans filled the Siren's nostrils once again. Yet, her attention was on getting them to the Pit.

Najah had to admit, the Siren's plan was gutsy but brilliant. If this worked, the assassin would question all of the training she received at the Egg. She'd be damned if a model could come up with a better plan than her. Still, as the Siren walked past the dying Humans lined along the cement walls, taking little care not to step on their appendages, Najah bit her tongue until she drew blood. No, she wouldn't let herself admire the woman for a second, even if she was bringing them to freedom. She was a Nextulus after all.

As they wound through the halls, Perri's grip on Najah's arm was a tad too tight. She wore the authority as if it were bestowed upon her by the Goddesses themselves. Najah took a breath. Even without the Alcorium in her head, in these blood stained halls she still needed to shove down her emotions or risk death. It was all too similar to the Egg. One prison for another. At least they would be out soon, and then she would find her sister.

Bass vibrated beneath their feet as they walked the slight incline that led to the tunnel into the Pit. Guards and employees buzzed about, eyeing the Human competitors that had just entered the arena to fight to their death. In this first round, the last Human standing would live to see another day. But as Perri and Najah approached the entrance, a voice rose above the music.

"She's got the exemption! She's not supposed to fight!" Cambrie screamed at the guards around them. "Get her out of there!"

"I'm just doing as I'm told, and they specifically told me she's fighting," a guard growled before turning to Perri and Najah. "What are you doing here? You're supposed to be at the east entrance. Hurry up, you're already late! The next match starts in fifteen minutes."

Perri turned away in her larger demon form, grumbling something about a mixup. Najah began to walk away but paused as she heard the guard turn to another and say:

"Watch the Halfling carefully. You heard what they did to their room the other day, and they don't go on until after this round."

Najah began to follow Perri, taking note that they may have more eyes on Cambrie than her when Cambrie lunged for her, grabbing her arm. Najah met the Halfling's desperate eyes.

"They've got Ella! They're making her fight. Najah, please, help me," Cambrie begged before being yanked away by the guards.

The announcer in the Pit began counting down for the match to begin. The crowd inside cheered, their voices vibrating inside rib cages. A guard hurried to close the door to the Pit.

"Get moving." Perri muttered as she grabbed Najah roughly. She tried to pull Najah away from the others.

But Najah stayed firmly in place and stared as the Halfling broke free of the guard's grip. With every ounce of desperate strength, Cambrie slid inside the closing doors just as the announcer shouted "One!" The doors automatically barred shut, leaving Cambrie locked inside. They wouldn't open now, not for anyone besides a Pit Master. Or Perri.

A millisecond of memory left Najah breathless as she watched the Halfling. A brief moment of mercy in a place not designed for such kindness. An act of humanity in the walls of the inhumane. She swallowed hard, allowing herself to wonder for just a second if she was going soft.

Najah shot Perri a pointed look as the guards around them began shouting.

"We're saving them," Najah hissed. "Open the door."

"What! No! We're not..." Perri's gruff whispers were cut off by a suddenly nightmarish Najah.

"We're saving them, otherwise I won't hesitate to slit your pretty little throat when we get out of here. And just to spite you, we're saving Ella too."

"This is going to get us killed," Perri hissed. "I swear to the Goddesses, you're risking our lives for some weak ass Human!"

Najah held out her hand, weaving in a subtle threat to her words. "Do it."

Perri rubbed her eyes and grit her teeth. "Fine, whatever, but after this my debt is paid. Take care of the guards."

# Seven

# She's a Runner, She's an Attack Star

## CW: Sexual harassment

Belle stood against the velvet wallpapered wall in the Master's booth, the scent of an untouched buffet teasing her nauseous stomach. The guards that stood sentry in the corners of the room had locked their gazes onto her, nearly ignoring the other assistants. Though, Belle couldn't quite figure out why she had acquired that target on her back. The past few days she had been on her best behavior. She had sat being primped and primed in the floor above, ever silent as they transformed her into someone she didn't recognize. She had been the perfect doll for them. And as Odastron's shiny new plaything, she had been at his beck and call during his workday. Always quiet, always attentive, always willing to please. Anything to save Ella.

The Masters all sat in their thrones, their banter unusually light-hearted. Their favored assistants lined the wall beside Belle, all silently gazing in the space in front of them until called. One of them sat on Pit Master Artemis's lap. Her obnoxious giggles accented every word the men said. But from the tenseness in her shoulders and the extra wide smile, everyone knew she wasn't there of her own volition. It was enough to make Belle want to gouge her own eyes out.

"Darling, get me a glass of wine would you?" Odastron called to Belle sweetly.

Belle pushed herself off the wall, resisting the urge to yank her skirt further down her legs. She brushed past one of her fellow assistants, his eyes focused on picking out the perfect cheeses for his Master. Belle shakily took a bottle of wine from the buffet table and poured it into a glass, nearly dumping half the bottle onto the pristine tablecloth. But the assistant beside her shielded her actions from view and used his empty hand to steady the bottle, ensuring it didn't splatter onto the linens. He didn't mutter a word or meet her thankful gaze, only walked away with plate in hand. Belle bit her tongue and scolded herself for being so on edge. Her anxiety had skyrocketed the past few days. She needed to keep a level head but her nerves were shot.

With trembling fingers she delivered the drink to her Master. He accepted his drink in one hand and with his other, pulled Belle into his lap. He took a sip of the wine before placing it on the side table. His hand wandered to Belle's bruised thigh and squeezed. Belle grit her teeth, forcing her gaze ahead. His other hand ran through her hair, almost like a mother to her child. The action repulsed Belle, and it took every bone in her body to remain still. She was doing this for Ella, for her safety. No matter what happened to herself, at least Ella would be safe.

"I was just telling everyone how I think you'll really enjoy watching this match." He paused as he sunk his fingers deeper into her bruised leg. "It's too bad that you won't be able to see Cambrie anymore." Belle refused to look at him, sure that if she did, she would be repulsed by the look on his face. "Oh look darling, the Humans are about to play."

Belle didn't glance down. She couldn't care for the careless slaughter about to take place. She had seen enough of it when she was a competitor herself. Out of the corner of her eye, she spotted the other Master's openly staring at her. She opened her mouth, then closed it, knowing better than to question them. Whatever the reason for their stares wasn't worth losing her tongue over.

"Look," Odastron hissed as he placed his hand on the back of Belle's head and forced her to look down towards the Pit.

Belle grit her teeth to avoid swearing at the man controlling her and disdainfully cast her gaze to the Pit below. From up high with her painfully Human senses, she struggled to make out the details. But just before she tore her eyes away she saw all too familiar rainbow braids. And as if right on cue the screens scanned across the Pit, zooming in on Ella.

Belle's heart stopped in that moment, her throat tight as the full shock of what happened hit her. She leapt to her feet and whirled around to face the Masters, her face flush with an indescribable rage.

"You promised you'd keep her safe!" She shouted. Damn the consequences. Damn everything. She had fallen right into his trap. The world spun as she breathlessly flew towards the door, yanking on the gilded handles. The doors wouldn't budge. She banged her fists against the solid wood. She looked to the statuesque assistants on the wall, the too attentive guards, the other Masters, begging them. Only the assistant from earlier indiscernibly shook his head. "Let me out! You promised!"

Odastron, with every ounce of his Siren charm, strolled up behind Belle and leaned over her, placing his hand on the door. She whipped around, eyes blazing. The Master cupped her chin in his hands, snickering slightly.

"You seem to forget that you're not a Champion anymore sweetheart, and I don't make promises with my...."

But before he could finish his sentence, the other Masters let out a collective gasp.

"Oh shit," the demon Master chuckled. "Hey Stron, that Halfling of yours is trying to get killed."

'What?" Odastron turned on his heel and took a few steps towards the window. They both saw it at the same time. Cambrie had slipped into the Pit.

It was as if the air had been sucked from the room. Belle felt the nausea rise in her throat, too many thoughts bombarding her brain. There was no time to comprehend the consequences that would behold them all at the end of this. There was only time for action.

Odastron let a flurry of curses fly from his lips as he used his Alcorium to unlock the doors. He shoved Belle aside as he threw them open, nearly knocking her into the buffet table.

"Guards, take care of her," he growled over his shoulder.

But Belle had already recovered and was out the door before the guards could move. Her running was muffled by the velvet carpet, pure adrenaline pumping through her veins. She pushed past Odastron. At the end of the hall was an elevator. She had to get there before him. She had to get to Ella.

The guards were thundering down the hall behind the Master, but their footsteps weren't the only ones. A few assistants trailed behind her, shoving the guards into the walls with a desperate fury. The guards' fingers were frantic as they slammed on their invisible screens, trying to shock Belle and the other assistants. But Belle kept running, electricity failing to course through her muscles. Little did the guards realize that her bracers had been unlocked moments ago, like every other prisoner's. Belle flew into the elevator. She jabbed the button, willing the doors to close faster. Odastron was only a few steps behind. He couldn't slip through the doors however. They slammed shut and Belle's stomach dropped as the elevator took her underground. She had to get to Cambrie.

## Eight

# Rules are Meant to be Broken, Smashed, and Just Generally Fucked

Cambrie recognized far too late that they were fucked. Their bracers were still tight on their wrists, the sudden weight hitting them in their chest. They didn't have time to think about that though.

A large man barreled towards them waving a jagged machete. His ribs stuck out and dirt was caked in his hair. His reasons for wanting to win were as numerous as the scars along his hands. Given his gall, he believed he could do it too.

Cambrie darted to the left as he charged. As he ran past, Cambrie caught a glimpse of Ella ducking behind a barrier. They sprinted towards the girl, the grunts of fighting filling the air. Blood pounded in their ears.

Ella crouched behind the cement block feeling nausea rise in her throat. No amount of training could have prepared her for this. Nothing she encountered in the Resistance had come close to this, this lone battle for survival. Across the Pit a woman screamed. Someone ran past her wielding a crossbow, narrowly avoiding her as they chased their prey. She had to find a weapon. The dust flew up around her in a cloud, coating her mouth and scratching her corneas. Nothing she had ever heard could compare to the desperation and frenzy around her. It was dizzying, and before she got on her hands and knees, she didn't know which way was up or down.

She scanned the dirt around her in the hopes of finding a glint of steel. And her prayers must have been answered because moments later she found herself sliding into the dirt, lunging for a knife. Just as her fingers slipped around the worn leather hilt, a towering, hulking man kicked it from her hand. She let out a yelp as she stared up at the man and scrambled to her feet.

With her back against the barrier she ducked under his swinging arm. She lurched forward, ready to run. If she could just last five minutes....

But just then, Cambrie delivered a swift kick to the back on the man's kneecaps. He tumbled to the dirt, a typhoon of curses spewing from his lips. He tried to stand, only to have his leg buckle beneath him. His face fell as he collapsed to the ground. A few stuttering pleas for mercy echoed through his trembling lips as he frantically scrambled away on his hands and knees. He only made it a few inches away by the time another competitor ran by wielding a knife, easily slicing the fallen man open.

Cambrie threw themselves in front of Ella and snarled at the knife wielder. The competitor hesitated, but upon second thought veered away from the pair.

"Are you okay?" Cambrie shouted over the fighting. Ella nodded just as ear shattering screams rose up throughout the arena. The noise from the audience that was normally blocked out by the safety dome echoed in full force. The pounding rock music however cut off, leaving an unusual emptiness in the air.

"Stay calm everyone! Remain in your seats," the announcer called out. "Competitors, put down your weapons! The match is over!"

The competitors hesitated, fingers still clenched around weapons. No one made a move to surrender first, wondering if this was perhaps a cruel trick. But with one glance Cambrie knew why. The safety dome had glitched, leaving the members of the audience victim to poorly fired arrows and stray throwing knives. In fact, a few medics were already hurrying around in the crowd. And on both ends of the arena doors had swung open. Guards rushed from the east door, running right for them.

Panic filled Cambrie. They had to get out of here. Once Odastron got ahold of them, they would be dead for tampering with his game, for daring to save Ella. But before the full force of those implications hit, a surge of familiar power flooded them. It nearly knocked them to the ground as they stumbled backwards into Ella. As Ella made a grab for Cambrie, an unlocked bracer fell from their wrist, tumbling to the dirt. Cambrie and Ella met each other's eyes, the realization hitting them at the same time.

A wicked smirk grew across the Halfling's cheeks as they grabbed Ella's hand. Then, they fired a fireball at the Masters' box.

# Nine

# Five Criminals Walk into a (Snack) Bar...

Najah's body sung with power as the last guard fell to the floor. She brushed off her palms and then wiped them on her pants as she waited for Perri to open the doors. Her mind spun a mile a minute, doubt tearing through the corners of her skull. She was wasting a surefire shot to get out of here. All because of one moment years ago.

Perri's large fingers quickly scrolled across the Alcorium. Frustration sat heavy in her stomach. She was wasting precious time saving these other assholes while her window of escape was closing. Her back was drenched with sweat, the stuffy guard's uniform clinging to her skin.

The metal doors scraped against the floor as they slid open. Dust hung in the air. They rushed into the Pit, met by guards pouring through from the other side. The Human competitors, as if recognizing their opportunity, rushed towards the uniformed men weapons raised.

Perri and Najah entered the Pit just in time to see Cambrie toss a fireball at the Masters' box. The fire scorched the glass, unfortunately doing nothing to the Masters remaining inside. A few fleeing patrons screamed as the heat licked their skin. Cambrie and Ella shoved through the onslaught of competitors towards Perri and Najah. Najah reached out and grabbed Cambrie, yanking them into the hall.

"Took you long enough," Perri muttered.

"Who are you?" Cambrie hissed, their tail flicking as they ran. "What's happening?"

"It's Perrianna, she hacked into a guard's Alcorium," Najah said before Perri could answer. "We're getting out of here."

"What? No! We have to find Belle!" Ella cried out.

The yelling of the dying rang out at a feverish pitch as they passed. Desperate hands reached for ankles, hands, anything they could grab to beg for a last chance at escape. Ella stumbled, gripping Cambrie's hand for dear life.

"No! We don't have time!" Perri screamed back as she hauled them through the hall. If they could make it to the elevator at the end of the hall, they could get to ground level and get out of here before they locked the place down. But she'd be damned if they kept saving people.

"Please!" Ella pleaded, trying not to gag on the scent of rotting flesh. She nearly stumbled again as more hands clung to her. Tears threatened to spill down her cheeks. She cast a pleading glance to Cambrie. Then she planted her feet to the ground, refusing to move any further. The group stumbled to a stop.

"We'll find her on our own," Cambrie said, pulling their wrist from Najah's grasp. They didn't need allies. Asking for her help in the first place had only been out of desperation. Not that they weren't eternally grateful to her. "Thank you, for everything." Cambrie starred into Najah's eyes in the hopes of conveying an impossible amount of gratitude. They didn't bother glancing towards Perri.

"Whatever," Perri sighed. She kicked at some of the hands descending from the shadows. "Go get yourselves killed. Damn Humans," she muttered. She rolled her eyes, ignoring the glare she got from Cambrie. She sniffed, the distinct scent of the guards' boots at the edge of her senses and approaching at a rapid pace. "The guards are coming. Let's go."

But then, at the end of the hall, the elevator doors opened and Belle rushed out. Her skin was flushed and marred, her eyes frenzied. She looked as if she hadn't taken a breath in days.

Ella noticed her first and took off running. She leapt into her sister's arms, nearly knocking Belle to the floor. Tears fell from the younger girl's face as she gripped Belle tight. Cambrie appeared beside them a moment later, letting out a sigh of relief.

"How did you get out? What happened?" Belle questioned. But then she spotted Perri, still disguised as a guard, and shoved Ella behind her. "Don't touch her," she snarled at the Siren.

"Are you that stupid?" Perri growled back. "If I wanted I could have already ripped her to shreds. I'm saving your asses. Now get in the elevator. They're coming." She shoved past the others and entered the elevator.

"It's Perrianna Nextulus," Cambrie supplied shortly. "Not a guard."

"Great, like that makes me feel any better," Belle huffed as she wrapped an arm around Ella and stepped into the lift.

The others crowded inside, the scent of sweat thick in the air. The heat was stifling. But none of that mattered because they were minutes away from escaping and seeing the night sky again. Minutes away from seeing friends, family, newfound freedom. But only if they could get out of the lobby. As the doors closed, Perri whirled around to face the others. Words flew from her mouth a mile a minute.

"Cambrie, go invisible or shift into someone else, whatever the fuck it is you do. We need to draw as little attention to ourselves as possible. So if anyone has any talents they haven't shared, make yourself useful."

"Love having you tell me what to do," Cambrie mumbled.

"Get rid of your bracers. Guards will be looking for them." Perri ignored Cambrie's comment, trying to get out everything she had to say in the few seconds she had. Bracers clanked as they fell to the floor. "I was able to get into a guard's mind earlier. They'll go on lockdown once they realize we're missing. I unlocked all the Champion's bracers so that should buy us time. Most of the guards will be covering the exits closest to the other Champions. I'll disable the elevators once we get there to slow more guards from coming. We're going to have to go out the front doors. It's the quickest way, and the last one they'll lock down because that's where all the patrons will gather."

"We're walking out the front doors?" Ella whispered. She shook as Perri shot her a look so deadly the Human wondered if the Siren developed a new power to kill with just intention. "I just thought that you had a plan that wouldn't involve us walking through a bunch of people that would recognize us and maybe get us caught since we...."

"I did, until *someone* decided to fuck it up. But now I have to try to get us out of here dressed like this, so blend in and shut up. If we gotta fight, then we gotta fight. But no matter what happens I'm getting out of here."

"Can't you persuade the guards to look the other way or something? You're a Siren after all." Belle asked, glaring at Perri. "I don't want to hurt innocent people."

"Like these people are innocent," Najah snorted.

Perri let out a little laugh, pressing her tongue to the back of her fang. "If that's your concern right now, go back to being Odastron's whore," the Siren huffed.

"Don't you dare! That's not her choice!" Cambrie snapped.

Perri ignored the Halfling. "Besides, I can only persuade one person at a time, and only if I touch them. Unless you have any powers you'd like to contribute to the group, Human?" She pursed her lips as she stared right back at Belle. It was a challenge and everyone knew it.

Belle remained silent but refused to drop her glare as the elevator stopped on the ground level. A last glance around revealed that Cambrie had silently turned invisible, although their judgment could still be felt.

The doors opened to reveal the atrium. Vibrant holograms of various Champions danced across the smooth walls of the room, their bodies larger than life as they fought in carefully animated battles. A Demon Champion wielding a large axe brought the weapon down on the head of her opponent. Realistic blood coated the walls, the dates of upcoming matches written over the crimson stain.

The smell of popcorn still lingered in the air, wafting through the geometric chandeliers dangling from the ceiling. A marble statue depicting the five Pit Masters stood sentry in the middle of the room. Soft pop music played from the speakers.

Patrons had calmly crowded in every crevice of the atrium waiting to hear news of continued matches or refunds, many Alcorium rings flashed green as they received their doses of CareFree. Alcoriums were already soothing those too distressed, quelling the rumors that floated around the room and substituting a more palatable narrative. The murmurs that floated around the room talked of planned stunts to spice up the show, hologram weapons, and a misfired pyrotechnic machine.

It was a more digestible alternative to the inattentive high paying clientele than saying that people had been injured or that there was a full on prison break going on. Any disputes would be drowned out by the collaborating news stories and a CareFree high anyways.

Perri's fingers were already at work on the Alcorium as everyone stepped from the elevator. The group stepped into the mass of people. Past the people in impeccably tailored clothes they went. As they passed the gift shop, Perri noted it did have more than just Aarlin's hair care line. Maybe they would have nail polish.

Najah was nothing more than a shadow, easily slipping through the crowd. She scanned the room, slipping into her old role as if it were a leather jacket. Guards were slow to fill in around the perimeter, but aimed to blend in with the others. This time, there were no distractions for them. They had just as much to lose as their charges if this went south.

Najah hissed a warning to the others. Belle gave a barely perceptible nod in response, her fingers wrapped tightly around Ella's wrist. She wasn't about to lose her sister again. Meanwhile, Perri forged ahead through the snack bar, her burly voice mumbling apologies. Once she got out of here, she was so going to ditch everyone and treat herself to a spa day. Dozens of threats lurked around despite her hacking, and everywhere she turned, another few guards were clamoring through entrances.

Cambrie scanned the room as their fingers slipped inside silken pouches and metal purses as they moved past. Their own pockets were full by the time they reached the middle of the room. But even with their nimble hands busy they kept up with the group, watching Ella's back in particular.

Ella's boots squeaked on the marble floors as she narrowly avoided collisions with the guests. Her stomach lurched with every step. No matter how she tried, she couldn't keep up with the dance of the strangers. The thoughts that intruded inside her mind refused to leave despite her pleas, despite her need to focus. They tattooed into her brain and cried out all of her 3am anxieties. This whole thing was her fault. They were putting themselves in danger for her, because she wasn't strong like them. If she had powers she could have fought. They were moving too fast. The others glided through the place like they were weightless entities while Ella stumbled over her own feet to keep up. Her heart pounded in her head. Every step she took felt like she was tip toeing around a bomb. One misstep could kill them all. And yet, she had to keep moving. Past the porcelain nails and subtle perfumes she was yanked, Belle's grip on her like a vice. She cursed her braids, the blood on her shoes, the itchy competitor's uniform she had been forced to wear. Even without disguises, Belle and Najah somehow managed to blend in with the crowd. But Ella, she felt like a toddler in a busy shopping center with her mother, overwhelmed, chest tight. So she kept her head down, staring at the golden veining on the floor. If she could just make it to the front doors....

But then a man backed into her. Belle was already being swept away with the tide of people when Ella was sent tumbling to the floor. The man's cocktail splashed like amber rain around her. All the color drained from her cheeks as droplets hit her head. She tried to scramble to her feet before he turned, tried to hide among the legs of patrons, but she was too slow. The Siren glanced down at the young girl, an easy smile on his face.

"Oh, sorry," he began, barely registering what he had done. He reached down in order to help her up, but paused as his bright blue eyes roamed over the bloodstains and dirt on her clothes. "Are you alright?"

"I...yeah..I'm fine," Ella stuttered. She stood, backing away from him, knocking into a woman. The woman turned, disgust written on her face.

"Is that blood?" the man asked loudly, his voice lulling into a familiar intonation as his CareFree began to kick in. "Are you okay?"

The patrons nearby turned at the spike in volume. Ella crossed her arms over her body as she tried to melt into the crowd, but she was only pushed back into place. She scanned the swarm for a familiar face, but the people only seemed to close in around her.

Her chest tightened as she searched for a way out. All eyes were on her. Her skin burned as she tried to stammer out a response, but only incoherent sounds fell from her lips.

"Wait," the man paused, his voice growing louder despite the smile on his face. "You look like one of those Human competitors, don't you think Mina?" He turned to his partner who nodded in agreement. They both peered down upon Ella like she was a caged animal on display, curiosity lining their faces instead of fear. "How did you get here?"

Cambrie shoved through the crowd, evident by the fact that a Siren woman was thrown to the ground. Their invisible hand wrapped around Ella, ready to run. Guards were already closing in. Cambrie sprinted towards the door, yanking Ella along with them.

Belle's heart was in her throat as she tore through the horde. Forget discretion. This entire plan had been idiotic. Patrons screamed in shock as she knocked them aside. The room was abuzz as people tried to get a closer look at the commotion. Body armored sentinels with newly acquired guns on their waists elbowed towards them.

Najah stopped as she watched Belle turn and run. There was a desperation in her eyes that created knots in the assassin's stomach, one that Najah herself knew all too well. That sisterly love had driven her to desperate lengths herself. She knew she should run and get out of here. Every fiber in her screamed out urging her to move. Surely, she was getting soft.

"Let's go," Perri hissed as Najah hesitated. "Leave them." Just a few more meters and they'd be out. The others were the perfect distraction. They could get out of there without a fight.

"No. Go ahead, leave, consider your debt paid," Najah said. With one last look at Perri, she took off towards Belle. She easily caught up with the Human, wordlessly fighting towards their companions.

Patrons clambered to get away as Belle, Najah, and the guards shoved through them. Now these were the easily recognizable faces of threats Alcoriums worked so hard to protect against. For a moment, people began to do the math. They all flooded towards the exit, green rings pulsing. But as the narrative was warped once again, everyone seemed to ridicule the idea of a prison break.

Meanwhile, pandemonium had completely broken out. Guards had multiplied. Guns were drawn. Orders were shouted but barely heard. Someone used their Alcorium to shut and lock the doors.

Cambrie and Ella managed to meet up with Belle and Najah. It came as no surprise that with no crowd to hide in, they were surrounded. Too many barrels to count aimed at their heads. So, Cambrie held out their palms and cast a ring of fire around the group. The flames arched and twisted tall above them. They spat towards the offenders with a repulsed hiss. Yet, the guards continued to push forward. Steel barrels aimed for the flames. They didn't intend to spare the prisoners.

Ella shrunk beside her sister. This was all her fault. She was going to get them killed. She should have tried harder, should have trained harder. Why did she have to be Human?

The flames tickled as Cambrie slipped out of the ring, their skin untouched. It was child's play to wrap the crook of their elbow around the first unsuspecting guard's throat and choke him out. He was out before he could move. Cambrie grabbed his pistol from his hand before he collapsed in their arms. They slammed the butt of the gun on his skull, then dropped him to the floor. The other guards realized their mistake as Cambrie threw the pistol inside the ring, making themselves an invisible threat once more.

Belle picked up the pistol, the metal warm. She traced the subtle curves of the grip with her fingers. Her ears strained for any sound of Cambrie as she flicked the safety off and waited.

Najah glanced towards Ella. The girl was practically trembling despite the heat. Shadows flickered on her cheeks. The assassin briefly wondered how she had gotten involved in the Saybrim Resistance, how she had gotten herself branded a terrorist. It mattered little though if they couldn't get out of here. With one hand she shot a vine up towards the ceiling and hooked it around a chandelier. She began to climb. Her hands gripped the thornless plants, rose petals falling to the flames below. She scaled the vine in seconds. From what Najah could tell, the guards weren't sure how to fight this new threat, some of them holstering their guns and deploying their billy clubs instead. They swung their clubs around wildly, hoping to hit Cambrie. Just as Najah was about to wrap her vines around one of the men, Perri hurried into view in her true form. And, she was wielding a gun, probably for the first time in her life. With only a single hand on the grip she aimed for a guard. The bullet hit the wall behind him. A smirk cemented on his face. His fingers moved on his own gun and Perri's face fell.

Najah's vine wrapped around the guard's body, pinning his arms to his torso too late. Perri screamed as a bullet struck her. The sound ricocheted through the air and caused Najah to cringe. To her credit though, Perri grit her teeth and fired another bullet into another guard's head as she clutched her side. Using that opening, Najah bound a guard as Cambrie took out another. Three more remained.

The flames below suddenly extinguished, leaving Belle and Ella exposed. The Pit Masters waltzed into the room. They looked more fit for a party than a prison break with their green Alcoriums and their golden clad necks. But nothing seemed to change about them as they were pumped full of CareFree. Whether it was the drug or their natures, they didn't seem to care about the carnage around them. All were unblinking as they stepped over the bodies of their employees. Instead, one grumbled about getting blood on his shoes.

Vitare Master Artemis was drenched with sweat, his skin pale. He stumbled into Master Odastron as they strolled into the room. It was clear that extinguishing the flames had taken a toll on him. The guards looked at each other, their hesitation allowing Cambrie to down another.

"What are you doing? Shoot them!" One of the Siren Masters screamed.

Belle and Ella were already scrambling towards the door. Just a few more steps and they'd be free. Their Human bodies were slow, giving them a disadvantage compared to Odastron, who was speeding after them.

"Don't shoot the Humans!" Odastron cried out. "They're mine!"

The guards, confused over the conflicting orders, hesitated once more. Najah easily bound the two remaining guards and sent them falling to the floor.

Cambrie launched themselves towards Odastron. A quick elbow to his side caused him to stumble and double over. As he regained his footing, the Halfling stuck out their leg and tripped him. His body splayed to the ground with all the grace of a newborn calf. As

Odastron tried to scramble to his feet, Cambrie delivered a swift kick to his chest.

"Stop you crippled b..." he began to bellow before Cambrie stomped on his throat. The man's voice gave out as he went limp beneath them.

"That's for Belle, *ilsqiam!*" Cambrie cried.

Just then, Ella and Belle smashed the glass on the front doors and ran through. The remaining patrons who didn't realize they could escape remained on the floor by the exit, engrossed by the drug.

Cambrie turned to run after the Human women, but then hesitated. Najah and Perri were still in the Masters' line of fire. The Halfling couldn't abandon Najah again.

Najah had swung off her vine and wrapped a Siren Master's legs together. He pried at the vines and turned to his co-workers for help, finding none. Something left his mouth, but not before he flew through the air like a child was playing particularly cruelly with a doll. His body collapsed to the floor with a sickening thud.

Perri was still standing, albeit rather pale and wobbly. One hand clutched her side, the other shakily gripping her pistol. She took her aim. But after a single unlucky shot the slide hung back over her wrist. The gun was empty. Still, she tried to fire the gun, her finger desperate against the trigger. She could practically feel the color drain from her face as she tossed the gun to the side. She reached out with her perception to try and invade the Vitare Master's memories, to search for some weak spot. But even though their mental walls were weak from CareFree use, she was fading fast and using her powers made her vision go black.

Cambrie cast a chest-high wall of fire across the room between the Masters and remaining women. Their invisibility fell away from them like a cloak as they wrapped their arm around Perri's left shoulder.

Najah joined and supported Perri on her right. Together they hurried across the room, past the unconscious guards, then past the content patrons. The room hung heavy with the scent of burning flesh.

Flames licked at the projected Champions on the walls and scurried across the floor. Chandeliers creaked as the fire crawled up towards the ceiling. The Vitare Master held out his hands in a last ditch effort to control the flames, but as his colleagues fled and the smoke began to wrap its tendrils around bare throats, he too abandoned his mission.

"Get out of here!" Cambrie cried as they passed by the patrons, but to no avail.

Najah threw the doors open, desperately gulping down the warm summer air. Cambrie lifted their hand up and the flames rose to engulf the stadium. The straggling patrons in the lot hardly seemed to notice. Cars were lined up at every exit but no one seemed to be in a hurry. Meanwhile, the shadows of fleeing prisoners could be seen in the distance. Behind them the building began to crumble.

"We have to get out of here!" Najah shouted hoarsely. "We can't go on foot! The cops will be here any minute and she's not gonna make it far." She nodded towards Perri as she readjusted her grip on the Siren. Perri was fading fast as blood dripped onto the pavement.

Cambrie searched the lot for any sign of Belle and Ella. Had they left? They couldn't have abandoned them. They wouldn't. But the Humans were nowhere to be seen. Overhead the whir of a helicopter sounded in the distance. Police sirens could be heard from every direction, coming ever closer.

Then a luxurious black sedan sped up across the lot and came to a screeching halt in front of them. Belle hung out the window of the driver's side.

"Get in!" she shouted.

The back doors swung open. Cambrie jumped in and guided Perri to the middle seat. Najah clambored in after, the doors slamming behind her. Then they sped off into the night, leaving the Pit and the people within to the mercy of the flames.

## Ten

# HUMANS DON'T MAKE GOOD MIDNIGHT SNACKS

## CW: Insinuation of domestic violence

The sedan shuddered as Belle took it off auto-pilot, then subsequently drove over the sidewalk. They sped past the line of cars winding out into the main road. The line pulsed like ants, seemingly never-ending. Perri groaned as they hit a patch of rough cement. Ella turned in her seat to keep her gaze on the Siren, grasping for her icy fingers.

"Is she gonna be okay?"

"We have to get the bullet out, then I can heal her," Cambrie said to Najah. They were sweating and pale, but their voice was steady. The assassin nodded as she met the Halfling's eyes.

"I'll get it out," Najah muttered. She had always had a distaste for bullets. They were crude, and shrapnel always managed to get everywhere. Somewhere in the back of her head she tried to recall the numerous first aid classes she had been forced to take.

"Do you need help? I took first aid classes in elementary school," Ella chimed in. "Plus I earned my first aid badge in Star Squad. And I

did some stuff in basic training for S.P.A.C.E and when I was in the
resistance and..."

"Shut up!" Belle hissed. "You're distracting them!"

"I was just trying to help..."

Najah held out her palm, rose oil dripping from her fingertips. She
shifted in her seat as Belle yanked the car back into the traffic, the
firetruck whizzing down the road. The air was filled with the scent of
smoke and rose.

"I'm going to sedate you with rose oil, okay Perri?" Najah asked as
she went to paint the Siren's forehead.

"Wait." Perri grabbed Najah's wrist. Her fingers trembled, eyes
glazed. "Alcorium...They can track us," she panted before tapping
the ring in her head six times. "Activate emergency protocol. Release
Alcorium." She yanked the device from her head with a wince before
dropping it into Cambrie's outstretched palm. Blood dripped from
her skull onto the leather seat.

As Cambrie tossed the device out the window, Najah spread the oil
across Perri's temples. The Siren's eyes fluttered shut.

"It's really cool how you can do that," Ella whispered.

"What?" Najah asked. Red and blue lights flashed across her face
as a cop rushed towards the chaos. Traffic had slowed to a crawl as
emergency personnel crowded onto the street. The road was abuzz
with the wailing of fire trucks and cop cars. Belle was jamming her
fingers across the dashboard of the car, disabling and wiping the many
cameras the car had.

Najah shook her head. She turned her attention to Perri. Her hands
were steady, her eyes sharp despite the darkness. She tore away the tank
top easily.

"Uh, Cam?"

"What?"

Cambrie peered across the Siren's flawless skin. Any wound that should have been there seemed to have disappeared. Only a small smattering of blood remained.

"How? I...didn't do that." Cambrie's brow knit into confusion as their fingers touched the flesh that should have been broken.

"I know," Najah whispered. "It shouldn't be possible."

"What's happening?" Belle asked, trying to catch a glimpse over wandering hands in the mirror. However, the others failed to hear her.

"She doesn't even have a scar on her face from the other day. Sirens don't suddenly have accelerated healing abilities, do they?" Cambrie continued, brushing aside the woman's hair in search of some mark.

"Not unless Triton genetically modified his family or something," Najah said.

"That wouldn't surprise me. But we still have to get this bullet out...unless this changes things?" Cambrie asked, meeting Najah's eyes.

"She helped save us. Why would it?"

"It...doesn't," Cambrie said, meeting Belle's eyes in the rearview mirror.

There was no hesitation as Najah responded. "You always were leaving me to do the dirty work. I don't suppose anyone has a knife?" When no one said anything, she sighed. "Then this isn't going to be pleasant."

She plunged her vines into Perri's side, the greenery easily piercing flesh. Ella gagged and looked away. Her stomach churned and she found herself eternally grateful that she wasn't at the receiving end of that treatment.

After what felt like minutes, Najah found the bullet and pulled it from the Siren just as an ambulance whizzed by. Warmth enveloped her as blood coated her hand. She took a breath as she went in again, fishing out pieces of shrapnel. A chill caught on her spine as she felt the flesh beneath her vines. It was all dizzying. But with a breath she shook it off, not letting this feeling settle into her bones. She dropped the metal into her palm and tossed the pieces out the window, wiping the blood on her pants.

Cambrie placed their hands on the Siren. They weren't sure how Perri's healing worked and they weren't going to take any chances of her bleeding out. They'd just heal her on their own, as much as they hated the idea. Blood seeped onto their skin as they began to chant in ancient Nirvana, the language of the Angels. The words floated through the air like music. Beneath Cambrie's fingers the body began to repair itself.

Najah watched, remembering the night Cambrie had touched her like that. They had knit broken flesh back together with a single touch. The incantation was so natural on their tongue, one of their few birthrights. Even with her fluency in the language, Najah would never be able to fully understand the words said, as it was a whisper meant for the Goddesses alone.

Traffic finally began to move again and Belle guided the car onto the highway. She set it to self drive mode and allowed the car to take over. The steering wheel moved without her touch as the machine easily merged into traffic. The other drivers on the road craned their necks to watch the fire blazing behind them. There was a raw, fiendish, beauty in the unkempt nature of the flames. If only one looked at the right angle.

Belle grabbed for Ella's hand and squeezed it tight. The familiarity brought her back to family road trips and childhood adventures. She let out a breath, finally realizing the startling tightness that clung around her ribcage. The reality of her body, all of the aches and pains, suddenly seemed all too present. And while she wanted to enjoy the chaos behind them, they had to be on alert. She traced her thumb across Ella's knuckles. Her other hand traced the grip of the pistol in the waistband of her pants.

When Cambrie ended their chant, an eerie silence settled into the car. They removed their hands from Perri, blood staining their fingers. There wasn't even a scar on Perri's side. She would be fine.

Cambrie would have admired their work if their vision weren't blurred from exhaustion. Hunger gnawed at their stomach. Every limb was three hundred kilos and they were drenched in sweat. The motion of the car made them nauseous as they shivered furiously.

Najah recognized Cambrie's burn out, the same burn out that Pit Master Artemis had pushed himself to back at the Pit. They were nearing the end of their energy supply. If pushed too far, death was a likely result. It was a point Najah and Cambrie knew all too well. Their time at the Egg had them teasing the edge often in the name of being better soldiers.

"Get some rest," Najah whispered to Cambrie. She hesitated before meeting the Halfling's eyes. There was more she could say, more she should say. But Belle's presence was too large in the small confines of the car. By the time Najah thought it over, Cambrie was asleep anyways.

Silence and sleep settled over the group so Belle turned on the radio. A woman's voice belted out something about newfound independence. Drums pounded, the feeling resounding in Belle's chest. Cars sped by, the Pit and its flames far behind them. With each passing minute, relief caused muscles to loosen and pulses to steady. They had been driving for a while when Belle finally looked over to Ella who was passed out against the window. She glanced in the rearview mirror at Najah before speaking up.

"So, what's your plan?" Perhaps it was exhaustion or stress, but Belle's tone wasn't exactly warm. She turned in her seat to face Najah, arms crossed over her chest.

"From here? I'm not sure. Why?" Najah raised her eyebrows and leaned back in her seat. Perri shifted in her lap but remained asleep. Najah found the weight oddly comforting.

"I figured you'd have a plan. You are the one working with a Nextulus."

"You say that like I had something to do with what they've done. In case you haven't heard, I was in that damned place because I was trying to kill Triton. I only worked with Perrianna because she offered to get me out."

"Oh?" Belle paused for a moment and pursed her lips. "I'm honestly surprised she had enough brain cells to come up with a plan that actually worked, even if it was a little...chaotic." The sound of a motorcycle whizzing by nearly drowned out her words, but Najah heard the condescension in her tone clearly. They sat in silence, the gray of the city whizzing by.

"What's your deal with her anyways? Are the rumors true?" Belle asked.

"I don't see how that's any of your business," Najah replied, pressing her tongue to her cheek. She glanced out the window. Dozens of flashing signs advertised fast food restaurants and stores. Crowded metal buildings fought for attention as they sped past. Najah knew the area. She had tracked an informant near here two summers ago. "Where are you taking us?"

"My ex's place." Belle must have sensed Najah's judgment, because she quickly elaborated. Although, a shadow flickered across Belle's face. Her eyes suddenly focused a tad too sharply on the road flashing by. "It's not far from here. It's not like any of us have credits to spend after all."

"I think you'll be fine in the morning when you can sell all the jewelry Cambrie managed to snatch," Najah said. She reached down to the floor and held up a diamond bracelet that had fallen from Cambrie's pocket. The piece shimmered as moonlight hit the stones.

"I should've known," Belle said with a small smile. Her hardened tone returned with her next comment however. "You two can stay the night and leave in the morning. I suppose it's the least I can do since you helped us." Her lips were pursed, her face taught. Her eyes pierced Najah's. "I know Cambrie seems to trust you but...I can't, and I won't trust the Siren."

Najah brushed off the coldness of Belle's tone. She had grown up with worse.

Belle wouldn't trust Najah either, not yet. The Human didn't know if she could trust the assassin's story. That was fine. Neither owed the other warmth or trust. They may have saved each other, but it's not as though they were friends.

"It's not like we're gonna turn you in." Najah knew full well that whispers to the authorities were never Belle's concern. She was a Human after all, a Human that had fought in the Saybrim resistance. She had seen the damage Triton had wrought. But Najah wanted to hear Belle say her fear aloud.

"I was more concerned about being murdered in my sleep by Nextulus." Belle's lips pursed, her throat dry.

For a moment, Najah raised her blood-stained hand to pat Belle's arm in some symbol of solidarity. A flurry of curiosity and compassion warmed Najah's chest as she paused, then brushed at her cheek as she thought better of the action. She pushed down all the questions she had, all the comments she could make about her shared experiences with Triton. No, she didn't know this woman. She shouldn't want to know this woman. She should only focus on getting to her sister. Instead, she settled on saying:

"If it's any consolation, she'd only make it a step before Cambrie and I woke up. I really didn't risk my life saving you just have her eat you for a midnight snack."

There was a moment of silence between the two. The city blurred by them, the lights like flickering bugs. The car slowed as it turned onto the offramp.

"You and Cambrie... you met in the Egg right?" Belle inquired, her tone softer, perhaps even sympathetic.

"Yeah." Najah wouldn't elaborate, not to her, not to anyone.

The road glided beneath them as if it were made of the smoothest silk. The car slowed in front of a large row of glimmering steel apartment complexes. Holograms advertised various expensive restaurants and spa treatments. The faces indulging in the luxuries were too glossy, as if the smiles would slide right off. The decrepit apartments and stores Najah knew well were only a few blocks away, but the new buildings made it feel like a completely different world. The vehicle pulled off to the side of the road and stopped. Belle turned off the car. The lights flickered on, causing the others to stir. Ella rubbed her eyes, and yawned before looking up at the apartment.

"Wait, why are we at Brett's?" The moonlight highlighted Ella as her lips curled downwards and her nose wrinkled. She leaned forward to get a better look out the window only to be greeted by the looming jaws of the beast of a building. It had already claimed so much of their blood, yet it still stood with its starving mirrored teeth, waiting to drain them of everything they had.

"We don't have anywhere else to go tonight," Belle said shortly. She didn't want anyone's questions, especially not from Ella.

"We're not staying here. You promised me," Ella hissed.

"You've gotta be shitting me," Cambrie groaned sleepily. They rubbed their eyes with the back of their hands, trying to wake up. "We're not doing this."

"It won't be that bad," Belle said as she opened her door. "It's only for tonight anyways. We'll be safe here."

"Fuck, Belle, why was this your first thought?" Cambrie said, their head in their hands. Their nausea only increased, their vision still blurred. "We don't have to do this. We can figure something out."

"It's only for the night," Belle snapped. They wouldn't understand. They would never understand. Brett could provide what no one else could. He was what no gun or knife or prison or home had ever promised.

Perri sat up, confused. "What's wrong?" Her voice was groggy from sleep.

"Nothing. C'mon." Belle huffed and got out of the car before going to the passenger's side and pulling Ella from the car.

"I'm not going in there," Ella spat as she stumbled from her seat.

"Yes, you are. We just broke out of the fucking Pit. Does it look like we have a lot of options?" Belle hissed.

"I'd rather die than go back to him. You know how he-"

Belle whirled around, the word flying from her mouth like venom. "Shut up. You're a kid, and you made that pretty fucking obvious back there. You have no room to talk right now. And hell, you don't even understand how relationships work! So stay out of mine! We're staying here and that's fucking final."

"I can't believe you," Ella spat. "You talk about me all the time, but you're just an insecure, cowardly, ugly, toenail-looking rat!"

"Belle we don't–" Cambrie began.

"Did you not hear me?" Belle shouted, ignoring her sister's out-burst. "We're staying here! Now get your asses in here!" She began to stalk up the steps of the building, the slightest drizzle of rain dripping onto her hot cheeks.

"Yeah, I did, and I think you deserve to be alone forever instead of dragging everyone down with you!" Ella shouted, her body pulsing. A hand touched her shoulder but she shook it off. Quieter this time but with a newfound tinge of venom, the words slipped off her tongue. "I hope you're miserable."

When only silence responded, Ella seethed and turned to the others in hopes of a coup. But as Perri and Cambrie were leaning heavily on Najah, all hope of different accommodations was lost. Ella joined the mass in order to support each other's injuries as they made their way into the building, with Belle already dry in the lobby.

The warm glow of the lobby welcomed the weary group. Fortu-nately, the Human woman at the front desk didn't move. Her eyes didn't canvas the blood-soaked clothing. She was all too engrossed in whatever her Alcorium was showing her. The five escapees hurried past her towards the elevator.

Belle could have found the place with her eyes closed. The white hallway was still so immaculately polished that she could see her re-flection in the shine. Her stomach twisted as she jammed her finger on the all too familiar button for the thirteenth floor. Acid sat in her throat. She had made herself the same promise as Ella so many nights ago. But things were different now.

An uncomfortable silence weighed down on the tongues of the others as the elevator ascended upwards. The lights might as well have been miniature stars for how they melted their faces, but they still favored being blinded by them rather than risk glancing at one another. The smooth jazz only further fueled unspeakable rage, each note painstakingly longer than the last.

When at last, the elevator glided to a stop and the doors opened, Belle took the lead. Thankfully, there were no residents lingering about as she strode down this all too familiar corridor with false confidence. The others lagged behind, their shared glances speaking louder than words. When she stopped at the black door, she raised her fist, then hesitated.

"If you do this–" Ella began.

Belle's knock echoed too loudly for this place. Music could be heard through the thin walls, but there was no movement towards the door. Her heart was in her throat as she knocked again. Belle stared down at the doormat she had put there when she had first moved in. A wine stain still soiled the corner. She swallowed hard.

The floorboards inside creaked as he stomped towards the door. Belle heard a thud from Brett's apartment then an "Oh shit!" Something flooded her body– she couldn't quite place if it was adrenaline. If she hurried, she could make it to the elevator before he opened the door. But no. She would stay. She needed to stay. A few moments later, a Human man threw open the door, pants soaked on one side. His fingers gripped the door frame too tightly. He looked to the side, pre-occupied. That's when Belle noticed an Alcorium, which was new– given that the S.P.A.C.E program strictly forbade them.

"You're interrupting me." Brett's voice was low and agitated as he stared off at something in his apartment. "What?" He spit. His Alcorium ring turned green, immediately sending CareFree to calm the man. He yanked his gaze away from whatever was in the apartment and finally stared at his guests. His eyes widened, then he chuckled. "I always knew you'd come running back. You never could stay away."

## Eleven

# Don't Stand Between Perri and a Shower

## CW: Depictions of domestic violence, discussion of slavery

Brett's smile faded away instantly as he took in the sight of the others. His face paled as he eyed Cambrie and Najah, covered in blood. He bolted from the door further into his kitchen. Belle pursued him, the others following. He yanked a knife from the butcher block and flew behind his island, using it as a shield. A woman screamed as she jumped up from the couch.

"You can't kill me!" Brett shouted.

Cambrie slowly clambered up onto the island and crawled towards the man, baring their fangs. Belle and Najah blocked him on either side. He was pinned between them and the counters behind him.

"If we wanted to kill you, we would have done it already," Najah snarled.

"We're not here to kill you," Belle hissed. She placed her hand on the man's forearm and easily took the knife from his hand. "You need to listen to–"

"Oh fuck this!" Ella shouted, pushing past Belle. "Quit this! It's your fault we were in there! You can't just act like you're innocent! You treated us like shit and you know it! Just admit it!" She shoved Brett even harder against the counter, digging her nails into his chest.

"What are you talking about?" Brett retorted. He brushed Ella aside with a sweep of his arm. "Belle, what are you doing here? Who are these people?"

"Brett, look, don't listen to her. You know how she can get." Belle refused to look at the others, instead raising her hands in front of her and keeping her voice soft and slow like one would to a scared animal. "The whole thing's complicated, but we aren't here to kill you. We need a place to stay for the night, and we figured we'd stay here."

"Ooh, this is not a good look for you babe. You sound desperate," Perri said with a laugh.

"Excuse me?" Ella exclaimed, her eyes flickering between Perri and Belle.

Brett hesitated, anger flashing in his face for a moment. He eyed his opponents, as if sizing them up. Cambrie raised their eyebrows, tail flicking as they cocked their head. Najah shifted, readying her palms. Brett's Alcorium flashed green as he clenched and unclenched his fists.

"Where the hell have you been? Who are these people?" His voice was still agitated despite the continuous flow of CareFree in his system. His usual charming facade had fallen away. He couldn't care in the face of his potential reckoning.

"You're not exactly in the position to be asking questions," Najah stated.

Suddenly, the woman in the living room made a dash for the door. Perri grabbed her and began to sing quietly, with a command to forget interwoven into her song.

*"Tu nre tio dedisconé..."*

As the woman stumbled in Perri's arms, Brett was seemingly trying to shout but was reduced to gesturing vigorously, his voice at a regular volume.

"You can't just show up after a year and curse my girlfriend! Last I heard you were terrorists!"

"We aren't–babe, we aren't terrorists," Belle said, rolling her eyes. "You know us better than that."

"Just suck him off already, Goddess," Perri said. When everyone turned to stare at her, she just shrugged. "What?"

"I can't believe this. I'm fucking done," Cambrie sneered. "Someone take him out already." Their whole body trembled, although from rage or exhaustion they didn't know.

"Absolutely not, we're not killing–" Belle began, then swallowed hard as she glanced towards Cambrie. Her stomach twisted. She despised the part of herself that hated them for their threats towards him. She hated that she still felt anything besides resentment for him. Hated that she craved the familiarity that she had found in his arms instead of Cambrie's. The ropes of both hatred and love, fear and trust, bound her body. She glanced towards her lover, in the hopes that a silent apology for unspoken misdeeds would quell her guilt. But Cambrie didn't meet her eyes. Their gaze was still on her ex.

Brett took the opportunity to escape towards his living room. His footsteps were heavy against the kitchen tile. Without even so much as a glance towards the man, vines shot out towards Brett and pinned him to an armchair.

"I recommend you stay still," Najah warned.

"You can't do this to me!" The man fought against the vines as they tightened around torso and arms.

"I just did." Najah scooped a knife off the kitchen counter and stalked towards the man.

"Najah!" Belle hissed, rushing after the pair.

Brett swallowed hard and sunk into the chair, causing Najah to smirk and lean against the wall. Belle collapsed into the couch with her head in her hands. The couch was new, she noticed. Black, like an abyss, instead of the white one she had picked out with him. If she prayed hard enough, maybe it would swallow her whole so she didn't have to look at the people joining her.

Cambrie sunk into the couch beside Ella. Their limbs were heavy as they felt the cushions envelop them. Belle hesitated before joining on their other side. Perri however, rolled her eyes and walked past the others. The reality of escaping was hitting her, and she needed a moment alone to process the panic-preferably, in something other than government given grey.

"Do you guys still need a babysitter, or are you all done snapping at each other?" she asked, scrunching her nose.

"Oh yeah, because you've been so helpful so far," Belle huffed. Perri just ignored her and continued on.

"Well, I'm not gonna sit around while you all stare at each other." Perri turned to Brett with her lip turned out in disgust as she looked him up and down. She ran a shaking hand through her hair, intent on keeping up her façade. Her lungs struggled to take a full breath. "Where's your shower? I need to get out of these clothes."

Brett's face reddened. He glared at Perri, prompting Najah to take a step forward. "This is my house! How dare you come in and start just..."

Perri lept in front of Brett, towering over him. She roughly cupped his chin up, and forced him to look in her eyes. She stepped on his foot, forcing all of her weight on his toes. Perri then elongated her fangs. She was no longer shaking from fear–rage was all that was left from earlier. Brett paled.

"Let's get one thing straight. I'm doing whatever I damn well please, and some pathetic Human man isn't going to tell me what to do. So I ask again, where's your fucking shower?" Perri snapped.

"Down the hall, on your left," Brett replied quietly. Any bluster was gone as Perri dug her nails into his cheek.

"Was that so hard?" Perri crooned. She didn't release her grip as she stared deeper into his eyes. Brett swallowed hard as her breath tickled his lips.

Perri easily slipped into his mind. The CareFree and months of disuse had transformed his mental walls into tissue paper. One gentle poke and she was able to slip through. She stood amongst the sea of memories, unyielding to the darkness and desires that swirled around her. While she hadn't planned on looking at his memories, a couple caught her eye. Besides, time moved slower here. She had plenty of time to look before he noticed. She fished out a select few memories from the waves and shook her hands, soothing the onslaught into submission.

Perri let the first memory play out, watching as Brett and Belle met for the first time. His face was inches apart from hers, and sweat dripped down each of their faces. A line of baby-faced recruits stood off to the side, having already endured that day of torture.

"What's your name, recruit?" Brett barked, far louder than necessary. His spittle landed on Belle's cheek, but if she noticed, she didn't show it.

"Zennebelle Everard sir!" She responded, staring at his chest as he towered over her. Her gaze was steely, her lips pressed in a tight line.

"Everard, you're up."

Brett stepped back, allowing Perri to take in more of the area. He turned towards an obstacle course covered in metal obstacles. Belle approached the starting line, Brett's eyes lower than appropriate as he stood behind her.

He counted down and she was off. She scurried up a ladder, jumped down into the mud, and crawled through a tunnel. Brett glanced at the timer projected in the air, his arms crossed over his chest. Another Staff Sergeant came up beside Brett, surveying the course as Belle hurried through it.

"She's supposed to be the best out of everyone here. What do you think?"

Brett watched as she easily scaled a wall and lept over a set of hurdles. He was silent as she cleared the last obstacle.

"Personally, I think she'd do better as a man," the man continued.

Brett didn't respond as Belle crossed the finish line and the timer stopped. Fifty-four seconds. She had shattered all previous records. The Staff Sergeant uttered a string of curses as he began to walk away.

Belle put her hands on the back of her head, chest heaving as she met the passing Staff Sergeant's eyes and refused to tear her gaze away. Then she turned her stare towards Brett, a newfound confidence in her step.

"Everard, stay. Everyone else, go back to camp," Brett shouted.

The memory faded away and Perri dove back into the sea of memories. She pulled up another clip. Brett sat on the couch in his living room, the T.V. blaring. Moving boxes sat in the corner of the room, and a shattered lamp's porcelain pieces were scattered all across the floor in front of Belle.

"How could you break that? It was right there on the box!" Brett's voice was so loud that it hurt Perri's ears. "Why aren't you cleaning it up? Do I need to tell you everything? Hurry up!"

"Don't yell at me! I hate when you get like this!" Belle cried.

Belle bent down to pick up the pieces, carelessly collecting the shards in one palm. Her face was taut, her eyes downcast. As she picked up the last piece, the ceramic edge sliced her skin. She hissed and dropped some of the shards back into the carpet. She stood up and hurried down the hall, refusing to look at Brett.

Brett walked over to the spot Belle had previously stood. Amongst the shards was a small drop of blood. He made no move to clean up the mess. Instead, he braced himself on the fireplace, staring at the single picture on the mantle. The pixels made up a photo of Brett, Belle, and Ella at some park, posing in front of a large tree. Their faces smiled wide as the sun casted golden rays over their cheeks.

Belle returned with a bandaged palm. Brett cast a disgusted look over her body, clenching onto the mantle as if it were the only thing keeping him grounded.

"You got blood on the floor!" He yelled. "This is new carpet! If we have to get it replaced it's coming out of your pocket!"

"You could have cleaned it up!" Belle brushed past him to look at the spot. "And you can barely see it!" She scooped up the remaining shards and headed towards the kitchen. Before she could get far, Brett grabbed her arm roughly.

"Don't ever tell me what to do," he growled, his grip tightening on her. He raised his other hand above Belle's face as she struggled against his grip. Ella peeked out from the hallway and—

"Get out of my head!" Brett shouted, finally realizing there was an intruder. Only a second had passed from the initial moment of contact, but that had given Perri enough time.

The sound jolted Perri from his memory, and reminded her of the true reason she had gone inside his mind. Brett raised his arms, causing Najah to start. But before he could shove the Siren off, Perri uttered her song again.

*"Eri soporé et sina insomnefal crucia tu tacitla...."*

Brett fell limp in his chair, his eyelids slamming shut. Blood dripped down Perri's fingers as her nails pierced the man's skin. She didn't tear her gaze away from the man as she began to repeat the song.

"What are you doing?!" Belle exclaimed, rushing towards the pair. "Get away from him!" She shoved Perri away from Brett, breaking them apart. Perri stumbled backwards, holding up her hands as a sign of surrender.

"So you're fine with everyone else threatening to kill him, but when I put him to sleep you're on my case about it? He'll be fine. Relax, Human." Perri spat out the last word as if it were sour on her tongue.

"How am I supposed to know what you did? It's not like I can really trust your kind." Belle crossed her arms over her chest.

"Belle!" Ella cried, appalled by her sister's words.

"You seem to forget that I risked my life to save your ass. I don't know what more you want from me," Perri shrugged.

"I'm sorry, but I don't know how I'm supposed to trust the daughter of the man who enslaved millions of Saybrim people, drugs everybody, and allowed his people to kill innocent Humans? I don't give a damn if you helped us inadvertently. You would have left us if it weren't for the others. You're his daughter and I will never trust you around anyone I love," Belle spat.

"Oh, so you love hi-" Perri stopped her retort as she remembered the scene she saw and watched as Belle's face fell. The Human shook as tears formed in her eyes. Perri was a lot of things, but she wasn't cruel. She knew that despite the anger she felt at the Human's accusations, she had crossed an unspoken line.

"No, I didn't mean, I don't lo..." Belle stammered as she closed her eyes.

She rubbed her forehead, then turned to Cambrie. Cambrie was already up, distancing themselves from their girlfriend. They peered out the window, refusing to meet Belle's gaze. Ella simply stared at the carpet.

"I don't love him!" Belle shouted as she stood and stalked towards Perri, her hands balled. "Don't twist my words."

"I know. I shouldn't have said that," Perri whispered.

"But you did. Because you're a fucking Siren, and what's worse than that, is you're a fucking Nextulus. You're his daughter. You don't give a flying fuck about anyone but yourself."

Perri swallowed as she dug her nails into her palms. She poured every ounce of self control she had into keeping her tone even, her face neutral.

"I'm not his daughter, not anymore. The whole reason I was in that place is because I was trying to confront Triton about everything he's done. The slave trade, the Alcoriums, Carefree, the contracts with the Pit, everything. He's done so much more than you can possibly imagine. He killed my best friend because we got too close to the truth, then he tried to kill me. So, you'd be wrong if you thought I had some loyalty to him."

Belle didn't respond. Instead she swiped at her eyes and turned away from Perri, her hands trembling. She sunk back into the couch. How many nights had she spent in this living room staring at the wall? How many nights had she wished, she vowed, that she would escape? And yet, here she was.

Belle didn't even fully understand why this had been her first thought. She could logic her way out of it, sure. Brett's place had been close, but not too close to the Pit. Plus, despite the lofty price tag of his building, the cameras were notorious for not working. If the police traced their location here, she'd rather Brett take the heat than say, her parents, or any Resistance members. She could say she was only thinking about Ella, because the Goddesses knew she had made so many sacrifices for her sister. Yet, that would've been a lie.

Belle hadn't even asked any of her new companions if they had any ideas; and logic sure didn't work to explain why she didn't want anyone to murder him. It didn't explain why she felt anything other than pure rage towards him. No–this hadn't been about Ella or Cambrie or anyone else, and she hated herself for it.

She hadn't even realized that Najah, Ella, and Perri had left the room until Cambrie sank down into the couch beside her. The Halfling brushed a hair behind their ear and let out a heavy breath. Exhaustion still sat heavy in their bones, but Belle needed them more. She always needed them more. Careful not to let their own irritation slip into their words, they said:

"I'm sorry. I know there has to be more to this decision than you're letting on. I know you're hurting. But we don't have to stay here. We can find somewhere else. You don't have to stay here with him."

Belle opened her mouth as if to say something but a strange gasping noise came out in place of words. Tears streamed down her face. She flung herself against Cambrie, collapsing as if the entire world weighed down upon her.

Cambrie stiffened under her touch. They had anticipated this, yet it was still uncomfortable. They wrapped an arm around Belle as they scrunched up their eyes. If they didn't look perhaps they could stave off the imminent nightmares that refused to stay encapsulated in their sleep.

"I don't hate him," Belle breathed into Cambrie's shoulder. "I'm sorry." Broken sobs accentuated each apology. "I'm so sorry."

Cambrie knew, but hearing the words aloud still stabbed them in the heart. Somewhere inside themself they knew that Belle didn't mean to hurt them. But how could she not hate the man who left those scars along her soul? How could she run to him at her first chance of safety, even if it was only for a night? They would never understand that.

The looming silence that followed was louder to Belle than any anger or frustration Cambrie could have responded with. Both sat in their own separate but entangled worlds, clinging onto each other out of desperation and obligation.

Najah stared out across the half eaten pizza sprawled across the kitchen island. Ella sat across from her, munching on a cold slice. The young girl drummed her fingers on the marble countertop before tilting her head towards the assassin.

"So, you don't have to tell me if you don't want to because I know it can be a really personal thing... but I was just wondering...how do you know Perrianna? Are you friends? It really seems like you're friends. Not that I'm trying to assume anything." Ella huffed and took another bite of her pizza, glancing down at the veining on the marble.

Najah raised her eyebrows and crossed her arms over her chest. She asked herself again how this child had gotten herself involved in the Saybrim resistance. But the shimmer in Ella's eyes was so much like the one Najah imagined in her own sister's eyes. Genuine curiosity lay beneath her questions. This wasn't an interrogation.

"You had to have heard the rumors," Najah replied.

"Well, yeah, but you probably heard the rumors about us too. Do you think we're terrorists? Because we're not. I mean, that's what they call us because technically... But we're not. We just hijacked government ships that were transporting enslaved Saybrim and..."

"Yeah, I know. Trust me." Najah took a sip of her water while conflicting emotions built in her chest.

Ella wasn't a threat, at least she hadn't made herself one yet. But no matter how much Cambrie trusted this girl, and how much Ella resembled Najah's fantasy version of her own sister, the assassin still didn't know her.

"I just happened to help Perri out, and she, in turn, offered to get me out of the Pit. That hardly makes us friends. But you want to know if I trust her, don't you? Because if I trust her and Cambrie trusts me, then by extension, you think that there's some fragile safety in this group," Najah explained.

Ella glanced at her blood-stained pants, her fingers fiddling with a braid. She didn't meet Najah's eyes, giving the assassin enough confirmation to continue.

"I'm definitely not about to put a knife in someone's back without provocation, and I won't let Perri eat anyone here, but Belle's right not to trust us. You don't know us."

"How can you say she's right about any of this? She brought us here, back to him." Ella's voice broke as she looked away, swiping at her eyes. "She promised me."

Najah hesitated, her heart wrenching in her chest. A daunting, horrible thought crossed her mind regarding the promise she herself had made years ago. She shoved it down into the darkest depths. Maybe it would never resurface. She had to deal with the girl now.

"I know, but she's trying to keep you safe. That's why she went with the Pit Master right? And that's why she kept getting exemptions for you? This is just another part of that. She's your sister, and I know that this entire situation has been hard, but she's doing what she can. Even if that means breaking promises."

"But she's acting like she has to do this alone! She doesn't! She didn't even bother to ask any of us if we had any ideas, she just ran straight back to him. And I'm not some kid. I can defend myself just fine." Ella frowned and tossed her pizza onto the counter, having suddenly lost her appetite.

Cambrie and Belle, having heard raised voices, stumbled numbly into the blinding light of the kitchen. Belle clung to the island as if it were the only thing rooting her to the world. She tried to pat her sister's hand, only for Ella to pull away. Cambrie took to the other side besides Najah and slid onto a stool, rubbing their temples as if that would help to soothe the headache that had formed.

"Is everything alright?" Cambrie asked, rubbing at their eyes.

"Yeah," Ella said curtly. "Just peachy."

She stood from her stool in order to get as far away from everyone as possible. She stared at the flaking grey paint on the walls and the awful artwork of a clown that she swore had eyes that followed her. Mythos, she hated this place.

She wasn't a child. She could hold her own. As Ella turned to say as much, the words caught in her throat. Belle looked an absolute wreck. The woman's face was puffy and her hands were trembling. Guilt smothered Ella's anger–guilt for being angry, guilt for being a burden, guilt for existing. This was all her fault. She backed into the wall, overcome by emotion. It choked her and threatened to cause tears to spill. But no. A child would cry, and she wasn't a child anymore. So she struggled to take a breath, then another, and steeled herself.

Just then, Perri waltzed into the room, a towel piled on her head. A white jumpsuit that was a few inches too short clung to her body. She had obviously raided someone's closet, although the garment certainly wasn't in Ella's nor Belle's taste.

"Am I interrupting something?" The Siren asked, her eyes flitting between people. She could practically taste the sadness and resentment in the air. It made her stomach churn. When no one responded, she continued. "So... I was thinking..."

"Oh goddess, we should watch out, she was actually thinking for once," Belle muttered, although there was very little bite behind the words.

"...we should probably all stick together for a while." Before anyone could protest, Perri elaborated further. "I mean, think about it. We'll have power in numbers. And we all kind of have the same goal. We all want to–"

Ella's voice was deadpan as she finished the sentence: "To kill your father."

## Twelve

# MURDER? I'LL DRINK TO THAT

**CW: Mentions of pedophilia/human trafficking, mentions of slavery, mentions of medical experimention**

Everyone whipped around to face Ella. The young girl shrugged as if she had simply been commenting on the weather outside.

"What? He's the main factor in all of our problems." The words were bitter on Ella's tongue. She hated them, hated the implications. She had made her previous comment without thinking. It seemed the obvious choice, given the rumor that had been floating around Perri and Najah's arrest. She had thought that's what they wanted. A tough, ruthless, woman who would propose they fight. Not a scared child. But even if Ella was trying to put up a façade, the thought of taking a life repulsed her. Even if it was the life of a man who deserved it.

"I'm sorry, did *you* just suggest that we kill him? That wasn't exactly where I was going with my plan." Perri asked. The Siren scoffed, a grin forming on her face. "What in Inanis did he do to you?"

"Ella!" Belle felt the world slip from around her. Her sister who refused to even hold a gun had stared her right in the face and suggested death to the President. Nothing on this night made sense. "What the fuck is wrong with you?"

Cambrie reached towards the girl, their words getting drowned out by the din. "This isn't you."

"You know though, as shocking as it is, she has a point," Perri said. "Everything is much bigger than Triton himself, but getting him out of the way would be helpful for everyone."

Ella's stomach knotted. She should have kept her mouth shut. Stupid stupid stupid. Now she had put death on everyone's mind when no one else had thought it.

"I'm not helping you assassinate the fucking President," Belle hissed. "There's no fucking way I'm getting myself or my sister involved in that."

"Even though he's an instrumental part in the Saybrim slave trade? Taking him out would help the Resistance. I thought you wanted that," Perri replied.

"No." The words jumbled in Belle's head. On any other night she could have this conversation, could come up with a dozen reasons why this was a terrible idea, but her own thoughts weren't making sense. "Not like this." Her hands were cold against her temples.

Perri pressed on her crusade despite Belle's obvious exhaustion. "If the slave trade were disrupted it would mean a disruption in the production of CareFree, since Saybrim blood, as you know, is used to create it. If there's a shortage of CareFree-"

"-People would be forced to face the truth about everything." Ella's eyes went wide. "The fact that Triton manipulated them through the Alcoriums, that they're being drugged to sedate them, that Saybrim are being slaughtered to make CareFree, that there's a Resistance at all..." One death could be justified if it saved everyone else. Right?

"It would be great if you let me finish my thought for once," Perri huffed, but she was drowned out by Najah.

"It wouldn't be just the Resistance," Najah held up her hand, staring at the counter. "We'd be helping to cripple his other schemes."

"How so?" Ella asked.

Perri shook her head and rolled her eyes but said nothing.

"A lot of wealthy people find enjoyment in absolutely abhorrent things, and a lot of those things involve inflicting pain on other people simply as a show of power," Najah spat. "Some like the Pit. Others like renting out children by the hour. So the Egg, and therefore the government, have contracts with many rings in Sanctus. The creation of a Vitare is an incredibly expensive process, and it only has around a fifty percent success rate. The government needs Vitares to do their dirty work, but they would be bleeding money if they didn't do anything with the kids that don't bind and become Vitares, like my sister."

Najah pressed a tongue to the inside of her cheek, eyes tracing the veining on the countertop. She didn't want to look at the pity in their faces. She could practically feel it radiating off the walls. "So, the government supplies the children they aren't using, and the rings pay them half of the profits. The rings get wealthier clientele and a blind eye from their local governments."

Cambrie nodded in agreement, letting their gaze rest on Najah. "It's a huge problem in Sanctus."

"It's not just in Sanctus either," Najah muttered. She found her chest unusually tight. She shouldn't have mentioned her sister. Shouldn't have let it slip she had a personal connection. Not yet anyways. It was stupid. She was getting sloppy.

"And if we killed Triton it would-" Ella began. The invisible blood she had felt earlier washed away with the others' words. She could justify this death. She would have to justify it. She wouldn't let this be another weight to her already guilty conscience.

"Don't even finish that thought." Perri snorted, glaring at Belle as the Human cut her off.

"Mythos Ella, why are you so ready to kill him?" Belle asked.

"Why aren't you Belle?" Perri huffed before turning to Ella. "But do you really think killing one man would take down an entire multi-billion credit industry? The Egg, the experiments, the Pit, the trafficking of children, hell, even the Saybrim slave trade existed long before Triton was ever in the picture. What Triton did was create Alcoriums, and later CareFree to suppress and distract people from the issues so they didn't rebel. He didn't just suddenly create these industries. They've always been there."

"Think." Perri tapped on the side of her head and continued. "It's not like you have an Alcorium in your head."

"So tell me about it, tell me everything," Ella said. "I never had an Alcorium, I've never had CareFree. I don't know what they're like."

"You're going to listen to her?" Belle asked, her voice rising in pitch. She threw her hands up, running one through her hair. "Her of all people?"

"It doesn't hurt to listen," Ella said. She propped her elbow on the counter and leaned towards Perri. "If you don't like what she says afterwards, then fine. But if she can help the Resistance then it could be worth it."

"Finally someone with some common sense," Perri smirked.

"I would think not wanting to try to kill the fucking President after already failing once would be common sense!" Belle shouted. Her head throbbed. She just wanted to get out of this place. How was she losing her grip on everything?

"Can we not argue?" Cambrie asked. Goddess they wanted out of here. They were tired of having to listen, but they were terrified of the silence. "Let's all just have a conversation. Perri, go ahead and explain your side."

That earned the Halfling a killer glare from Belle. Cambrie simply avoided eye contact, staring at Najah, who, in turn, examined Perri as if she were an exhibit in a museum. When the room was silent, the Siren stood and walked to a large screen along one wall. It held many of the standard kitchen items inside. With the press of a few buttons, Perri dispensed a glass and a bottle of liquor. She poured herself an incredibly generous portion before returning to her seat and setting the bottle on the counter. Everyone stared as she brought the glass to her lips.

"Are you ready, or should we wait for you to finish the whole bottle?" Belle asked as Perri swallowed and set down the glass.

"I may need the whole bottle if I have to listen to you all night," Perri said as she rolled her eyes. "Goddess. Fine. Let's get started. Triton created Alcoriums to manipulate the media and the world around you. Of course, he marketed it as a mental health treatment option because limiting negative media stories and pushing good news helped to decrease depression and anxiety."

"Well then if Alcoriums worked, why did he need CareFree?" Belle asked, crossing her arms over her chest.

"Can you give me a damn minute?" Perri took another swig of her drink. She was tired of being interrupted. Back at the Manor no one had dared to speak over her. "Mabo rudees can`es."

"Perri," Najah growled. "Play nice." She instinctively found herself prepping her powers, ready to build a barrier of vines between the two women. The insult would've launched a fight instantaneously had

Belle been able to understand it, hence Perri's use of her native tongue, Solaska.

"What did she call me?" Belle snapped, her eyes bearing into the Siren. The stool beneath her clattered to the floor as she stood, her body shaking.

"Nothing," both Perri and Najah said simultaneously.

"Continuing on," Perri said before Belle could get a word in edge-wise. "I'll get to CareFree in a minute. But-"

"No, I want to know what you called me!" Belle snarled. Her eyes darted around as she searched for support. No one met her gaze.

"-first, let me talk about Triton's motives," Perri continued on, unfazed. "His original idea-"

"*What...did...you...call...me?*" Belle spat, taking care to punctuate every syllable as she pulled the gun from the waistband of her pants.

"Just let it go," Ella hissed.

"Belle, threatening her is going to make things a lot worse," Cambrie said, wrapping an arm around Ella and pulling her away from the crowd.

Perri however just laughed as she leaned against the kitchen counter. She picked up her drink, a smirk painted on her face. "Is that all you've got? Really, it's kinda sad."

"You're a privileged racist brat," Belle snarled, spit flying from her lips as she aimed for Perri's chest, hands trembling.

Perri's face darkened, the playfulness falling from her face. She stood, somehow seeming to tower over the Human despite being shorter.

"Oh, that's right, that's what I called you: A fucking stupid bitch." As those words left Perri's lips, Belle flipped off the safety. "Go ahead, shoot me. I dare you."

Najah's vines ripped the gun from Belle's hand. Belle glared at her, but said nothing, crossing her arms over her chest. Perri rolled her eyes, throwing herself back against the counter.

The assassin raised an eyebrow, huffing. "I'm not here to babysit you two. This is absolutely ridiculous."

"I completely agree," Cambrie muttered. "I really don't know how this is going to work. It's obvious that we aren't going to work together."

"Of course you'd agree with her. You'd agree with anyone besides me," Belle muttered.

Cambrie rubbed their eyes, a strangled noise coming from their throat. In that moment they found themselves longing for the warm embrace of slumber. Dear Goddess this was exhausting. How did they always mess this up?

Perri chuckled at the exchange and took a sip of her liquor. But the amber liquid barely touched her lips before Najah snatched the glass out of her hand with a vine and tossed it into the sink behind her. It shattered into a thousand pieces.

"Hey!" The Siren shouted. "What was that for? That's disrespectful!"

"This isn't some party for your entertainment," Najah said. "I was sick of you sitting there watching us with that dumbass smirk on your face like you're better than us. You're one of us now, princess. You're a criminal, and all of us here know you aren't ready for this life. You can't take Triton down alone. So, you have one last chance to tell us everything you know, without the insults."

"I'm..." The words died in Perri's throat. Najah was right. Tightness built in her chest, her head spinning. She had no place to go. Her face was plastered on billboards and yet she had zero credits to her name. The police already had to be searching for her. When word got out to Triton that she had escaped, any security around him would get tighter. She needed them. "Fine."

"I don't want to work with her!" Belle shouted. "I don't want to work with any of you!"

"You don't have to. You don't even have to listen," Najah shrugged. She knew that the woman would, even if she pretended not to. She cared too much about the others and the cause not to. But she deserved a choice in the matter. "Here. If you're leaving, you're going to need this." The assassin flicked the safety back on and slid the gun across the counter to Belle.

Perri bit her tongue but raised her eyebrows at Najah as if to say *"She gets her gun back, but I don't get my drink back?"*

In a silent response, Najah rolled her eyes. Belle scooped up her gun and slid it into her waistband as if she were afraid someone was going to take it from her, eyes never leaving Perri.

"I'm staying here," Ella said, her voice suddenly small. "I want to know what they're talking about."

Cambrie looked up with tired eyes at the group, analyzing. If things went south again, someone needed to be here to be a moderator, and that certainly wouldn't be Ella. They didn't know why they needed to be having this conversation anyways when they kept butting heads. Why couldn't they all just go their separate ways? Seeing Najah again was nice and all but she made things...complicated. They had repaid their own secret debt to her by helping to get her out of the Pit. They didn't need more allies, not now, not ever. Still, someone needed to be here to make sure there wasn't any bloodshed.

"I'm staying too I guess," the Halfling said.

Belle silently set up her stool again, but didn't sit, instead perching one of her legs on the bars as if she were still deciding if she wanted to stay or run.

"So, Perri, enlighten us. What were Triton's motives for creating Alcoriums?" Najah asked, perching her elbows on the counter.

Perri swallowed, the usual bluster gone from her voice. "The Alcorium was created to control the media Humans consumed because the tensions between Sirens and Humans were high. Humans were continuing to take over Siren land, which meant that more Sirens felt entitled to break the treaty that said they'd only feed off Human prisoners, which left Human civilians terrified. Triton, at the time, had just been elected to the Arayvia Council, and if he wanted to keep his position, he had to figure out a way to allow Sirens to feed off Human civilians while keeping them peaceful."

"I think you mean allow Sirens to *murder* Humans," Najah said. "Sirens don't have to kill them to feed. But they do."

Cambrie took a breath, digging their nails into their palms. Najah was right, of course. But she was egging the Siren on. The Halfling was prepping themself to play referee. Except, Perri didn't have a witty remark.

"You're right." The Siren gave a defeated shrug. "And Humans don't fight back because of Alcoriums. Triton was successful in manipulating the media to convey that Humans were safe, that Sirens weren't a threat, and to convince Humans to move from Siren land. But he realized the power that he held, especially as Alcoriums moved beyond just the Human market. So he used that power to manipulate the media to keep his position on the Council and later, President."

"It's disgusting," Belle muttered. She placed her shin on top of the stool, letting her elbows rest on the countertop. Her eyes narrowed as she stared at the Siren as if she were trying to discern if this were the truth. "Wait, why didn't the Council Members stop him? Wouldn't they have realized that he had too much power? Wouldn't his opponents try to stop him?" She rubbed at her temples, her mouth dry.

Perri had to resist the urge to laugh. She pressed a tongue to her cheek, running a finger along her bottom lip. This woman. If Perri was lucky, Belle would run. Still, the Siren had to watch what she said.

"First of all, you have to realize that at the time, no one cared what edge they needed. The Assimilation of Inanis had just happened. You know what that is right?" Perri asked as she looked around. 'You have to know what that is. They teach it to babies."

"No, they neglected to teach us world history in the Egg," Najah rolled her eyes. "That and things like how to draw puppies. I mean, how can you get anywhere in life without knowing how to make those cute little paws?

Cambrie snorted. "Oh, so your Handler probably didn't let you take the baking course right after your class in advanced torture techniques? Such a shame." But as soon as the words left their mouth regret settled in their bones. No. They didn't need to make friends. Not with the assassin.

Najah let out a chuckle, her eyes sparkling with approval. Perri's face however, flickered with poorly contained annoyance.

"Ha ha. Very funny." The Siren crossed her arms over her chest. "Right. So to give a very quick history lesson, essentially, Angels were the first ones to live on Inanis. Then, according to the religion of Theralaan, the Goddesses helped some Angels survive and escape the cave in of Jerilee by bestowing upon them some powers and taking away some others to keep the balance, and they later were dubbed Demons. I'm skeptical about that but whatever."

"Anyways," Perri continued. "Demons were treated pretty badly and a lot of other stuff happened, but then this big 100 Year War happened and the Demons pushed Angels from their land. Meanwhile Humans and Sirens were still back on Mars, fighting because Humans killed yet another planet. Demons and Angels have by this point stopped the war, and established their own countries with their own separate governments but they're both really weak. That's when Humans and Sirens decided that they're going to work together for once to take over this country. So they did, and they split it up into the countries we have today. The Assimilation of Inanis essentially had just given the Angels and Demons time to transfer their models of government into the model of government that Sirens and Humans had established when we came here. They had up until 2458, the day before Triton was officially elected to officially change over their state models even though Humans and Sirens arrived in 2442."

"So, wait, wait, Sirens came here, kicked Angels and Demons off their land, then turned on their Human allies and continued to murder them?" Najah asked, her voice rising in pitch. "Typical. Why am I not surprised?"

"Colonizer," Belle spat as she stared at Perri. The Human's eyes were daggers, deadly sharp against the Siren's skin.

Ella raised her hand tentatively. "I mean, technically, wouldn't Humans be col-"

"Okay, I'm sure this would be an intriguing discussion, but it's getting late and I'd like to finish the original discussion if you wouldn't mind." Perri forced a smile as she cut the girl off. "So, to answer Belle's original question, the reason why the Assimilation was so crucial to the election is because everyone was forced to assimilate to these state Councils, and no one was entirely sure if that would impact the national Presidential election. They could guess, but no one knew for sure. So, if Triton's fellow Council Members had to play dirty to help get him elected, they didn't care. They'd deal with the consequences later. I don't think they really realized the extent that they'd be giving up their political ambitions, but when the options are to ally with or make an enemy of arguably one of the most powerful men in the country, what are you going to choose? And as for his competitors, that was easy. They just got Alcoriums and they practically gave him the election."

Before Perri could take a breath, questions were raining down upon her. They practically smothered her, making her head spin.

"What about CareFree? What are Alcoriums like? What do they really do? I just know what they say in the commercials." Ella asked, the words falling from her lips as soon as the Siren finished her sentence.

"Alcoriums are an incredibly smart piece of technology," Perri began after a moment, her voice smooth and light as if she were in awe. "It's addictive. It predicts your every need, and that's without CareFree. The thing can quite literally block out your vision with positive videos and stories if you're walking past a homeless person, and the GPS will even reroute you to avoid the poorer neighborhoods, since that would ruin the perception that people are flourishing under Triton's rule."

"Don't forget that it also does things like order the food you've been craving for days or play your favorite song when you're upset," Cambrie added. "They're pretty invasive when you think about it, but it's all about making you happy."

"You had an Alcorium?" Belle asked as she sat fully on the stool, tilting her head. A sinking feeling settled in her stomach.

"Yeah. I mean, I had one for the few years between the Egg and the Pit that I was living in Sanctus," Cambrie shrugged. They weren't surprised that Belle didn't know.

The Halfling had never really talked about their time outside the Pit. It was better that way. "It's kind of hard to avoid having one. You use them for everything. Talking to people, paying for things, using the internet, it's nearly impossible to live a normal life without one."

"Oh." Belle's face clouded over as she stared down at her hands. There were so many things she didn't know about Cambrie.

"Anyways," Perri continued. "The Alcorium's manipulation made it easier for Triton to do a lot of things, like work with the Saybrim King, and expand the slave trade without scrutiny from the public."

The mention of Saybrim seemed to get Belle to perk up because her head instantly snapped up and her face was hot.

"Ahithophel is a bastard," Belle spat, referencing the Saybrim King. "Selling off his own people to be slaughtered and enslaved for his own profit."

"A bastard that needs to be stopped, no matter the cost." Najah crossed her arms over her chest. Despite the obvious threat, no one seemed shocked by her words, unlike Ella.

Ella let her shoulders fall, her body slumping. It was no surprise that the assassin could get away with threatening people. No, if she did it everyone freaked out.

"I agree," Perri said. "And the thing is, because of Alcoriums, people think Saybrim are happy. Public perception was changed to see Saybrim as lesser than, as some subrace that doesn't have the capacity to understand enslavement. It's the same thing for everything else. Alcoriums block out the news that Triton and his team don't want shown, so the Egg, the clubs, everything evil and unsavory is blocked out. Most people think everything is genuinely fine and that Triton is the reason behind it all. I used to. If it weren't for my friend Anna, I would have stayed brainwashed too."

"Yeah, those filters are pretty effective," Cambrie sighed.

"Then if everything was fine with the Alcoriums, why bother with CareFree?" Belle asked again. " I was in S.P.A.C.E by the time it came out. I heard different stories about how CareFree was developed. The way you're framing it, with the Alcoriums, it just seems like a waste of time and credits."

"Because there was an issue," Perri said. She pulled the towel off of her head and ran her fingers through her hair. "People in poor neighborhoods didn't have the credits for Alcoriums and they were witnessing the damage they did first hand. They were being left behind by every relief effort and non-profit that had ever tried to help them because everything said they were fine. Businesses were leaving because people weren't coming through their neighborhoods. Problems they already had were getting worse. These people weren't going to be easily manipulated into spending their hard earned money on something they didn't trust. That's when CareFree was introduced. The government funded it and marketed it as an inexpensive and completely safe treatment for just about every mental illness, and pushed it to doctors that worked in those poor neighborhoods."

"Because there are higher rates of mental illness in impoverished neighborhoods, which tend to be predominantly Human neighborhoods," Ella recited as if it were a line from a textbook that was painted on the wall in front of her.

"Right," Perri nodded, her lips pursed tight. "And since CareFree inhibits feelings of anger, sadness, stress, and fear, and increases feelings of happiness, it did help mental illness; but those people grew numb to any resistance they had against the government and many ended up getting Alcoriums, especially as the government funded free Alcorium implants for those communities. What the government didn't bother to tell people is that CareFree weakened their natural powers."

"Which is why it's not allowed in the Egg or the Pit," Najah added.

Perri swallowed her frustration as she continued on. Her fingers curled into fists. "So, Demons, Angels, and Sirens, anyone with powers, if they took CareFree, the Saybrim blood in it would cause them to slowly lose their abilities. If anyone noticed-which many didn't because of the distractions Alcoriums brought-they were already in the clutches of addiction, and losing their powers seemed like a good trade for happiness."

Perri continued. "That part was the final nail in the coffin for any hope at rebellion. Because even if someone managed to break through to their friends about the manipulation and sedation, they'd be weaponless and unable to do much against it. Of course, like any addictive drug, CareFree spread. Then it was implemented into Alcoriums, as it only helped the government manipulate people more."

Everyone seemed to take a collective breath, finally waiting for Perri to continue. There were no quick witted comments or interruptions. Now all eyes were on the Siren, as if she held some magical answer to the problem at hand. Which, fortunately for them, she did.

"So, this is all to say that killing Triton would be a powerful symbol, might slow some things down, and it would make me feel a hell of a lot better, but it has always been a lot bigger than one man. The people in his Cabinet, his potential successors, local governments, they're all involved and they'd make sure that everything he's done stays standing. So if we really want to fix it all, we have to disable Alcoriums, stop the manufacture of CareFree, and get people to stand with us to destroy the existing government."

The Siren paused, taking in the faces of her companions. Each one seemed to be taking in the vast wealth of information she had presented to them. Cambrie and Najah's faces were virtually unreadable. Ella's eyes were narrowed, her lips pursed in a look of determination. Belle, however, was bouncing between shock and rage. Perfect.

Perri brushed some hair out of her face and let out a breath.

"I should mention that if we do this, we will be dragging an entire country through withdrawal at the same time so we will probably be absolutely despised and they'll be miserable. But, I'm still up for it."

"We're smart! We can figure it out! We can do this!" Ella said, banging her fist on the table.

"Absolutely not! She's proposing a revolution!" Belle shouted, her face red. She turned to Perri, spit flying from her mouth onto the Siren's cheek. "How do I even know you're telling the truth? This could be some elaborate set up! You're his daughter! You could be luring us to him! You could be using this to your advantage, to take over and become President! Besides, we're criminals and Ella's a kid! We can't lead a revolution!"

"I'm not a kid!" Ella shouted. "We can do this Belle! Please!"

Perri reached up, eyes closed, and swiped at the spit on her cheek. Her voice was deadly calm. "I don't know what else you want from me. I've answered all of your questions. If you don't trust me, fine. But Najah was there when I tried to confront Triton and he, for the last fucking time, *tried to kill me.* Why would I go to all of these lengths to make up these stories, and why the hell would I ever want to run a country? Have you seen me? That sounds like hell. If you don't want anything to do with this, that's fine but use your brain. You were already leading a revolution weren't you? With the Saybrim?"

"Yeah, but we had help then! This...things...they're different now," Belle stammered.

"Face it, it's not the revolution that scares you. It's me," Perri snarled.

"Can you blame me for not trusting you? Even if you're telling the truth, your kind has been eating Humans for forever! And you've never had to work for a thing in your damn life! You'll just leave the second shit gets hard!"

"You act like I-" Perri began. She closed the gap between herself and the Human, her chest heaving.

"Stop! Both of you!" Cambrie shouted over the chaos. They shoved the two women apart, taking Belle by the shoulder. Belle wrenched herself from their grasp, disgust in her eyes. Cambrie met her gaze. "Look, this whole plan involves trusting and working with each other, and it's pretty obvious that you're not going to be able to do that."

"Don't tell me what I can and cannot do," Belle spat as she stalked as far away as she possibly could get from her partner. The light flickered for a moment, casting shadows over her face.

Najah surveyed the scene, crossing her arms over her chest. She pressed her tongue to her cheek. Cambrie knew just as well as she did that Perri had told the truth about everything. Both of them could spot a liar within a second. Even when Najah had pressed about things she had in fact known, Perri didn't bother to lie. It was enough for the assassin to trust her, for now. But why hadn't Cambrie bothered to reassure Belle that the Siren was telling the truth? What game were they playing?

"Excuse me, but didn't we all just escape from our death sentences by working together?" Ella spoke up, holding her hands out to her side. Her eyes were wide with disappointment. "This fighting is absolutely ridiculous. There were points where we all could've left each other to save ourselves but we stuck together and got out of there. If that didn't solidify your trust in one another, I don't know what your problem is. But honestly, even if you don't trust each other, what other option do you have? We're gonna be on the run for the rest of our lives anyways and we want the same things. We want to put an end to slavery, tyranny, and oppression. Do you really want to do that on your own? Because we all tried that before and it didn't go well."

Perri turned to face Ella, a small smile on her face. "You know, I'm starting to like you."

"She has a point. We should work together," Najah said, watching Cambrie's face.

But Cambrie's face was a practiced mask of unreadable emotions as they turned towards Belle. The Human woman's tears streamed down her cheeks in silent rage.

"You're just going to let her listen to that murderer and get herself killed? You're not going to say anything?"

"She's not a kid, not anymore," Cambrie said, trying to ignore the guilt in their heart. It was a lose-lose scenario. This is why they didn't try. They always hurt people. "She was in the Resistance. She saw what it was like. She can make her own decisions."

Belle stared at her partner for a moment longer, the knife of betrayal wedging deeper into her heart. For a moment, as her heart palpitated, she wondered if this would be the thing that killed her. But no. Not this. So she grit her teeth and turned towards Perri, yanking the invisible knife from her heart and turning it upon the Siren.

"You've had the privilege of living in an ivory tower your whole life with zero regard for what your actions do to others. You want to kill your dad? Great. Go ahead. I hope the bastard dies. But innocent people are going to die because you think playing soldier will be fun, and I'm not going to let that be my sister. "

"Hey!" Ella cried. No, she was sick of being the child. She wasn't powerless. "You know all of this is true, and you just don't want to admit it! It all makes sense! It adds up with everything the Resistance told us! We can't just stand by and let people be drugged into submission! Not when we can do something. Not when it can help the Saybrim. You risked everything when you joined the Resistance, not just for yourself, but for me, for our parents. You got me dragged into it when I didn't even know it existed. You got me arrested. And never once did I tell you you were stupid or that we couldn't face it together. ”

Ella's words hit Belle like an icy slap across the face. She could take a lot, but not that. That was it. How could she throw that in her face? She had to get out of here before they saw her break, because this time there would be no one to catch her.

"It's not the same, and you just keep proving to me just how stupid I was to think you could ever handle any of this! Tomorrow I'm dropping you off with Mom and Dad, and you'll be their problem! I'm tired of listening to this shit. I'm going to bed. We're leaving in the morning." Belle stalked across the kitchen, swiping at her face. It was no use. More tears replaced the ones she wiped away. "If the rest of you want to play savior, that's your problem, but you're not dragging us into it." She turned to Cambrie, eyes cold. "Tell me you're coming."

Cambrie opened their mouth to speak, then shut it. They had fucked up. They stared between Ella and Belle. Ella wouldn't go willingly, that much was clear. So if the choice was between the two women...Their silence was enough for Belle who choked back a stifled sob.

"Fuck you too then."

The Human stormed out of the kitchen and down the hall, slamming a door. Ella followed on her heels, screaming incoherently as she pounded on the door. Cambrie stiffly sat on a stool, avoiding eye contact with the others as Najah massaged her temples. Perri stood and retrieved another bottle of liquor from the dispenser on the wall.

"Well, we could all definitely use a drink after that."

## Thirteen

# CRIME IS HARD, RELATIONSHIPS ARE HARDER

## CW: Insinuation of kidnapping

"Get out of my room Belle!" Ella screamed. The doorframe shook beneath her fists. "Get out here! What's wrong with you? Why are you treating them like that?"

Belle was silent as she listened to her sister outside the room. Darkness engulfed her as she sat on the bed, the bedspread new. The posters that had hung on her sister's walls had been torn down, bare walls in their place. The stuffed animals and knickknacks Ella had spent so much time collecting were nowhere to be seen. It was just as well. Neither of them were the same people who had lived here a little over a year ago.

She stared up at the ceiling into the eternal darkness. Maybe she was wrong about it all. But how was she supposed to dwell on whether she was right or wrong? Everything but the blood on her hands remained in shades of gray. How was she supposed to sort through the emotions that just kept forming tighter knots in her mind the more she kept running?

They wouldn't understand. The curses of girlhood that were whispered about by every woman before her had thrown the noose around her neck. But she had picked herself up and made the sacrifices necessary. That's what women do. At least, that's what people always said.

Silent sobs racked her body. Mucus dripped down her throat, her face aching, her temples throbbing. Every muscle screamed out in agony but they weren't louder than her conscious. Her lungs begged, but they were greedy. No matter how many breaths she took it was never enough. She tried so hard and it wasn't enough. She had done everything and it wasn't enough.

Little did anyone realize, but the higher ups in the Saybrim Resistance knew all about the corruption, the Alcoriums, the CareFree. How could they not? They had told her all of it before her arrest. She had just tried to spare her sister the details, because she knew Ella would get it in her head that she had to save the world. But Ella wasn't capable of doing what needed to be done. It's why she had spent so many nights awake trying to figure out how to send Ella away, how to keep her safe.

And now, all of that work had been done in vain. She failed-she endangered Ella multiple times, and then brought them all back here. Fighting with this group had been some last ditch effort to keep Ella safe from herself, even if it meant hurting her. And once again, she had failed. So, it just meant that she would have to take more drastic measures. Ella wouldn't ever go with her willingly. She had made that clear. But, she was a heavy sleeper. She probably wouldn't even wake up until they were in the car.

Another sob racked Belle's body as she realized what she was planning. She had to, even if it destroyed her relationship with her sister. It was better than finding out she was dead. But it also meant leaving Cambrie behind. They wouldn't be complicit in kidnapping Ella.

Time and time again, Cambrie had stepped up for the girl. Cambrie had offered to give up everything, all their points and perks to give Ella another exemption. It hadn't worked, but then they helped train with her every morning. And of course, they risked their life to save her. Belle hadn't even thanked them.

But Cambrie had still sided with the others over her. They were so ready to stay, to listen to that god awful Siren. They had agreed with Perri and even joked with Najah. They were supposed to be her partner. She was supposed to come first and have their unwavering support, but they hadn't supported her at all. And Belle hated them for that.

Most of all though, she despised herself. If she had only worked harder, if she had been more attentive, faster, stronger, smarter, prettier...

If only she wasn't Human.

The thoughts smothered her long into the night, wrapping their tendrils around her mind and squeezing her heart.

After Belle's exit, everyone had decided sleep was desperately needed, although no one had been particularly keen to claim the main bedroom. It was too far away from everyone else.

Perri shuddered in the armchair, having shoved Brett to the floor before curling up and passing out. In her dream she found herself back in the Manor standing over Anna's body. A knife was heavy in her hands, blood thick on her fingers. Flames built up around her, the screams of her mother and of her boyfriend Finn somewhere in the

distance. She tried to run, tried to search for them, tried to cry out.
But the smoke choked out the cries, turning into a literal fist around
her throat. Triton stepped from the flames, his eyes blazing.

"I am a God amongst mortals. You have nothing. You are nothing."
With every word he spoke, the screams of her loved ones grew louder.
"All that anyone will ever see you as is my daughter."

Najah awoke with a start. Hair stood up on her arms as adrenaline flooded her system. Something was rustling, a soft thud echoing
through the room. She glanced around as her eyes adjusted to the
darkness. No one else stirred from where they had collapsed in the
living room.

The sound of a car running over a manhole cover emanated from
outside. The scent of weed hung in the air, having seeped through the
walls from the neighbors. She stood from the couch and soon located
the source of the noise. Brett had woken up. He squirmed on the floor,
his screams muffled behind the duct tape Perri had slapped over his
mouth after his sleep talking became too much. Najah deftly avoided
the garbage on the floor as she approached the man. She gripped the
mantle, searching for the flashlight she had seen earlier. When she
found it, she switched it on and blinded him.

Cambrie woke from the floor after sensing the movement in the
room, thankful for the reprieve from the nightmare that plagued
them. They cracked their neck as they joined Najah, who stood above
Brett. Of course, the assassin had sensed the thief's movements as soon
as they had left the couch so their accompaniment was little surprise.

Cambrie stared down at the squirming man. His eyes bulged. If they were to ungag him they had no doubt that he would begin spewing profanities at them. He would probably lunge and try to bite their ankles as well. He acted enough like a child anyways.

"You wanna put him out, or should I?" Najah whispered.

"Go for it." Cambrie gestured towards Brett. " I'm not wasting any energy on him, as much fun as it would be."

Najah bent down and gripped Brett's vine bound wrists, her palms secreting rose oil. The scent overwhelmed the musk in the room. Cambrie bit their lip. Something about the scent caused them to flush. Maybe they had been too focused earlier on Perri that they hadn't noticed the profuse odor. Maybe it had been the exhaustion. But the room suddenly seemed too warm as heat coursed through their body. They swallowed hard.

Brett instantly calmed and laid still. His eyes fluttered shut. Najah stood and wiped her hands on her shorts. She angled the flashlight towards Cambrie's face, which caused the Halfling to squint. The assassin opened her mouth as if she were going to taunt Cambrie for the flush in their cheeks, but then thought better of it.

Cambrie turned their back and approached the window. Anything to get away from that incessant rose smell. Headlights of a car shone in as it drove past. They used their fingers to separate the blinds. As they scanned the street, the darkness of hundreds of windows of apartments greeted them. Any one of the occupants of the buildings could be a cop. Anyone could be lurking in the alleyways. Still, nothing popped out as being suspicious. But their mind was hazy, and it wasn't from exhaustion. They had slept enough for the symptoms of their burnout to subside.

"We'll need to deal with the car once we figure out what we're doing," Najah murmured as she came up beside Cambrie. Her golden eyes glimmered in the moonlight. She was careful not to touch the Halfling as she too glanced outside.

"What?" Cambrie whispered, trying to focus on something other than the assassin. But their gaze kept wandering up her bare arms, tracing the lines of her tattoos up to her shoulders, across her collarbones and...They tore their gaze away. What was wrong with them? They shook their head, swallowing hard.

"The car? The one we stole? The cops will be looking for it. But we can deal with it once the others wake up."

"Oh, yeah." Cambrie rubbed at their eyes, trying to step away from Najah once more.

"Sorry, I didn't mean to catch you in the crossfire. I didn't think you'd be in the headspace to be affected by my oil." She gave a small, knowing smile.

"What? What do you mean?"

"Did you forget? Rose oil has more uses than just the sedative. You just weren't affected earlier because you weren't relaxed enough. Trying to save someone's life will do that."

Cambrie stayed silent, suddenly wishing they could melt into the floor. Their cheeks burned red with embarrassment as they ran a hand through their hair. They were just about to turn and find somewhere to hide until their feelings died down when Najah cleared her throat.

"Look, we need to talk," Najah said, the seriousness back in her voice. "We should go somewhere where we won't wake the others."

*Talk? About what?* Cambrie thought. They weren't friends. They were never friends. But the thought of talking alone with her brought back memories of a time when they were certainly something. Not friends. Never friends. That wasn't ever allowed. But talking now-friends now-in this world, that was complicated.

Cambrie glanced towards Ella who was hanging half off the couch, dead to the world, then towards the hall where Belle slept. Once the Halfling followed the assassin, they were afraid there would be no turning back.

"Don't worry, you'll hear them waking up before they even take a step," Najah said as she headed towards the hall. As she glided down the hall, she tried to navigate the feelings in her stomach. Logic and emotion had no holds barred here. They were going head to head in her chest. But before she could pick a winner, she had to know that she could trust Cambrie.

Najah entered the main bedroom and flicked on the light. The drapes were already drawn over the window and the dresser drawers were ajar with half folded clothes. If she had to guess, Perri had already gone through this room in search of an outfit earlier. Luxury perfume and even more expensive jewelry was scattered amongst the top of the dresser, neither in Belle's taste. Gifts to whatever new woman was in Brett's life. Abstract digital art that she didn't understand covered one wall, the random splatters of pixels making up semi-shapes that shifted between 2-D and 3-D. The bed was half made, the duvet barely covering a large crack in the right side of the bed frame.

As Cambrie entered the room, their stomach churned. The bedroom was just as repulsive as the rest of the house. It served as a reminder. The room was representative of him. Maybe it hadn't looked like this when she lived here, but this was where she had slept with him. And she was just a few yards away, in this awful place, dealing with tonight alone. Cambrie didn't even know if they wanted to go to her or if they wanted to leave her be.

"Why didn't you reassure Belle that Perri was telling the truth about everything?" Najah asked from where she sat on the bed. "About the

Alcoriums and CareFree and all of that? You could've saved everyone a lot of fighting. Because you ended up driving Ella and Belle apart."

Cambrie didn't dare to look at the Vitare. Instead, they went to the closet in search of a safe. Upon finding one, they began tossing out the shoes, making room for themself to sit on the floor. In truth, they didn't have a good answer, or at least an answer they wanted to admit out loud. The fog in their brain had subsided slightly, but they knew better than to try and lie to Najah on their best day, nevermind tonight. The leather of a boot smooshed between their fingers as the bed creaked and footsteps sounded behind them.

"I don't know," Cambrie said as they tried to toss the boot over their shoulder without looking.

Najah grabbed it from them, her fingers brushing theirs ever so slightly. "We both know that's a lie. You don't do things without thinking of the consequences. You can't afford to." She set the boot on the ground, carelessly shoving the shoes around her to the side so she'd have space to sit beside Cambrie. "Now watch where you're tossing those and try answering the question again."

Cambrie's fingers absentmindedly spun the safe's dial as they considered their options. They could leave. It wasn't as if Najah were holding them hostage. Yet, if they planned to stay with Ella, and if Najah didn't trust them, it could make things difficult.

"I don't know who you think I am, but I'm not the same person I was back when we knew each other," Cambrie said. "We aren't, and we shouldn't be, friends."

They spun the dial to zero, then to another zero, then to zero again. They pulled the safe open. Out came a large sack of plastic credits, the colorful coins rather heavy. Najah swiftly pulled a pistol from the safe and checked the magazine. Seventeen rounds stared back at her. She loaded the gun once more and rested it on her lap, staring at Cambrie.

"Don't give me this bullshit. I asked you a question. Is it really that hard to give me a straight answer?"

Cambrie glanced down at the pistol then rolled their eyes. They turned back to the safe and began to dig through files.

"I should have told Belle. I should've told her. I should've done a lot of things. But I didn't because I didn't want us-" they gestured to themself and Najah, "-to work together. If I told her, I was afraid that she would be more willing to listen. But then, I couldn't crush Ella. I couldn't tell her that she shouldn't fight, that she's not capable. So I don't know what to do. I don't want to keep them apart. I fucked up, like I do everything else. Is that what you wanted?" Cambrie tossed aside the papers with disgust, refusing to look at Najah as they stood. "Are we done?"

Najah stared up at the Halfling. She couldn't tell if Cambrie was telling the whole truth, but she didn't know if they knew the full truth either.

As Cambrie began to walk away, Najah reached inside the safe and pulled out a small velvet box nestled in the corner. She flipped open the lid. A gaudy diamond sat atop a plain golden band. Najah's eyes flitted to the doorway where Cambrie had paused. She rolled her eyes as she held it out to them.

"It's ugly."

Cambrie took the box with trembling fingers. Why were they shaking? They didn't even know if it was for her. And it didn't matter. It shouldn't have mattered. But as they looked closer, the tiniest of initials were engraved upon the inside of the band. ZE and BK. Zennebelle and Brett's initials. Cambrie swallowed hard. It shouldn't have mattered. But it did.

They slammed the box shut and shoved it in their pocket. They had to get out of here. They had to shove down their feelings. They had to figure out how to convince Ella to leave. They couldn't afford to put Najah in danger. Then they'd worry about Belle.

The walls were closing in around them. They felt as if they were ascending above their body. Pins crawled across their phantom limbs as they crossed the bedroom. Everything moved in slow motion. If they could just get out of here...

"What happened to Tenajh wasn't your fault, you know."

Cambrie stumbled to a stop. They couldn't have heard Najah correctly. She couldn't know about Tenajh.

"What?" The word seemed to come from far away, as if it weren't Cambrie speaking.

"I kept tabs on you when you had escaped, while I was still in the Egg. They had this plan to set you up." Najah's voice was softer than normal, gentle. "They knew you were working with Tenajh and Arix, and they knew you were too dangerous to be walking free. The file I managed to read said that they planned on taking all of you down at that gala. They drugged you. You couldn't have known how the rest of that night went down."

The floor rushed up to meet Cambrie, their knees giving way beneath them. The carpet cradled them as they tried to cling to this reality and the truths Najah was revealing. That night had haunted them forever. They had thought it was Arix setting them up all along. They thought they had missed the signs of betrayal, of subterfuge. If it had been the work of the government all along then it was an entirely different story.

When Cambrie had escaped the Egg, they had worked with a group of minor thieves. Arix, their leader, got word of a particularly valuable necklace being worn by a Councilman's wife at the Northexxe Gala. Cambrie was supposed to be the one to grab the necklace-but in the midst of their mingling, their drink had gotten drugged. They recognized the signs and told Tenajh who had been running technological interference. Tenajh told them to get out, but Arix cut in and threatened their life over the jewels. He'd fulfilled that promise to others.

So Cambrie got the necklace. It wasn't their best work, but they got out. They were supposed to meet up with Tenajh a few blocks from the gala. But the next thing they knew, they woke up in handcuffs, watching Tenajh be beaten by the same hands that had once beaten them. The hands demanded information that Cambrie didn't have.

The hands wouldn't touch them. They were too hardened for torture, and too tainted by the drugs and CareFree to be a useful experiment anymore. Whatever happened to Arix, Cambrie didn't care. What happened to Tenajh after they shipped him off to the Human prisons however, they didn't want to think about.

The Vitare crouched down next to the trembling Halfling. For a moment she remembered that night when their roles had been reversed. She couldn't leave them like this. She didn't have their healing touch, but she had to try.

"It's not your fault." Najah swallowed hard, ignoring the knot in her stomach. She was going soft, no doubt about it. "You don't have to push me away because you're afraid of hurting me. I can handle myself. I know between the Egg and Tenajh you're scared, but don't make rash decisions today because of it. And please, don't blame yourself for what happened. It's not your fault."

Cambrie stared up at Najah for a moment, their eyes dull. If only they could believe that. They stood, not quite sure if they could trust their legs. They braced themselves against the wall to test their strength before looking down at the assassin.

"I have to go."

But as Cambrie said those words, footsteps sounded from the other bedroom. They pressed their tongue to their fang. They were out of time.

"Stay here," Cambrie breathed. They didn't bother to look at Najah as they walked out the door. "I need to do this alone."

"Are you leaving?"

But the assassin's whisper went unanswered, fading into the night.

## Fourteen

# No One Had Kidnapping on Their Records, Okay?

## CW: Kidnapping attempt

Belle slipped her feet from under the covers, the chill caressing her bare legs. She flicked on the light and dug through the closet. Cardboard boxes were piled high, packed against the walls of the space. She wasn't surprised. Brett had always had a bit of an issue getting rid of junk. She was searching for some clothes, some valuables, something. Anything she could take with her, to reclaim.

The first box was full of holiday decorations, the second box full of records. Finally, as she dug through the third she found some of her old clothes. It was nothing more than a few old t-shirts and leggings, intermixed with some of Ella's favorite dresses. He had held onto it as if they'd come back. He had been right.

She shoved back her fury and shame. She would deal with it all later. She didn't have time to think.

She changed into clothes, shoving her uniform into the box. She shut the closet door with a heavy breath. This was it. She was leaving them behind.

Her heart was in her throat as she made her way into the living room. Despite the darkness, the apartment was too familiar. Even after all this time, she could still remember the spots where the floor squeaked. She tiptoed around them, her breath baited.

The moonlight cascaded across Ella's cheeks as she slumbered. She looked peaceful. She wouldn't wake up, not even if Perri were to hold a knife to her throat. She was too trusting, too naive for this world.

It was too easy to scoop her up from the couch and carry her. Perri slumbered in the armchair, Brett slumped on the floor. Najah and Cambrie were nowhere to be found. She wouldn't think about that now. She made it two steps before a chill went up her spine.

"I was hoping I'd be wrong," a low voice called from the corner. "You don't want to do this. She'll never forgive you." Cambrie stepped from the shadows, carelessly stepping over Brett.

"I have to keep her safe," Belle said curtly, moving towards the kitchen. She was never any good at goodbyes. It's why she ran, every time. "You don't know what I want anyways."

"This isn't doing her any favors. Regardless of your intentions, you've beaten her down and belittled her. You may be keeping her physically safe, but you've instilled a lot of emotional damage on her. She's going to despise you." Cambrie was faster and stood in front of the front door. Damned Halfling powers. They lowered their voice, almost begging the woman. "Please. I can't go with you if you do this and I-."

"You don't think I know all of that?" Belle snapped. "I don't care. I don't care about any of it. At least she won't be dead. Now get out of my way." Belle growled, her voice low. She needed to get out of this place.

"And what about you? Where are you going?" Cambrie asked. "You can't save the world on your own."

"Why do you care? You were never going to go with me. You've made it abundantly clear you don't care about me." Belle knew she had gone too far. She could tell by the way Cambrie's face fell, the way they recoiled away from them as if they had been struck. But she needed to leave, to get Ella to safety, even if it meant tearing apart every relationship she had built.

"Is that really how you feel? I..." Cambrie's voice was weaker than they intended. It didn't matter. They looked away and stepped away from the door, their voice suddenly icy. They were never going to let Belle leave with Ella anyways. "Whatever. Just put Ella down and leave."

"No, never," Belle growled.

Cambrie reached for Ella, but Belle turned away, causing Cambrie to stumble back. They fell back, their only wing hitting the door. Panic filled their body. Their lungs ached for a breath, but they found themself choking on air, unable to utter a sound. The screams and beeping machines intertwined with the other voices. They braced themselves against the door, trying to keep a grasp on reality.

Ella jerked awake, suddenly alert. She flailed and tumbled from Belle's arms, catching herself on the counter.

"What's going on?" Ella asked, despite knowing the answer.

"Ella I couldn't just leave you here with..." Belle began desperately trying to plead with her sister. "Please, you have to realize... You can't just..."

"Don't try to tell me what I can't do!" Ella shouted, shoving Belle into the fridge. "Go ahead! Run away. We don't want you here!"

"Ella..." Belle went to grab her hand, but Ella pulled it away. "Ple ase..."

But Ella was no longer paying attention. She had turned to Cambrie. She rushed to them, stopping short of touching them. They had slouched to the ground, covering their face with their hands. Their back screamed in agony, as if they were having their wing cut off once again. They chanted indiscernible words to themself as if it would stave off the hallucinations.

"It's okay, you're having a flashback. We're all here. We're in Brett's kitchen. Take a breath, just breathe."

"What's wrong with them?" Perri asked, wrinkling her nose.

"You're the most insensitive person I know and I was raised with fucking assassins, Goddess," Najah hissed as she came up beside Perri.

"Shit!" The Siren exclaimed, slapping Najah in the arm. "You could give a girl some warning before sneaking up like that."

Najah rolled her eyes. Perri looked to the others for an explanation of Cambrie's behavior, but everyone was too enthralled watching Ella to notice. The Siren groaned and returned to the living room.

Belle reached around Ella to try and touch Cambrie, trying to embrace them. Ella whipped around and shoved her sister back, shielding the shaking Halfling as well as she could.

"Don't touch them! You'll make it worse!" Ella snarled, breathing hard. "If you cared, you'd know that." She turned back towards Cambrie. Tears were streaming down their cheeks. "It's okay. What are three things you can touch?"

It took a few moments of harsh, jagged, breaths, but Cambrie managed to choke out: "Floor... door...my...face."

"Good, good. Now, name two things you can see. You can do this," Ella coached, her voice calm. The bags beneath her eyes were dark and her cheeks were still covered in blood.

Cambrie brought their hands away from their face, staring up at Ella. Their eyes were hazy and unfocused. "You... and the...counter."

"Good! You're doing great." Ella hurriedly stood and threw open the freezer. She grabbed a fistful of ice cubes. She squatted down and dropped one into Cambrie's outstretched palm. They jolted as the cold shocked them.

"Feel that? You're not there. You're with me. You're safe. Focus on the cold."

As color returned to Cambrie's cheeks and their breathing steadied, Ella stood and dumped the rest of the ice in the sink. Belle reached for her shoulder. Ella whipped around, eyes blazing.

"Does that...are they okay?"

"They will be. But that should've been you. But you're so wrapped up in doing whatever you want, whatever you think is best, that you don't notice what's going on with the rest of us. So go. Do what you want, without us."

Cambrie stood and took shaky steps to steady themselves against the island, watching the argument with exhausted eyes. They knew they had to make a decision. They had torn the sisters apart. But words were slow to mind and felt weak against the growing fissure. So instead, they settled for making it to the sink as their stomach emptied in a humiliating display.

"Ella, this just goes to show that I can't leave you with them. You're not safe. What happens when they do that in the middle of a fight?" Belle wanted to sob once more. She was playing a losing game. She couldn't look at her partner, not when she was throwing dirty punches.

"Then I'll be there for them, like they will for me. That's what friends do," she spat. "It's disgusting you'd use their trauma against them." Ella stood beside Cambrie, pressing a cold towel to their forehead and eyeing her sister with disdain. "You know what? Get out. You're not my sister, not anymore."

Too shocked for words, Belle stood rooted to her spot, unable to comprehend the words Ella had uttered. After everything Belle had done for her, how could she not see the sacrifices? How could she not see what she was trying to do? How could Ella take the only thing Belle had left?

"Get. Out." Ella growled, pointing towards the door.

This was it. There was no more begging or persuasion that could be done. Belle slowly made her way out the door, glancing back at her sister before shutting the door behind her. Her throat was tight, her eyes watery.

"El..." Cambrie whispered. "I'm sorry..." The apology would never convey the weight of the guilt that they felt. Nothing ever would. But it didn't matter. Ella wouldn't blame them, and somehow that made it all so much worse.

"Don't," Ella shook her head softly. "We both know she deserved that."

Najah's heart sank for Belle but she bit her tongue. She wanted to defend the Human- wanted the others to see Belle like how she saw her. But now was not the time nor the place.

Ella turned to the others. Her voice suddenly became steely.

"So, what now?"

# Fifteen

## At Least Breakfast Sandwiches Don't Scream

### CW: Mentions of domestic violence, mentions of slavery/human trafficking

The subtle quiet after the chaos could have been mistaken for a family preparing for vacation. Showers were had and new clothes were procured. Bags were packed and lined up at the door. Newfound treasures were stuffed into pockets. And although the smoke from the previous night still hadn't cleared their lungs, there was an air of hope that surrounded them.

After some discussion, it was obvious that the best course of action would be to head to Sanctus. Due to various treaties written during the Assimilation of Inanis, the Demon run city had its own laws; even though it was in the state of Vitana, neither the Vitana police force nor the federal government could touch it, at least not without a dozen hoops to jump through. The Sanctus police force weren't known for their speedy or fair policing either, which made it a criminal safe haven. Plus, Cambrie had old contacts in the city.

But as the sun teased over the horizon, an increasing, Brett-sized weight seemed to bare down on the group more and more.

Cambrie's gaze kept lingering on the man, as if they were trying to come up with a dozen new ways to make him suffer each time they saw him. It was as if he had disappeared from Ella's vision completely, while Perri continued to kick him at every opportunity. So it came as no surprise when the Siren dropped to her knees where Brett laid and licked her lips.

"What the hell are you doing?" Najah asked, dropping the backpack she was stuffing onto the couch.

"Eating breakfast, obviously." The Siren gestured to the man whose muffled screams resounded beneath the tape. He writhed against the floor, thrashing against his bound limbs. She rolled her eyes as she stared down at him. "Yesterday was exhausting. I need to feed before we go."

"Yeah, we're killing him right?" Cambrie muttered as they came from the hallway. "What's the issue?"

"Are we talking about Brett? Go ahead, he deserves it," Ella called from the bathroom. She placed her palms on the counter as she stared at herself in the mirror. This would be the first test to prove that she could handle this. As she spat bile into the sink, she tried to bar the gruesome images she had seen of Sirens feeding from her mind.

"As much as I understand the appeal, Belle said not to," Najah cried, looking from Perri to Cambrie. Cambrie stared at the floor. What cue was she missing?

"Does that mean nothing? I want to kill him too, but if we don't have to, I feel like we should honor one of the few choices she's gotten to make about the whole thing."

When neither responded, she rolled her eyes. Maybe she was wrong. The knots of conflicted emotions building within her were so difficult to untangle.

"If nothing else, we'll have a body to worry about on top of everything else?"

"You're an assassin aren't you?" Perri mocked, her eyes wide. "I'm sure you've dealt with plenty of bodies before. Besides, I'm sure everyone would rather me feed on this asshole than some random innocent Human. So if you'll excuse me." She carried Brett into the kitchen, his body suddenly heavy as he made himself deadweight.

Najah could have stopped Perri, could have ripped Brett from her arms. But as she quite literally dropped him onto the tile floor, the assassin just watched Cambrie. The Halfling didn't make a move to stop the murder and yet, they hadn't offered to kill him first. If anyone here had a claim over the man's life, it should have been Ella, then Cambrie, but their compliance had sealed his fate just as much as any weapon. Maybe they were right. But that thought did nothing to ease up the tension in her chest.

"I mean I guess I could leave him alive, but I think it's safer for us if I just kill him. Wouldn't want him getting away and telling people that we were here. Besides, this is more fun." Perri shrugged as she shifted into her bird form, then knelt down to Brett and tore into him.

Cambrie silently beelined to the bathroom. They couldn't stand the nagging voice in their head, the one that begged them to intervene because they knew Belle would've wanted them to. But this was to protect her, to protect Ella, to protect everyone.

They glanced up to where Ella had perched on the counter and began digging beneath the sink for cleaning supplies. Multicolored bottles awaited them as they opened the cabinet door. Ella shifted slightly so she didn't whack them in the face with her foot.

"We shouldn't feel bad, right? He deserved it?" The girl asked as she stared down at the Halfling.

Cambrie gripped a bottle at random, taking too much care reading the label. "He deserved it."

They reached back in the cabinet. Another bottle, another label. The words all blurred together, but it was still better than looking up at Ella. And hiding in here was better than shrinking under Najah's disappointed gaze. Goddess, what were they doing? It had been so much easier when everything was numb, when they hadn't had to think outside the highs.

"And we shouldn't feel bad?" Ella frowned, jumping off the counter. She sat on the floor beside Cambrie, taking the bottle from their shaking hand. In that moment, they were far from the steady hands of the master thief.

"You shouldn't. Not about any of this." Cambrie dug their nails into their palms.

Brett's muffled screams made their skin crawl, the guilt weighing down on their heart. Had Tonajh sounded like that? No, they couldn't think of him. They wouldn't think of him. But he had met a similar fate because of them. He had trusted them. Belle had trusted them. Ella trusted them.

"Cam, you shouldn't feel bad either. You know that right? We're doing the right thing." Ella had to make them see that. She had to show them what she saw. "You protected me, you believed in me when she didn't. We're going to be okay. We're going to get through this together."

But Cambrie just shook their head and stood, grabbing random bottles from the cabinet. The screams had deadened, but a knot still sat heavy in their stomach. They left the bathroom wordlessly. They'd worry about the body. The body they could control. That blood they could wash away.

Perri had just shifted back into her Humanesque form when Cambrie entered the kitchen. Very little evidence remained to the naked eye of the crime that had been committed. Just small smatterings of blood splashed around the tile. Apparently Perri had taken care to be neat.

"Good, you found stuff to clean up," Perri remarked as she saw Cambrie. "Najah just took the rest of the body down to the car and she said she'd take care of both of them. She acted like she didn't have to do this shit all the time back at the Egg. It's not a big deal." The Siren glanced at the blood on her hands, grimacing at the small stain on her sleeve. She gestured to the kitchen around her. "I'll leave you to clean this then. I suspect you have more experience in this area than I do."

Cambrie didn't have the energy to protest as Perri left the room. So, they set down the cleaning supplies, then they got to their hands and knees, eyes closed, and for a moment they asked for guidance from the deities they had long ago forsaken. Then they got to work cleaning up the murder scene.

Everyone left the apartment on foot just as the sun began to rise. Najah didn't say a word about where she dumped the evidence, but returned with breakfast sandwiches for everyone except Perri to eat along the way. Cambrie didn't touch theirs though, and instead gave it to Ella. Once again they avoided Najah's gaze.

Cambrie and Perri had already shifted into their Human forms. Perri stood tall as a purple haired vixen with bright green eyes and a nose piercing. Cambrie had taken a subtler route and gone for curly black locks with song lyrics tattooed along their dark skin. Both felt the pressure, as they would only be in those forms for an hour. It should be just enough time to get to Sanctus.

They clung to the shadows of the empty streets. Their footsteps were drowned out by the noise of construction a few blocks over. Even in the early morning, machines were at work putting up new office buildings that would push tenants in low income apartments out of the neighborhood.

Soon the new and old apartments made way for coffee shops and fitness boutiques. More cameras hung from the corners of buildings which caused stomachs to knot and feet to move faster. Somewhere in the distance birds began to rise from their slumber and called out to each other. The morning breeze swept back Perri's hair and spread her stolen perfume in the wind. Ella nearly tripped over a crack in the concrete, Cambrie catching her before she face-planted. Najah grit her teeth as she kept her face downturned away from a camera.

The sidewalk widened and an escalator leading underground sat, awaiting the hustle and bustle of the day. They hurried down the moving stairs and into the Line station, which provided shelter from the wind. They were going to catch a train to Sanctus using the public transport system that ran through all the major cities in Inanis.

A single robotic security guard stood watch over the station. Its white plastic body rolled back and forth as if it was pacing. A screen with a cute emoticon face on it turned as it heard the group approach. It stood watch from afar as they congregated around an antiquated ticket machine.

The dim green lighting of the screen on the ticket machine flickered. The rusted beige metal groaned as Ella leaned against it. Najah grabbed Ella's wrist and pulled her away from it, as if the machine would collapse with a single touch.

A man jogged down the stairs just as a train pulled into the station. The man moved his fingers in front of him, paused for a moment, and then stepped into the car as the doors swung open for him.

Najah pulled the credits from her backpack and fed the coins into the machine. She rushed, wanting to catch this train. Yet, the tickets dispensed painstakingly slowly. One by one the plastic cards spit out from the machine. She handed one to each companion, tapping her foot as she waited for the last one to dispense. The full body jumpsuit she had found covered her tell-tale golden tattoos, but was unbelievably warm. The turtleneck was a slow fist around her throat. The train pulled out with tremendous speed just as the final ticket printed.

"Dammit," she muttered as the rush of air from the train rushed over her. The robot with its deceptively charming face was beginning to creep her out. "When's the next train?"

"In three minutes," Perri replied, adjusting her hair. She drummed her long pierced acrylics against the ticket dispenser. The silver hoops that hung from her nails threatened to catch on the corner of the machine and rip as she did so.

The robot began to roll over in their direction. Everyone felt their breath hitch and their stomachs drop. The room was suddenly hot, the air stagnant. Cambrie raised their palm towards the robot. Najah's hand dropped towards the knife hidden in her thigh pocket. The four little wheels whirled loudly as the robot approached. Its side displayed bright blue stickers that read "A.I.S."

"Hello, you seem to be on edge. Is there something the matter?"

Of course, the damned machine could sense emotions. Cambrie had heard about these upgrades in the major stations in Zerephil but they must have made their way here. Sensing emotions in people without Alcoriums was a key part in preventing crime, they said, since non-Alcorium users supposedly committed more crime.

"No, we're simply running late," Najah said with a practiced calm, grinning at the smiling emoticon on the screen.

"I sense a growing anxiety," it chirped. "Would you like to talk to a customer service representative to talk about de-escalation tactics?"

"No," Najah said with a smile still plastered on her face. She stepped in front of Ella with the hopes that a physical barrier would make her tics harder to read. The girl was practically a walking neon sign that said "ANXIOUS." Her leg bounced, her hands scratched at her arms, and her eyes darted around. Najah wanted to grab her and force her still. "We're fine."

"My programming dictates I cannot leave until you are calm. You are being recorded for your safety," the robot chimed, its face replaced with a live feed of the group. "Would you like to speak to a customer service representative?"

Perri was visibly biting her tongue, her annoyance clear as day. Other passengers were milling about the station now. A few spared glances over towards the group but most were too preoccupied with their Alcoriums. The Line sped down the tracks, the brakes squealing as the cars stopped in front of the waiting passengers.

The group hurried away from the robot and onto the Line. Its chirping voice calling for customer service could still be heard as the doors closed. Only two other passengers were seated in their car, and they sat as far away as possible. One Human wore a incredibly tight pants and a dress shirt made of the cheapest silk, with a single button buttoned in the wrong hole. The other Human narrowly avoided plopping down in a puddle of mysterious liquid in their form-fitting dress. Shoes had apparently been abandoned elsewhere during the night.

As everyone found a seat, Najah surveyed the car. Hairs stood up on her arms and the back of her neck. A breeze caressed her spine. She found her leg bouncing uncontrollably on the train seat.

"Keep an eye out for anything suspicious," she muttered to Ella and Perri. "I feel like we're being followed."

"I agree," Cambrie whispered. "I feel it too."

"We just got on a train," Perri responded. "How do you know that? It could be a coincidence. Besides, I would have recognized those two's repulsive scent from our walk over, and I don't."

The other passengers did, in fact, smell of vomit, vodka, and sweat. Their legs entangled with each other as they began to make out rather passionately for six-thirty on a Sunday morning. They didn't notice an open bottle of soda splashing by their feet.

"It's not them I'm talking about," Najah said. "And it wouldn't be too far-fetched to assume that we're being followed, given the circumstances. Just, watch out."

Ella was uncharacteristically quiet as she stared at the screens embedded high in the car's walls. Silent video compilations of baby animals playing flickered past. The colors reflected in her glassy eyes. But there was no joy written in the lines of her cheeks as she watched a bunny hug a kitten.

"Ella," Cambrie said. "Ella." When the girl didn't respond, they waved their hand in front of her eyes. "Ella."

The girl blinked a few times and turned. "Yeah?"

"It's going to be okay, you know. We're going to get through this together." Cambrie gently took Ella's hand. It was the same thing Ella had told them earlier right? And even if they hadn't believed her, maybe it was what she needed to hear, maybe it was why she had said it.

"I know. I just-" Her voice broke. She crossed her leg over her knee and rolled up the hem of her leggings to reveal a small sun tattoo on her ankle. Belle had a small crescent moon in the same spot. "We got these when we first moved in there, when I first got accepted into the S.P.A.C.E program. Everything was going great. Brett was actually...nice, or pretending at least. I was doing well in basic training. She said that she was proud of me, and that no matter what happened, she'd always be by my side."

Tears had begun to fall down her cheeks. She looked up to Cambrie, her chest quivering. She swallowed hard. "Then everything started to go wrong. I flunked out of the program. Brett, he..."

She pressed her tongue to her cheek and closed her eyes. She took a breath to compose herself, to stop her tears. "You know. Plus, he took control of her paychecks so she couldn't get out. It's not like our parents had the money to help. When she asked me to take over her shift, I didn't want to. I knew it was a bad idea. But she said Brett was going to propose and she would pawn the ring and we'd leave."

She went silent for a moment as she stared up at the screen. A kitten was riding a toy car. As the train squealed to a stop in another station, a breeze caused Ella to shudder. More people entered the car, squeezing into the seats farthest from the rancid smelling couple. The group examined the new passengers with critical eyes but the riders were all too involved with their Alcoriums to notice. Still, Ella lowered her voice as she continued.

"Belle mixed up her dates and I saw the shipment of Saybrim. In her uniform, I looked enough like her. They thought I was her. I hadn't realized that we... that S.P.A.C.E soldiers had to transport them. I knew our job was to protect the border, to protect shipments of supplies, to keep the peace. But be part of the slave trade? That was part of a secret taskforce I didn't know existed, and I never would have signed up for had I known. But the Saybrim, since they thought I was her, started thanking me and telling me how I was saving their lives. They told me to undo their shackles. So I did. I wasn't going to deliver them to wherever they needed to go. But I had no idea what I was doing, I had no idea they all had trackers in their Alcoriums. I didn't even know where we were going, but I couldn't go to the coordinates set in the plane. So I started flying like they taught me in training. I guess flying off course set off a lot of alarms. Belle had already realized her mistake when I called. She told me where to land, so I did. But by the time she got there, the other soldiers had already caught up to us. You know how she managed to get us all out of there. Then, she took us to Kolasi and told me she worked for the Resistance."

Ella looked at the ground with a stare that threatened to crack the epicenter of the planet. That day would be forever imprinted in her memory. She had never felt such a feeling. The very memory of it still made her skin flush, made her chest tighten.

"I was enraged that she hadn't told me. She could have died, and I would never have known why. I was terrified for her. I was distraught that she didn't trust me enough to tell me. But then we started working together and I had thought that things were better. I thought she learned how to trust me. I thought we were finally sisters again. But I guess I was wrong."

Cambrie leaned in to hug Ella. Their stomach churned at the action, although not for the usual reasons physical contact brought. The full weight of the role they were to play in the girl's life finally hit them. In another life perhaps it would have been an honor. Perhaps they would have loved to have someone akin to a little sister. But here and now, this was irresponsible. It was foolish. It was dangerous. They only ever hurt people, and she was too in need to see that. But what other choice did they have?

"She's gone through a lot, I can't deny that. But you have gone through just as much and she doesn't seem to realize that. Not believing in you is the biggest mistake she's made so far," Cambrie whispered. "You may not have powers, but you have so many other strengths. If there's going to be any of us that can save this world, it's going to be you."

"Thank you." Ella gave a small smile. The words did little, but the warmth of Cambrie's embrace heated her soul and allowed for a glimmer of sunshine to return to her cheeks.

Perri was staring up at the screens with a look of permanent annoyance plastered onto her cheeks as a man tapped his foot in the seat beside her. Najah had been polite enough to pretend to not be eavesdropping on the conversation, but both knew she was too well trained not to be.

A silence followed them for a few stops. More Humans got on and off of the car in wave after wave of bodies. Some were headed to their low paying careers, others just getting home. There was a common tiredness among them. Most looked at their Alcoriums with dead eyes. Only one or two didn't seem to have the implant, so they were forced to stare at the screens above. The screens had switched to a channel bombarded with advertisements as the throng of bodies had grown in mass. Foods that couldn't possibly be natural stuck out, promising the results of a dream body or perfect meal. Their neon colors flashed for moments before they were washed away among hues of makeup that all blended together.

Najah had stood and gone to the other side of the car a few stops ago. She couldn't keep still, as that age old sensation of paranoia clawed at her gut. She had since gathered the stories of everyone on the train.

All of them were somebody, she was sure, but their features blurred with every passing second, their relevancy lessening. She couldn't taste the tang of acuity, the bitterness of false pretenses in the air. None of them had the barrel pointed at her back. And it was that fact that made her uneasy.

Ella kept her eyes on the mind-numbing screens, but kept her fingers intertwined in Cambrie's. The Halfling couldn't settle back into their skin. Their legs stiffened as the doors opened, their feet pointed towards the exit. Their eyes darted rapidly through the car as more people began to fill it up.

"You need to relax," Perri grumbled as she watched the Halfling curl into their seat.

"And you need to mind your own business," Ella retorted.

"It's all of our business now if we're going to be a team," she snapped. "What's wrong with you anyways?"

"Shut..." Ella began but Cambrie held up their hand, swallowing hard.

They certainly didn't want to tell the Siren. The thought of trusting her with something so intimate felt wrong. It made their chest tight. But they needed to be responsible and they couldn't-they wouldn't-rely on Ella.

"She's right. She should know." They turned to Perri, trying to control their breathing. "I don't know. It just started a few months ago, after I got sent to the Pit. I have my guesses but it's not like I've had a lot of time to see a therapist. Just being touched sometimes or seeing people upset can fuck with my head. It's like, I'm back at the Egg sometimes. Other times I'm just really paranoid. I don't get it." They danced around the symptoms that scared them, shrugging and staring at a discarded wrapper on the floor.

"That sounds fucked up. Are you sure you're okay to do this? I agree with Belle, I don't need you freaking out in the middle of something important."

"Perri!" Ella exclaimed. "That's so rude."

"It's fine. She and Belle were right to be concerned. But I can do this. I won't let this get in the way of what needs to be done." Cambrie stared up at Perri, eyes steely. "I've fought off worse than my own brain."

"Okay," Perri said, pressing her tongue to her cheek. Whether or not she believed it, she dropped the topic. A look of disdain crossed her face as a Human stepped on her foot.

"We really need to get you some help. Maybe we could..." Ella began but Cambrie shook their head.

"We don't have the time, or the resources," they said gently. "We'll figure it out together, but we have bigger issues right now. Besides, they'd probably just recommend CareFree."

Najah made her way towards her companions, eyes still darting around as if afraid of missing a critical detail. She stood before them, a chill going up her spine despite the stuffy air.

"We're here, we're in Sanctus."

## Sixteen

# THIS IS STARTING TO SOUND LIKE THE BEGINNING OF A BAD JOKE

The city was hazy and the sky was dark as clouds cloaked the sun. Between the wings of the Demons flying overhead and the giant resorts, the sun was nowhere to be seen. The neon signs adorning the fronts of buildings provided plenty of light however. With each step there was discarded garbage underfoot. A few graffitied, beat up, robots scurried about with brooms attached to their arms, but they couldn't keep up with the plastic cups that rained from the sky.

To their relief, nobody seemed to notice Cambrie and Perri shifting back to themselves. The throngs of people that flooded the streets were too involved in their Alcoriums. Rings flashed green everywhere they looked. Screens with holographic projections towered on the sides of gray buildings, playing advertisements that Alcorium users could interact with on their screens. Various drugs and drinks held promises for a good time. Those same screens easily hid the rapid decay of the buildings.

The group's plan was simple. They would find a pawn shop to sell off all of the newly acquired jewelry. Then, they would find Cambrie's contact.

"This place never changes," Najah whispered as they passed through a particularly rowdy group of intoxicated Sirens. To her left, a fountain sprayed bourbon from the lips of fish. Some party-goers had taken off their shoes and were bathing in the basin under the amber rain. "Do you still sense them Cam?"

"Yeah, we're still being followed," they muttered. They kicked a cup down the road. "But I can't figure out who it is. There's too many people. Perri? You have any ideas?"

"This place reeks. I couldn't tell the difference between a Human and a Siren in this haze. I can't believe I used to have fun here." Perri wrapped her arms around herself as if to protect herself from the filth. Shadows cascaded over her skin as someone bumped into her. From all around people seemed to swarm her. Except, these weren't fans. These were ignorant, bumbling fools. She swallowed hard as she ducked her head. It was better this way.

"What are you guys talking about?" Ella asked, her ears straining to hear the conversation. "It's so loud!" For a moment, a flash of red nylon caught her eye amongst the crowd of neutrals. But before she could catch a second glance, it had disappeared.

"We're trying to figure out who's following us," Cambrie practically shouted.

"Well the cops can't get us here, right?" She shouted back. "We're safe right? Unless it's not a cop!" Ella's heart began to race as she searched the crowds frantically.

"Relax, we'll lose them," Najah said. "Don't draw attention to us. Cam, if it will make you more comfortable, we can get around you.

But if we want to lose this tail, we should try to get in with the crowds. Is that okay?"

Cambrie bit their cheek but nodded. In the midst of the crowd, the group got into formation.

Najah watched Cambrie's back while Perri and Ella surrounded their sides. Footsteps echoed all around in a senseless din. They tried to make out faces amongst the indistinguishable, but every foggy feature seemed the same. Frustration clung to their chest. They could do better. They had to do better.

Perri's head pounded. She had come to Sanctus almost a year and a half ago for her seventeenth birthday. Back then, the lights hadn't been as blinding, and the drugs had lessened the noise. CareFree had made the grunge on the street disappear, and made the Demons seem fun instead of destructive. Her friends had partied with her for days on end. She could have been wrapped in bedsheets and she would have styled it thinking she was going to traipse around the city in a satin gown. Even now, she swore she had glitter from that weekend still stuck in the crevices of her eyelids.

Cambrie traversed the familiar street with ease. The eternal night of the city was comforting despite the growing anxiety in their chest. It had been here that they worked on finessing their pickpocketing, targeting the teenage children of wealthy politicians and businessmen here to spend the weekend partying. It had been easy enough to master, given their previous training at the Egg.

With Tonajh at their side, the two of them had been an unstoppable duo. So many nights had been spent dancing under pounding lights. Among the sweaty bodies and powder filled noses, it had been a little safe haven. What they wouldn't give to be in his arms again, hearing the reassurances he whispered.

It would be too easy to be swept away forever in this crowd. Cambrie gripped Ella's hand tightly, swallowing hard. Ella's head was on a swivel, her fingers loose against Cambrie's. The buildings towered high above her in colors that she had only seen in movies. And yet, there was no red.

"Watch your pockets," Najah said, smirking as she cast a glance towards Cambrie. "There's a lot of thieves around here."

Cambrie didn't respond to the jab as they continued navigating through the crowds. Perri however, frowned and peered around at the crowd. A Demon was dancing in the street to some music only they could hear. Gaggles of Siren women squealed as a group of Demon performers juggled fire balls on a small stage beside a bar.

Another flash of red caught Ella's eye. This time, as she turned, she caught a glance of a hooded figure slipping into the crowd far beside them.

"I think we lost them," Najah muttered. "I don't sense them now."

"Me either. Let's get out of here," Cambrie swallowed hard as they navigated out of the massive swarms of people. As they emerged, they were able to breathe again.

"I think I saw-" Ella began before cutting herself off. If the others didn't see anything suspicious, she was probably just being paranoid.

"Did you say something?" Najah asked, double checking the area around them as Ella shook her head. "If you think you saw something, we could've missed it. What did you see?"

"It's nothing. Just someone in a red jacket."

"Red is hardly a discreet color," Perri muttered. "Probably nothing."

"We'll keep an eye out then," Cambrie said as they ignored Perri.

Past the crowded clubs, bars, casinos, and hotels, the street curved into rows of shops. Holograms showed off tattoos in front of body modification shops. Liquor stores had set up vending machines full of shots. Nestled in between a tacky clothing boutique and a drug store was a small pawn shop. Its neon sign was burned out in some spots. In order to get to the door, Cambrie had to cut through the line of people waiting for the CareFree station six doors down.

A bell rang through the tiny store, but it didn't seem to alert the Demon sitting behind an impenetrable shield behind the counter. He didn't look up from his Alcorium, which was for the best. He knew his clientele preferred a silent, inattentive shopkeep. Within the counter display were a few cheap pieces of jewelry and a few worthless relics called cell-phones from the old planet-Earth. This way, if someone were to come in and rob the place, which no doubt happened at least once a month, they wouldn't be able to smash the glass and get away with valuables.

Two machines sat upon the counter. One was a slick white plastic rectangle with a touch screen, hologram projector, and dispenser slot. It had a catalog of every item currently in stock. The other was a similarly designed machine except it had a pull out drawer where customers could place their unwanted belongings. Najah unzipped the backpack and began pulling out handful after handful of jewelry. It clanked as it fell into the drawer.

Perri scrunched her nose. The place reeked of cat urine and she didn't want to know what lurked in the corners of the musty carpet. A large faded poster along the back wall advertised an out of business beer company. The peeling edges of the advertisement revealed spots of mold on the wall. She supposed that slapping a poster on it was cheaper than removal.

Ella bounced on her toes as she tried to stand in front of the shopkeeper's view. She didn't want him looking up and asking questions, because she certainly didn't have an excuse for the reason they had piles of expensive bracelets and rings.

The machine took the items and analyzed them before giving a quote for a rather generous sum of credits. Cambrie hit a few buttons and the machine loudly dispensed handfuls of plastic coins. They scooped them into the bag with the other coins they had taken from Brett and turned to the others.

"Let's go," Cambrie said, casting a look towards the shopkeep. It was like he hadn't noticed they were there. Perfect.

As the stale air hit their faces and candy flavored vapors wafted up into their noses, an exhausted looking Human in the CareFree line reached out and grabbed Perri. The bags under his eyes told of quite a few sleepless nights, and he appeared as if he had just finished rolling on the floor of a pest-infested restaurant's kitchen. Perri gagged and ripped her arm away from the man.

"Aren't you that model from Mirror?" His voice was garbled as he reached towards her again, eyes wide.

"You've got me confused for someone else," she said as she walked away, repulsion written all over on her face.

He opened his mouth to respond but Najah shook her head. He huffed and turned away, but not before sneaking one last glance at Perri.

"Layla, my contact-her house is this way," Cambrie said as they navigated away from the crowds, unfazed. "Let me talk with her. She can be... a lot."

They turned down an alleyway where the neon blurred and time seemed to slow. Two Demons pressed against each other, their limbs banging against a dumpster as they entered into their own ecstasy. The group hurried past, descending into the intentional mind-fuckery of the East neighborhood. Designed by some sadistic genius, the labyrinth hid every kind of soul that dared to enter. With each house, each street, more a reflection of the last, it promised the secrecy normally reserved for politicians. But here, without a way to tell one from the other-or a way to escape the winding roads that only multiplied-who was to tell what lurked inside?

The scent of garbage was inescapable. Something large scurried past Perri's foot, but her shriek was drowned out by the thumping music in the air. Around and around they went past manicured lawns and white walls. Wrought iron fences and tinted glass dared to look down upon them. As they walked, bugs swarmed around them. A foolhardy woman's diamond jewelry clinked on her wrist as she passed.

When they reached Cambrie's destination, it stood no differently than any of the other houses they had passed. It was truly unremarkable. The air was humid and sweat began to drip down Cambrie's cheeks, although it wasn't all from the heat. Cambrie raised their fist to the door and knocked. The sound reverberated through the air and joined the classical music that played somewhere in the distance.

The stairs creaked inside the house. Butterflies fluttered furiously in the pit of Cambrie's stomach. The door squealed as it opened. They could barely make out the figure in the dark doorway, but the cool metal of a pistol on their chest was unmistakable even through their clothes. Before anyone could react, Cambrie held up their hands and called out over their shoulder:

"Don't do anything."

Najah stood with her palms at the ready. Perri's eyes were closed, searching for a connection, just in case. Ella got ready to run.

"What are you doing here?" A female voice called out from the doorframe, her voice flat.

Cambrie swallowed hard. "Is Arix here?"

"None of your business. Answer my question."

"We need your help."

"And you came here?" The Demon woman began to laugh. The sound rang out and danced in the air, joining the music. It rose, raucous and uncontrolled. She dropped the pistol from Cambrie's chest and doubled over. "I didn't...realize...that you're that... dumb," she said between breaths.

Cambrie crossed their arms over their chest and stared down at the woman. They were too exposed here. They longed for the security that walls brought. Sweat dripped down their back, their palms slick.

The woman stood, catching her breath. "Goddess, you're so lucky Arix is dead, because if he were here, he would've beat your ass." She stood aside and gestured inside with her pistol. "I gotta know why the fuck you're here. Hurry up, you're letting in the mosquitos."

Ella cast a glance towards Najah. Were they seriously going to go into this woman's house? But Najah seemed unconcerned as she headed up the deck.

The tiles squeaked as they shuffled into the house. The wallpaper that had once adorned the house was slashed through and burned in spots. Instead, antique posters of half nude Angels were haphazardly pinned along the walls and ceiling. The crystal chandelier that had once been a statement piece of the home now had become an abstract art piece. Pieces of clothing and scraps of metal now hung haphazardly off of it. Piles of impractical heels and boots lay by the door.

"I see you've done some redecorating," Cambrie said, taking in every inch of the place.

"Yeah, well, let's be real. Arix was shit at design. He never had an eye like I do." Layla led them further into the house, down the hall, past moving mugshots she had edited to have all her friends' faces on them.

"Absolutely," Cambrie agreed, resisting the urge to snort as they stepped over a pelted rug made of genuine tattooed pig skin, complete with the head.

"I'm still pissed he had me sell that Gregori Tsundi ruby. That would have made the best finishing piece on my choker."

Perri's jaw visibly dropped and her eyes widened. "You're the ones who-"

Najah swiftly delivered a killer glare which silenced Perri, but it was too late.

"Yeah, we are. You should really guard your stuff better. Especially around here."

As Cambrie mouthed an apology to the Siren, Layla continued on. "But that was so long ago. Go ahead, sit."

Perri sat stiffly as Layla gestured to the couch with her gun. The Demon flopped into a tufted armchair and draped her legs over the arm. Her eyes glimmered like the stolen ruby. As she unfurled her charcoal wings, she flicked her tail like a cat and inhaled a puff from a silver atomizer. The haze curled around her head in a shimmering halo. It would have been easy for someone inexperienced to fall into her.

Cambrie had seen it happen, and would be a liar if they said they hadn't been tempted by her when they first joined the syndicate. With how the low light reflected off the curves of her soft dark skin, she was gorgeously reminiscent of the women in the ancient artwork she had studied in university. But, she was a thief through and through, and most hearts were nothing but blackmail to her.

Layla tossed her gun to the coffee table where the head of an old toy was being used as a bowl to hold a conglomeration of pills. Priceless art pieces lay on the coffee table, with half drunk glasses of rum balancing on top. Her jet black bob fell to the side to reveal an Alcorium, which she used to shut off her T.V. that had been playing a fashion show.

The group took their seats on the pair of red velvet sofas that sat in the middle of the room. Another glance around would reveal a confusing series of taxidermied Human hands mounted onto the far wall, reaching out from the abyss for help.

"Has anyone told you you look like shit Cam?" Layla asked.

"Sorry, I've been a bit busy not dying," Cambrie responded, rolling their eyes.

"It's too bad you can't stay for one of our self care nights. It's been too quiet around here."

"Yeah, I really wish we could, but we can't."

Layla swung her legs off the chair and slunk towards Cambrie, leaning in close. Her woody perfume lingered as she traced a strand of Cambrie's hair through her fingers.

"The buzzcut suited you more. I can take care of this if you like."

Cambrie stiffened and pulled away from the woman, voice breathy. "I like it like this Layla."

Najah and Ella shared a look somewhere between appalled and shocked before returning to their observation of the art on the walls.

The Demon frowned and stepped back before shrugging and grinning. "Whatever. But my offer stands anytime you want. Honestly, I've been bored without Arix, so I'm kind of glad you and your friends popped in for some entertainment. Don't get me wrong though, I'm still pissed at you babe, so you better tell me why you're here." She pointed a finger towards Cambrie and shook it like an upset mother, rouged lips in a pout.

Cambrie sucked on their lip, deciding to take a risk. "Look, before we get into the real reason we're here, do you have my wing?"

"What?"

"My wing, my prosthetic. It was here when I got arrested with the rest of my stuff." Their heart pounded as they awaited an answer, fingers furiously rubbing against the edge of the couch.

"Oh, that metal thing? Yeah, turns out that piece of shit actually sells for quite a few credits. Sorry. I figured you didn't really need it where you were going and, uh, you do owe me. You didn't bring me credits did you?"

As Cambrie's face fell, Layla's lips pressed together and turned upwards, slight dimples forming as her cheeks rose. But the façade never reached her eyes.

"I didn't think so, but really, it doesn't matter. So, you presumably escaped the Pit and you brought a bunch of people to my door. I mean, do you know how much attention this is going to draw to me? This whole thing is like a bad joke. An assassin, the President's daughter, a little girl, and a terrible thief walk into a bar..." She trailed off as if expecting a reaction, then shook her head and continued, gesturing towards Najah.

"You better have a damn good reason to be here. The only reason I haven't killed you is because I've heard The Duchess over there can fight. That, and you amuse me."

Najah raised her eyebrows and opened her mouth to say something, but Layla beat her to it.

"Yeah, I know who you are. You're a bit of a celebrity in this town. Killing Amani with her own fork? Legendary. In other circumstances, I would've taken you to dinner just to get the details on how the Picilin Conference went down."

"I'm open to it," Najah said with a small smile. She shifted in her seat, letting her fist clench as she reached for her bag. A vice crushed her lungs as the scent of death clung to her nostrils, only for a moment.

Najah curled her tongue before fishing out a decent sum of colored coins for the woman. "But here. Here's some of the credits you're owed."

Layla sneered, smacking away Najah's outstretched hand. "I don't want them from you. I thought you'd know better. They need to be the one to pay me back." She then turned her attention back to Cambrie.

"So, why are you acting like you didn't cost me four hundred thousand credits and the crew? You know just as well as I do that there's a bullet with your name on it, just waiting for the day you came around."

"You know I didn't mean for it to end up like that," Cambrie's eyes darkened. They looked away from Layla in an attempt to look hurt. They'd play her game if it got them help.

"Maybe, but Arix was never convinced. They went after him right after they got Tenajh, you know. Besides, does it really fucking matter? Whether you meant to or not, you still cost us the job-and a really good man." Layla muttered the last bit, looking towards the floor.

An Aravyian shepherd trotted into the room and nuzzled under Cambrie's dangling hand. They absentmindedly ran their fingers through the dog's familiar black and auburn fur. The dog licked their hand, tail thumping against the floor.

"I know. I'm sorry." Cambrie paused, as if the apology would be heard by the man they really meant it for. But despite the fractures between the two of them, Cambrie couldn't help but feel some empathy for Layla. She too had felt the pang of loss deep within her soul. So, their shoulders softened and they leaned forward. "I need you to help us launch an attack against the people who did this. With your intel and weapons we could take down-"

"So against you? I'm down."

"No. The ones actually responsible: the government, the Councilmembers, Triton. I was set up at the gala by the operatives out of the Egg, and they had planned on taking us all down that night, but really, it's all a small part of a bigger plan to-"

Najah stared at Cambrie, her glare conveying far more than words ever could.

"Do you really expect me to..." Layla trailed off and her eyes glossed over. "What? What do you mean?" She shook her head as if to clear the fog that had settled over her brain. "What are you doing here?" Her chest rose rapidly as if she couldn't draw in enough air.

As the woman's hair fell out of the way, purple light refracted in the dark as it circled around her Alcorium. She stumbled backwards.

"Cambrie? What are you doing here?" Layla's eyes darted from Cambrie to the others. "Who-who are you?" She lunged across the table for her gun with the ferocity of a leopard.

Najah was faster. Her fingers curled around the grip, whipping it towards Layla.

"Sit down!" Najah yelled.

"What are you doing in my house?!" Layla screamed. She took a step forward, her knees banging into the coffee table. "Get the fuck out of here!"

Perri stood and yanked Ella to her feet.

"Go, go," Perri hissed as she hustled towards the door with Ella in a vice grip. The dog got up to follow them.

Cambrie looked towards their old colleague with confusion. "Layla I..."

"Don't! Come on!" Perri yelled. This had been stupid. She had been stupid. She pulled Ella out the door just as Layla lodged a weak burst of flame into the wall.

The tendrils licked away at the wallpaper for just a moment before dissipating into the air. Cambrie glanced back towards Layla, a dozen unsaid words on their lips. But Najah shook her head and found her fingers locked on Cambrie's wrist. Past the priceless artwork they ran, and the incoherent screams of Layla swirled with the night haze.

The warm air kissed their faces as they retreated from the house where memories flooded. No one looked back as Layla slammed the door in their faces.

Perri didn't release her grip on Ella until she determined that they were safe in a nearby alleyway. Ella wheezed, her lungs aching. The smokey air burned as it went down her throat, but she was thankful for it regardless. A pair of eyes spray painted onto the side of one of the buildings watched diligently over them. Small swarms of insects buzzed past Ella's cheeks. As the others entered the alley, Najah threw out her arms, lips pulled taut. She glanced between Perri and Cambrie.

"What was that?"

Perri took a tentative breath, her hands raised to the back of her head. "I-I think they're listening to us. For us."

"What?" Ella asked, her stomach twisted.

"They had the technology centuries ago, before Alcoriums existed. Governments back on Earth used it before it was outlawed. It wouldn't be a stretch to think they brought it back, especially to search for all the Pit escapees here in Sanctus."

"But that doesn't explain why she freaked out!" Cambrie exclaimed. "She completely forgot who we were."

"Yeah, I know! I don't have all the answers, okay?" Perri shouted as she threw her hands in the air, racking her brain. She paced towards the wall and placed a fist against the brick. Her forehead rested on her hand. "I'm trying to figure this out...it's just...her ring was purple...that usually signals some form of communication."

"Does that mean that anyone could be listening to us? At any time?" Ella asked. Her blood ran cold at the implications of it all.

"There have to be too many users for them to listen all the time," Cambrie muttered. "Maybe there's keywords that trigger them to tune in?"

"That would make sense," Najah said. "It wasn't the most discreet conversation."

Laughter rose up from the street. Colorful lights flickered on the walls of the alley. The scent of rotting garbage and dried vomit created a nauseating odor.

"Shit! Shit, shit, shit!" Perri hit the wall as she cried out. "How did I not think of that?" She turned to the others, dread in her eyes. "It was one of the last things Anna told me. There was talk of an Alcorium update that was messing with the beta tester's memories. They were severely confused, they were forgetful, entire memories gone."

The words hung in the air for a moment. They weighed down lungs and hearts, knotting stomachs and shaking limbs. The implications of that power...Najah swallowed hard, and Cambrie crossed their arms over their chest. Ella felt the anxiety rising in her throat, tears forming. She couldn't do this, what was she doing there? Her breathing quickened and her heart raced.

"How is that even possible?" Cambrie asked, mouth agape.

"I'm not sure. The technology has advanced so quickly, I can't keep up. But if they were able to control the update and listen in to conversations, and then erase any memory they want, it will be nearly impossible for us to find anyone to help us."

"And, it means we have an entire city of people listening to us, potentially exposing we're here," Najah hissed. "We may not be able to be arrested here, but the second we step out of this city, they can catch us."

"We've been in worse spots before," Cambrie reassured. "We just have to be careful. We can't ask anyone for help, or mention anything about Triton, CareFree, or Alcoriums. We can figure this out."

"We have to," Perri said. "There's not another option."

Ella crossed her arms over her stomach, feeling nausea rise in her throat. She swallowed it back down and stared into the faces of the others. They seemed so at ease in this city, in this life of crime. But all she really wanted to do was curl up in bed. Standing with the Saybrim Resistance was one thing, but now, on the run, with an entire city potentially spying on them, all of their eyes on her...She just barely had time to turn her head before she felt the bile in her mouth. She vomited, her sick hitting the concrete with a disgusting splat.

Perri took a step back and wrinkled her nose. "Gross."

"You okay?" Cambrie asked.

Ella nodded, tears of embarrassment prickling at her eyes. She wouldn't cry. She wouldn't cry, not here. It would only embarrass her more. She fought back the waterworks and stared at the entrance of the alleyway where dozens of people wandered past without a single glance into the alley. She took a breath, then stared towards her companions.

"So, what do we do now?"

Najah brushed a hand across her face. "Let's go find a place to stay for now. Then, we're getting my sister."

There was a solemn nod from the others as they peered out into the city. Then, Cambrie wrapped an arm around Ella and headed out of the alley. Najah followed, watching the crowds of people as usual. Perri trailed behind, casting a glance up to the eyes on the wall. And as they walked away, she could've sworn that the eyes were still following them.

## Seventeen

# Scars Tell Stories

## CW: Discussion of sex trafficking/pedophilia

Ella sucked down a bottle of juice and bounced her leg. The hotel comforter scratched at her bare skin, the sweetness of apples contrasting with the bitterness of the air in the back of her throat. The beginnings of a headache formed at the top of her neck.

"Belle do-" she began, before stopping and chewing on the inside of her cheek. "Does anyone have a Ploferin I can take?"

"Perri took the last one for her period," Cambrie grumbled, rubbing at their knee. "Trust me, I looked."

"I'm sorry everyone, I wasn't aware that I'm not allowed to be in pain," Perri mumbled. "Fucking hell. Do you know how long it's been since I've had mine? Unless you're gonna go out and inject me with-"

"We can get some more meds when we go out," Najah interjected. "Now, can we focus please? We can't stay here forever. We have to get my sister and get the hell out of Sanctus before they find us."

"At least here we're safe from the cops-" Ella began before getting cut off by Najah.

"Yeah, I'd rather deal with them. You're acting as if they won't send assassins after us here. And trust me, they're not going to be cool like me."

"Fine. So, what's your plan then?" Ella asked. "Are we going to be rushing into the club like Alexa did in Spy Mind 4?"

Najah stared at the girl, narrowing her eyes and letting her jaw fall open. Her throat was thick but she gave a slight shake of her head and turned to Cambrie.

"I was hoping we could brainstorm together."

"Of course," Cambrie nodded. "We'll come up with something guaranteed to work."

"Well, can you give us a little more information then?" Perri asked quietly. "We can't really help plan without knowing more."

"I would've thought-" Najah spat before biting her tongue. Acid flooded her mouth and she wiped at her lips, wishing she could wipe away the years. "Nevermind. What do you want to know?"

"How do the kids get kidnapped? What happens to the kidnappers?" Ella asked, her eyes wide, fingers gripping the bed frame. The setting sun cast shadows around the others, illuminating their eyes.

"How do you think this works? Do you really think there's an epidemic of kids getting snatched from the arms of their moms?" Najah fought back her screams, staring at the silver wallpaper behind Ella before continuing.

"You really bought into that? Fuck. Sure, that can happen, I'm proof of that. But, it's mostly kids who were given up under the guise of subsidized adoption. At Human hospitals it's common for large families on social welfare programs to be given the option of adoption in exchange for a one time fee so that the government doesn't have to increase their assistance. But, of course, those adoption services are often designed to traffick said children. It's either that or families will just traffick children themselves. That's common too, especially outside of Sanctus," Najah closed her eyes, trying to wipe the memories of all she'd seen from behind her skull. She wanted the black shag carpet to swallow her whole, to engulf her into its furry tongue. But alas, when it didn't, she continued.

"The rings they've formed...it's atrocious. But I suppose it is nicer to just imagine that it's a scary kidnapper prowling around in the darkness, because then it seems like it can't possibly happen in your neighborhood, like your friends and family aren't participating in it," Najah spat towards Perri. For once, the Siren didn't answer.

"I'm sorry," Ella whispered into the sudden darkness that had fallen. No one got up to turn on the lights. Her quiet voice spoke up once more. "So we have to plan on getting a bunch of kids out, not just one."

"Ella, we're not getting them all out. We can't return them to their families, and we can't take them with us."

"But they're kids! We can't leave them! You said it yourself, you've seen how awful it is, and yet you want to leave them?" Ella stood from her spot, her shadow spreading out to eclipse Cambrie and Perri.

"She's right Ella, if they travel with us it'll put them and us in more danger," Cambrie said gently, reaching up to touch the girl's arm. Ella shook them off.

"Exactly. Traveling with a dozen or so kids isn't exactly discrete, and it's not like we can drop them off with the cops," Najah rolled her eyes. "Especially not with Alcoriums tracking every move. What do you think Perri? You've been pretty quiet over there. Got any thoughts you so desperately want to get off your chest?"

"I-" Perri began before she was cut off by Ella.

"Well, what's going to happen to them after we break Maggie out? Don't you think there's a good chance those kids could get killed?

That the traffickers get angry with them for letting Maggie get away, or maybe they'll think the kids said something-"

"It's a risk we'll have to take, Ella," Najah said.

The rainbow around Ella faded into red as she gripped the sink. Her fingers trembled against the counter as she stared down the others in the mirror, wishing the glass would give way and she would find herself lying in bed. The ire was too big in her chest, the venom that eroded her sensibility into spitfire threatening to spill from her eyes. The words exploded from her chest before she could stop them.

"I guess all of you only stand for freedom when it's worth the risk for you then!" Risks be damned. They may be right, but so was she. "I knew you killed people, but I thought you at least had some morals. I thought you cared."

"That's not fair," Najah began.

"Fuck it though, I'll do it. Since I'm obviously outnumbered, I'll go along with your plan. I know that's your concern, isn't it?" Ella cut off the assassin with all the vitriol she could manage. "Don't worry, I won't be another risk you'll have to take."

"You're-" Cambrie began.

"I mean, she has a point, it is a little hypocritical of us to leave those kids. But, I'm also not about to be a babysitter," Perri called out over the noise.

"Did I ask?" Najah rolled her eyes. "Anyways Ella-"

"Yeah, you did ask, actually, and I feel like we should all have an equal say in what's happening," Perri retorted.

"Yeah, let's let everyone speak their mind, why don't we?" Ella said, a sickeningly sweet smile plastered on her cheeks.

"Thanks babe," Perri sighed. "As much as I hate to admit it, she's right. We shouldn't leave those kids. But if we can't bring them with us now safely, then we shouldn't risk it. I have a contact that may be able to keep an eye on them until we can come back to get them."

"You've had contacts this whole time and haven't mentioned them?" Najah huffed. "You know, nevermind, whatever." Her eyes bored into Perri's. "Are you sure this contact won't betray you? Do you trust them with your life?"

"Yes."

"Good. Because if they do betray us, I'll kill you first. Call them."

## Eighteen

# The Monster's Facade

## CW: Sex trafficking, pedophilia, slavery

The city pulsed with the leeched blood of a beautifully cursed thing. The air that had seemed so spirited and carefree upon arrival now clawed at the innards of every passerby with a silent screech. The red silk and diamond dancers that spiraled around each other with lips so supple were just another enchanting sacrifice for the never ending appetite of that place.

As the group of four wandered down the neon bleached sidewalk, rain seeped down their temples and into their socks. Only the squelching of shoes sounded between them, hoods were pulled over strained, guilty eyes. Everything else was unimportant. Every other sound was unintelligible muttering, every building blurred to be the same. Every face was nothing more than an advertisement for a life they could've had. It had to be this way. It had to be. Right?

A few more blocks left them teetering on the edge of the East district of Sanctus. The main streets where tourists came to party and corrupt business people set up their hotels sat adjacent to the streets of art thieves' galleries and millionaires' mansions. The pounding music and blinding lights weren't as violent here, but the four of them still had no issues finding crowds to blend in with.

Perri gripped Ella's arm as they approached the apartment building. Secrets were held in by thousands of windows and scandal dripped from the golden balconies. Towering glass and metal archways intertwined to frame the doorway, standing nearly ten stories tall, beckoning them to enter. Cambrie and Perri had changed their appearances somewhere amongst the swarms of people. With a nod to each other, they went their separate ways, Perri with Ella and Cambrie with Najah.

Ella had conjured up an image of the place to be full of signs pointing towards the traffickers, or at least heavy perfumes and velvet draped windows to mask what horrors happened here. It was never that obvious though. Instead, warm light bounced off imported tiles that had to have been hand polished. Plants she couldn't name bloomed around a fountain that created the outline of sea creatures as water danced in the air. Crystals dangled from the ceiling as if they were stars, shining on the few residents milling about in the lobby. It was a place of luxury like she had always dreamed of living in, and now she never wanted to set foot in another apartment again.

A man cleared his throat from behind the front desk. "Hello, how may I help you today?"

"I have a delivery for Elenor in 227," Perri said, suddenly wishing she had prayed to the Goddesses earlier. The words were a struggle to form as her mouth was as dry as the Wiverian Desert. The well-worn blouse she had been forced into clung to her back as she sweated. Her heart pounded behind her eyes, her fingers digging into Ella's arm.

The doorman peered over the counter at Ella who was busy tugging at the hem of her dress, avoiding his gaze. He paused a moment, taking in the Human forms before him, before pressing a button on the desk and gesturing down the hall.

"The elevator is down that hall, on your left. Take the one on your left, not your right. Press the button for floor two twice. She'll be expecting you."

"Thanks, have a good one," Perri muttered.

She briskly strolled down the hall, making sure to keep a grip on Ella and keep her head high. No one would question her. She was Perrianna Nextulus after all, even if no one knew it. She didn't need her powers. As she made it to the elevator, she just barely caught Cambrie's gaze as they made it to the doorway. Things were going according to plan.

"Can you let go of me? You're gonna break my arm," Ella hissed as they waited for the elevator.

"Shut up you brat," Perri muttered back, her eyes darting between Ella and an approaching Demon family. Ella seemed to get the hint. Perri loosened her grip and gave a polite smile to the mother and son.

"Why can Ashtien have his birthday party at Polaris Pit but I can't?" The boy whined.

"You know that place isn't for people like us," his mother sighed, rubbing her eyes. "Look, you can spend another half hour on your game if you agree to let this go."

"Fine, but only if we can go to Inertia Overlord instead for the party." The bargaining of childhood was truly unmatched as the child gave a coy grin, knowing he had worn down his mother enough to win. He pushed the elevator button again in his impatience, apparently having the lucky touch.

The elevator arrived and the four of them stepped inside. For a moment, Ella's breath hitched as she watched the mother reach for the buttons. If they headed to floor two as well, did that mean the boy...?

But before she could even finish that thought she was pulled out of the elevator and the family was whisked away into the sky. She would never know if the boy ended up having the party after all, but he soon became the last thought on her mind.

An eerie silence encased them as they stood in the grey hallway. Only a single door loomed before them. It was encased in light, as if trying to showcase the exclusivity of the place.

"Look at me," Perri said, her hand leaving Ella's arm for the first time. She met the girl's eyes. Something in her shifted, because as she looked, she realized Ella's eyes reflected none of her own fear. Instead there was only a wild fierceness. Perri raised an eyebrow, letting her words take on their own meaning. "Are you ready?"

Ella only nodded, which left Perri to take a breath and open the door.

To any unsuspecting person, to any poor soul who may have accidentally stumbled upon this place, it was as if the people who lived here were immensely wealthy, beyond generous. As Ella peeked across the foyer into the sitting room, a rainbow of unopened gifts sat in the corner and a shimmering banner of a name she couldn't quite read ran across the t.v. A few children of various ages sat among the large furniture, eating tiny pastries.

"Welcome, you must be the guests I was told about. You're just in time," a Saybrim woman greeted them instantly, her smile faltering for a millisecond upon seeing Ella. "Let me take your coats," she held out her hands expectantly. Familiar gold bracers wrapped around her wrists. Right above them, a serial number had been etched into her forearm, along with a spiderweb of bruising.

"It's okay, thank you," Perri smiled, clutching her jacket close around her.

"Please, you're soaking wet, I'd hate for you to catch a cold." The woman glanced over her shoulder, searching. "Please."

Ella had the garment in her hand, ready to give it up. But before she did so, something changed in the woman's demeanor, her head tilted downwards in curiosity. The woman stumbled forward as if her heels had caught on the tile and grabbed the girl's forearm to steady herself. But as the woman met Ella's eyes, a moment of realization sat heavy in the girl's stomach. All those nights ago, her and Belle had been given tattoos in ink only visible to Saybrim. She didn't even know what it looked like herself. It had been a ritual, signifying them as true allies, family even, to the Resistance and the people within it. But forgetting that mark could have just outed them.

Instead, as she grabbed the coat from Ella, the Saybrim woman's nail ran across the girl's skin, leaving a shallow gash that just missed the tattoo.

"I'm incredibly sorry. Oh, you're bleeding, I'm so sorry." she apologized, wrapping an arm around Ella. "Neshevellie," she then muttered under her breath, one of the few words that Ella knew in a language even fewer understood. But they stopped Ella's world momentarily. Perhaps she should have called out to Perri, or searched for another plan, but instead she let the woman take her by the wrist.

"Here, you can come with me and I'll get you cleaned up. And I'll have Iya take you to Elenor now," the woman said off-handedly to Perri, already dragging Ella off into the depths of the apartment.

"But I-" Perri began, feeling the plan come apart at the seams. She had to pull this together again somehow.

"Thank you," Ella cut off Perri, suddenly coming to her senses and understanding what was about to take place.

Through the sitting room, into a sterile kitchen, and shoved into a cramped bathroom, Ella was torn between closing her eyes to block out the children everywhere, and searching for possible escape routes. She soon found her back pressed against the basin of a sink, the cool porcelain making her shiver. A scent too cool and foreign to her stuck to the back of her throat.

"Ella Everard, what are you doing here? Is that woman forcing you?"

The use of her full name sent adrenaline coursing through her veins. It was a biological force of habit. She glanced at the woman, wondering just how much she knew. Perhaps it was risky telling her the plan, but she hadn't sounded the alarms yet.

"No, she's my friend. It's a long story," Ella said as the woman began to apply the bandage. "I appreciate you checking in, but we're just trying to get a kid out of here. Perri and I were going to distract Elenor while our other friend comes up here and acts like the guest and gets Maggie out of here."

"Maggie? Maggie Irozi?" The woman turned away, but her face was still visible in the mirror. She rifled through another drawer, her lips spread in a thin line. She began to wrap a ribbon around the tentacles that protruded from her head, then stuffed something in the folds of the fabric that wrapped around her stomach.

"Yeah, why?"

"So you're wrapped up with Najah Irozi, huh? Figures." By the way the woman rolled her eyes, Ella took it that it was a sore topic. "Where's Zennbelle?"

"I'm not sure. What's your name?"

"Swenulu. I'll help the best I can. You're just getting Maggie out, right?"

"This isn't going to work if you're not there!" Najah exclaimed, her hands covering her eyes.

"I'm sorry. I didn't know they'd have an Angel barrier," Cambrie replied, referencing the technology still in place from the Hundred Year War that prevented Angels from entering certain areas.

"I should have known! How did I not know? I should be in there. I should be the one getting her. What if they don't get her? What if we're just putting her in more danger?" The words rolled off Najah's tongue in waves, her voice cracking as it knocked down the hardened exterior she had forced herself to put up.

Cambrie wrapped their arms around Najah, trying to shield her from herself as she shivered in the rain. "We just need to adjust a bit. We can figure out another plan. We always did and we always will. We're going to get her."

"I know-I'm sorry. I just need this to go perfectly," she gasped into Cambrie's shoulder.

"I know, you don't need to apologize to me, Oraësiana." The name was a careless slip of the tongue, something that the Halfling prayed would be washed out under the drone of cars from the city street.

Lips parted, Najah took a step back, breaking the embrace. She swiped at her cheeks, trying to swallow the repulsive lump in her throat. "It's been a long time since I've heard that name." Najah pressed her tongue against her cheek, staring out across the street.

"I didn't-" Cambrie began, brow furrowed, the apology for crossed boundaries already on their lips. It had only been in those stolen moments so long ago that the nickname had been uttered. They had no place saying such an intimate phrase anymore to her, not when their heart was supposed to belong to another. But Najah just squeezed their hand, smiled, and shook her head.

"Don't. We've got bigger things to worry about right now," she said, pulling her hand back and tracing the raised skin on the back of her shoulder.

In that moment between the thunder and the raindrops, Najah tucked her imperfect storm of emotions away to feel later. Across the street, the apartments taunted her as the only foe she hadn't yet defeated. Mice scurried around her feet as she stood squeezed between two brick walls built up so thick they threatened to crush her. Blue and green hued people milled around, partaking in the upscale nightlife without a clue as to what lurked in the shadows.

In the neon moonlight, Cambrie's eyes shimmered like gems as they let curiosity dance along their face. They hadn't missed her nervous habit of following the scars along her skin. "What are you thinking?"

"This reminds me of that training mission we did in Ofarin. The one where we thought we kept messing up so we ended up digging through the dumpster..."

"Yeah, I remember that! Goddess, that was terrible," they paused, tracing their bottom lip with their tongue. "I think we could try it here though, minus the dumpster diving. There's only two perimeter guards. You could go up to the third floor and I'll stay on the ground?"

Najah stared out at the building, then back to Cambrie, grinning. "This is why I love working with you."

Perri sunk down into the chair across from Elenor, every single bone in her body wanting to lean across the desk and inflict unimaginable pain upon the woman. Golden flame tattoos dotted her arms in a dime a dozen pattern. Everything from the way she dressed to the way she talked made Perri's skin crawl, which only made rage flame higher. Her jewelry were all pieces Perri had modeled, her lacy top with exorbitant feathers extending off the shoulders a favorite of the Siren. But Perri couldn't allow herself to be distracted. Any Vitare this old who made it outside of a government career had to either be working in a partnership with the government or was too influential for the government to catch. Either way, she wasn't keen on finding out which one.

She wouldn't ever recount the details of the encounter to the others, nor did she particularly want to remember what was said. But it was far too easy to let her tongue form the words she needed, to smile as Elenor offered her a drink, and to pocket the credits given to her.

Meanwhile, Ella leaned against a locked closet door while Swenulu jammed a chair beneath the handle. Muffled shouting emanated from within.

"Are you sure Iya won't help?" Ella asked as the other Saybrim woman slammed against the door.

"She's an informant for Elenor," Swenulu said, shaking her head. "C'mon. Where's your friend? We have to block the front door so the building security doesn't come in."

"They're supposed to have been here by now," Ella said. "We just have to get the kids out of here. Where's Maggie's room?"

"Upstairs, third door on the right. Go, I'll send all the kids up to you, and I'll get your friend."

"Thank you," Ella said breathlessly as she ran toward the stairs.

She tore through the hallway as quickly as her silent footsteps could manage. Blurs of jagged murals and brass numbers, the scent of lavender, pop music. It would all play out later in some haunted house nightmare she was sure. But as she swung open the door to Maggie's room, all she could focus on was Najah snapping a man's neck.

The sound forced itself into Ella's brain. A hole created by the wall's bent steel and Najah's broken vines let in bitter air that chilled her to her bones. Her stomach churned and threatened to empty right on the stained carpet. But she shook her head, biting back the contents. It didn't matter now.

"What's going on? Where's Cambrie?"

"Where's Maggie? Why are you here?"

"You first."

Najah rolled her eyes. "The perimeter guard's too nosey for his own good. Cambrie's outside, they couldn't get in the building. They're taking care of security. Now you."

"We had a change of plans. Cambrie didn't show obviously, and the Saybrim woman in here recognized me and said she'd help. So she's getting Maggie and the others."

"The others? Ella, if you mean to tell me that the other-" At that Najah was cut off by children running into the room. "No, no, absolutely not! They're gonna get hurt!"

Voices rose up around them as eight children took in the scene. There wasn't time for emotion though. Smoke was crawling through the crack under the door, the tendrils rising to the ceiling.

"Something's wrong! Where are the others?" Najah shouted. "Cambrie's losing control of the flames! It has to be Elenor!"

"They set a fire?!" Ella screamed. "Why?"

"Where are the others?"

"Perri's still with Elenor! Swenulu was supposed to get her!"

A small slide made of vines had appeared in the hole in the wall. Among the terrified cries came hurried footsteps down the hall. From somewhere an alarm sounded and muffled yelling shook the walls.

"We have to get them out," Ella called out at the assassin as she shoveled kids into the slide. "C'mon!"

"I don't see Maggie!" Najah screamed, trying to look at each remaining kid as the smoke grew heavier.

As she said that, the door flung open, exposing Perri, Swenulu, and two children.

"Maggie!" Najah screamed upon seeing her sister. "Thank goddess, come on, we have to go."

Maggie, holding the hand of a boy barely out of diapers, didn't even give her sister a second glance as she stepped up to the slide. Maggie followed the boy down, her buns bouncing as she disappeared from Najah's sight. Najah faltered for a moment, watching the girl go, before following down the slide.

"You're coming with us, right Swenulu?" Ella asked. "We need someone like you!"

She shook her head, holding up her wrists in reply. The heat was nearly unbearable. Sweat dripped down their faces. If Cambrie couldn't gain control, they knew what would happen soon.

"Perri, you can fix this, right?" Ella begged. "Right?"

Perri's mind was torn away from where she was staring at a doll on Maggie's floor, the doll with the purple dress. The same one Artemis had given her as a child.

"I'm sorry?" Perri's voice was small, every part of her trembling as she fought back sensations she couldn't describe.

"Can you get Swenulu out of the bracers?"

"I-I can try. But we need to get to Elenor first."

As they raced out the door, Perri snatched up the doll and tossed it into the flames.

The finery on the walls peeled away like decaying flesh, an eerie darkness creeping along the place as the electricity went out. Silence marked another headstone in the surrounding apartments, racking up row after row where frantic cries should have been.

Elenor tugged at the flames around her as they descended the stairs. The woman's eyes glinted as she played tug of war with Cambrie's powers, carelessly letting the flames catch on her surroundings. It was a tricky game to play, a calculated bet, only reserved for the top players.

Cambrie forced the flames forward in an attempt to throw Elenor off balance. If they could pitch her backwards into her crumbling office, perhaps they could get an upper hand. But as cement rained from above, the woman didn't lose her focus. She kept her hands out, trying with all of her might to control the flames. The wind whipped her hair in a hurricane around her face as she looked out on the massacre with a sneer on her face.

"I should've known it was a fucking half-breed taking out the barrier. What, you're willing to take out the whole building just to get in here? You're sick! Let it go!"

"That's rich coming from you!" Cambrie yelled. "Save yourself! Let go!" They waved their hands, desperate to extinguish the blazes around them, but to no avail.

"Hey!" Ella choked out as she picked up rubble. She chucked it at Elenor, the rocks hitting the woman straight in the head. "Take that!"

This time, Elenor fell backwards, clutching at her temple. She dropped the tendrils of flames that she had gripped so tightly, leaving them free for Cambrie. They tried to extinguish the flames, but it already ate the walls with desperate mouths. Beneath their feet, the building creaked.

"Get out of here!" Cambrie yelled to Ella and Perri. Their voice broke as the smoke only rose higher.

"Go!" Perri said as she shoved Ella towards the crumbling exit. "I'll take care of Swenulu and... right behind you!" A fit of coughing broke up her words.

Ella glanced towards her friends one last time as the wall beside her crumbled. She bit her lip, last words and regrets filling her throat. But it was all too late as her feet carried her towards safety.

Perri dragged Swenulu towards Elenor who still laid on the ground. With an arm around the woman's throat and a few choked out words in Solaska, the bracers around Swenulu's wrists fell to the ground. Perri was on all fours, chest heaving, mucus running down her nose. Swenulu wasn't faring much better.

"C'mon! The building isn't going to last much longer! Finish her off!" Cambrie shouted, sweat pouring down their forehead. Their vision wavered for a moment as the flames inched ever closer to Perri and Swenulu.

"Go," Swenulu choked out to Cambrie. "They need you."

The building creaked once more and Swenulu pushed Cambrie, causing them to stumble over a beam and into the abyss of the floors below.

"What-"

But before Perri could finish her sentence, the belly of the beast lurched forward with one last breath and the building collapsed.

## Nineteen

# It's Not Nice to Run From Old Friends

## CW: Discussions of survivors of sex trafficking/pedophilia

The red linens flowed around her like the wine she so desperately craved. It was as she glanced around at the neon illuminated faces that she cursed herself for being so careless. The cloak she had snatched in the low light of a stage show had been perfect for concealing the lack of her Alcorium, her sweaty brow, but it had caught her too much attention from the prying eyes around her. But as she ducked away from curiosity and concern, she lost them in the crowds.

Just as Belle was about to give up wandering around the soggy streets of Sanctus, a burning building sent up a beacon. She pushed past the begging Humans on the fringes of her vision, their hollow figures little more than ghosts. The crackle of the fire and the moans of metal called her ever closer. Ash poured down upon the vacationers like forsaken glitter. Then, tiny bobbing heads pressed against the crowd making her targets easier to follow. It was evident as she got closer though, that Ella and Cambrie were nowhere to be found.

"Where are they?" she roared, pushing past the children entering the hotel room. The fraying curtains swayed as the door flew back and hit the scuffed wall. Najah turned, rolling her eyes.

"You're who's been following us," Najah exclaimed, throwing her hands in the air. "Great! Just what I need."

"Where's Ella?!"

"When you find her, let me know. I'll be first in line to strangle her." Najah's eyes roamed over the kids as if she were counting them for the twelfth time that evening.

"You don't know where she is?" Belle's limbs went numb, her tongue leaden. She was suddenly aware of her own heartbeat.

"No, I was suddenly being handed a bunch of kids from a burning building while the other three decided to run back inside. This-" Najah gestured around her "-wasn't exactly in the plans."

"What happened? What were you doing?" But as Belle looked around, the pieces began to click. Too many little Human faces stared up at her, their eyes terrified and exhausted. A few clutched blankets tightly around themselves. A Human girl who couldn't be more than ten wrapped her arms around an even younger Human boy. Another girl who looked eerily similar to Najah sipped from a water bottle from her spot on the bed. Belle's mouth went dry as realization hit her.

"You let her go in there? With those monsters? And you left her?" Belle shoved Najah against the wall. "She's a kid!" She reached out towards the assassin's throat but her hand was smacked away.

"She said she'd do it," Najah snarled, back pressed to cheap wallpaper. Her nostrils flared. "Besides, do you really think Cambrie would let anything happen to her? They haven't left her side once through all this, unlike you. Hell, even Perri protected her more than you did."

Belle pushed Najah once again, her palms bouncing off the woman's chest as she stood immobile. So Belle spat in Najah's face, wet saliva sliding down the assassin's cheek.

"Fuck you. I will never fucking trust you! She could be dead for all you know and you wouldn't give a damn because you only think about yourself!" Belle's breath was hot on the other woman's cheek, and as the Human turned her back to storm away, Najah yanked her backwards.

"I'm going to say this to you once, so listen carefully: I have more important things to deal with right now, but if you dare disrespect me like that one more time, you're not going to have the chance to walk out of here again, understand?" Najah hissed to Belle. She could barely hear herself over the blood pounding in her head. If she could, perhaps the whispers of the children behind her would have changed her tone.

"You don't scare me. Now let go of me so I can go find my fucking sister. I thought you, of all people, would understand that."

It was then with baited breath that she took off into the night once more.

As the building came down, Demons swarmed around the fiery rubble. They scooped the flames up with their bare hands, tossing them in the air like they were in some new exhibition. They squealed at each other in their substance induced hazes. They tossed the fiery rubble to each other, nearly singing each other's wings off in the process; although given a Demon's propensity for fire, they were probably enjoying the thrill.

Ella considered herself fortunate. The concrete hadn't crushed her, and only a few marks would leave her bleeding. There were plenty of bodies. The smell alone told her that. But there was no sign of the living among the charred skin and crushed bones.

She squeezed her way through the crowd of patrons and staff that had formed. Her heart pounded, her lungs clenching as smoke filled the sky. Blood filled her mouth, a result of a bitten tongue. Her throat tightened and as the crowd grew around her, she found it more difficult to breathe, although from the pollution or the people she couldn't know. She scanned the scene around her. Amongst the silhouettes and the shadows she couldn't find the familiar figures of her friends. The crowd pushed in on her, all the tourists looking for the impromptu show. The Demons above her had swarmed like bats. Their wings blocked out the moonlight as the fire raged on.

Ella managed to elbow her way to the edge of the crowd. She finally could take a breath. The air was cool in the back of her throat. It startled her lungs as she finally gave into the coughing fit that had been building. She fell to the glass littered pavement. As it felt like pieces of her lungs would pierce through her throat, people paid her no mind. They swarmed around her like ants on candy. Their Alcoriums flashed green. Instead of fear, it was as if this was new and exciting. Even the lucky few residents who had been inside didn't seem at all rattled. They all stared up at the show above them. As more of the building crumbled and flames began to lick the walls of the neighboring structures, the demons ramped up their show. It would be ages before the firefighters showed up, and soon half the street would be ravaged. But, the people didn't seem to care at all.

Ella dragged herself up, searching once more for her companions. Metal crunched beneath her weight. She wiped at her lips as the salt and metal taste became unbearable. More tourists hurried up the street towards the spectacle, brushing past her. Her lungs protested against her quickening movements but she ignored them. Sweat poured down her back as her soot covered clothes clung to her. And as much as the city had the lifeblood of an exhibitionist, Ella was once again reminded that the prowling dangers of the darkness could easily wrap her up and devour her alive. Down along an alley were people shaking hands and tangling tongues under crimson lights. The decaying bricks were adorned with self-proclaimed artwork. As the rich sighed in sin, it took the breath of the dying with it.

It hit her as she reached the intersection. The streets were too similar, too blinding. The labyrinth of a city had twisted in her mind. She was lost without even the stars to guide her.

Suddenly, a shaking hand clamped down on her wrist. Ella choked back a scream as she looked into Cambrie's bitter and bruised face. She opened her mouth to say something, but Cambrie simply shook their head and dragged her along.

As they made it to a quieter street lined with cheap hotels, a Siren in a short white dress with a "Just Married" sash took a spill to the pavement in front of them. Another Siren in a suit helped them to their feet, laughing.

"Are they okay?" Ella asked, turning to Cambrie.

A pause, a bitten cheek, then Cambrie whispered. "I don't know." They refused to look in her eyes.

"What? What do you mean? I-" Ella began.

"Not here," Cambrie shook their head.

"We have to go back!" Ella hissed. "We have to make sure they got out!"

"No. We're going to the hotel. We can't go back there now."

"I can't-"

"Ella, please," Cambrie begged, their voice breaking. "They should be there. It's the first place they'd go."

"And if they're not?"

Cambrie's somber face was enough of a response. The remaining walk back was silent. Ella stared at the cracks on the sidewalk, counting each one as if it would save her life one day. Anything to take her mind off the possibilities that lay ahead.

As they approached the hotel, Belle tore down the sidewalk. Icy puddles splashed at her exposed ankle but it didn't jolt her out of her stride. Belle wrapped her arms around Ella, letting every bit of anxiety roll off her back. Air rushed back into her lungs at warp speed, choking her as tears rolled down her cheeks. Her knees buckled, forcing her to rely on Ella's weight to keep her upright.

Ella however, never got a chance to comprehend who had latched onto her. She shoved off her sister, heart skipping a few beats. And as she took in Belle's red cloak, her lips pursed.

"What are you doing here?" Ella's disgust was written on every inch of her face.

"I had to make sure you were safe," Belle murmured. She looked towards Cambrie and opened her mouth, but they were already heading towards the room.

"I don't know how to say it any clearer. We don't want you here," Ella said as she brushed past her sister.

Headlights illuminated Belle from the parking lot. She stood solo under the branches of a metal tree, raindrops dropping onto her cheeks. She said something, only for the words to be lost on the ashen wind. She could feel the electric hotel sign buzzing in her veins, her limbs quivering much like the fading "O."

Ella hurried into the room behind Cambrie only to be greeted by ten pairs of eyes and one dangerous smile. Perrianna Nextulus was nowhere in sight, but the Duchess had come out in her fully realized form. The girl shivered under the air conditioning, only vaguely aware of her sister slipping in behind her and shutting the door.

"Hello Ella," Najah said, her words sickly sweet. "Zennebelle. Let's go to the bathroom so we can have a quick conversation."

"Najah-" Cambrie began.

"You can say whatever you want here," Belle spat.

"Please. This isn't meant for them," Najah said, glancing towards the girl with uncannily similar features. Her stomach dropped at the acidic gaze her sister threw back. The things Maggie had said in the others' absence had made her regret her earlier confrontation with Belle. And Maggie sure wasn't shy about her opinions.

"What? You're planning on abandoning us again?" Maggie asked as she crossed her scarred arms.

"You know I don't-I didn't-" Najah stammered, the color leaving her face.

Maggie just shook her head and opened a drink for another child. They all hovered around her, taking shelter in the shaking strength of her despite the slimness of her frame. But as Najah opened her mouth again, Maggie turned to the panes which only framed the blaze in a macabre painting.

"I don't care about a damn talk right now, I need to know where Perri and Swenulu are!" Ella cried.

Najah ignored the outburst and pulled Ella and Belle into the bathroom, every fiber of her being shaking. The door slammed shut but not before Cambrie could slip inside. The fluorescent lights weren't kind to any faces, the mirrors on opposite walls reflecting on their frenzied anger. Sweat dripped from the assassin's brow as she clutched the black sink, hanging her head as the others found their places. One look in around at the black floors, black walls, black tub, and toilet, and she felt as if she weren't careful, this black hole of a nonsensical hell might swallow her whole.

"Do you have a plan for how to take down the government with a fucking three year old in your arms? Anywhere you're going to take these kids that you've neglected to share?" Najah hissed as she whipped around. She leaned forward, forcing Ella to press herself deeper into the tub, nearly falling in.

"No, but I couldn't just leave them there! Perri said she had connections that could watch them! Maybe they could take them! Besides, you set the building on the fire! They would've-" Ella replied. She stood sturdier, pushing herself off the porcelain. She swallowed hard. "Where is Perri? Swenulu?"

"I don't know, but all you've proven is that you're a risk to us, both of you. You need to leave. Now." Najah snapped.

"Great! We will!" Belle said, grabbing Ella's wrist. Her voice was echoed back by the shadows. Ella shook off the hold and perched herself back on the side of the tub.

"I'm the one who fucked up. I'm the one you should be mad at!" Cambrie hissed. "She saved innocent people, I killed them!" Cambrie closed the gap between them, forcing Najah to look at the blood on their hands. "It was me."

"At least you-" Najah began quietly, shutting her eyes.

"At least what? The plan failed. If you're gonna be pissed at someone, be pissed at me. She's part of the reason we're all still alive, that Maggie's alive. They're both staying. We need each other."

Then Cambrie whispered something only Najah would understand, their breath caressing the nape of her neck. The assassin swallowed hard before leaning back into the sink and looking into Cambrie's eyes. She clenched her shaking hands at her side before glancing at Ella.

"Thank you for saving them. You did the right thing."

"Great, apologize all you want, but we're still not staying," Belle spat at Najah, her gaze venomous. "Obviously, you're not as great as we thought, right Ella? Since you were perfectly fine murdering a bunch of kids? So-"

"I didn't want them to die, I just didn't want them to come with us," Najah said, letting her tongue press against her cheek.

"Don't you dare touch me," Ella snapped as Belle reached towards her. "I'm not leaving. Don't you see? At least here I have a use."

"Ella Rosemary Everard, I swear-" Belle began before being cut off by a cacophony of screaming in the other room.

They all burst through the bathroom door only to see Perri holding the severed head of Elenor, blood dripping down her arm and onto the welcome mat. She swayed in place, her eyes glassy. Her clothes were tattered, burns and dirt marred her skin. Specks of blood were splashed along her cheeks, her hair matted with crimson.

"Where have you been? Get in here!" Cambrie cried. "Goddess, did you walk here?"

"What's wrong with her?" Najah asked as she noticed Swenulu behind Perri, pale and covering her eyes.

Ella and Belle gathered the newcomers inside before shutting the door. Perri held the head an arm's length in front of her, body stiff and face deadpan. Some of the children cowered against the wall, while others desperately clung to Swenulu.

"Perri, talk to us. What's going on?" Cambrie asked before turning to Swenulu, gesturing to the Siren. "Do you know anything?"

"She hasn't said a thing since the building came down on top of us. At least, not that I can remember. But I don't know how we got here, now that I'm thinking about it. Last thing I remember, she was holding up part of the building." The Saybrim woman shook out her wrists and stepped away from Perri, looking towards the children. She knelt down to their level, hugging one of the young boys.

"What do you mean she-" Belle began.

Perri shrieked, tossing the head across the room with a sickening splat. "What did I do?"

"We're trying to figure that out. But the good news is, Elenor's dead. The bad news is, that means we have to go. Now. There's going to be a lot of people after us. The fire was one thing, but ten missing kids and Elenor's death means we're going to have a whole network of people trying to track us down," Najah said, rubbing a hand over her mouth. "I'm going to find a car. You deal with this," she gestured towards Perri.

The children all shrieked out a cacophony of high pitched questions and concerns as the assassin slipped out of the room. The cool summer air had taken on a dangerous heat, smoke still heavy on the wind. Her fingers trembled as they slid across the dark paint of a party bus.

"Najah," Maggie called out. No one else could make her heart leap as though it were doing a somersault off the tallest Arayvian building only to fall through the cracks of unbound sinew. "Wait." As the young girl strode across the parking lot, Najah collected every detail of her face. From their mothers' brown eyes to high set cheekbones to a wide nose, it was all like the assassin had pictured. "What's your plan?"

"Right now, we all have to get out of here. After that, honestly, I have no idea."

"Great. So glad to see that my entire family was almost killed by someone who doesn't even have any fucking idea what she's doing. Do you even know what happened to Iya? Did she get out?" The hotel sign flickered on and off, illuminating Maggie's gritted teeth.

"Who's Iya?"

"The other Saybrim woman. You didn't know about her?"

"I had no idea, but I'm sure she got out," Najah said, her voice weak. She glanced over her shoulder, aware of the visitors that could be arriving at any moment. There were far too many things to tell the girl in front of her and too little time. "I was just trying to keep you safe."

"I was safe before you came along!"

"What do you mean?"

"I was safe! I didn't need you to save me! I've never needed you!"

The words were jagged against Najah's heart as she tried to clutch for something, anything, that made sense. She turned away from Maggie, holding herself tight.

"I'm sorry," she whispered. The words were wrong on her tongue. She wasn't sorry, not for that, but what else could she say?

"Yeah, like that matters!" Maggie cried. "Just get us out of here."

The ground tilted under Najah's feet as she tried to suck in oxygen. She nodded, her heart beating in her chest. She needed to get them out of here. Then she could deal with this.

Colorful lasers blinded Najah as she fumbled with the computer system, her fingers feeling too big for her body as she tried to override the party bus. The sticky lyrics of a pop song clung to her eardrums and made her fumble with the buttons. The warmth of frustration and rage coursed through her veins and made her jaw stiffen.

"Not to rush you, but we've got company!" Perri said, racing up the stairs. "There's at least two Vitares headed our way, coming fast!" She held onto two kids' hands and led them to their seats.

"Fuck!" Najah shouted, running a hand over her face. Her teeth were grit so hard she swore they would shatter. She continued to try and stumble her way through hotwiring the bus.

"We gotta get moving!" Belle said as she corralled kids onto the bus. "What's taking so long?"

"I've got it," Cambrie said as they leapt up the stairs. They easily pressed a series of buttons over Najah's shoulder. "You're driving Belle."

"Fine. What's taking Ella so long?" Belle muttered as she swapped spots with Najah.

"I'm here, Mythos," Ella huffed as she and Maggie ran onto the bus. "This is what we're taking? This isn't exactly discreet."

"Oh, you're gonna-" Najah began.

But just then tires squealed as a sedan pulled up to block the driveway. A heavily golden tattooed man leaned out the window. His golden eyes glistened in the light as he smirked.

"Hey Duchess! It's not nice to run from an old friend!"

Then, he pulled out a rifle and aimed at the bus.

## Twenty

# WHY DID IT HAVE TO BE BUGS?

"Get down!" Belle screamed as she veered over a curb. The bus jolted as it hit the road. Bullets hit the metal and cracked the back window. Shrieks filled the car as Belle sped down the road. "Who are they?" She screamed as she swerved at breakneck speed. She blew past a red light causing the other cars on the road to squeal to a stop.

"Slate controls stone, Blair electricity, Juke bugs," Najah shouted as she watched the sedan pull up beside them. The distinct faces of her fellow Vitares stared back at her as they leaned out windows. "Keep the windows rolled up and step on it!"

Cambrie paled at the names. They had seen the damage these Vitares had done at the Egg. They still had nightmares of spiders laying eggs in their mouth.

"Bugs?" Ella whispered, a shiver creeping down her spine.

"I can't get anything!" Perri said, slamming into the wall as the car whipped around a corner. The streets were growing emptier with each turn. The bus pulled them farther and farther away from the city, the blaze growing smaller in the distance.

"Their mental walls are too strong!"

"We're not going to outrun them! Whatever you do, Ella, protect the kids!" Najah shouted, the color-changing lights pulsing with her words. "It takes Blair time to charge her attacks, use that to your advantage! Slate will wear stone armor but there's weak spots in it, especially around the eyes! Juke will summon deadly bugs to swarm you, so it's a good idea to stay close to his teammates!"

"Keep your mouth shut for the bugs too! Slate can cause earthquakes! Feel for vibrations! Blair can-" Cambrie shouted before being thrown against the door. They winced as their bruises throbbed.

As Belle threw the bus around another corner, the children all let out a collective screech. But with a glance in the mirrors, a rush of relief filled her body. The sedan was nowhere to be found. As she hurled the bus around another corner, she let herself sink into the driver's seat. She had shaken them. For a moment, she wanted to laugh at the bitter irony of the airy voice from the speakers that sang about being rescued from some darkness. But then, the gang was thrust into silence as the pop music stopped. Fear bubbled up in Belle's chest as she searched every mirror, gripping the wheel as if it would bring some answers.

"What happened?" Perri managed to get out before all the lights went out, plunging them into the darkness of the abandoned roads.

Then, the vehicle shut off. Adrenaline flooded the bus as it hurtled down the road at breakneck speed. Belle yanked at the wheel, but it had locked up with no hope of her gaining control. Even as she desperately slammed her finger on the ignition button, the engine made no effort to turn over. She slammed on the brakes. People screamed. The bus jerked, but the brakes seemed to have no effect.

"Don't stop!" Najah yelled, knowing it was hopeless.

But Belle had little choice. They still sped down the road at a dangerous pace and now a curved road loomed ahead. Belle threw on the parking brake. The bus squealed in protest. She was roughly thrown into the steering wheel, the seat belt yanking her backwards. There were thuds as everyone else was thrown about. The bus skidded across the road, the tail end swerving out from behind so that the vehicle slid sideways over the centerline.

The Vitare's car appeared, speeding in front of them just as the bus hit a dilapidated apartment building. The impact jolted everyone. Teeth rattled and spines ached. No doubt there would be lasting marks in the morning. But there was no time to consider the wounds.

The Vitares stormed from the car. A hulking man with biceps the size of basketballs towered over the smashed bus. His body was jagged as if he was covered in stone armor. His palms were raised as he formed a boulder in front of him. Pieces of rock flew around him as if they were in his own personal orbit.

"Get out of the car!" Najah screamed.

She threw open the door and scrambled out into the darkness. Children shrieked as they piled out of the vehicle. A round of bullets sprayed the area, accounting for a couple very close calls. Just as the group threw themselves from the bus, Slate tossed the rifle aside and tossed a boulder into the vehicle. It completely smashed the car between the building. The sound was deafening, so much so that the gang didn't hear the buzzing until it was too late.

A swarm of insects bore their stingers into the flesh of the group. Children shrieked as they felt the bugs fly past them onto the bigger targets. In the darkness it was hard to see what was attacking them, the streetlights giving little insight.

Cambrie hurriedly cast a wall of fire between their companions and their assailants. The flames stood chest high and illuminated the faces of their enemies. It singed the wings of some of the insects. Cambrie took a breath of smokey air as another shot of epinephrine coursed through their body. It was welcome, as the exhaustion was already present in their limbs. The flames were weaker than normal, the wall flickering.

Ella made the mistake of opening her mouth in a scream. A few insects flew past her lips. They vibrated against her gums. Her throat lurched. But she found herself lucky because as she froze, the bugs swiftly found their exit.

Vines shot from Najah's palms as she focused on Juke, a slender person with an intense aura and a purple buzzcut. The plants wrapped around their wrists and bound them together. Even as the insects swarmed around Najah, she kept her focus, her jaw clenched. She had trained for this. The bugs stopped pouring from Juke's palms but the insects that they had already unleashed still swarmed. And while she had been given plenty of injections of anti-toxins at the Egg to ensure she would never be killed by the menaces, it didn't stop them from attacking her. They stung at her arms, her neck, her face. But she bit her tongue, ignoring the searing pain they unleashed within her. Instead, she used her vines to lift the Vitare off the ground and swung them into the car. The metal dented beneath them as they slammed into the machine. They let out a groan. Before they could react, the Duchess yanked them through the air again. This time she flung them into the sky. They flailed wildly. Their arms flapped as if they were some insect themself. Their eyes bulged.

In some desperate attempt to save themselves, Juke summoned a gargantuan moth-like insect. Its wingspan was easily the size of a car. Juke managed to grip the bug's wing, but they couldn't pull himself onto the back of the insect. One of Najah's vines swung at them like a fly swatter and sent them and the insect flying. Another vine pierced them in the throat and they slid to the ground, impaled.

The female Vitare rolled her neck and grinned, unfazed by the chaos around her. Her golden hair matched the lightning bolts along her arms and neck. The white of her teeth shone in the firelight. She lazily leaned up against the car and flicked her finger towards Perri. The air crackled. Perri stumbled backwards, clutching at her chest. Her eyes rolled backwards and she gave a small gasp before falling to the ground. Blair's laugh echoed through the air.

Somewhere in the chaos children shrieked. Smoke lingered in lungs and sweat poured down faces. Rubble lined the ground in a precarious fashion. The ground shook.

Cambrie rushed to Perri's side. They had seen the damage Blair's attacks had done in the Egg. The Vitare had figured out how to short-circuit the heart's electrical system. While it took Blair time to charge, it was a potentially lethal one shot attack. Cambrie dragged Perri around the corner of the rocking apartment building, out of the line of fire, and began muttering a chant as they started chest compressions. Their heart pounded fiercely. A boulder landed inches from them with a crash. This had to work.

Ella had rounded up all the children and put them behind the safety of the building with Swenulu. Her mouth had begun to swell as she yanked a stinger from the roof of her mouth. She bounced on her toes as she watched Cambrie work on Perri. She had to do something, anything.

Belle's hands were steady on the trigger of her gun. She readjusted her grip. Sweat dripped down her forehead. She fired off a shot towards Blair, but the Vitare easily sidestepped the bullet. Instead, the shot lodged itself into the car. Blair raised her eyebrows and brandished her finger towards Belle. Electricity sizzled through the air but Belle threw herself out of the way. Her face met the road with a thud.

Jagged stalagmites ruptured from the road around Belle. They passed the wall of flame, past where Slate could properly see. But his shot in the dark worked. She tried to scramble out of the way but rock pierced her leg clean through. Her scream echoed throughout the street, more from shock than pain. The adrenaline pulsing through her numbed the wound. Her finger trembled on the trigger of her gun as she fired another round towards Slate. A single bullet managed to lodge itself in the gaps of his armor. He growled and launched a boulder towards Belle.

"Watch out!" Ella called.

Najah wrapped her vines around the boulder right before it bashed Belle's head into the concrete. She flung it back towards Blair who was just a second too slow. It smashed her between the car. The sound of crushing flesh and bone was chilling. Blair's shriek caused the streetlights to flare and burn out. Najah nearly pitied her, as the blow hadn't been an instant death. Then again, pity was an awfully strong emotion.

Cambrie felt the rhythm of Perri's heart return to normal beneath their fingertips. They took a breath of relief, lightheaded as they stood. The world spun as they ran to Belle who was desperately trying to free herself from the rock. Blood stained her hands as an ever increasing puddle pooled around her, her moves frantic. She let out a scream as she tried to lift her leg upwards, tears streaming. The heat of the flames only added to her misery. Cambrie waved their hands and created a type of flaming saw, cleanly cutting the stalagmite. A boulder flew centimeters above their heads.

"I'm sorry, I've been awful to you," Belle cried, breathing hard. She clutched at her leg.

Cambrie wordlessly gathered her in their arms, Belle weighing them down. But they carried her to safety regardless and let the wall of flames die down. They set about stopping the bleeding, letting their fingers slide over Belle's jagged flesh.

"Cam-" Ella wheezed out through puffed up lips. She collapsed beside the Halfling.

Cambrie didn't look up as they reached out and let their words heal the Human. Their powers pulsed, threatening to give into the exhaustion. But they had to keep going. The swelling went down and Ella coughed out her gratitude before running out into the line of fire.

Najah was playing defense against Slate, her vines hurriedly catching the rocks he was throwing. Swenulu had taken Belle's gun and was taking aim at the man, although the bullets only ricocheted off his body. She stood tall, staring Slate down as each bullet left the chamber. It was only when Ella ran past her, knives in both hands, that she stopped shooting.

"Ella, wait!" Belle cried, fighting against Cambrie's grip on her.

Slate was distracted by the bullets and the dangerous game of catch he was playing with Najah, tossing round after round of boulders at her. He didn't notice Ella running towards him. Blair pointed at Ella weakly, but the Human was able to dive to the side as electricity singed the air beside her.

She knew what she had to do. It had been a year since she had done anything like this, but she prayed her muscles would remember. She got a running start, letting the wind whip her braids through the air. Then she firmly planted her foot on the hood of the Vitare's car. She pushed off hard and lept, twisting in the sky as if she were a gymnast. For a moment, she thought she was going to make it. She was going to land on Slate's shoulders. But she missed. Her leg slipped off his shoulder, his jagged armor slicing into her thigh. She tried to save herself, but it was too late. She was falling. She dropped her knives to the ground as she scrambled to hold onto his upper arm. She grit her teeth as the rock scraped her sweaty palms. If she tumbled to the ground below she could easily be crushed under his foot.

With a bit of luck, she found a hold in between the patchwork armor. She wedged her fingers into the crack, letting her nails scratch into the flesh beneath and draw blood. She wrapped her legs around his arm as he began to try and shake her off. She felt bile rise in her throat and she closed her eyes. She seriously regretted the sandwich she had eaten earlier that day as she was shook up and down. Her head spun. Before Slate could pluck her off with his other arm, Najah wrapped his arm in vines and pulled. A horrible pop could be heard, followed by a roar of agony.

Slate instinctively went to cradle his dislocated shoulder, allowing Ella to quickly grab onto his good shoulder. She climbed onto his shoulders and wrapped her legs around his neck. He realized too late what her plan was. Desperation surged through her body as she wrapped her arms around his head and drove her fingers into his eyes.

He roared in agony and bucked, throwing Ella off with his good arm. Her bones rattled as she hit the ground. The sting of scraped knees and palms made her grit her teeth, and she shuddered as she continued to feel the squish of his eyeballs under her fingertips. Slate clutched at his face as blood poured from his eye sockets. He began to shift back to his Human form, the rocky surface transforming into flesh.

Ella shook as she looked at the brutality she had caused. She scrambled to her feet watching Slate's blood drip to the pavement. Her own hands were covered in gore. She wiped them on her pants, feeling her stomach flip at the repulsive sight.

Najah ran through the chaos, scooped up a knife, and launched herself at Slate without a glance at Ella. As Slate was still transforming, Najah hurtled the knife with great precision into Slate's fleshy throat.

A crude gurgle filled the air, and he flailed for a moment before going limp. When he fell, Najah finished the job and sawed the blade across his neck. His head rolled slightly upwards, his hollow eyes staring up at the moon above.

Najah stormed up to Blair who was still pinned. She was pale and blood dripped onto the pavement. Her breathing was shallow. She didn't try to fight.

"Please, kill me," she whispered so only Najah could hear.

In an act of what was perhaps both mercy and self-preservation, Najah gripped the woman's hair and dragged the blade across her throat. Every Vitare knew the tales of what torture awaited a failed mission. It would be cruel to leave anyone to that fate. The Duchess let the head roll to the ground and strutted towards where Juke was still impaled. They twitched, groaning.

Ella shivered in the warm air at the ease of which Najah murdered the Vitares. There were no second thoughts, no warmth for her former classmates. As she tossed the head of Juke to the ground, her eyes shimmered. As blood dripped down the assassin's hand, Ella couldn't help but notice a slight golden hue to the crimson. In the fire light it glittered as it mixed with the gold from Najah's tattoos.

Najah wiped her hands on her clothes and placed a hand on Ella's shoulder. With the other she returned the knives to Ella's shaking palm. Ella only frowned and began to turn away. "Wait Ella! I-" Najah began. "I shouldn't have said that stuff earlier. I'm sorry. I'm just-It doesn't matter. Good job out there." With another pat of Ella's shoulder, Najah left the girl.

"Ella! You could've died! Don't pull that shit again!" Belle began to yell as she hobbled over to her sister. Then she seemed to think and shook her head, embracing Ella. She let out a breath of relief. "Thank the Mythos you're safe."

Ella swallowed hard before returning the embrace. "Are you okay? Is everyone okay?"

"We're all alive," Perri called, leaning heavily against the wall. She was pale and her body ached, but was otherwise okay. "I'd love a nap though."

Cambrie, trembling, sat on the pavement with their head in their knees. Any movement caused them to feel as though they were pressing molten nails onto their skin. They struggled to keep their eyes open, conversations making little sense.

Najah rolled her neck to the side. She picked up the empty gun carelessly, the metal glinting in the moonlight. She went to return it to Belle. With blood stained cheeks and a busted lip, Najah looked as if she had been there a thousand times. It shouldn't have been shocking, but the way she wore violence was unsettling, even to a soldier like Belle. Belle could tell the assassin wanted to say something as the gun exchanged hands, but with one piercing gaze from her, Najah rethought it.

The street had been completely abandoned for some time, all traffic rerouted away from the dilapidated buildings. It would be a miracle if someone even noticed the new destruction they had wrought. Belle turned her attention away from the destruction to her companions.

This could have ended so much worse. They had been inches from death. Yet, here they stood in the aftermath, a team of misfits who had stepped up for one another without hesitation. Not to mention Ella's role in the bloodshed.

"Well, we need another car," Najah sighed. "I know where we can get one. I'll be back in a few minutes, just wait here."

Swenulu slumped down against the wall besides the children, many of whom clung to each other. They cried and whined, which did nothing to help Cambrie's massive headache. Ella took up the job of consoling them in whatever way she knew how. She handed out water from a discarded bag and tried to shield their view from the chaos in the street. She knew that none of the words she said mattered to them. They needed so much more support than what she could offer.

"What do we do now?" Ella asked quietly as she approached Perri and Belle. "Do you think your contacts can watch them?"

"No," Perri said, staring at the ground. "I don't- I don't know who was involved...or who I can trust anymore. It runs deeper than I thought."

There was a moment of silence, then Ella spoke up. "It's okay. We can take them to our parents' house."

"What? We can't do that! That'll be one of the first places anyone looks for us. We'll be putting them in danger!" Belle hissed, gesturing with her hands.

"What other options do we have?" Ella asked. "Anyone else have any suggestions?" When nobody spoke up, she shrugged. "It's a risk they'd be willing to take, one we have to take."

"I can't believe you," Belle said, pressing her tongue to her cheek. "You're not acting like yourself. You're being reckless."

"No Belle, I'm not. I'm just doing the things that you don't have the guts to do yourself."

With that, Ella turned on her heel and walked towards Swenulu and the children.

"Damn," Perri said, a hint of a smile on her face. "I really didn't think she had it in her." She balanced all of her weight on one leg and placed her hands on her hips as she turned her attention to Belle. "You have any regrets yet?"

"What's it matter to you if I do?"

"Because you can't do this. You're hurting people. You can't just follow along in the shadows and show up at the last minute. You either have to leave for good or shut up and stick around."

"I thought you didn't care about them. I thought you wanted me gone," Belle tilted her head, meeting the Siren's eyes.

"I don't care about them. I care about the function of this team. I need everyone to focus on what we need to do, and we can't do that if we're being followed and screamed at constantly. We have enough to worry about without you adding to our problems." Perri frowned, crossing her arms over her chest. "Don't get it twisted, I don't care about you or Ella."

"Sure, keep telling yourself that," Belle said.

"I don't, I really..."

Before she could finish her thought a black SUV pulled up. The front bumper hung off, nearly dragging on the ground. A large dent resided in its passenger door. The headlights illuminated the bodies on the road. Najah expertly avoided most of the carnage and the car rolled to a stop. She hopped out of the driver's seat.

"Where did that come from?" Belle asked.

"Don't ask questions you don't want the answer to," Najah replied. "But if it makes you feel better, I think stealing another car is pretty low on our list of crimes right now. Especially since I already took care of the cameras and sensors."

Belle rolled her eyes. "Whatever. I'll drive."

Everyone piled into the car and drove back towards the crowded downtown. The fire department was working to put out the fire that had already spread to half the buildings on the street. It was slow going getting out of the city, as traffic crawled through the streets.

"You know, we can't continue to make a habit of setting things on fire," Perri muttered as they finally left the city and its fires in their wake.

# Twenty-One

# WHO BECOMES A HERO, WHO BECOMES A VILLIAN?

No one dared to speak until they were far from the wreckage they caused. As they passed the border from Vitana into Gerecae, the desert wasteland turned into a lush expanse of greenery. In the darkness of the early morning, everyone felt the effects of the night's battle. It was too cramped and too hot to sleep though, and slowly, the quiet turned into whines of exhaustion, fear, and discomfort.

Ella was ready to bash her head into the window. She couldn't get all the death she had seen out of her head. She could still feel the ease with which her fingers sunk into Slate's eyes. The knives were heavy in her pocket, her body stained. Today had been too much. She wanted to sleep, but the overwhelming voices of the children kept dragging her back to reality. Her own mind branded her some kind of sadist, and repetition continued to drill that fact into her. The trees outside blurred together, her hands detached from her body as she covered her ears to block out the noise.

Belle rested her fingers on the steering wheel, allowing the car's automatic driving to take over. She had dozens of questions and dozens more apologies. The words were on the tip of her tongue, but held them back as she looked at the others. Cambrie was nodding in and out of consciousness in the back seat besides Najah, and Ella looked as if she had just lived through multiple world wars. Najah was buried somewhere beneath a pile of limbs, her face unreadable to Belle. A glance over to Perri in the passenger seat revealed she was about ready to slaughter the children if another one asked for more food. The boy sitting by her feet was bumping into her repeatedly as he cried, and it was visibly taking all of her strength not to kick him. Swenulu was sitting in the middle row, kids piled around her. She was taking the time to brush out a girl's hair with her fingertips.

Najah sat in the backseat squished between Maggie and Cambrie. Two little kids sat on the floor in front of her, another on Maggie's lap and the other squished between Cambrie and Ella. The air was rank, not helped by the fact that one of the toddlers had had an accident. Between the smoke curled in her lungs, the smell, and the crowd, her breathing was short and shallow.

"Are the bad guys gonna try to hurt us again?" A girl cried as she gripped the seat in front of her. The bow in her hair had come loose and she was fiddling with it.

"I want another sandwich!" Another yelled, kicking the boy next to them.

"Ow! They kicked me!" The boy screamed.

Cambrie shifted as the girl beside them dug her elbow into the Halfling's thigh. They desperately chased after sleep, trying to block out the sensations around them. Their limbs were heavy, but the kids squirming around them did nothing to calm their overactive mind. They scooched closer to Najah in hopes of getting away from the children.

With Cambrie practically on her lap, their hand brushing her thigh, Najah felt her breath hitch-although that also may have been from a boy who suddenly placed his cold fingers on her shin. She pressed her tongue to her cheek as an idea formed.

"Hey, kids, I've got something to show everyone, but you have to be quiet for me, okay?"

As all of the small faces turned towards Najah, she held a finger to her lips. They all nodded in agreement, craning their necks for a closer look at her. She closed her eyes for a moment and formed a rose in her palm. It unfurled gently, the flower releasing a sweet aroma into the air. The children oohed and ahhed, smiling for the first time that night. Cambrie turned and met Najah's eyes. They pushed a strand of hair back from their face, a flush creeping into their cheeks. Their other hand brushed against Najah's knee, their fingers lingering just a second too long. Najah took the rose and tossed it into the air. It danced around, swirling around Cambrie's head, then Maggie's. After it circled, Najah took it and handed it to Maggie who stuck it behind her ear.

"I want one!" A young girl with bright brown eyes chimed in. "Please?"

"I want one too!" Another girl cried.

Blossoms formed one after another in Najah's palm. Soon she held a bouquet of roses, one for each child. Each child took the roses from her, their fingers clinging to the fraile stems which would secrete the sedating rose oil. As Maggie fell asleep, Najah smiled down at her sister. And in those moments after the chaos, it was as if nothing was wrong.

After the children had fallen asleep and the rays of the morning sun were just beginning to peek over the horizon, Belle finally was able to break the silence.

"Who sent those Vitares?" she said quietly. "Elenor, as like a final, if I'm ever murdered, go find my killers kind of deal? Or the government?" She turned around in her seat to talk to her companions as the car drove itself down the road.

"The government," Najah said without hesitation. "Those three were still working at the Egg when I left."

"Besides, there aren't that many Vitares in the wild, and all of them, besides Najah, are still under contract for the government. So Elenor, or any other Vitare wouldn't have the authority to just send three Vitares after us. Her allies, anyone coming after us on her behalf, would be Demons or Sirens," Cambrie added.

"So the government is sending assassins after us now? They just forwent the whole police thing?" Belle asked, digging her nails into her leg.

"Yeah," Najah, Cambrie, and Perri all said in unison.

"It's not surprising really. They couldn't legally reach us in Sanctus but assassins don't really fall into the category of legality," Perri said. "Besides, Triton's an ass like that."

"But if they sent assassins, they knew we were in Sanctus. Does that mean they know about the kids?" Ella spoke up, suddenly wide awake.

"Probably," Najah said. "Vitare handlers, the ones in charge of keeping Vitares in check, monitor the emotions of their charge, their location, and, now probably, their audio. If any of them said anything about there being kids in the car, the handlers heard it. Even if they didn't, the handlers know where their dead assassins are, and they'll hear that there was a giant fire at the trafficking ring, I'm sure they'll figure it out pretty quickly."

"So how do we know that they don't know where we're going right now?" Belle hissed, ready to yank the car off their current course.

"Considering there aren't many cameras on the streets of Sanctus and I swept this car for any tracking devices and yanked out the security systems, we should be fine for now. But they aren't dumb. We all know they'll track down your parents and investigate them. They shouldn't keep these kids very long," Najah sighed. The car sailed onto the offramp and stopped at a stoplight. "The government will search through every inch of their lives, if they haven't already. You're the only two here with a decent family. It won't be hard to suspect we're running there."

"I know-it's why I didn't want to go there in the first place," Belle muttered.

"I'm still open to any other suggestions," Ella said.

"There's no one in the Saybrim Resistance who could take them?" Perri asked.

"I'm not exposing them to more dangers on our behalf again. Besides, it's a rebellion, not a daycare," Belle said.

"The Resistance stands and protects everyone in need of freedom," Swenulu offered up quietly. "They would take care of these kids."

"I know, but I can't ask that of them. And it's not a place for kids. These kids should get a normal childhood, or at least, as normal as they can get." Belle bit her lip, staring out over the vast fields.

"I understand, but know you have help whenever you need it," Swenulu said.

The car continued to drive down a road that eventually turned to dirt. Ella's heart was in her throat as the SUV hit the rough terrain. Her stomach twisted in knots. She stared down at the sleeping children. It wasn't regret that lived within her. No. She would have regretted it far more if she hadn't saved them. But she was tired of treading the fine line, of falling into the gray matter. Nothing was black and white anymore. She had gouged a man's eyes out and watched him die, and had left people to die in the fires they created. They had stolen cars and ran from prison. She was putting the people she loved most in danger. She couldn't rely on the books she had read or the laws put in place anymore, couldn't tell if she had fallen too far from grace. Had she become the villain in a story she had so desperately wanted to be the hero in?

As the car turned down a winding dirt driveway, she was jolted back into reality. Her stomach lurched and her legs felt weak. She was home.

## Twenty-Two

# Hᴏᴍᴇ ɪꜱ Wʜᴇʀᴇ ᴛʜᴇ Sɴᴀᴄᴋꜱ Aʀᴇ

It was as if she had stepped back through the portals of her dreams. The house still looked as though it would collapse at any moment. Eggshell colored siding hung off the house, swaying in the wind. Paint chipped shudders framed the dirt smudged windows. Puddles sat in the dips of the driveway as flies lazily flew about. It was too familiar. Nothing had changed from their childhood home. A constant in an otherwise rapidly changing world. Yet, Ella couldn't smile as she stepped from the car.

Belle was careful to shut the door to the car quietly, a wave of un-usual anxiety washing over her. The woods surrounding their house were silent. There was no sign of the creatures that used to accompany her on her adventures, used to watch over her as she climbed up trees. Flies touched her shoulder, seemingly finding their treasure on their search for remnants of the past. She shook them off, along with the resentment in her building in her gut. This was home. It was supposed to be home. That was why, even after Belle sent more than half of her paychecks to her parents, they refused to leave.

The family sedan was missing from the driveway, as it almost always was. Her parents were most likely working. That was for the better, Belle told herself. It would make this easier.

The kids grumbled as they stretched their limbs. They wiped at tired eyes and exchanged contagious yawns. Belle and Ella walked up the rickety porch, each in their own thoughts. Ella knocked twice although she knew no one was home. There were no lights on in the windows, no movement over the creaking floors. Belle reached in front of her sister and pressed her finger to the fingerprint scanner on the door. With a quiet click, the door unlocked.

"They never changed the locks," Ella said quietly. "Does that mean they don't think we're-?"

"Hopefully," Belle muttered. "Either that, or they think we're dead." She turned to the others, her voice shakier than she intended. "C'mon, we don't have all day."

"We'll stay out here!" Najah called as Belle and Ella entered the house. There was something far too claustrophobic, too intimate, about crossing that threshold. "There's no need for us to leave any more evidence we were here."

As Maggie went to join her friends on the porch, Najah reached out to her, then stopped.

"Hey, can I talk to you for a minute?"

Maggie paused and turned her shoulders to face Najah. Yet, she didn't meet her sister's eyes. She stared past her, as if Najah were a ghost. This public moment was the most she was willing to give. The other children lingered on the porch, watching over their leader. For once they came out from beneath Swenulu's shadow with crossed arms and stares made of steel, ready to shield Maggie from this intruder.

The words on Najah's lips were small, and if she could have given it all up for a magical antidote, she would have. Because nothing, no amount of words, could undo this.

"I'm sorry, for more than you can imagine. I can't pretend to know what you've been through, but I'm sorry you had to go through it. I'm sorry I couldn't come sooner, and I'm sorry I have to leave now. I know you don't know me, but I love you. You're my sister and I'll always love you."

"I know."

Maggie turned towards the house with no regard for Najah. Her eyes were dark in the sunlight, her shoulders heavy with a burden that she should never have had to bear.

"I'll be back for you, I promise. As soon as it's safe, I'll find you," Najah wanted to reach out towards her sister, to grab her and never let her go. But she didn't. She couldn't.

"Okay," Maggie shrugged as she climbed up the porch.

Najah had to look away as Maggie left. She had lost all control. Tears flooded down her cheeks. Her chest ached in ways that she had never felt, and she swore that it was about to shatter. Without a word, she entered the backseat of the car, throat tight. Attacked by her very own mind, she buried her head in her hands to try and muffle out her thoughts. She had been stupid, she should have known better than to think Maggie would be happy to see her. She would never have a relationship with her sister. She would never be loved. She didn't deserve-

The door slid open. The breeze hit her face, causing a chill to go down her spine.

"Hey, do you want company?" Cambrie tentatively poked their head into the car.

Najah didn't respond. She stared out the window, motionless. Cambrie climbed in the backseat, sliding next to the Duchess. They reached for her hand, slowly taking it. When she didn't pull away, Cambrie squeezed.

"I should've known that she wouldn't remember me, wouldn't trust me. I just...I've spent every waking moment trying to get back to her and now I have to leave her again. And she'll never understand...that I love her...and that I didn't want to leave her there," Najah took a breath, trying to patch the growing cracks in the walls of her emotions. "That I didn't mean to abandon her..." Her voice was thick as mucus dripped down her throat. She wiped at her face, avoiding Cambrie's gaze. It was always with them, wasn't it?

"I should have saved her sooner."

She shook as sobs racked her body. She gasped not only for air, but for relief from the overwhelming guilt. Cambrie wrapped their arms around their friend and pulled her close.

"You were a kid, and you were trapped too. You didn't have a choice Najah, and as soon as you did, you went to her. That means something," Cambrie held tight to the assassin, like they had that night in the Egg. "You risked everything to go to her and you brought her to safety. And even though you have to leave her now, you'll get back to her one day and you'll have a chance to have a relationship with her then. You'll just have to give her time."

Najah tried to get out the words but nothing she said made sense. Snot dripped from her nose, her face puffy. The words Cambrie said were meaningless. Nothing would ever repair their relationship. It would be impossible. Nothing she had done mattered. Maggie had still been abandoned. Those thoughts made her bawl harder, unable to draw breath.

"It doesn't make it hurt any less. I know," Cambrie nodded. "It's okay to feel this way. You haven't been allowed to be sad in a long time."

They recognized this. It was the first time Najah had been able to react how she needed. The Egg had made sure to suppress all emotions, including sadness. Cambrie had experienced it themselves. The first time sadness had reared its ugly head, they ended up locked in their room for days, horrified by the sheer pain of it all. It had been a miracle that Najah had felt a love and determination for her sister so strong they couldn't suppress it all.

Najah attempted to say something else but just ended up blubbering. She couldn't breathe. The world was crashing in on itself. She longed for a weapon that could keep this enemy at bay because she felt like a child: defenseless, weak, and hopeless. She sank deeper into Cambrie's arms, the warmth of their shoulder the only thing keeping her from being washed away in the storm.

"I can't stop you from hurting. But I'll be here for you every step of the way. Cry because you need to. Get angry. Let yourself feel the hurt. It sucks, but it's a part of a life you haven't gotten to experience," Cambrie's voice got quiet as they remembered Tanajh reciting these exact words to them.

"You deserve to experience all of it, even if it's the worst thing you can imagine. It will get better."

Najah sat gasping in Cambrie's arms for a few minutes. She had no more tears to shed. Her head throbbed and the light filtering through the window hurt her eyes.

She looked at Cambrie and sniffled. "Whole lotta good you are," she let out a sad smile.

"What?" They tilted their head, blinking twice.

"You can't stop me from hurting. Great healer you are," Najah murmured.

"I'm sorry," the Halfling whispered, reaching up to wipe away the last tear that clung to Najah's cheek. As if suddenly realizing what they did, they yanked their hand back.

They sat in silence for a bit. Both snuck glances at each other, examining scars both visible and invisible. Cambrie bit the inside of their cheek until they tasted blood. It wasn't until both of them turned to each other that it hit them.

"I should've gotten you..." Cambrie began.

"You need to..." Najah said at the same time. She gestured to Cambrie. "Go ahead, you first."

Cambrie felt their face flush and they tucked a strand of their hair behind their ear. "When I was escaping the Egg, I thought about taking you with me. I should have. I would have had enough time. I knew I could trust you and I knew you wanted out of there. But I was terrified that I would get caught. I didn't want you to get caught with me. You had a chance there, as much of a chance as you could get. I didn't. But when I left I regretted not bringing you. I'm sorry."

Najah was silent for a moment as she pondered her words. The words were thick in her throat. "That was the first time anyone had ever escaped the Egg, you know. It gave me hope that one day I could get out of there. That was the first time I had felt any hope, any happiness, in such a long time. Your escape inspired me." She hesitantly reached for Cambrie's hand, looking for any discomfort as she did so. "I'm glad you got out of there. Don't feel guilty for leaving. And don't feel guilty for doing what's best for you."

Cambrie was suddenly aware of the heat that radiated off the leather interior, the blood rushing to their cheeks, and the fact that Perri still sat on the porch alone outside. Their hands were still entangled with

Najah's, her words already being analyzed in their head. They pulled away, a feeling they couldn't name beginning in their stomach.

"I better go, otherwise Perri will start getting suspicious that we're plotting against her or something," Cambrie said, blinking rapidly as if it would erase the thoughts they had forbidden. As they opened the door, they looked over their shoulder. "We're going to get through all of this together, you know."

As Ella tended to the children in the kitchen, Belle headed upstairs. Digital family pictures watched over her as she took the stairs two at a time. When she hit the second floor, she paused. A picture of her parents, Ella, and an unsure child stared back at her. They were at some ice cream shop, chocolate smeared all over a baby Ella's cheeks. All Belle could focus on though was the frown on the child's face, the slicked back hair, the bowtie. As she pulled her attention away from that picture, she marveled at the child's transition seen in every photo afterwards. Her transition. Young Belle's smile grew in every photo as the name typed in school pictures changed. If only that kid could see her now. She nearly laughed at the thought. Her younger self might have loved the new name, pronouns, and body, but certainly not the new lifestyle.

There were fewer family pictures as the girls got older. As Belle reached double digits, the only pictures began to come on holidays. As work began to take them away with double shifts and second jobs, her parents fought to keep them fed, leaving her in charge with little time for photos. Alas, there was nothing recent on the walls.

She tore her attention away from the pictures and found her old room. Her heart pounded as she turned the knob, as if she was going to find someone waiting for her. But no, the room was empty besides memories of playdates and afternoon tea parties.

The walls had been repainted to a light gray, but if Belle looked close enough, she could still see specks of purple beneath the new paint. The furniture has been moved to accommodate a small screen and a desk. This had been transformed into a study for her father, who was a professor in Ancient Earth History at local universities. Tablets littered the floor, the contents of a bag threatening to spill with one misplaced step. Yet, a few childhood remnants remained. A S.P.A.C.E program recruiting poster hung on the wall, its corners curled. The two twin beds had been shoved together in the corner, a pile of linens sitting atop the mattress. A purple unicorn lamp sat on the desk. On Ella's old side of the room hung a digital poster of her favorite teenage band, silently watching over Belle. A collection of stuffed animals sat on a shelf.

Belle began to rummage through the closet where boxes were stuffed on top of shelves. She stood on her tiptoes to reach the top shelves. As she dragged down the boxes, a smaller box fell to the ground and burst open. Letters, physical letters, scattered across the carpet. Belle scrambled to collect the papers. They were crisp beneath her fingertips. Stationary had become such a rarity. She only knew of it from her textbooks in school. The faintest smell of perfume still lingered on some of the letters. Her eyes poured over the notes, her heart swelling as she realized they were love letters from her parents. Her mother's shaky handwriting had scribbled hearts in the margins of the paper, her signature wobbly. Her father's steady, sprawling print spun poetic verses for his love, his name taking up two lines. They both told stories of first dates and first kisses, of sweet dreams and future plans. It felt deeply intimate, as if she were holding their physical hearts in her hands.

Belle clutched the letters to her chest, swallowing hard. She missed them, missed the family dinners, missed the game nights. She missed her mom's warm embrace and her dad's laugh. For a moment she considered staying to see them, considered staying to talk to them, to try and reconcile. Maybe if she did, these kids would get a taste of the parents they deserved.

But no, they would ask too many questions, and the longer she was here the more danger everyone was in. Besides, if they came home and didn't believe her story, thought her a terrorist, her heart would shatter. If they welcomed her however, she didn't think she could leave.

She placed all the letters back in the box except for one. She found the pen that had been stowed away with them, tore off the blank half of the letter, and wrote a note. In tight lettering she told the short-ened version of her story, gave directions for their safety, apologized for everything, and most importantly, told them they'd be back. She tucked the note into her pocket and dug through the box she had pulled down. She easily located what she was looking for.

The small transparent rectangles powered on with her touch. Her fingers traced over the screens. They were much older versions of a communicator, but she prayed they would work. As they booted up, she replaced the cardboard box onto the shelf. She snatched up a backpack lying on the floor of the closet and began to fill it with old clothes and anything else she could find.

"Belle, are you coming?" Ella called from downstairs. "It's getting late!"

"Yeah, I'll be down in a second!"

Belle zipped up the bag and slipped the communicators in her pocket. She rushed down the stairs to find all the kids crowded in the living room munching on snacks. Ella stood amongst them with Swenulu, telling them how to work the T.V.

"And this button is how you change the volume. You should be good to go! My parents will be back soon. They'll take care of you." She turned to Swenulu. "Are you sure you're going to stay?"

"Yes, we need each other," Swenulu said, gesturing to the children. "Besides, I can help make sure everyone stays safe."

"Thank you then, for everything," Ella smiled.

"No, thank you for everything you've done, Ella."

"I want more fruity hoops!" a child cried, pulling on Swenulu's leg, diverting her attention away.

"Do you have any credits on you?" Belle asked as she approached Ella. "We should leave them something since we're dumping a bunch of kids with them."

"Yeah, I have some I think." Ella walked through the sea of kids and fumbled around in her pockets for a moment before pulling out a few credits. "Here. Did you get everything?"

"Yeah, I did. Are you ready?" Belle walked towards the kitchen where she left the credits and her note on the faded tablecloth. There were still four chairs sitting around the table. Packages of snack foods were scattered across the countertops. Memories of baking cookies and holiday dinners were etched into the cracks in the stove and the burns in the table. A small tree with baubles and lights still sat on the corner, left over from the Creation celebration weeks ago.

"I wish we could see them," Ella whispered.

"I know. But we can't. This is already so risky."

"I know," Ella sighed. "Are you gonna stay this time?" She grabbed a granola bar from the counter. "

"Yeah, I am," Belle said, touching Ella's shoulder. "I'm sorry. I've been really shitty to you. I just-I don't know how to do this. I'm terrified, and I'm terrified of losing you."

"I get that, and I'm scared too, but the things you did sucked. You hurt everyone. Especially Cambrie. If we're doing this, we have to actually work together. Give the others a shot. " Ella focused on struggling to open the granola bar, her fingers trembling slightly.

"I know. I'm sorry. I'm going to talk to everyone, and I'm going to do better," Belle took the bar and opened the wrapper, handing it back to her sister.

"Okay," Ella said. She tossed the wrapper into the trash slot in the wall then approached her sister. "I do want you to be here, you know. I'm sorry for the stuff I said too. I love you."

Belle nodded in acceptance and embraced Ella tight. "I love you too." As they broke the embrace, for a moment everything felt like it balanced out. But then they had to return to reality. "We have to go."

So past the hall closet that stored old sports equipment and extra coats they walked. Past the living room that had hosted many games of play pretend. They paused at the front door, not wanting to say goodbye to the house and its memories.

"Bye guys! I'll miss you!" Ella called out to the kids. "Take care of each other. Thanks again, Swenulu!"

As they exited the house, birdsong played in the distance. Najah's face was puffy and she was taking extra care to not make eye contact with anyone as she stared at the dirt driveway. Cambrie was sitting on the hood of the car, talking with Perri as she picked at her nails. Ella hung back on the porch, leaning against the rotting railing. Belle sheepishly stood on the porch as if it were a pulpit. She pulled the sleeves of her cape over her palms.

"So, I know things haven't been great between all of us. I've said and done a lot of terrible things, and I'm sorry. In the end, all of you have protected Ella and I, and you've done nothing but prove yourself trustworthy. I'm hoping that we can start over and put this behind us. If you'll let me, I'd like to prove that I can be better."

Her heart palpitated as she waited for a response. She crossed her arms around herself as if it would protect her from the potential outcomes. Her eyes darted between her companions, examining Najah, Perri, and finally Cambrie's faces. They were unreadable, at least until Najah stepped forward.

"Okay," she shrugged, her throat still warbly. "We need people on our side. Start acting like you are and we'll be good."

"You've only proven to be more trouble than you're worth. I find you insufferable and irresponsible." Perri pressed her tongue to the inside of her lip and shifted her weight to one leg. "But, Najah's right. There's power in numbers and it's not like we have many options. Besides, Ella's kinda okay, I guess." She let a small smile form on her face as Ella grinned and leapt off the porch into Perri's arms. "Just try not to be so damn annoying."

Belle nodded, then looked towards Cambrie's directions. They refused to meet her eyes, instead finding the dirt rather interesting.

"You don't need my approval or my forgiveness to stay," Cambrie murmured. "You're your own person. Prove that you can be better for yourself."

The words were icy across Belle's cheeks, even if they weren't meant to be. But as Cambrie clambered into the SUV, she was left standing in the shadow of her past, wondering if she was wrong about it all.

## Twenty-Three

# A Cake for Every Occasion

Ella set about the tiny kitchen of the hotel room with a mission, trying to balance multiple pans between her fingers. She sweat profusely, her brows furrowed, lip bitten as she tried not to lose the bread on the floor. Enough garlic to slay a vampire filled her nostrils. She slid the pans across the top of the island, taking care to finish off her masterpieces with a hefty sprinkle of spices. She kicked the oven door shut behind her, being careful not to burn herself. From the row of appliances behind her, she gathered butter from the vendi-fridge.

Meanwhile, Perri sat on the barstool, sucking icing off her pointer finger. "Do you think she's gonna be able to tell that it says 'Sorry I cheated?' I couldn't really scrape it off."

"I think it'll be fi-" Ella began before looking over at the hot pink cake that had been scooped up from the custom order shelf of a bakery. The yellow icing that had originally been etched into the top had been dug at with a fork, then covered with blood red script reading 'Happy Birthday Najah.' "It's the thought that counts."

"Who the hell gets a 'Sorry I cheated' cake anyways? If Finn cheated on me and got a cake, I'd throw the cake in his damn face and eat him instead."

Ella's eyes widened as she focused on scooping pasta onto plates. She nearly bumped her head on the floating cabinets above the island as she sat atop the counter. "Has anyone ever told you that you're really intense to be around?"

"Better than being boring, darling," Perri smirked as she swirled wine around in her glass. She spread her legs across all the barstools.

"So I told him that I was-" Najah stopped mid-sentence as she entered the hotel suite, turning to look behind her at Belle and Cambrie. "What's happening?"

Belle shrugged, dropping her shopping bag onto the floor. She murmured something unintelligible before pulling out a bottle of pain medication from the bag. But Cambrie just grinned and dimmed the lights, then pulled Najah towards the spread. Without looking, they flicked their hand towards the birthday cake. Perri pulled her hands back from placing the candles just as the flames found the wicks.

"Happy birthday!" Cambrie and Ella said in unison.

"This is for me?" Najah asked, her tongue suddenly feeling as if it had been tied in knots.

"Obviously. Is there anyone else here named Najah?" Perri said, gesturing to the cake.

Najah tilted her head, squinting in the candlelight. Against the stark white walls, her golden eyes were reminiscent of the sunset. Her new leather jacket that fit like a second skin smelled of iron, sweat, and someone's signature cologne. And if one were to look past the stolen clothes and the bruised fists, there was a delicacy in the strength of her form. She stood on the tips of her toes to read the lettering of her cake, the softness of her lips trying to sound out the syllables. The dark bags beneath her eyes, the tension in her shoulders, all were subtle reminders of the fractures in her diamond exterior. But all of it, all of her, well, she was beautiful-the epitome of a masterpiece.

"Is that what it says?" Najah smiled.

"Shut up and just blow out the damn candles before we set something else on fire," Perri muttered.

"I'm joking!" Najah closed her eyes and blew out the candles. Then she turned towards her companions and let her arms fold around Cambrie and Ella, pulling them into a hug without hesitation. She looked towards the others, urging them to join her. They relented, Perri rolling her eyes and Belle stiffly patting Najah's arm. "Thank you. This is the nicest thing anyone has ever done for me."

"Well, I said we needed a reason to break out some wine," Perri shrugged as she began to pass out wine.

"We have a chance at a new beginning, I say we celebrate what we can," Ella said.

Perri began to hand Ella a glass before pulling her hand back with a smirk. "Wait, you're only sixteen right?" She took a sip of what was supposed to be Ella's glass. "Damn, sucks to be the baby here. More for me I guess."

"Give the girl a drink if she wants some, damn," Cambrie said as they snatched the glass from her hand. "Underage drinking is literally the least of our worries. Besides, I got harder stuff, you greedy bi-"

"Eey! Now it's a party!" Perri grinned, cutting off Cambrie as they pulled out two bottles of swirling purple liquor from beneath their jacket.. She handed the glass to Ella before reaching for the bottles.

Ella swirled the red around in the glass, her eyes darting towards her sister. Belle raised an eyebrow but said nothing as the girl raised it to her lips. It was bitter against her tongue, and she choked back a cough.

"How about we eat some of this food before it gets cold?" Belle said, arms crossed over her chest. She gripped her glass so tightly it threatened to shatter.

"Yeah, I haven't had something like this in forever," Najah said, trying to let herself take in the moment. There was still a lingering despair that weighed down her heart, but those feelings were quickly mixing with something that she could only describe as the gentle glow of lightning bugs illuminating her body.

Plates were laden with pasta and bread, hands warmed by bowls of pale beige soup. As soon as they poured a drizzle of cabbage and pumpkin reduction into the soup, it turned red. Bodies spread out across the spacious hotel room with content silence radiating off the plush furniture. White spoons were scraped against their matching white bowls, then set upon the criminally designed white rabbit fur table. With so much potential scarlet on their hands, they were careful not to stain the crisp snow bedding. But as their meal finished and their thoughts began to devolve, conversation began to flow again, much like the drinks.

"So," Perri began, pouring herself an incredibly generous glass of tequila. "Doesn't your, like, Human religion have a holiday soon?" she gestured towards Ella and Belle, her limbs seeming a little heavier than usual. "When can you make more of this soup?"

"I can make it whenever really, but we're Isapolians, kinda, so we don't have another holiday for a while," Ella responded. "Creation Day was a few weeks ago. I'm pretty sure the Vuheins' have their Festival of Lights next month, but of course we don't celebrate that."

"Can you make more food anyways? Or could we do a late celebration for Creation Day and Demi-Birth Day?" Perri asked, her lips in a pout and a slight whine in her voice.

"I didn't take you for the religious type," Cambrie said, taking a sip of their wine.

"Excuse you, I've been the perfect little Theralaanian my entire life." Ignoring the snort Cambrie let out, Perri elaborated. "My mom was obsessed with it when I was a kid. But let's be real, there are perks. I mean, the celebrations? The gifts? And the food is the best."

"Fair enough," Cambrie said. "I just never understood religion, or the deal with the Goddesses...or whatever."

"Yeah, and there are plenty of reasons to make food other than religious holidays," Najah chimed in.

"So, what's our plan guys," Belle asked. "Like, what are we doing? We got the kids out, when are we focusing on taking out Triton and the Alcorium factories? Or taking out Ahitophel?"

"Chill Belle, it's a party. I like that you're eager but we can talk about this later," Perri said.

"Yeah, let's just celebrate for now," Cambrie said.

Belle rolled her eyes and bit her cheek but said nothing.

Najah put aside her plate and put her elbows on her knees. "Look, if we're going to celebrate the right way, I'm going to need another shot and some music."

"I think we can manage that," Cambrie said, rising from their spot on the bed.

They set about fiddling with the hotel T.V. while Perri began to dole out another round of drinks. Ella and Belle slid around the marble floor, collecting the dishes. Belle grabbed her sister's arm, pulling her into the kitchen as she got the last plate.

"Why didn't you tell me about this? I thought we were going to try and be a team." Belle leaned against the counter. A 3-D abstract painting of five converging lines hung along the wall blocking off the main living space from the kitchen, but she still kept her voice down.

"I was trying to keep it a surprise for Najah," Ella hissed. "Cambrie told me it was her birthday and that we all should celebrate. Then the three of you have been gone all night so I didn't have a chance to get you away from Najah. I didn't think it was that big of a deal. I'm sorry."

"It's whatever. Go enjoy the party," Belle said as she waved Ella off, putting the dishes into the wall to be cleaned. They clinked against each other as the music began in the other room.

"Why are you acting like this? Go, take a break, prove yourself to them like you said you would." Ella's face fell, frustration set in the subtle lines of her forehead.

"Please, just go. I can't do this right now." Later she'd gather up enough pieces of her mangled heart and finally shove them back together into a façade. She had said she'd play nice, that she'd forgiven this team, and those were truths. She would. But she couldn't forget what she had seen, had done, and what she knew was still to come. That was something Ella couldn't understand.

"Fine, be like that," Ella sighed before returning to the rest of the group.

Bass thumped and rattled in the cavities of her chest. Liquor rained down in her glass, splashes of lavender falling to the floor. The lights flashed rainbows down from the heavens, the colors prismatic as they shifted and bounced off the walls. It was blinding, enough to drown out the concerns of the day, and she was ravenous for it. So she let the alcohol sting the back of her throat and twisted her hips to the rhythm.

Perri sang the words as Cambrie danced with her. They pressed their body close to hers, grinding their hips into hers. Perri exaggeratedly swayed and giggled, grabbing them closer. She shimmied down, trailing her hands down their body as the lyrics suggested. Then, she spun Cambrie around, trying on a suggestive pout and come hither gesture, but moments later she broke character and fell into a fit of giggles. The warmth of the buzz was flush on Cambrie's cheeks and their chest hurt as they doubled over in laughter. They stumbled backwards into the couch, clutching their stomach. Fireworks set off in their brain, the splashes of color illuminating their smile.

The birthday girl danced atop the coffee table as if it were her stage, letting the music take over her body. She moved as if she were enchanted, a spell thrown over her mind so nothing else mattered tonight besides the music and the movement. As she shouted the lyrics to the songs, or at least tried to, a fist came unclenched from around her throat. Freedom poured from her veins.

Cambrie danced below her, a vision in black and white. Ella shimmied beside them, having lost any sense of rhythm she had. She had her hands raised in the air, spilling her drink down to the floor. As the song changed though, she gasped, flapping her hands and bouncing on her toes.

"Mavis Midnight!" she shouted, referencing the singer. She ran her hands down her body. The music was punchy, electric, and upbeat, sensuality dripping from the lyrics. She wanted to infuse it into her blood. "Did you know that we have the same birthday?" When she realized Cambrie wasn't paying attention, she beelined towards Perri who lounged on the couch. "She's my favorite singer of all time! Last time I heard, she's supposed to make her new album debut at the Blue Diamond festival next month!"

"Mavis? Yeah, we're friends," Perri said casually. "It's a great album, better than the last one."

"You're friends? You're joking! I can't believe it, and I can't believe that her new album is better than *Black Pearls, Black Heart*!"

"Yeah, she's pretty okay," Perri smirked, turning her attention to Najah and Cambrie now dancing alone in the middle of the room.

Cambrie pulled Najah off the table, the pair giggling as the woman fell into Cambrie. She probably could have stopped herself, but instead she let herself be wrapped in their arms for a moment. As she pulled away, a grin graced Cambrie's cheekbones. They swirled their bodies together, their breath ragged. For a few moments, it was them and only them.

They were lightning, sparks passing between their fingertips as they met. If there was such a thing as euphoria, it was in the laughter that passed between them, in the thundering heartbeats in their chests. Sweat glittered on Najah's collarbone, her curls bouncing as she swung her head back.

Belle came twirling into the picture, wine in hand. She took her partner's hand, pulling them closer. She held their hips close, grinding on them. With a hand on their cheek, she leaned in, mouth centimeters from theirs. But they backed away, subtly shaking their head.

Belle swallowed back the shock of rejection and turned away, a thin smile pressed on her face as she went to sit with Ella. She tried to wash away the dryness in her mouth with another swig of wine. But the aching loneliness was too familiar, and Ella's rambles were quickly slicing away at her patience. She had turned towards Perri, but the Siren already got up to dance. So, Belle got up and wandered into the kitchen.

The world spun beneath her feet. She needed to breathe. But all she could do was replay every vital moment in her head until nothing made sense. It was only when Cambrie wandered into the kitchen, the music faded into dull noise, that she returned to reality.

Cambrie opened their mouth to say something, anything that would make it better. But there was nothing they could think of in the fog that would help the woman before them.

Belle stared at the wall over their shoulder. "We're over, aren't we?" She croaked out the words, feeling them spill like dust to the floor.

Cambrie pressed their tongue to the back of their teeth, hands on the back of their neck, wishing it hadn't come to this point. "Yeahhhh, I'm sorry," they slurred. Shit. Their face reddened as they desperately tried to not sound as drunk as they were. "I stillllll s-care 'bout you, I just-"

Belle held up her hand, closing her eyes. "Don't. Just don't." If another drunken word left their mouth, she didn't think she'd be able to stop herself from doing something she'd regret. Her fingers went numb as they curled into fists at her side.

Cambrie stared at their ex for a moment before letting out a heavy sigh and stumbling into the bedroom. They rolled their shoulders, feeling as though weight had been lifted from them. But as Belle crawled into bed cradling the rest of the wine, they couldn't help but feel the room shrink in on them.

They entered the bathroom, hoping for the peaceful respite of cool water against their skin. Instead, they were confronted by Najah, washing the day off her face. She turned, water dripping off her lips and eyelashes under the low light. The door slammed shut behind, causing Cambrie to jump.

"Shitttttt, sorry," Cambrie muttered, turning to leave.

Najah took in her friend's jittery form, aware of the drink still swirling in her stomach. "Wait, are things alright?"

"Yes, no, I mean-" Words were turning to putty in Cambrie's mouth as they tried to focus on anything other than Najah. "We broke-broke-kup."

"Oh, I'm sorry," Najah said, turning from Cambrie to wipe her face on the towel.

"It's fine, it's fine," they waved off the comment. There was a moment of silence and a bitten lip. They took a step closer to the woman, letting their fingers brush against hers. "Are you okay?"

Najah let in a sharp breath, cursing every deity for making them so damned divine. If they were to stand on the brink between here and heaven, it was only with them that she would gladly go. She could trace every faint freckle of theirs behind her eyelids as if they were constellations. The strawberry tinge to their lips she had dreamt of tasting, the aroma of smoke and cedar that lingered in their hair she wanted to bury herself in, it was more intoxicating than the tequila in her veins. Every breath they took was a poem that put the greatest works of art to shame.

But the words she had uttered earlier in anger resounded in her head, and their desperate whispers were on repeat. *"Please, Oraësiana, you know what you said in your vow. This isn't you. You're not a cold-hearted killer. Neither is she. You promised me."*

No, they belonged behind the stained glass windows of ancient churches, where rainbows would cascade along their body and hymns would be sung in their worship; where they would be protected from her sacrilegious hands. So with a stare that lingered just a moment too long, she said:

"I'm fine, I'm good. Today has just been...a lot. Thank you though, for everything."

"That's swhat friends sare for," Cambrie mumbled.

"But you've always been-"

Before Najah could get out the rest of her sentence, the sound of glass shattering rang out from the other room, followed by a bitter scream from Belle.

Najah poked her head out from the bathroom, only to find Belle staring at the wine bottle in pieces against the wall. The woman sat atop the bed and buried her head in her lap, letting out another screech. Najah eyed the others in the room, holding out her hands in question. They gestured back, exaggeratedly mouthing out the scenario in a terrible game of charades.

"I should go," Najah said, turning back to Cambrie. "Maybe you should sleep on the couch tonight."

Cambrie winced, their chest aching. "S'that bad?"

"Not great." There was a moment of hesitation as Najah leaned out the door. "Thanks for the party too. It was fun."

"Happy birthday." And as the door shut, Cambrie stared at the emptiness in the mirror.

## Twenty-Four

# Death Day Dances and Disastrous Dyeing

"Look at this!" Perri exclaimed as she held out her arms, her lips pursed in distaste. The black hair dye that she had managed to splotch onto her blue was faded in patches. Uneven fringe framed her forehead, locks now choppily hitting her chin. Tears snuck into the corners of her eyes and her voice went up an octave. "What, was that dye made back on Earth? I look like a fucking disaster! And now all of the negativity in this room is making me break out in hives." When no one looked up, she frowned. "Fine. You can all sit in here with your sadness and dark circles. I'll be outside. Oh, and Ella?" She gestured to the three interlaced circles known as the trine that hung on the wall, the symbol that represented the Goddesses. "If your gods or mine were going to help us, they would've by now."

The afternoon breeze tickled her face as she stepped out the door. Ella followed her, asking if she was okay, then mumbled something about running to the store next door. From here Perri could see the skyscrapers of Zerephil, the capital city of Inanis. After they had slept off the party, they had to wake up to the familiar faces of hangover and regret, then shove together in a car. It had been tense, to say the least. At one point, when Cambrie had had the audacity to ask for water from Najah, Belle had nearly driven them into the barrier. So no one had particularly cared when they stopped at the cheapest hotel they could find. While a significant downgrade from the previous night, it meant they could at least breathe again.

She sat on the curb in front of the hotel door, watching the un-moving parking lot. She took a breath, letting her emotions settle back into their boxes. She couldn't be like the others. She couldn't break down like them. If she had to be the one to keep the mission going, she would, for Anna. Except...

The sun beat down on her bare shoulders, threatening to burn her if she stayed too long. But for the moment she basked in the warmth and dug in her backpack, searching for the communicators that Belle had grabbed from her parents' house.

Her dyed fingertips sailed across the glass screens. With just a few clicks she had made the device untraceable. Given how out of date the technology was, she knew a toddler could've done it. But even though she figured it out, she couldn't bring herself to type in the number she had memorized.

It had only been two weeks since her arrest, but the world had managed to collapse around her. She was eighteen. She should have been spending the summer traveling with her friends, working on beauty campaigns, and preparing to go to Arayvia University in the fall. Instead, she was struggling to type in her boyfriend's number, wondering if he thought of her as a murderer or not. She almost longed for the days of CareFree.

She typed in his number, deleted it, then typed it in again. As she held the device to her ear, her breath caught in her chest. In that moment, her heart seemed to stop.

From behind her, the hotel door opened and out came Cambrie. They came to join her on the sidewalk, tilting their head as they noticed Perri on the communicator. She held out a finger as it rang a third time, and then:

"Hello?" His ragged voice was akin to a health potion for her exhausted body.

"Finn," she breathed, as if any louder would prove disastrous for them both. "It's me."

There was the sound of movement on the other line and a muffled excuse. His breathing was labored and the pit of her stomach dropped. He could be doing anything on the other side of the line. He could be getting his supervisor. There could've been a new policy for President's guards to have Alcoriums implanted. If so, anyone could be listening. She should've hung up. But then a door closed on the other side and he returned to the line, his voice a whisper.

"Are you okay? Where are you? What happened?"

"I'm fine," she whispered back. The lump in her throat had only gotten bigger. "You know I'm not-I didn't try to kill him, right, at least I didn't want to? It was never my plan. He tried to kill me."

"I know, I believe you. You're not like that." In any other circumstance, those words leaving Finn's mouth would have had Perri rolling on the floor. But today they were a security blanket around her shoulders. "They're trying to pretend like it never happened over here. But there's weird shit going on over here. They alerted the other politicians that this happened, and to be on the look out, but I heard they're going to fake your death to the general public. What's weird though, is I heard Ahitophel was alerted too, and even invited to the Lantern Ball." As Finn mentioned the Saybrim King, Perri's stomach dropped.

"What? Wait, that makes no sense! What do you mean? And what the hell do you mean they're still holding the Ball? They're going to have the audacity to announce my death, then throw a party? Think about the optics of that. Fucking assholes."

"It doesn't make sense to me either, love," Finn sighed. "But if Ahitophel is invited to the Ball, then there has to be a reason. I can try to find out."

"Nuh uh, if they're throwing a party for my 'death,' I'm crashing it." Perri ignored the confusion written on Cambrie's face as she said that. "I-and four of my friends-are going to that ball. Can you help us get in?"

"But they know you're alive, and they're looking for you. Besides, you know how well they guard this thing. If you get caught, it's not prison anymore. You're getting killed."

It was an opportunity for intel. An opportunity to get close to Triton. That's all it was. She had to do this. It didn't matter that she would get to see Finn again. And her mother-how was her mother? Did her mother even know the full extent of what happened? She was as addicted to Alcoriums and CareFree as everyone else, so Perri wouldn't doubt it if the woman hadn't even noticed her absence. Still, even if she only caught a glimpse of the woman, it would be like a breath of fresh air.

"I know. But I have to do this. Please babe," Perri begged.

There was hesitation on the other side of the line. Finn's voice was weak, his resolve gone. "Fine. I'll help. I'll call you again in a few days to sort out the details."

"Thank you." She gave a heartbeat of consideration as she tried to sort out the most important words, knowing time was running thin. "I love you."

"I love you too. Be safe out there."

The line went dead and Perri felt her stomach knot. At least he was alive. That much she could tell herself. But as she turned towards Cambrie, their eyebrows raised, she couldn't help but feel that maybe she had made a mistake.

"Who was that?" Cambrie asked as they stared at the person walking through the parking lot, blowing a haze of fruity nicotine through the air.

"Finn, my boyfriend," Perri began. "He was my bodyguard."

"They let you date your bodyguard? And you decided to call him?"

"They didn't know about us. And yes I decided to call him. He knows about everything, about the Alcoriums, about...a certain someone's plans, everything. So he seemed safe enough to call." Perri curled her knees to her chest, avoiding their gaze.

"And he's not going to give us away, or give you fake information?"

"No, he's not like that!" Perri said sharply. "Do you want to talk about your relationship?"

"Sure, why not?" Cambrie threw up their hands. "Tell me, what are your thoughts? Did I do the right thing?"

"Breaking up with Belle? Goddess yeah. I wish you had done it earlier. If it weren't for the fact that everyone here would kill me, I probably would've eaten her already." At that, Cambrie rolled their eyes. "I'm joking of course...mostly. Although, the whole thing does put a bit of a negative vibe on the group. I could do without all the crying. But, the whole thing with you and Najah-"

"There's no thing with Najah and I!" Cambrie said, turning a deep shade of red.

Perri smirked and raised her eyebrows. "Oh really? Doesn't seem like it. But I gotta give it to the Human, she's handling it a lot better than I would in this scenario. Ya'll are being kinda...mean, flaunting it in her face like that."

"There's nothing going on!"

"Whatever you say," Perri shrugged.

There was silence as Cambrie pondered what Perri had said, the words hitting them in their gut. They stared out across the parking lot, drumming their fingers on their leg. In an attempt to distract, or perhaps break the awkward silence, they added "I am grateful you got us out of there, you know."

"Oh, trust me, I know. But I do like hearing you say it," Perri smirked. "Without me y'all would have died."

"And without me, you would have died too. So I think we're even," Cambrie grinned.

"Mm, you would have died first, so any saving you did afterwards is kind of canceled out by that fact. Without me saving you, you wouldn't have been able to save me."

"What kind of logic is that? I heard you gave a life debt to Najah for her saving you. What, I don't get one of those?"

Perri snorted. "Hell no! Those aren't even really a thing anymore. It's just an old tradition that's more of a legend than anything. I just needed an excuse to stick by Najah so we could help each other escape and we could..." she suddenly looked around, making sure no one heard her. "You know."

"So that's why you stayed. I heard you say your life debt was up after saving us, but you still stayed. It definitely wasn't because deep down you're a decent person who cares about us."

"You're imagining things," she smirked, then glanced around. "Where's Ella? Wasn't she just getting snacks from next door?"

"I'm right here!" Ella said, arms noticeably empty of snacks as she rounded the corner.

"What happened? Where did you go?" Cambrie asked.

"You know that guy from the Pit? The announcer guy with the loopy hair? What's his name?" Ella snapped her fingers a few times before Perri supplied his name.

"Aarlin?"

"Yeah, that dude. He's across the street at the bar. I saw him go in."

They all peered at the run-down establishment, graffiti coating the plywood door. The holograms that were meant to dance along the windows glitched in and out, the signs offering specials now misspelled and burnt out.

"No, I can't see a guy like that in that place," Perri muttered.

"You never know. I've seen rich people in shadier places," Cambrie shrugged. "He's probably having an affair, or meeting his dealer."

"We should see what he's up to," Ella said.

"Why in the hell would we go up to one of the few people who knows we're alive?" Perri asked, staring at the girl.

"Look closer at the symbols on the door," Ella gestured towards the purple sigil in the middle of the door. It resembled a backwards crescent moon with an arrow through it. "It's not just a bar. It's a Saybrim Resistance safehouse. I don't think it's an accident that he wandered into that specific bar."

"And what if you're wrong? What if he just randomly wandered in and he recognizes us?"

"What do you even want to do?" Cambrie asked.

"If he's a part of it, then we have an ally, a big one. We should know."

"Go if you want, but I can't be part of this," Perri shook her head. "Sorry. It's stupid."

Cambrie hesitated and shook their head. "It's too risky. We can't."

Ella rolled her eyes, tapping on her forearm. "Fine. But we should at least keep it in mind."

Perri stood, brushing off her pants. "Okay, well since we got that figured out, I'm going to go feed, and then we'll actually plan."

"Didn't you just feed-" Cambrie began, but Perri was already walking into the shadows of the building to shift.

She flew as high into the atmosphere as she could, letting the thin air clear her head and cool her body. Among the clouds, she lazily flapped her wings, floating in among the golden particles the sun spread around her body. This close to her Goddesses, she closed her eyes, raising her arms towards the heavens for the first time in years. As her words were suspended in time, she asked-begged-for safety, for guidance, and for forgiveness. And for a fools moment, as she dove closer to the city line, she could've sworn she saw them smile.

Zerephil was her city and yet, she still tucked her wings and dove in between the tallest buildings. Her feathers blended in with the murky shadows lining alleyways. As others flew freely above the city, she couldn't help but stare up at them with envy. They weren't nearly as powerful as her, weren't nearly as knowledgeable as her, and yet, they were so free. And the people who milled around on the streets, those who lost all of their powers to the hands of CareFree, they didn't even glance up. She shouldn't be here. She didn't need to feed. She just needed to feel the pulse of the city again, to prove she wasn't dead.

She took off between alleyways, in her Humanesque form again, the scent of sewage mixing with fresh cooked meats and candied nuts. She ducked her head past the line of dayclub goers, past the crocodillo tear infusion center, past the cuddleduck party place. She let her feet carry her until she found the heartbeat of the city.

Her home lay towering above the streets before her, built to stare over the main square and its businesses. From the windows of her bedroom in the Manor, she would normally enjoy the view of the bustling city. But being down here, among the alleys where starving Humans begged for spare credits, she couldn't help but feel the desperation build in her veins. Here, amongst the scraps of fabric, the dead eyes of CareFree addiction, and the people who never had a fair chance, here was the opportunity to take down Triton. And they were dying. So many were dying. She stared down at a sleeping woman and her child and tucked a credit into their blanket before rushing away.

The shops she had once ran through taunted her and the CEOs she shook hands with had turned their backs. She wanted to scream the truth from the iron spires of the history museum that was so ready to paste her death date. And among the silver buildings that all seemed the same, she was met with a familiar face. Hers. Projected high in some twisted, sick joke from the universe, a hologram sat on the side of a building. Her blue hair had been painstakingly pinned to resemble a birdcage, sitting atop her head. As Perri applied a layer of shimmering pink gloss, tiny hearts appeared on her lips. She blew a kiss and the tiny hearts exploded from the hologram and transformed into colorful birds of paradise, which flew around her and into the cage on her head. And as the larger version stared down upon her smaller self, eyes chock full of glitter, the tagline appeared. *Love yourself. Stay in your head.*

Her body shook violently, and for a moment she swore her heart was going to shutter to a stop. *You caused this. And now you're powerless to fix it.* She shoved down her stomach contents, bracing herself on a wall. And then she ran. She ran for the danger, for the power, for the fall, because stopping had proven devastating.

Somewhere along the way, she had shifted back into her Siren form, yearning for the power of her wings again. So she wasn't exactly surprised to find herself here, although her bitten cheek and the pit in her stomach told a story of guilt.

The restaurant had no menu posted outside, no signage, no windows. It was squished between a coffee shop and a narrow alleyway.

For all intents and purposes it was simply an abandoned building. But Perri knew better. She let her fingers grip the door handle, then stopped. She could smell the Human blood inside. It was tantalizing, fresh, pure. But she didn't live the life she once did, and both the price of a meal and the price of getting caught were too high.

She turned and kicked the bins lined against the wall, her talons easily knocking over the row of metal bins. The contents spilled out onto the dirt. The scraps of half eaten meals came tumbling out. A femur with a bit of remaining meat rolled by Perri's foot.

Just then, a rather ragged looking Human stumbled down the alley. But she didn't even have time to turn around as she made eye contact with Perri. A shifted Siren was never a good omen.

She tried to run, but the Siren was faster. Her talons wrapped around the woman, crushing her before she could let out a scream. But as the life drained out of the woman, Perri didn't feel powerful. Instead, she shook more.

She let out a shriek that bounced off the walls and was drowned out by the traffic. The woman's blood now turned her stomach queasy. She looked down at her victim, swallowing hard. What was done was done. There would be no point leaving the woman without feeding. Perri closed her eyes.

"Thank you for your service and sacrifice," she whispered. "May the Goddesses guide you."

Then, she tore into the woman's body. The blood was bitter on her tongue.

## Twenty-Five

# Anything is Free if You Can Run Fast Enough (Please, This is Not Legal Advice)

"If none of you go with me, I'll make sure that you're forced to wear bedsheets to this ball," Perri said as she stared at herself in the mirror, wrinkling her nose. She took the hair tie from her wrist and wrapped it around her hair into a tiny ponytail. Then she yanked the tie out and tossed it outside, running her fingers through her hair with a scowl. The circles under her eyes matched the various bruises along her arms.

"Honestly, sounds good to me," Belle muttered from the bed, bedding strewn on the ground. She put her arm back over her eyelids, filtering out the dim orange light. "I don't need anything fancy to beat Ahitophel's ass."

She didn't need to play dress up. If no one else was going to watch her back, she would take back up the mantle her mother gave her. She would cover herself in the ripped perceptions of her past in camouflaging armor. She needed to let herself down in the graves she had dug and take her rightful place as the reaper.

"I'll go with you," Cambrie said, the words rushing from their lips. If they had to spend another second in the room with Belle, they were going to crack. Their shoes were on and they were at the door in seconds.

Perri nodded. "Anyone else coming?"

"I would, but I have to coordinate our entrance and exit plans, and double check the security detail," Najah sighed as she poured over the tiny communicator screen. She laid on the extremely outdated brown carpet, picking at a crumb in the shag.

"I told you that Finn has all of that handled, Najah," Perri said, her voice picking up a bit of a bite.

"Yeah, but it never hurts to have a backup plan," she said off-hand-edly. Her feet kicked into the brown floral walls as someone outside yelled. Cambrie jumped and glanced out the window.

Ella just shook her head and shrugged. "I'm gonna stay here and help."

"Fine, suit yourselves. Let's go."

Perri slid into the passenger's seat and turned up the music so that it rattled her ribcage. With the windows cracked to let the breeze in, she took a drag of Cambrie's atomizer. She let the smoke curl in her lungs before exhaling out her nose. As Cambrie climbed into the SUV, she passed it back.

"Thanks for letting me borrow it. I've been craving this," Perri said.

"It's a bad habit," Cambrie chuckled as they took a hit and put it back in their pocket. "Ella would kill me if she saw I got another one."

"Yeah, well, seems better than any of the alternatives," Perri muttered as they pulled out of the parking lot.

The car wove in and out of traffic as the A.I took control of the wheel. It sped towards the address imputed. Thin smoke filled the car as Cambrie puffed on their atomizer, mango dancing on their taste buds. Perri sung along to the music and danced in her seat, enjoying the disappearing sun on her face.

Before they pulled into the parking lot of an apartment building, cheekbones shifted and noses contorted, hair grew and eyes changed. Despite the changes, they were careful to keep their bodies the same sizes.

"So, you're using your persuasion right?"

"Yeah, that's the goal," Perri said, picking at her abnormally short nails.

"Great, want me to do anything?"

"Just bypass the locks, I'll do the rest." Perri took a breath as she stared up at the building, dark clouds forming above the towers. "Goddess, I've been dying to do this to him honestly. Trust me, the designer is a real bitch. His name is Tyrone. He was busted for not paying his workers a few months back, and when I walked his show, he built all the models into this pyramid and walked on our backs with heels on. It was his 'aesthetic vision.' What kind of fucked up asshole does that?"

Cambrie's eyes widened, their mouth agape. "Yeah, that's pretty fucked up."

"Right? C'mon, let's go."

The apartment was just like every other luxury building Cambrie had robbed. It was completely and utterly tasteless. Boring. The same lock system which was easy enough to override with the crossing of wires. They waltzed into the back door, peering into the empty lobby as they waited for the elevator. Unnecessary fountains and a mountain climbing simulator stood sentry over the community meeting space.

Unused couches littered the floor, and a room full of fitness mirrors sat encased in glass in the corner. Gentle music resounded off the pristine white tiles that had been painstakingly hand placed on the towering walls. And above, prismatic glass let in the faux sunshine of the day. It was always sunny here. Holographic silver butterflies fluttered too close to the glass, swarming each other in a frenzy.

They entered the elevator and its jaws closed around them. Soft instrumental music piped from the speakers above as they were shot upwards. Their likeness contorted in the mirrored walls, reflecting their truths back to them.

As the doors opened, Perri strutted down the halls of the familiar hallway, letting her heels echo. Two doors stood on opposing ends of the hall. The plants that grew along the walls seemed to reach out towards her with greedy palms and the gilded wall sconces seemed to whisper secrets. She knew the cameras in the corners would be tracking her every move. But she ignored it all, gliding towards the door at the left end.

"He has this side of the floor," Perri explained.

Then, she simply knocked. Then she waited. And waited some more. She placed her hands on her hips.

"Are you sure he's-" Cambrie began.

But Perri held up her hand as she heard movement on the other side of the door and it swung open.

"I wasn't expecting guests today. Who are you?" Tyrone was steady on his sky-high boots as he towered down over his guests. His mustache was thin and protruded from his face, only to angle upwards and create a three-dimensional triangle around his nose. It was truly a horrendous work of art. A double pair of glasses, one with blue lenses and one with rose lenses connected by golden rims sat atop the bridge of his spindly nose. An old naked doll with coarse colorful hair hung around his neck on a gold chain. His vintage hot pink track jacket hung off his shoulders, revealing a tattoo of a large feline.

"Tu nre tio sina nosill ne e facied nosill clestidas. Tu nre ausculté ot mehe," Perri demanded of the man in her native tongue.

As the man's eyes glazed over, Perri grinned and entered the apartment. Wealth oozed from every corner. Abstract modern artwork Cambrie had only dreamed about attaining hung on the walls. The living room was basked in artificial sunlight from the wall of windows that overlooked the city. A large couch sat in the middle, below a balcony which held a large table and a variety of instruments, perfect for the parties he undoubtedly held. Off to the left side, a large open bar sat, the bottles of booze more than generous. A smaller sitting area with a ginormous T.V. was tucked away to the right, underneath the balcony.

"Do you want a drink?" Tyrone asked as he approached the bar. "You're welcome to anything I have."

They both shook their heads, but Cambrie smirked at the comment. In another life, perhaps they would have found the artwork a new home or worn out some of his designer bags. But not today. Tyrone shrugged and poured himself a bourbon. Then, he stood in front of the couch and waved his hand on his Alcorium, projecting his screen to a larger screen on his windows.

"With such a short time frame, I can only do semi-custom outfits. I'm going to need measurements for everyone. It would've been nice if they all came, but I can make it work," he sighed. "Stand here for me, arms out."

Perri stood in front of him, reminiscing of the time she had done this for Fashion Week. She knew he was under her influence, but she still wanted to spit in his face as the measuring laser spun around her body.

Cambrie did the same, and they reported the other's measurements approximately based off their own. Tyrone grumbled as he typed in the numbers. Veiled insults about presumed body types were on his tongue.

"I'm sorry, what was that?" Perri asked.

"What?" Tyrone said, glancing up from his Alcorium.

"Watch your mouth," Perri snarled.

A shaken man backed away, sucking on his lips. He turned towards his Alcorium again, the ring switching to green as he received Care-Free. With a breath and a smile, he continued with the design process.

"Great, now you just have to pick your fabrics and accouterments from this list," he gestured to the large screen before him. 3-D samples of fabric protruded from the screen. "Pick something that inspires you. I'll fashion them into a style that flatters you best."

Perri scrolled through the list on the screen. Silks and satins and tulles passed under her fingertips in a sensory carousel.

"That one is cool," Cambrie butted in as Perri passed a color changing leather.

"Yeah, but not the most discrete. I'm looking for something I can hide in."

"Eh, fair enough." Cambrie said. "Ooh, what about this one?"

"I think that's perfect for you!" Perri exclaimed as Cambrie held up the scrap of fabric.

"Ah yes, I can make a good suit out of this," Tyrone said as he took the scrap from Cambrie. "What are your thoughts on snail teeth? I just got a shipment in and I think they'd make a cool accent piece on the collar. They're all the rage these days."

"Snail teeth?" Cambrie asked, eyebrows raised.

"Yeah, they harvest them from these giant snails. They're super valuable because they're the strongest material in nature. Stronger than diamond."

"You harvest them from giant snails?"

"Well I definitely don't. Have you seen me? But yeah, obviously someone does," Tyrone chuckled.

"What happens to the snails after? I-yeah, no, nevermind. I don't want the teeth. Just give me diamonds or emeralds or something normal," Cambrie cringed.

"Fucking purist," Tyrone muttered. "Fashion is built on sacrifices. What's wrong with people these days?" He turned, his hands busy with his Alcorium. He threw the fabric down on the table and kicked at the coffee table. Another flash of green and a calm aura came over the room once more.

Perri's face was pressed in a thin line as she handed over her materials. Her eyes bored into his. "These will be fine for mine. I already set the other's aside. I don't want to hear anything about them. Just make the outfits silently."

He opened his mouth, then closed it as if he had eaten something particularly sticky. He took the pile and ascended the glass staircase to the balcony where he sat and worked. His gaze however, never left his new clients.

Perri pulled Cambrie over to the bar. Under the clinking of glasses and ice, she whispered:

"We have to get out of here asap. My persuasion is already wearing off, I can feel it. It's why he's getting angry, and why he hasn't stopped looking at us. He's suspicious."

"I don't suppose you can persuade him again," Cambrie said.

"Yeah, no. Since he's suspicious, he's got his mental walls up. And yeah, they're weak as hell, but he's gonna know I broke through them again and get even more suspicious and stop working with me. It's a vicious cycle. We gotta find some pre-made stuff here."

Perri poured a top shelf whiskey in her glass and offered some to Cambrie. They shrugged and took the other glass Perri poured. It went down smooth as they sipped it. Then, they smiled, knowing they needed to throw down one of the oldest cards in the book.

"Can I use your bathroom?" Cambrie called up to the man.

He rolled his eyes and nodded, waving his hand in the general direction of a hallway in the back of the apartment. Cambrie walked in that direction, whiskey in hand. But they began to toss open every door until they found what they were looking for.

A spare two story bedroom had been renovated into a custom walk in closet. Hats hung from the ceiling. Bags that cost more than the apartment stood encased in glass along one wall on the second story loft, shoes showcased the same below. Gold, silver, and jewels sat in the middle, tempting in their velvet dresser drawers. Only an easily bypassable thumbprint lock kept them safe. Luxurious gowns of Tyrone's design hung along one wall, and as Cambrie moved further into the room, they realized the closet would rotate through them based on color. They tried to focus, knowing time was of the essence. But the wealth was overwhelming. They yanked gown after gown down off the rack, doing their best to shove them in various handbags they knew people would kill for. Into a tote bag went every pair of shoes they could manage. Then, under their clothes, went the dress shirt and pants. They slipped the jacket over their arm, over one of the purses that had grown rather large. They slid rings onto their fingers as easily as they had slid the lock off the dresser, and dropped just about every piece of jewelry into their pockets. It was more than they needed, more than anyone needed. But as they shut the door, they shrugged. They'd consider it a donation to the cause.

Perri sat with Tyrone, her arm slung around his shoulders. He was stiff, his fingers moving along the Alcorium as he paid no attention to what Perri said.

"Let me work, let me think," he said, voice gruff.

"I wanna watch," Perri whined from where she sat. But as she saw Cambrie emerge from below, she stood. "But I guess I should let you work, since you're doing me a favor."

She walked down the stairs, her steps hurried. She met up with Cambrie, her heart racing.

"Is it okay if we step out for a bit? We're going to go get a bite to eat and come back,"

"Wait, no, no where are you going?" Tyrone called as he rushed down the stairs, taking in Cambrie's now full arms. "Those are mine!"

Perri said as she crossed the threshold. She gripped two bottles of top shelf liquor by the neck and shuffled towards the door.

"By the way, tu nre tio dedisconé nosill. Tu no dedimem tun bonia," she laughed.

Tyrone paused long enough that they managed to pass the threshold and shut the door. They dashed to the elevator, hearts in their throats, adrenaline pumping in their veins, arms weighed down by their treasures.

Perri let out a laugh in the safety of the lift. "I can't believe we did that!"

"I know," Cambrie said, much more reserved. They knew not to celebrate too early. "What did you tell him?"

"Oh, just to forget that we were there and that he ever had any of that stuff."

"Will that work? The last thing we need is him saying something to the cops."

"Hopefully. It's never guaranteed, but forgetting is one of the easier things to persuade someone to do. Besides, he's not coming after us, is he? I'm betting he already forgot we were there. C'mon, quit worrying! We pulled it off!"

Cambrie nodded as the elevator opened and they were able to waltz to the car. It had begun to rain, and lightning struck in the distance. As the car began to drive, Cambrie unloaded their arms. Five bags stuffed to the brims sat on their lap. The jewelry sat heavy in their pocket. A grin etched on their face. They had never set out to be a thief, and they had sworn they'd give it up, but by Goddess were they good at it.

"I can't wait to see what you got, oh my Goddess, even the bags you got are phenomenal."

Perri reached for a red handbag with silver hardware shaped like hearts. There was a hand painted scene that continued to warp and change as a woman kissed another woman, then ascended to the clouds and gained a set of wings, while her lover stayed along the river where they kissed, a tail growing along her bottom half.

"It's been so long since I've seen a mermaid, oh my Goddess. I can't believe Tyrone would make this. Damn Humans."

"Perri," Cambrie warned.

"I know, but Humans killed out Mermaids by polluting the water. They killed an entire race and we never talk about it. I know this generation of Humans is different, and I'm trying real hard to respect them, but damn. We have history."

"I didn't know that," Cambrie said quietly. "When was that?"

"272 years ago. Mermaids were the first victims of the pollution that Humans created on Earth, then Sirens were next. Ya know, it's a lot of the reason why there's that myth that Mermaids and Sirens are the same thing."

"Damn," Cambrie said. "Still, not all Humans are bad. Ella will fight with you to the ends of the planet."

"I know, and I get that...it's why I'm not going to feed anymore."

"What? Don't you have to do that to live?" Cambrie was running through every textbook they had read in their mind. Nothing was adding up. Their brow furrowed, mouth agape.

"I've heard of Sirens that manage to go without feeding. It's incredibly rare, but I can't hurt people like that anymore. I'll go through the withdrawal process. I'll be weaker. But if I can make it through, it'll be worth it." She took a breath. This had been sitting in her gut since her last feeding, but saying it out loud made it all too real. She was doing it.

"That's huge. Are you sure?" Cambrie stared at their partner in crime, unsure if this was just a spur of the moment decision fueled by adrenaline.

"Yes. I need to do this," There was no reserve in Perri's voice. She didn't waver.

"Okay then. Good for you!"

As they pulled into the hotel parking lot, Perri took hold of their treasures, cradling the mermaid handbag if it were her firstborn child. She giddily dumped the bag onto the bed, unveiling a silken gown and jewelry, suit jacket and heels soon following.

Ella giggled as she picked up a gown for herself, holding it up to her body. She spun around, imagining herself in the middle of the ball. Najah picked up a headpiece and placed it on her head.

"There you go. Now you're the Queen of the Lantern Ball."

Najah bowed exaggeratedly and smiled, before examining the goods before her.

"So, these are gorgeous, but uh, I vaguely remember hearing that you were going to get us custom gowns, not just rob this guy blind. Is everything good?" Najah asked.

"Look, we got what we needed and we probably won't be caught. That's all you need to know," Perri said with a sly smile. "He's not going to remember that we were there."

"Okay, that's all I care about," Najah said, raising her hands in innocence.

After hearing that, Belle finally stood from the other bed and looked down upon the remaining outfits. More gowns remained than people.

"This is a lot of stuff. It is really nice though. Are we going to sell the rest of it?"

"Probably. We could use the credits," Cambrie said.

Belle shrugged and picked out a black number, running the fabric through her fingers. She bit her lip. She would go along with this plan, she told herself. She would. But as her stomach dropped and she felt above her body, it was getting harder to keep it together. While the other showered in the luxuries they had wrought, she hit the shower and let the water fall over her shoulders. But it did nothing to bring her back. And as she slipped beneath the sheets, she prayed for respite. But it never came.

As her breaths came shorter and the sweat trickled down her chest, Belle kicked off the sheets and yanked off her bonnet. Nighttime had always come as a blessing and a curse. With another bang from outside, her heart kicked into her throat. With a glance, she realized Ella slept soundly beside her. Perri spread fully on the other bed, nearly kicking Najah onto the floor. Cambrie sat awake, circles under their eyes, flipping a knife in their palm.

Cambrie gave a sympathetic smile and a nod as Belle passed them. She welcomed the sudden breeze on her bare skin, pulling at her thin tank top as she shut the door behind her. A pink lightning bug lazily flew by her to join the other insects flocking towards the flickering light in the overhang. From beneath the dim lighting of the parking lot, she found the source of the noise. A group of Humans sat around their sports cars, smoking and tossing a ball to one another. Music pounded from the color-changing interiors, neon coating the pavement.

She pulled her locs to the side to cover her bare head and let her hips fall into a sultry swing. She had seen one of them earlier. The veins on his hands were evident as he spun the ball on his ring clad fingertips. He didn't belong here. His silver chains and bands wove around him like armor, though he didn't need it. His body was one designed by the greatest warriors and athletes, an image that would instill jealousy into anyone who saw. And as he leaned on the front of a purple sports car, smoke circling around him, he grinned and waved two fingers towards Belle, welcoming her forward.

She couldn't remember the words that were spoken. But the atomizer left mint on her tongue and her mind in the clouds. The other men passed the ball around her until she managed to grab it and toss it to the silver man. He casually tossed the ball to the side and took a hit of the atomizer, blowing the smoke in an 'O' to the stars. A woman in ripped shorts ran her hand across his shoulder as she swirled past him, but he ignored her, laser focused on Belle. She let her hips move with the music, one thing on her mind. It couldn't come from the strangers that held her waist, or the ones that tried to slip tablets between her lips.

So she let him watch as the parking lot began to empty. And then his hands came up around her, picking her up and placing her atop the sports car. His hands rested on her cheek. His thumb curled around the bottom of her jaw, his palm at the edge of her throat. Her pulse raced. Bare, vulnerable, it would be so easy for him to just crush her trachea. But those hands could do so much more, could keep the nighttime and its horrors away. His fingers pulled her close, his breath tickling her lips. For a moment, the world went quiet. As she melted into him, craving the raw strength of him, she wondered if this is what CareFree felt like. He pulled her hair, trailing kisses on her neck to erase the marks of the strangers who had touched her.

As they stumbled towards his hotel room intertwined in each other's arms, a brief glimmer of shame rose in her chest. The walls were thin and Cambrie, at the very least, would know. But that thought was quickly washed away as her shirt was shed and he pulled her on his lap. Her lips met his in a desperate attempt to convey everything she needed in the wordless exchange of breath. Here, in this room, she was able to be bright, neon, and gave up all control as she slid to her knees. She burned like a fire, sparking and spiraling under the watchful eye of this man. She just prayed she wouldn't die out.

## Twenty-Six

# THEY'RE JUST MASKING FOR TROUBLE

## CW: Self-harm

"I swear to the Goddesses, if you move one more time, I'm going to stab your eye out!" Perri exclaimed. She waved the mascara wand in the air as if it were a weapon of mass destruction.

"Sorry!" Ella said as she blinked rapidly and shook her body out. "Okay. I'm ready, hit me."

Perri coated the girl's lashes a few times before dropping the wand and pressing pigment into her cheeks. Some of the blush fell into the chipped sink, alongside strands of someone's hair. As Ella sat on the bathroom counter, she tried to ignore the spider forming a web in the corner of the room. With all of the stolen items sold off, they could have afforded themselves nicer accommodations, and yet, they had decided to reserve their credits for more important things. So here they sat in another motel room, trying not to look too closely at the stains on the bedding.

"There," Perri said as she sprayed a mist aggressively into Ella's face. Then she leaned back to admire her masterpiece. "You look gorgeous!

Too bad we have to cover my work." She helped Ella settle a mask atop her cheekbones made of gold and citrine, tying it into the shimmering headdress set atop her head.

"Why is this thing a masquerade anyways? Doesn't that seem dumb for security?"

"It's a tradition. You're supposed to stay masked until the lantern launch, then everyone unmasks. It's symbolic for bringing your true self to light or something. Security is so strict with these things I guess. Everyone has to send in unmasked pictures in their costumes to the security team, and unmask at the door with their invites. Finn just forged ours and put our names-or the fake names I gave you-on the list. We should be good to go. Now move, I have to finish my own makeup."

Ella shrugged and walked from the bathroom, strutting as she framed her face with her hands and gave a smile. Yellow chiffon shimmered through the air, the A-line gown falling off her shoulders. Golden chains crossed around her arms and laced behind her back in an intricate illusion of wings. She practically floated as she spun to face her sister, her gown changing from yellow to orange as she did so. She was the sweetness, the hope, in the wishes whispered to a shooting star, reminiscent of the star charms that hung from her braids.

"What do you think?" she asked as Belle finished slipping on her dress.

She gave a small smile. Ella, who had missed all of her school formals, stood before her looking like a dream in the dingy orange lighting. But now there were daggers attached to the girl's legs. "You look phenomenal."

Belle's black satin gown was far too constrictive for her liking. She would've preferred a jumpsuit, or even better, a good pair of pants. There wasn't a great reason for dressing up, not one that would warrant the loss of her life if she couldn't fight if need be. But Perri had insisted, and she had to admit, she looked damn good. The dress clung to her body in all the right places. The v-neck dipped down to her stomach, giving just a tantalizing taste to what laid below. The slit that crept up her thigh gave her access to the gun and blade on her hip. White lights dotted the hem of the fabric, kissing her breasts, descending over her shoulders into a cape. With the pull of some fabric, a black iridescent hood appeared attached to the cape, lights attached to the edge. Silver jewels had been pressed to her skin so that she shimmered like the night.

As Perri stepped from the bathroom, she raised her eyebrows. "Damn, have you ever thought about modeling?"

"I haven't exactly had the chance," Belle muttered. "Nice to know I have a backup career though if this revolution shit ever goes south."

Perri smirked. "Yeah, it would be easy for you with that resting 'I'm superior to you' face.'"

Belle opened her mouth, then shut it with a cheeky grin. But she just couldn't help herself. "That's coming from the world's top su- permodel, huh?"

"Touche," Perri replied as she gave a little bow.

Her gown looked as though it was created from her other form. Sleek black feathers wrapped around her chest and cascaded down her body. The dress hugged her every curve and accentuated her best parts. A diagonal cut out around the side of her stomach revealed part of her perfectly toned abs while another on the other side revealed part of her upper thigh. She had painted elaborate black makeup and jewels across her cheekbones. Her hair had been touched up into braided, interwoven curls. She clutched an intricate wire mask in her hand. If she was going to attend the party replacing her 'funeral,' she was going to look drop dead gorgeous.

She applied her lipstick in the mirror before frowning. "This isn't the right color! Dammit! Ella, will you go out and get me a different shade after we finish briefing?"

"Yeah, sure," Ella said as she picked at a clump in her mascara through the eyeholes of her mask.

"Nah, I'll go get it," Belle muttered from where she sat on the bathroom counter. "But hurry up with the briefing if you want it. We're running out of time."

"Fine. So us three," she gestured to herself, Belle, and Ella. "We're finding any and all records that could help us. The priorities being the plans for the CareFree factories, anything on the Egg, Alcorium updates, and anything on the Resistance. We're taking pictures with these."

She held up a device with a dozen circles on one side and a screen on the other. Then she turned her attention to her other companions.

"Najah, Cambrie, you're sneaking into Than and Triton's meeting. See what they say, what they do. Do your secret spy shit, I don't know. Then keep an eye on them for the rest of the night. We'll go in through the tunnels in route A. Finn should be meeting us there. I hope you all memorized the other routes though. You're only going to have an hour in disguise Cambrie, so don't waste it. Any questions?"

"Did we ever come to a decision about whether or not we're going to...take the shot?" Najah asked from where she stood, setting her makeup brush aside.

Perri ran her fingers through her hair as everyone looked at her. Her mouth went dry as she pressed her tongue to her cheek. "As much as I want to be the one to take him out, I'll leave that up to your discretion, if you get a chance. But if we fuck up, we fuck up our whole mission. It's not just him who lives. So if you pull that trigger, don't you dare miss."

Najah nodded, taking a breath as the air grew solemn. Belle let the door shut behind them with a thud, causing Cambrie to jump. Cloaked in a dark teal suit and sheer dress shirt, they sunk into the corner of the motel room, finding solace amongst the water-stained wallpaper.

Cambrie fiddled with their bowtie, the golden serpent rings on their fingers clinking together. A black veil cascaded down their head, the edges tattered. Their simplistic answers to the questions that everyone continued to throw around had worn thin. They had already lost their temper this morning and lodged a knife into the bathroom wall, and when that hadn't proven enough, lodged it into their thigh instead. Still, it wasn't enough to drown it out. So now, in a nauseating cacophony of their thoughts, they waited.

Najah shimmied into her gown with an irritated sigh as body make-up she had been forced to slather onto her tattoos rubbed off onto the inside of the dress. A translucent fabric made up the torso with tiny gold diamonds dotted around the stomach and curling around the breasts in swirling patterns. The diamonds traveled diagonally up the collarbone into a beaded choker that wrapped around the neck. Soft metal, high-waisted, and high cut, underwear she had managed to squeeze herself into lay beneath a shimmering translucent gold skirt.

The woman sat on the arm of Cambrie's chair, trying not to mess up the golden eyelashes that were longer than her finger. Her lips were heavy, laden with rhinestones that Perri had painstakingly placed one by one.

"Hey, what's going on?"

"Nothing. I'm fine," Cambrie muttered. They rubbed at their neck, nearly catching their black and gold pierced nails on the veil.

"Don't lie to me, c'mon," Najah whispered.

There was a pause and Cambrie sucked on their lips. "I can't do this. I killed him last time. I can't kill you guys."

Najah nodded, realizing it was bigger than nerves or the people there. The Northexxe gala was where they had been drugged, where Tenajh had been killed. Of course going to this ball would be a trigger to Cambrie.

"I get it. If you can't go to this, no one is going to make you," Najah said. "But know his death wasn't your fault. You can't keep holding yourself responsible."

"But if I had been more aware-" Cambrie began before shaking their head. "I have to go tonight. I have to make sure you're all safe. But what if I mess up again? What if I fuck it up and-"

"You're not going to be alone this time Cam. We're going to be together. I'm going to be with you every step of the way. You aren't going to fuck up, and if things do go according to plan, we'll deal with it, like we always do. Together, as a team. And for Mythos sake, you're Cambrie. You can do absolutely anything you put your mind to. Honestly, they should be petrified that we're going together."

Najah could tell she hadn't fixed the issue, that she hadn't managed to bat away the thoughts in their head. But still, they gave a tight-lipped smile and nodded.

"You're right. Thank you."

As Belle returned and everyone put the final touches on their looks, Perri looked upon them all. Her procession strutted on heels, ready to set out towards the night.

"Well, everyone, let's go see my family."

## Twenty-Seven

# WITHIN THE SILENCE OF THE LAMBS AND THE LIONHEARTS

"Okay, next time we do this, can we not change into heels and then walk two kilometers?" Ella whined, holding her gown above her ankles.

"It's only one and half kilometers actually," Perri muttered as they arrived at the iron door to the entrance. "Trust me, I know."

While the tunnels were supposed to be used to evacuate the Manor officials in the event of an emergency, they hadn't yet been used for that. Instead, Perri had spent many of her teenage years navigating the tunnels to sneak out of her room. They were dark and damp, smelling of old rain. Cambrie's face was blank as they illuminated the place with a small flame.

"C'mon, let's get going," Perri said as she opened the door.

As she stepped into her closet and walked past her walls of gifted clothes, the faint smell of her signature perfume still hung in the air. As the others filed into the closet, she saw him.

It was evident that he hadn't slept in weeks. Whatever nightmares had plagued him still clung to his face, a new beard along his jawline.

His black coils had grown out longer than she knew he liked. His normally pressed suit was slightly wrinkled. But it was Finn, her Finn.

"It's me," Perri said as she flung her arms around his neck. He stiffened, uncertainty clinging to his limbs, at least until she whispered her codename into his ear. "Pythoness."

Finn grinned, the dimples that Perri loved indented into his cheeks. His blue eyes crinkled at the corners. She wanted to fall into them again like the night they met, and wanted to cling to him until his nightmares turned to dreams. She wanted to utter a thousand little words that did nothing to sufficiently convey the level of her affection. But as she pulled away, she knew they had work to do and that words would be a waste of precious time.

Introductions were quick and invitations were slipped into pockets. As they exited the closet, Finn wrapped his arm around Perri's waist. His gaze kept wandering to Najah though. As she turned to meet his stare, she noticed the man holding back tears.

"Thank you for saving her," Finn told Najah, his voice welling with sincerity.

Najah gave a small smile and a nod in acknowledgement. Perri on the other hand, barely heard him as she saw her room.

The past had come back and slapped her in the face. It shouldn't have been any surprise that her quarters would remain unchanged. But the walls were still covered in digital posters of her favorite bands. Her bed was still made up with her dozens of throw pillows, her filming station still set up exactly as she liked it. The tablets by her desk however had obviously been tampered with as they were discarded on the ground. The flowers in the vase on her bedside table had wilted. If she looked close enough, she could still make out the faint bloodstain from Anna's murder soaked into the light wood floor, her scent still faint in the edges of the room.

Moonlight poured in from her windows and danced on her skin. She needed to get out of here. She had shoved the grief and loss into the heaviest safes of her mind and continued on with life with all the practice of a starlet, but every inch of this room was an assault on those metal boxes. She tore her gaze away from her room that only seemed to echo with Anna's voice and followed Finn out the door.

The halls were devoid of their usual staff. Only their footsteps could be heard on the marble floors, bouncing off the gilded golden arches that touched the ceiling. In the corners of the halls, inset in the walls, were miniscule cameras. There would be no avoiding them, but Perri had managed to put them on a loop showing empty footage for the next hour, so they should be safe. She supposed she should have been thankful Triton was cocky. Nextulus Industries made all of the security systems put into place here by the President's own request, but since he left his company to play politics, he failed to realize many of the loopholes in his systems. All of which Perri knew how to exploit.

Elaborate scenes of the country's history were painted on the walls. The chemicals within the paint made the scenes move in a loop. The first scene was an artist's interpretation of the Three Goddesses creating Odnecus. The cloaked deities held hands around a spinning planet. Another scene depicted the Hundred Year War between the Angels and Demons. Blood continually sprayed across the battlefield, masses of bodies dotting out the sky. Perri's favorite showed the arrival of Humans and Sirens together to Sanctus. It was one of the few times in history they worked together as they strutted side by side, the sun shining in the background. Except, the colors in the scenes seemed more muted now than before, the eyes of the portraits hollow.

As they turned the corner and they left the residential wing behind, the faint sound of music could be heard. Perri slipped her hand into Finn's as they walked, hoping to steady her trembling fingers. Finn squeezed her hand but it only felt like a vice when Triton's office loomed ahead. It was in this hall that she had heard the rush of guards coming to arrest her. It was here where she had been escorted out of the Manor, into an armored car, and sent to an interrogation room. She swore she could still hear her screams bouncing off the walls.

Najah and Cambrie departed from the group as Finn opened the door to Perri's personal hell. The acid that rose in her throat burned a hole so large she clutched at it, her desperate fingers trying to cover the gap so she could take in air. But as she touched her delicate skin, she could only remember the pressure of his hand on her trachea, holding her high above the ground. Her knees quivered and gave out so she was forced to slump against the doorframe. They had washed away the signs of her, but the place looked just as it had that night. They had cleaned up the whiskey spilled on the large desk and the custom rug beneath it. Glass had been swept up from where Najah had broken through the window along the left wall. The chair that was awfully reminiscent of a throne with its high back and gilded details had been tucked into the desk. Couches that had been shoved during the fiasco had been returned to their normal spots, throw pillows straightened and fluffed. The letter opener, a gift from some Council Member, that had pressed against her heart was sitting in its stand on the built-ins along the back wall. Everything was perfect. He had scrubbed any memories of that night from the walls of the room. But he wouldn't take hers.

She could replay the moment over and over as she stood in the room, letting the emotions brew back up inside her. But she couldn't stew in them. Not yet. So she got to work, tossing open desk drawers and taking out stacks of paper with shaking hands.

"You go through those, carefully. Make sure you don't mess up the order," she ordered Belle and Ella quietly. "Finn, help me with this."

Perri pulled up the tablet built into the desk that projected a holo-gram of a screen into the air. Finn leaned in, his breath brushing her cheek. The hologram flashed, demanding password after password. But Perri, instead of giving the device what it wanted, placed another device on the side of the tablet. It changed the hologram into a fizzling screen of pink pixels. Then, Triton's unrestricted files were copied onto the device. Every piece of information he had ever stored: files on Egg experiments, Alcorium updates, blueprints of the CareFree plants, it all was in the palm of her hand. The weight of it made her breathless, her heart trembling.

"Is this all of it?" she asked Finn quietly.

"That and those papers," Finn replied, surveying the other two women who were busy taking pictures.

"Then stay here and help them. I-I have to see my mother." There was a desperation that clung to her like the tears of a newborn. Perhaps it was the list of sins that she held in her hands that made time feel so much more precious.

"That wasn't in the plan," Belle spoke up as she gestured to the piles of papers around her. "Besides, we have all this to go through."

"You can't go babe," Finn sighed. "She's already in the ball. You'd be risking getting seen by everybody."

"But-" Perri knew they were right, and the words died in her throat. She slid the device full of files in her dress, pressed against her heart. "You're right." She cleared her throat before calling out to the sisters. "How are you doing over there?"

"They have less on us than I thought they would, but they still know about us," Ella said. She hoped the pictures she was taking were coming out readable. "There's another group they're watching called the Horsemen, which I think they're more concerned about."

"I feel like I've heard about them. I don't know where though. Whatever. I'll figure it out later," Perri said.

"They seem pretty nasty. They're some supremacist-" Belle stopped as she heard footsteps from outside the door.

Everyone clutched papers to their chests as they bolted towards hiding spots. The door handle jiggled as if someone was unlocking it. Finn and Perri ducked beneath the desk. Ella and Belle launched themselves behind the couches.

A thud shook the door, voices from outside harmonized in drunken laughter. It was jovial and familiar in the way that the warm embrace of summer should be. But it moved on too quickly, the bluesy quiet setting in once more.

"That was close," Ella breathed as she got to her feet.

Perri exhaled and brushed stray hair from her cheeks. "Yeah, too close. Let's hurry up."

Ella glanced down to Belle and held out her hand to help her up. But Belle's eyes were welded to the page on the ground. She made no move to stand. Her chest shuddered.

"Belle? What's wrong?" Ella asked as she crouched down to look at the paper.

The wind was knocked from the girl's lungs as she saw the words. It was as if cold water had been poured on her head and froze right around her brain. The ice slipped into her muscles and veins. She couldn't move, couldn't think. It was her fault. Her fault.

"What's wrong?" Perri asked as she strode across the room towards them.

"The resistance...they're gone," Belle whispered. "They slaughtered the members of the Saybrim Resistance."

## Twenty-Eight

# The Words of Kings and Thieves and Everyone in Between

### CW: Mentions of slavery

"My deepest condolences for your daughter."

The words bounced through the lounge only to be met with silence. It scratched its nails along the glass of the ceiling. Moonlight poured over the leather lounge chairs and liquored lips. But then, chuckles and the clinking of glasses filled the room with a ruddy warmth.

Despite the violins and laughter that could be heard from outside, Triton didn't worry about his absence. Control flowed between his arsenic fingertips as he took his place before Ahitophel. He lifted bourbon to his lips. As he bathed in the signature of the self-indulgent booze, he rolled his shoulders. The nightmare black of mourning that his tailor had designed pooled around him like a shield. His skin was like the dark sands of time that latched into the crevices of each visitor, impossible to get rid of completely; his very presence unmistakably timeless. No, nobody would miss his presence for the moment. Not tonight.

Ahitophel had disregarded the traditions of the night by not concealing his face with a mask. Had it been anyone else, Triton would have had them thrown from the ball for the sheer disrespect. But, he supposed, the sweeping golden ceremonial gown the King wore would have given him away anyways. It hung loosely on his body, the sleeves so large that they were nearly the size of the man's ego. The tendrils on his head were tied up with silver chains that draped down his back to his waist and tied around the gown. The garment trailed so far behind him that he had to have two young Saybrim women carry the extra fabric. They had come into the room to help him sit, and then they hastily exited without saying a word. It was far too gaudy for Triton's liking, but he remained silent on the topic.

The excavated remains of a winged beast hung from the rafters. It was a beast that used to dwarf and swallow the fiercest men whole. But Triton ensured he would conquer even the bones of the deceased, so he had suspended his prize as a chandelier.

"Goddesses help me Ahitophel, I forgot how much I appreciate having you around. This whole thing has been a disaster," Triton said. He sighed, looking towards the door, and then back to the King before him. He lowered his voice. "Fortunately, the public was perfectly receptive to the news yesterday and all of the programming seems to be working perfectly. But we still haven't caught up with her and that degenerate group of hers since that little incident in Sanctus. To be honest with you, if Perrianna had any critical thinking skills, she would've just kept her mouth shut. This benefits us, it benefitted her. I don't understand why she was so upset about it. And people are happy, I-" After receiving a seething look from the Saybrim sitting before him, Triton quickly corrected himself. "-we, I mean-make people happy, happier than they've ever been. There is no nobler pursuit than what we're doing."

"Yeah, I don't understand it. You clearly gave her everything. Some people just don't align as they should, I suppose," Ahitophel muttered into his glass. Then he looked up, meeting the man's gaze. "How is Elisa taking the news?"

"She's barely even noticed," Triton smirked, his legs spread out as he leaned forward over the coffee table. "I understand your hesitations about marriage...but let me tell you, you give 'em a ring," he pointed to his head, "and that bitch is only good for two things."

Ahitophel's nostrils flared and his lips raised for a moment, eyebrows lowering. Then, his lips raised into a smile, he cocked his head to the side, and he raised his glass. "Truer words have never been spoken."

"But we should get onto business, I suppose. We have to ramp up CareFree production significantly. Did you get the opportunity to read the re-negotiations I proposed about our trade agreement?"

"I did, but I have some amendments I'd like to make. I understand you need the blood for production of CareFree, but I'd like to make an example of some of the Resistance members. So I'd like to keep the ones who are on this list," Ahitophel handed over a piece of paper to Triton, then continued. "In exchange for your assistance with this little issue, as long as you're able to deliver on what was originally promised, I'm going to open the second donation bank as well as institute the banning of all creative arts in schools, and lower the age of service."

"I can promise you in-"

A faint knock at the door interrupted them. A young servant poked into the room, her hands shaking as she bowed. "I'm so sorry for intruding, but there has been an incident that-"

Triton held up his hand. "Is this truly urgent? I told you I was in the middle of this meeting."

"Yes, it should only take a few moments sir." Her voice wavered as she stared at the floor, refusing to look at either man in the room.

Ahitophel waved his hand. "Take care of it, Triton. We can finish up this discussion later."

With that, Triton stormed out the door, the tail of his suit jacket swishing behind him. He followed the servant, hissing orders at her as they walked. But before Ahitophel could do a thing, Elisa slipped into the room.

"Hello Toph," she said as she glided across the room.

"Elisa, what are you doing here?" The man asked as he stood, confusion written in the lines of his face.

"I needed a moment to myself," she said. "These events are always overwhelming, and I swear, nothing can dull the noise for me." She raised a hand to her temples, hand brushing over her Alcorium, eyelids nearly closed. Through her eyelashes, her gaze darted towards the cameras hidden amongst the bookshelves.

She resisted all temptations, bit back everything that echoed around in her head, and remained opposite of the man before her. She picked up her husband's liquor glass from the table, refilled it, and downed it all in a single gulp, then stared at Ahitophel. Her gaze ran down his body, lingering longer than appropriate. Not that he wasn't doing the same.

"How are you finding the party?" Elisa asked, resting her arms over the back of the armchair, pushing out her chest. She let her hair fall over her shoulder.

"It's lovely, as always," Ahitophel murmured. He sipped on the liquor in his glass. "You always put on the most beautiful events."

"Thank you. Although, I can't help notice that you never bring a guest to any of them. You know that they would be welcome here with you, right?"

"I appreciate the offer Elisa. I suppose I just haven't found the right person to accompany me," Ahitophel said, hiking up the gown around him as he walked closer to her.

"Maybe one day you'll find them." Elisa smirked as she stood up, letting her mourning gown fall around her. The black accentuated her curves, the diamonds around her neck a sparkling noose. In her stilettos, she stood taller than the man before her. Her perfume lingered between them, the scent of sandalwood and frankincense heavy in the air.

"You know, I've been looking forward to our next dinner. The last one was delightful," Elisa purred, letting her hand linger on his shoulder. "We should have one again soon."

"It was perfect. Next time, you should bring some of that dessert that you always talk about making."

"I will, just for you," Elisa smiled coyly.

"But, I suppose I should leave. I need to get back. Besides, I would really hate for there to be... rumors." The last word stuck to her full lips as she turned to leave.

"Elisa, wait-" Ahitophel reached out for the woman. She paused, brow raised, as she took a step closer to him. Her hand brushed the fabric of his gown, her fingers finding the edge of his pocket in an instant. She left her mark on him. "Please, accept my deepest sympathies for your loss."

And with that, Elisa nodded and reached the threshold, disappearing into the party once more. But as Ahitophel remained behind with a drink in hand and fingers in his pocket. He didn't think to look upwards towards the rafters.

A live band was playing a rather moving rendition of one of their most popular songs as Najah and Cambrie slipped into the ballroom after dusting themselves off from the rafters in the study. They exchanged wordless glances, not daring to discuss what they had seen amongst the swarms of politicians and celebrities. Fortunately, they went unnoticed in the crowds. This was, after all, the social event of the season. It was the time for a parade of wealth, the exchange of business cards, and clandestine meetings.

Everywhere they looked, there was the glow of Alcorium rings from beneath coils of hair. On every wall were dozens of guards, even more stationed high in the balconies above. Even though Cambrie had shifted, the risk of discovery made their steps more purposeful, their gazes heightened.

Amongst the columned archways stood infidelity wrapped in imported silk and silver. Blackmail curled up the scrolls of the three custom chandeliers, the chains that anchored the lights to the gilded ceiling threatened to wrap around the throats of the victims unless they complied. Bribes passed through the manicured fingertips of the moving portraits on the wall. Underpaid waitstaff and marble statues alike kept their ears peeled for secrets that may prove more valuable than any sum of credits. Down the massive staircase came guests wielding their invisible daggers of their enemies' potential ruin.

Cambrie tried to control the tremors in their fingertips. They had spent so many years training for these scenarios. Yet, that training now felt lightyears away. They pulled the veil closer to their body. Their fingertips pierced tiny holes into the lace.

They snatched a drink from the waiter in the crowd and downed it in one gulp. It was too sweet, the bubbles popping in their throat. They replaced the glass on another waitress' tray as they followed Najah to the center of the room. Trails of perfume masked greed, and elaborate makeup hid people's true motivations as they walked. But as satin brushed Cambrie's shoulders, their breath hitched. The towering figures around them paid more attention to the performers hanging from silks suspended from the ceiling, but they still would've sworn spindly fingers were reaching for their throat.

Off to the side, Ahitophel had made his reappearance. His servants's heads dipped to avoid taking in the extravagance around them. The King paid no mind to the crowd forming over in the side room. His people milled about the velvet couches, donning rented ribbons and needles in their veins while wealthy patrons mixed the blood in blue vials provided to them. An extra potent shot of CareFree combined with the gentle touches of the Saybrim "attendants" were nothing Ahitophel hadn't seen before. Yet, he didn't indulge. Instead, he brushed past them and found himself enclasped in another Council Member's handshake.

Cambrie had watched the man with his casual cruelty pass by the suffering and felt the nausea in their stomach. He was a monster, but not the monster of tonight. So instead they bit their cheek until blood filled their mouth. They hadn't even noticed the glass in their hand until the chilled wine washed away the blood. Najah raised her eyebrow.

"How are you doing?" She kept a careful watch out of the corners of her eyes for both her target and her friend. She saw the drink, the frantic look in their eye, the increase in breath.

"I'll be fine," Cambrie muttered. It was a lie and they both knew it. But maybe they could stave off the panic until they were out of here.

"We can leave," Najah said. She turned to Cambrie, meeting their eyes. She lowered her voice. "You don't need to pretend with me."

"I'll live." They downed the remainder of their drink. "This is a special night after all."

"But-"

The Halfling forced a smile at their partner, shaking their head. They were sure to choose their words with care. After all, there were far more listening ears than just those of the guests. "Darling, come on. You wanted to come here, and we haven't even had a single dance."

With that, Najah conceded and held out her hand as the song changed. Cambrie accepted and placed a hand on her shoulder. Najah held Cambrie's waist and began leading them through the motions. They moved together like the ocean, gliding as one through the crowds like the crest of a wave. The jewels that blended together around them couldn't hold a candle to the beauty between them. Among the pulsing beat, Najah stared into Cambrie's eyes which shimmered like freshly fallen snow. Najah could see beneath the disguise they wore with ease, their beauty interwoven into their very DNA. Cambrie found the calming respite between her hands while they admired her. She was lightning, striking, illuminating, and deadly gorgeous.

It was in the breaths shared between them that tangled together in something far more intimate than either could have imagined. Their bodies pressed closer together, the heat tickling each other's lips. Sound and sight blurred together in a vibrant harmony. A flutter of joy had taken hold in Najah's heart. As her feet glided across the marble floor, she felt a glimmer of hope at the realization that this, this is what life could be like. She had never felt anything like it. It was ecstasy. Her vigilance melted away as she found herself completely immersed in this moment. Nothing could take away the rush she felt. It was better than any drug she had ever been forced to consume. She doubted even CareFree could compare to this.

As the music began to crescendo, a Siren's silky voice soothed away any worries. Cambrie closed their eyes, just for a moment. Their heart raced and they felt as if they had stepped into the sun's warm embrace.

Sweat dripped down their back, their cheeks flushed, but for a few breaths, they smiled as they swayed. Subtle notes of champagne and chocolate interlaced in their nostrils. This was the reality they wanted. This was the moment they wanted to stay in forever, with her.

But it was just a cover. That was all this was. And as if to emphasize this point, the song came to an end. A murmur raised up over the crowd as Triton and Elisa appeared at the top of the staircase. From somewhere in the ballroom, a voice rose up.

"Now welcoming President Triton Nextulus and Lady Elisa Nextulus."

Then, as the pair descended, music began and they took the floor. The people who they had seen just moments before appeared so different now.

They had donned tiny masks, making them easily distinguishable, but Elisa appeared little more than a ghost in Triton's arms. Her gown seemed to swallow her whole. The light pink lipstick that lined her lips was untouched, her eyes lifeless. The Siren danced with a careful gentleness as if trying not to outshine her husband. Triton, trying to keep up appearances, kept his eyes in her direction, an easy smile on his face, but he seemed to see right through her. A subtle beauty was etched into her skin that was like the honey-colored glass liquor bottles that held the last dregs of celebratory bourbon-a beauty that while initially savored and displayed on the highest shelf, was completely and utterly forgettable.

Triton, on the other hand, was the eye of the hurricane. He wore calmness like a second skin, frighteningly easy, practiced. He was the pure power that nature flaunted, the dangerous alluring beauty that bloomed. Meanwhile, a simple tilt in any direction would have him wielding the chaos he created.

The other attendees began to fill in the dance floor around them. The song's tempo began to pick up once again. Najah and Cambrie joined in with the crowd, inching their way towards the spotlighted couple. If they could just get closer, then they could assess the guards, could eavesdrop on any conversation, and could potentially take a shot at the President. It was a dizzying thought. It was intoxicating. Najah could taste the adrenaline on her lips. She was so close.

But as she took the lead, they bumped into the other guests. The shadows began to swirl. Cambrie's fingers trembled ever so slightly in Najah's hand. Najah peered into Cambrie's eyes, only to find confusion and fear take hold.

The song and dance ended. As Cambrie stared over their shoulder, Najah gripped their wrist and began to pull them towards the exit.

"Okay, we need to leave," Najah hissed.

"They're here, they're here, they're here," Cambrie muttered, trembling under Najah's grip.

"Just give me five minutes love, and we'll be outta here," Najah whispered as panic bloomed in her chest. "I promise you're safe."

But the guests swarmed against them, crowding towards the President who had begun to ascend the stairs. Despite Najah's strong-arming, there were too many people to make quick progress. So, Najah stared upwards at the man, locking her gaze on the door behind him as he bowed his head, the shimmer of tears on his cheekbones.

"As many of you may know, I recently lost my only daughter in a tragic accident. I-I-" He wiped at his cheeks as his voice cracked. "I apologize. This was her favorite event. I felt it was only appropriate to still hold this event in her honor. So tonight, as we launch these lanterns to the sky, I hope you'll join me in observing her legacy. Please, pay your respects at her pyre, dedicate a lantern to her, and hold your loved ones a bit closer tonight."

The doors behind him were thrown open and through them, thousands of lanterns were laid out on the lawn. A blaze stood in the center of the manicured grass. A hologram of Perri overlooked the pyre, purple flowers reminiscent of five pronged stars with golden centers were scattered at the base. Themed cocktails and gold trimmed hors d'oeuvres were piled high among a buffet table. It wasn't a wake, but the finale in exclusive entertainment.

As Triton moved outside and the crowd followed, the guards pushed Najah and Cambrie back into the fray. On the fringes, Cambrie covered their ears as the bang of a drum cued the music to begin again. The light burned into their corneas, the shadows of the night sliding into Human forms.

Cambrie walked amongst the party-goers as shapeshifters wielded weapons and lab coats. Logic and reality were slipping away with every passing second. If they stopped moving for even a moment, the hands were going to close around their throat. Their steps had turned sloppy, and the assassin was practically holding them up as she pushed towards the edge of the party.

Najah had been too distracted, so stupid to enjoy the moment. And now the colors that had been so rare and gorgeous were too vibrant against the dark. She couldn't hear herself think against the pounding bass and grating strings. She should've been better. She should be able to get out of here. God dammit. It had been so much easier to do her job without these emotions, these distractions. If she could just find the fountain signaling the tunnel that was on the map...

At least, until she bumped into Triton Nextulus.

His face contorted as he took in the people before him. Najah was sure they looked a sight. There was nothing more she wanted to do than launch herself onto the man, wrapping her vines around his throat. But they needed to run as fast and far as possible.

He was the nightmare that haunted them every night, the reason for their scarred gums and rotting liver. Cambrie couldn't fight with him anymore and gave into the fall. Their disguise was slipping off of them, the tell-tale shimmer of a shift radiating around them.

Unintelligible noises fell from Cambrie's lips as they tried to tear away from Najah's iron grip. But Najah managed to hold her partner in place, her palm slick with rose oil. It was a desperate attempt at sedation that made sure to lodge guilt into her stomach lining. But as Cambrie went limp by her side, Najah was faced with Triton and that guilt was put aside. Her only prayer was that in the darkness, Triton couldn't tell Cambrie was nearly asleep at her side.

"Pardon me Sir," Najah mumbled. "I'm so sorry, and I'm so sorry for your loss. This has been a lovely event, but we must get going."

Najah instantly understood his appeal. His ebony hair might as well have been a crown atop his head. His body must have been sculpted out of the finest marble by the Goddesses themselves.

As Triton took a step closer, Najah could feel the power and charisma radiating off of him. She wouldn't have been shocked if he commanded the shadows that danced in the candlelight. He approached as if he was a god amongst mortals, his gaze cast downward as if he already knew her sins. If the fist of terror hadn't closed around her throat, grounding her to this reality, Najah would have been swept away in his façade.

"Thank you," Triton murmured.

For a moment, Najah swore she was going to be let off easy.

But then he continued. "I owe you an apology as well. I seem to have forgotten your names."

Najah plastered a smile on her cheeks, thankful she had recited their alibis so many times in her head. "Of course, with these masks and all, I completely understand. I'm Katrina Swiftheart, Sir. We met at the

Arayvia state dinner a few years back. And this is Alathlis Billivard, my partner. But, we really should be going. We have to get back to the sitter."

Triton's eyes narrowed as he stared at the pair but he nodded. "Of course. It was nice to see you again Katrina. I'm looking forward to our next meeting."

He stepped back into the shadows to play mourning, allowing Najah to force Cambrie ahead. She was hyper-aware of the guards staring at her as she left, feeling their invisible blades in the small of her back. Cambrie's shuffle echoed against the melody. But with each step Najah felt she could breathe.

Except, the President turned once more, his eyes piercing Najah's back.

"Katrina, it wasn't the state dinner we met at. It was the Triple W Convention."

## Twenty-Nine

# TIL YOUR DAD'S DEATH DO US PART

"Shit," Finn hissed as he glanced at his communicator. "There was some kind of incident. I have to go." He started to gather up the papers and shoved them into Perri's hands.

"What kind of incident?" Perri asked, her eyes wide.

"I don't know, I just know there's two guests involved. I'm supposed to be there. Can you get out of here without me?"

"Are they okay? It could be them! Cambrie and Najah?" Ella asked, scrambling to her feet. Air was thick in her throat, the worst of the worst thoughts stuck in her teeth like rotting bubblegum. The room spun around her. "We have to go and make sure they're okay!"

"We're not going anywhere," Belle hissed. "They're probably fine!" She set the remaining files on the desk, trying to stop her fingers from trembling. The Resistance was dead. They were slaughtered in cold blood. They couldn't possibly all be dead. She shook her head as if it would clear the thoughts lingering there. She had to push through the fog of heartbreak.

"Yeah, we'll be fine getting out of here." Perri swallowed hard as a knot formed in her stomach. She shoved the files back into their respective spots. "Just, be safe okay?"

Finn gave a small smile and leaned down to kiss her. It was the pastel crumbs of crushed candy hearts, brittle and fleeting sweetness on her lips. She would savor it, replay the memory again and again in her head, but it would never be enough to satisfy her. Her throat tightened as she pulled away.

"Come with us," she breathed, eyes damp. She traced her thumb over his lip to wipe away her lipstick. "Please."

"You know I can't. I can't abandon my family." He took a step back, shaking his head. It was the denial she knew was coming, but still shattered her heart.

"Please Finn. If they find out that you helped us they'll kill you." Mascara ran down Perri's cheeks as she reached for his hand.

"I have to go." Finn began to pull away but then stopped, reaching inside his jacket pocket. He pulled out a simple gold band with a sapphire inlaid in the center. It was tiny in his fingers. "Take this and know that we're going to be together again soon." He slipped the ring onto Perri's finger. "No matter what happens, no matter where we end up, I promise to love you every second of my life." He placed a kiss on her forehead and turned away as if scared that if he stayed a moment longer he would stay forever in her spell. "Now go. I'll take care of your friends. Stay safe."

"I love you too," Perri whispered as he rushed out the door.

A sinking feeling settled in her gut, anchoring her to the floor. She shouldn't have let him go. She should have forced him to stay. But as much as she wanted to consume him whole so he'd always be a part of her, she couldn't be so greedy.

Belle cleared her throat loudly, knocking the Siren out of her thoughts. Perri wiped at her cheeks, then turned to Belle and Ella who were already at the door.

"Let's get out of here."

They hurried down the halls, the journey seeming to take longer than when they had arrived. The colors blurred together with each anxiety-provoking step.

"Are we sure they're okay?" Ella asked as they entered the closet once more. "What if they really need our help?"

"Finn has it under control," Perri muttered, playing with the ring on her finger. She traced every detail of his face behind her eyelids to store in her memory. Just in case.

"They're dead, they can't all be dead," Belle muttered as they entered the tunnel. It seemed so much darker, so much more ominous. "I can't believe they're all dead."

"They're not," Ella said with too much confidence. Denial. "They're smart. They're probably just hiding somewhere. We haven't even read through the whole file yet. It has to be wrong." She took off her mask and rubbed at her eyes, messing up her makeup.

Perri stayed silent, letting the cool air of the tunnels chill her skin. The ring weighed heavy on her finger. He was risking everything for her, and she hadn't even thanked him. She hadn't even thanked him.

The guards watched her closely as Najah dragged Cambrie into the car she hailed. She climbed into the backseat-the driver's seat was empty. The steering wheel moved by itself as the car pulled out of the driveway and drove down the busy city streets. Music from a nearby bar did nothing to dampen the thoughts in her head. She had so many unanswered questions and the possible answers only left her with more questions.

As they slowed to a stop at a light, Najah peered out the window. People stumbled between the bars and restaurants, their colorful faces glittering as they stared at the lanterns above. Perrianna stared down on them in an advertisement, selling her face as her funeral raged on. The Sirens that were done up in luxury stepped over the homeless Humans that sat along the sidewalk, unmoving. They didn't even notice them. They were all too busy with the screens in front of their faces.

Najah glanced towards Cambrie, who stirred against the window. They let out a sigh in their sleep. She tore her gaze away, hating how the sight of them made her stomach flutter. She had been stupid. She had put all of them in danger. She shouldn't have been distracted. It was a mission, nothing more. But as they passed by a dilapidated toy store, she couldn't help but smile at a stuffed bear wearing a pink shirt in the window. There was something childlike about the joy she had felt tonight. She had been the child in the toy store. It had been wondrous. But still, she had been stupid.

As the car pulled off into a more secluded street and parked, Najah stared up at the warehouse. It had been a little over an hour ago that they had arrived here and taken the tunnels to the Manor. But the night felt so much darker now. She had such little news to bear to her companions and so much guilt weighing on her ribcage.

"Cam, c'mon," she said quietly. "We're here."

Cambrie stretched and opened their eyes. They blinked a few times in an attempt to clear the sleep from their eyes. A yawn tore from their throat.

"Where are we? What happened?"

"We're at the warehouse. We're meeting up with the others now. C'mon. Let's get inside before anyone sees us. I'll explain later."

The pair hurried into the abandoned warehouse after the assassin entered an elaborate passcode. Urine had replaced the champagne that had flowed so freely just hours before. Najah, while used to worse conditions, certainly didn't want to know what squished beneath her feet. The lack of windows only added to her racing heart, the large boxes and old machines scattered around the room giving too many hiding spaces. The only saving grace was the lack of cameras here, the devices having been ripped from the walls.

She kept a watchful eye on Cambrie who was paler and slower than normal. The flame they had tried to ignite flickered out, leaving them in darkness. They hung their head, the scurrying of a large rat made them jump. They stared too intently at the graffiti on the brick walls as if they couldn't quite recognize the space they were in despite walking through this very spot earlier.

"It's okay. You're safe," Najah whispered as she pushed open a metal door. It screeched in protest. She held it open for Cambrie.

"What happened? I don't remember how we got here."

"You had an episode at the ball." Dripping water echoed through the narrow hallway lined with barren metal shelves. The cement was slick beneath Najah's feet.

"No," Cambrie whispered. They buried their face in their hands, looking up at Najah through their fingers. "Did I make us...What did I do?"

"It's okay. I should have recognized what was happening sooner. But we got out okay, that's what's important. I just had to sedate you at the end with my oil so we could get out."

"Did we get everything?"

"Mostly," Najah nodded. "We got some intel, but Triton got interrupted in his meeting so we didn't hear everything. Elisa had her own meeting with Ahitophel so that was a surprise. But we did bump into Triton at the end and things got a little dicey, so I ended up sedating you to get out of there without confrontation." Najah said gently. "But we got out and we're okay now."

"No, no, no!" Cambrie slumped over against the wall, looking completely defeated. "What do you mean? What did I do?"

"We were dancing and I was trying to get closer to Triton. I noticed you were starting to have an episode. We should've just left at the first signs. But when we were leaving, I was just trying to find the quickest and easiest way out, which ended up being outside where the lantern lighting was. I ran into Triton. You were already starting to repeat yourself and shake and stuff, and then you started trying to shift back, so I sedated you. Triton was suspicious of us, and had the guards watch us to make sure we left. But we're fine. We got out."

"Goddess. I could've gotten you killed. What is wrong with me?" They kicked at the wall and dug their nails into their palms so hard that they bled.

"It's okay. We got out of there safe. We're fine." Najah felt the urge to embrace Cambrie but refrained. She looked over her shoulder at the door that separated them from the tunnels. There was no sign of the others yet.

"How can you be so okay with this? Why aren't you angry at me?" Cambrie's eyes shone in the darkness. They gripped Najah's wrist hard. "I could've gotten us killed! I could've gotten the others...oh Goddess are they okay? Where are they?"

"They'll be here soon." Najah gazed into the Halfling's eyes. "I'm not angry at you because none of this is your fault. You can't help it."

"Belle and Perri were right. I'm a liability, I shouldn't..."

"Stop." Najah's voice got lower as she shook her head. "We're a team. We all have things we need to work on, but that doesn't make you a liability. You have helped us so much, and more importantly, you're our friend. You have every right to be here. I think-"

Najah and Cambrie both snapped to the ready as they heard footsteps from the other side of the door. Cambrie shook, their palms sweaty. Najah stole a glance towards them and whispered a prayer that it was just the others.

The door opened slowly as Perri stepped into the hall. She had shifted back to her true form, her eyes red. The others stood gripping their shoes in their hands, leaning on each other, shoulders slumped.

"What happened? Are you all okay?" Perri asked, her voice tired. She stared at Cambrie, as if she knew that the answer would fall from their lips.

But Najah spoke up, however, letting a smile grace her face. "Yeah, we're fine. Unfortunately Triton's still up and walking around, but we got some intel from his meeting before it got interrupted. Did you get anything?"

"We got everything," Perri said.

Belle muttered something under her breath that even Najah couldn't hear. Cambrie shifted back into their true form, staring diligently at the cracks on the floor.

"Good," Najah said. "Anything helpful?"

"We still have to go over a lot of the files," Perri said as she walked towards the entrance of the hall. She wrinkled her nose as the smell of urine reached her nostrils.

"The Resistance is dead," Belle murmured.

"We don't know that!" Ella cried. "We haven't read the whole file yet!"

"Oh shit," Najah said, unsure of how to respond.

Everyone remained silent as they followed Perri out into the main room. Every unaccounted for noise set them all further on edge. They stayed close to each other as they hurried out of the warehouse.

"Did you see my mom?" Perri asked quietly.

"Yeah," Najah replied, shifting her weight between her feet. She really wasn't sure how to deliver the news.

"How was she? Did she look okay?"

"Uh, yeah, she looked fine," Najah grumbled. "But-"

Just then, the SUV rolled up and Perri smiled, cutting off Najah. She didn't need to hear any 'buts' tonight. If she was alive and well, she needed the fantasy.

"Well, I'm glad she's safe. We're going to have to find a new place to stay tonight," Perri said as they arrived at the SUV. She opened up the door to the passenger seat and hopped in.

Everyone else stumbled into the car, the adrenaline finally settling in their bodies. They all longed for rest but they knew they were too on edge to think of sleep. Amongst the luxurious fabrics and makeup, loss settled in between ribs and coursed through veins. Loss of friends, of love, of trust. And while they had run out of tears, the tears on their souls just ripped deeper with every moment of silence.

## Thirty

# We Are the Novulan and We Are Never Getting Back Together

"I feel like we need some kind of superhero squad name," Ella said in an effort to lift everyone's spirits.

She took a handful of gummy robots and shoved them into her mouth. She had hoped the sweetness would take away the bitterness in her mouth, but it did little to help. She needed respite from the melancholy air hanging around the room, a distraction. She needed hope. *The Resistance couldn't be dead. They weren't dead. They weren't.* She would refuse to believe it.

The group was running low on credits for luxuries- and this new motel they had found smelled of old laundry and sweat. When they had moved the furniture to check for anything that could creep on them, they had found quite a few insects. It only added to the feeling of something creeping along her spine. She tried to push that thought far from her mind.

"I mean, what are they calling us anyways?" Ella rolled her chair over to where Belle sat on the bed, reaching for the camera that she held. Belle sat still, staring at the same report that told of the rebellion's slaughter. Ella tried to pry the camera from Belle's hands but her sister held tight.

"A group of escaped convicts with intimate knowledge of the inner workings of the Odnecus government," Perri responded, her voice deadpan.

She stared at her ring for a moment before sighing, letting her hand fall back onto the arm of the faux leather chair. The air was cool on her bare skin as she curled her legs to her chest, her gown feeling much tighter around her body. Still, she didn't want to get up and change. Doing so would mean discarding pieces of tonight-wiping Finn's kiss off her lips, and washing his touch off her hand.

"It really doesn't have a good ring to it, does it?" The Siren leaned back in the chair, letting her head dangle off the back. She closed her eyes only to be greeted with the memory of Anna's corpse, nearly dismembered.

Her beauty had been brutalized by the hands of man. Her lifeless eyes, her mouth opened in a scream. It was a macabre monster's dream and Perri had been meant to find her. It had been a punishment. She jolted up, catching Ella's attention. The girl tilted her head, silently asking what happened. Perri took a breath. She needed to think of something else.

"We could have a cool name like the 'Horsemen,' only better."

"You did not just say a racial hate group has a cool name," Najah groaned, glaring at Perri. She looked towards Cambrie who was sitting on the bed beside her, silently pouring over all the files on the camera in an attempt to redeem themselves. Guilt nagged at Najah's stomach.

"Hey, I don't support what they're doing, but it is a badass name," Perri held up her hands and sipped on her water.

Najah rolled her eyes. "Whatever."

"How about the 'Freaks of Nature?'" Ella proposed.

"Absolutely not. You can call yourself that, but I'm not a freak," Perri scoffed.

"Belle? Cam?" Ella asked. Neither responded.

"Sorry, but no," Najah said as she stole a gummy robot from Ella. "I've been called a freak enough, I don't need to call myself one." As the gummy passed her lips, her face lit up. She had never had candy like this before. The sweetness danced on her taste buds, the texture surprisingly satisfying. As she contemplated the candy, she tried to think of a name for the girl's wishes. She paused, her mind wandering back to the bear in the toy store window. "What about the Novulan?"

"Like the fairytale?" Ella inquired. Najah leaned over to steal another piece of candy from where it sat on Ella's lap but the girl wrapped her arm around it protectively.

"Yeah," Najah grinned, knowing the girl's fixation on ancient mythology and fairytales would have her understand why.

"Oh, you mean the movie! Yeah, that was my favorite as a kid! I always cried when all the animals finally came together and worked together to take down the King to save their resources and the world…Wait, is that why you suggested it?" Perri smiled.

Najah just nodded, then turned to Cambrie. "Cam," she said gently. "What do you think?"

"It's good," they said quietly, staring at a hole in the comforter.

"Belle?" Najah asked.

The Human ignored her and stood from the bed, her hands shaking. Her breath was quick and she was pale.

"Belle?" Ella asked. "You okay?"

"Yeah, whatever, I don't care what we're called," Belle said in a voice seemingly far away, ignoring her sister.

"You okay?" Ella asked again.

"I'm fine! This whole conversation is just stupid! You should be focusing on something that's actually important," Belle snapped. "Like, when are we going to make sure the Resistance is actually dead? When are we going to kill Ahithophel?"

Everyone exchanged looks and Ella's shoulders fell.

"I don't know that it would be the smartest idea to go to Kolasi right now," Najah said gently. "They'll be expecting you to run there, and..."

"Maybe if you would've been decent at your job tonight, we could know what Triton was planning!" Belle snapped.

Cambrie began to speak up, but Najah spoke over them. "I get it. It sucks that you lost people. You're hurt. But as we've all said before, lashing out at us doesn't help anyone."

"I just..." Belle buried her head in her hands before hissing in resignation. "Fine, then what brilliant plan do you have?"

"We need to get out of here, first of all. We're not far away enough from Zerephil. I say we break out the people from the Egg and then they can help us destroy the CareFree plants."

"Yeah, that seems like the best option right now," Perri said. "We can also have them help us infiltrate the Alcorium building so that I can corrupt their system and destroy the programming."

"But what if the Resistance isn't actually dead?" Belle asked, face hardened. "They could be useful."

"They could, but-" Najah began.

"Not if they're dead," Perri said. "We only have so much time and-"

As Ella swatted Perri on the arm, Belle stormed off into the bathroom and locked the door.

*They're dead. They can't be dead.* She had already lost her dinner to the porcelain bowl, and the sweat that poured down her face chilled her to her bones. Her lungs still ached as her heart returned to a slightly slower pace. Her fingers shook as she cupped water to her face and massaged her cheeks. Her sinuses drained down the back of her throat.

*They're dead.*

As the others laughed in the other room, she slid down the bathroom wall. She couldn't stay here with them. She needed an escape from this. She needed to surrender.

So Belle stood up from the floor and fixed her makeup, layering on borrowed lipstick and concealer to put on a façade. She pinned her hair back up and adjusted her dress. Then she emerged from the bathroom. Heads turned and the conversation about the night paused as she crossed the threshold. Without a word, she left down the hall, leaving the group behind.

Belle had seen her earlier with her snake-bitten smile, ripped tights, and faded purple hair. Well, *ran* into her would have been more accurate. On the desperate search for lipstick that would prevent a meltdown from Perri, Belle had been sent to search the motel and the surrounding shops for a match. But in her hurry, she collided into a woman whose tattoos crawled up her legs and around her forearms in blooming florals and fungi. The stuff in her arms went sprawling to the floor. As Belle helped her pick up her belongings, the woman introduced herself. Nyx, that was her name. After hearing about Belle's mission, Nyx then slipped a tube of lipstick and a room number into the Human's fingertips with a smirk, with the promise to see her soon.

So now, in search of a distraction, Belle stood on the motel doorstep, fiddling with the lipstick in her palm. As the door opened, Belle's heart faltered. Nyx was the poetry in the ink-stained diaries of her ancestors, her innermost thoughts laid bare in the doodles of the margins. She was gorgeous, but more importantly-intimidating-ly-held a world of stories in her umber eyes. The thread of the Fates had to have been woven into her veins, for the way she suddenly took Belle's breath away and became her destiny was ethereal.

In black lipstick and lace that covered up the raised lines on her brown skin, she welcomed Belle into the room that seemed so different from her own. Patchouli and lavender filled the air in a dizzying aroma.

"Here, this is yours," Belle said, her mouth suddenly dry. She placed the lipstick in Nyx's open palm.

"Thanks, but you should keep it. It looks better on you," Nyx's gaze flitted down to Belle's lips in the dim lighting. She took her time letting her eyes rake over the fitted gown before taking Belle's hand and gesturing towards the bed. "Go ahead, sit, make yourself comfortable."

Belle bit her lip, her cheeks warming. She sunk into the bed, trying to ignore the lump in her throat. Nyx sat beside her, their thighs touching. She was too aware of the warmth between them.

"You're gorgeous," Nyx said gently, placing her hand on her guest's knee. "Did you have a good evening?"

Belle hesitated, staring at the hand on her leg, then into the woman's eyes. The lie was thick on her tongue. "The best. Although, I would've preferred it if you were there."

She suspected that Nyx saw right through her lie but was too polite to say anything. With her lips pursed into a small smile, the woman nodded. The lavender tattoo along her fingertips danced as she traced a pattern along Belle's skin. Her breath was warm along the delicate skin of Belle's neck, causing the hairs to stand up along the Human's spine.

"What is it that you want, darling?" In her ear, Nyx left unspoken promises behind like a trail of stardust.

"You," Belle breathed, her stomach flipping. "I want you."

Nyx swung her leg over Belle's waist. Her hand rested on the back of Belle's neck, the other on her cheek. She was gentle, sweet, her lips tasting of pure rain and cool amber. Her body fit like a missing puzzle piece as she pushed Belle backwards onto the bed.

But as Belle closed her eyes, Nyx only felt cold and heavy atop her. Her heart faltered and her breath hitched as an onslaught of bloodied images flashed before her eyelids. She tried to push them back, and took a breath, kissing Nyx back. She wanted her. She wanted this. She wrapped her legs between the woman's, reaching up to pull her closer. She tried to lose herself in the silk slipping from her body, the gentle kisses on her collarbones, the desperation between them.

But the night was already filled with so many shadows, and she couldn't shake the words she had read. In this room-at no fault of the woman before her-she couldn't help but watch the corners and wonder what other horrors the night might bring. She didn't even notice when Nyx stopped and clambored off of her shaking body.

"Are you okay? What's wrong? Did I go too far? I'm sorry. I didn't mean-"

"What?" Belle asked, her words breathy. "No, no, it's not you, there's nothing wrong. You can keep going-"

Nyx raised her eyebrow, shaking her head. "You're crying."

"Shit, sorry," Belle sniffed, wiping at her eyes.

"Are you okay?" Nyx asked again as she adjusted her top and stood from the bed. She offered a tissue to Belle. "We can just talk, or if you need space, you can go, no hard feelings."

"Really, I'm okay," Belle said quietly as she wiped at her face with the tissue. She stood, bunching the paper in her fist and slipping the dress back over her shoulder. How would she ever explain to this woman the massacre she had learned about? How could she ever explain the truth? So, instead, the lie of 'okay' would suffice. "Really, it's not you. I promise. You seem great. I'm just in my own head tonight. I should go though. I'm sorry."

A faint nod left the woman behind in her room and Belle in the chilled moonlit air. She choked back her sobs, her hands on her head. She wandered along the parking lot in search of answers to her unanswerable questions. She kicked at a lightpost, welcoming the blunt pain that shot up her foot. She kicked it again, then again. The tears streamed down her face. And for a moment, as the light flickered out above her and hid her cheeks, she welcomed the darkness.

Ella had since stolen all of the cameras and was pouring over them under the covers of the bed. She laid out, pillow atop her head to block out the noise from the others, and was trying to find hope somewhere in the stolen text. Perri, on the other hand, sang while doing her seventeen step shower routine.

Najah and Cambrie had stolen away outside and sat on the curb. The stars twinkled above in fully formed constellations. The lanterns from the ball were still visible amongst them if one were to squint hard enough.

"How are you doing?" Najah asked, her voice soft. She rolled a pebble beneath her foot, her body turned towards Cambrie.

"I'm doing better," they said, giving a small smile. "Thank you, again, for everything tonight."

"Of course. You're my friend." Najah paused before continuing. "I was wondering though, how are you doing with, uh, Belle." Her eyes wandered towards the other block of motel rooms where she had seen Belle wander off to earlier.

"I'm just worried about her. She's not doing too well. I feel bad, but... I just wish we could have some space. Being this close to each other isn't great for either of us. But whatever. We've gotta do what we've gotta do." They scooched closer towards Najah. "You made this whole night bearable, you know. It might not seem like much but without you-"

"I had a great time," Najah said, her thigh brushing theirs. "It made me wish it had been a normal ball and not some mission. Goddess, the things I would do for one normal night."

"I don't think people like us get normal," Cambrie chuckled.

"You're right. We don't get normal. We get the monsters, the death, the tragedy that would drown anyone else. We don't get the storybook endings. But that doesn't mean we can't find some semblance of happiness in between the chapters."

A silence fell across the pair as they listened to the noises from the cars and the rooms behind them. They were both trained to never let their guard down, to never form attachments, to stay ever vigilant. But maybe, here in the darkness, they could forget for a moment.

"Oraësiana, I think I lo-"

Najah cut them off, breathless. No one had said those words to her, and they had to mean something. "Cam, please, I'm not that special."

And she was right, not because she wasn't special, but because she was far too remarkable a woman. Because love was too simple a phrase, too easy to fumble off the lips of a reckless ingénue.

Couldn't she see? It had always been them, they and she, she and them, together, as some fantastical, primordial legend. And if they were asked to describe her for the books of scripture, Cambrie would be rendered speechless, for no words could begin to adequately encapsulate the stardust woman who had shot into their life once more.

"No, I don't think, I know. I know I love you Najah. I'm sorry if that's too much, I just-"

Najah's lips crashed into theirs. The air was pulled from both of their lungs. Deep in both of their hearts they both knew that they were playing with fire. Crossing this line so soon was reckless. But the rose that lingered and intermixed with smoked wood was intoxicating, and the breathless desperation that fluttered in both of their hearts made the giant red flag look like a Love Day card. As one of the few lights from somewhere else in the parking lot went dark and left them submerged in a halo of pale moonlight, they couldn't help but feel the divine touch down between them. Color burst through their stained glass hearts and illuminated their bodies in a radiant glow. Even between unbelievers, it was hard to deny that there wasn't something holy between them.

But as they parted, lips only a centimeter from each other, an all too familiar voice tore them apart. She wasn't supposed to be back yet. She was supposed to be with that woman. But there Belle stood, towering over them, her makeup running down her face. She didn't smell like herself and dark lipstick clung to her like a curse.

"I should've known," she spat. "How long? How long have you two been fucking behind my back?"

"We aren't-we haven't-" Cambrie stammered as they stood. "We only kissed tonight Belle. I'm sorry, I never meant-!

"Yeah, sure! I've seen the way you look at her. You've been cheating on me ever since you two met again!" Belle was inconsolable, and as the light above her flickered, her eyes went dark. Her fists balled up at her sides. Her chest was millimeters from Cambrie's. She pushed forward. She went toe to toe with them.

"I never cheated on you! I would never do that!" Cambrie exclaimed as they backed into the wall behind them. All the bliss they had felt sunk and transformed into the werewolves of dread. Her breath was too hot on their cheeks. Her spittle landed on their lip as she spat accusations at them.

"I can't believe you'd lie to me! Tonight of all nights? When I find out all my friends died? I mean, what an absolute whore! You couldn't even wait a week to jump in her fucking pants!" Hot tears tore down her face. The acid in her stomach spilled out into her words. Her own blood was burning her. If she could have torn out her heart to stop the fire, she would have. Let them see the ashen husk that they had helped create.

"Oh, because that's not hypocritical at all," Cambrie huffed as they rolled their eyes.

"You wouldn't understand the shit I've gone through! Fuck, I should've known better than to date a fucking thief. All you know how to do is lie and make everything about your damn self! You've never once had a gram of empathy for me! You've never cared!"

"How dare you?" Najah exclaimed, her mouth set in a thin line. Her hands were on Belle's shoulders. She tried to push Belle away from Cambrie.

At the commotion, Ella emerged from the room. Her eyes went wide at the sight of her sister. Pale and tired, she approached with caution.

"What's going on?"

Belle ducked the assassin's hold and tried to land a punch. Najah grabbed her fist with a snarl. Ella stood beside Cambrie in abject horror.

"Hey!" Ella shouted, loud enough that their ears rang. "This is ridiculous! People are dying and you're fighting each other! I'm sick of it!"

Belle dropped her fists, blood draining from her face as reality came crashing back around her. Her sister's disgust imprinted inside of her brain. She was right. She was wasting her time fighting the wrong people.

"You're right," Belle muttered.

"Great," Ella said, her inflection more like a question due to Belle's sudden change of heart. "Then come back inside. I think I found evidence that some of the Resistance is still alive. We can-"

"I'm leaving," Belle interrupted, not registering what her sister had said.

"No, no, not this again," Ella said, a hysterical laugh entering her voice. "You promised me. I swear to the Mythos Belle, you're..."

"I'm leaving. I can't do this anymore." With that, Belle stormed off towards the SUV sitting in the parking lot.

"I-" Ella began, unsure of what to say as she looked at the others. "Take care. I have to go with her."

She dashed into the motel room and snatched up their bags that sat by the door. Perri stood in just a towel, looking at her through the mirror.

"Hey is something-" Perri began.

"Thanks for everything," Ella said as she rushed back out the door and across the parking lot. She pounded on the window of the car just as Belle began to pull out. "Hey! Hey!"

"Get out of the way!" Belle screamed, her voice breaking.

"I'm coming with you!"

Ella slid into the car and held on for dear life as Belle peeled out from the parking lot. Meanwhile, Najah and Cambrie watched in silence as the sisters tore down the street and disappeared from sight. After a few moments of silence, they returned to the motel room, where Perri stood at the doorway.

"So, wanna explain why they're stealing our car?"

## Thirty-One

# Tears Are Best Shed Together

The air was stifling as Belle clutched at her chest, begging the universe to rip out the carcass of her heart. The world blurred around her as she picked up speed at a nauseating rate. Forget the autopilot, she needed the control. She swerved in and out of traffic, chipping the paint on a few parked cars. Alarms screeched out curses behind them. The few vehicles driving along the road trailed behind as their automation saved them.

"Belle, please, slow down," Ella begged as she clung to the door. She closed her eyes, her stomach close to emptying on the floor. The moonlight was too bright against her closed eyelids, causing the pounding in her head to escalate with every jolt in the road.

Flashes of violence, of death, of escape all played out in front of Belle's eyes. She was done playing dress up. She was going to murder them. She needed a drink, or twelve. She needed to kill the leaders who did this. She needed to confirm that the Resistance was dead. She needed the hardest drugs she could find. She needed to finish her job.

"We can't do anything if we get pulled over by the cops! Just slow down!" Ella cried out.

The girl jammed her finger on the autopilot button, a confirmation box popping up on the screen. Belle tried to bat Ella's hand away but was too slow. The car took over and glided like butter to the proper speed, centering itself in the middle of the lane.

Belle shook in her seat as the car took over. Ella was right, but it didn't stop a scream from tearing through her body. It rattled her ribcage and left her ears ringing, her vocal cords raw and near bloody. The tears that streamed down her cheeks felt foreign but gave her a release as her vision blurred.

Ella wanted to comfort her, to say something profound to stop the pain. But nothing could take away the loss she felt when looking at her sister. How could she say anything when all the words in the common tongue would only rub more salt on gaping wounds? Everything would be hollow and meaningless. So, she cried too.

Ella mourned her losses with gasping sobs and curses to the Mythos above. She hadn't had any time to process the year, as her life had turned upside down. She had been forced to flee her life and join the Resistance she hadn't even known existed. Her unanswered prayers were left behind for a reality where near death experiences were the norm, where the shrieks of children were a haunting gospel, while reading the list of those murdered became her religious text. She had picked shrapnel from her sister's chest with her bare fingers and stood frozen as her best friend's body splattered in the dust. Then she was cuffed, branded a terrorist, and thrown in the Pit only to watch that reality play out once more. All for nothing but someone else's selfish gain. And through it all, she had put up a happy façade. If it wasn't for Belle's reassurance, it was for her own shallow hope that she could fool her brain.

She could still feel the squish of Slate's eyeballs beneath her fingers and the smoke in her lungs that swirled around like the ashes of those left behind. And when she tried to give into her heavy eyelids, she was only met with the eyes of all those children looking up at her as their reality collapsed around them too. It all gripped her in a vice so tight she swore it would suffocate her. When the bile left her stomach to congregate on the floorboard, she didn't feel any better. Instead, her hands were left clammy and cold, feeling untouchable when that was the last thing she desired.

How long Ella and Belle sat in their own wells of sorrow they didn't know-and neither bothered to ask. The silence between them was natural; sacred. At some point in their journey, the tears were replaced by solemn stares towards the dead trees outside, until they both fell off into a restless sleep.

"Wake up El," Belle said quietly, shaking her sister awake. The type of moonlight only found in the lonely hours of the morning cascaded over the sisters as they sat in the driveway of an old friend.

Ella rubbed her eyes, wiping at the eye boogers that had formed. "Where are we?" The words were thick on her tongue, despite her knowing exactly where they were.

"Alfred's place," Belle said. "C'mon. You can sleep on the boat."

Belle climbed out of the car, the cool salty breeze caressing her cheeks. Soft dirt caked the soles of her boots. It felt as though she had weights strapped to every limb as she stared at the tiny white cabin.

Her throat ached from screaming. Days of little sleep were taking their toll since the adrenaline had dissipated long ago.

Ella stumbled towards the house, fumbling with the backpack slung over her shoulder. She struggled to slip her arm through the second strap, her head pounding. Her own vomit clung to her shoes. She dragged her feet along the driveway, feeling as though she could fall asleep at any moment. She wanted to be angry, wanted to protest, wanted to tell Belle to go back to the others. She knew once they talked to Alfred there would be no going back. They would remain in the Saybrim country of Kolasi, forced to act as if these past days had never happened. But she couldn't blame Belle, and thoughts were like molasses in her brain. More than anything, she wanted to sleep.

As Belle found her footing on the creaking porch, a small light hanging on the side of the peeling siding flickered on. Her heart fluttered. She hadn't been here in well over a year, and yet it was as if this little piece of land were stuck in a time loop, completely unchanged.

The sound of slow footsteps approached the door, the familiar click of ancient locks unlocking filled the air. An Angel with graying hair and hands opened the door and stared at the sisters through the screen.

"Huh, you aren't dead. Damn. Good for you." Alfred, with zir skin as dark and tired as the midnight sky, let out a heavy sigh. "You do realize it's three in the morning right?" Ze tugged zir threadbare blue robe tighter around themselves. Ze glanced at Ella, then towards the car. "Did you kill someone? You know I don't dispose of bodies." When the pair shook their heads, ze shrugged. "Well, c'mon in I guess. This had better be good. I was having a dream about Princeton teaching me how to play the piano." Ze opened the screen door and stepped aside, muttering something about how Princeton had played a detective on the latest episode of zir favorite show.

A lanky, berry-purple creature rubbed up against Ella's ankle as she crossed the threshold. The tiny pet known as an asla looked like a cross between a ferret and an otter; obscenely adorable with stubby little legs, round head, and large nose. Its dark brown eyes rolled back with contentment as Ella reached down to pet it. It let out a little mew and licked her finger with its rough tongue.

"It's been a long time since we've had guests," the Angel said, gesturing to zir asla. "She always did love you though, El." Alfred took two steps forward into zir cramped kitchen, waving zir hand towards the dining table with a missing leg that was wedged into the corner. "Want anything to drink? I've got water....and water. Maybe I can find that teabag I brought back from my hospital trip in February?" Ze leaned heavily against the tiled counter, making it clear that ze had no plans to move.

"You know how my heart can be. The damn thing stopped for the fourth time. They say it's stress, but how can I not be stressed? They keep wanting to put one of those rings in me, but I know better." Ze sighed, tapping the side of hir head where an Alcorium would reside. "Besides, with my heart issues, and my Angel blood, they said there'd probably be some side effects. So, water?"

"We're fine," Belle said quickly.

"Sorry it's so late...or early," Ella yawned. She slumped against the wall, nearly knocking a painting of a ship off the wall.

"Yeah, if it could've waited we would have but..." Belle trailed off as a tall Saybrim man silently emerged from the hallway.

He cocked his head at the guests standing in the kitchen, one of his tendrils falling into his face. He brushed it away, sliding next to Alfred. "You're Belle right?" He asked, looking at Ella. "And you're Ella?" He gestured towards Belle.

"Actually, that's Belle, and that's Ella," the Angel said, smiling up at the man as ze corrected him.

"Oh, my sincerest apologies," the man said as he bowed his head. " I hope you'll forgive me." He held out his hand to Belle, holding her gaze. "I'm Stig, Alfred's fiancee. You probably don't remember me, but I was one of the people on 137."

After shaking both of their hands, he slid his arm around Alfred. "So, how can we help you?"

"We need your help getting across the border," Belle said.

The Angel let out a chuckle that under any other circumstances might have been considered cold or callous. But in the cramped confines of this place, it was just curious.

"Why? It's not like there's anything left over there for you, you realize that, right? I haven't smuggled anyone over that border since the last time I saw you," Alfred said.

"What happened to them?" Belle asked, deadpan. She needed to hear it in zir words.

Alfred glanced towards Ella, then towards Belle. "I guess you wouldn't know. Ahitophel dropped about a dozen bombs on the stronghold the day after you got captured. Anyone who lived through that was gunned down by both his army and S.P.A.C.E soldiers." The Angel paused, glancing towards Stig.

"There's rumors of survivors, but we don't know where they are," Stig said. "We haven't heard from anyone over there. Even Nat-" he trailed off as he stared at the floor.

"Could-" Ella began, her voice wobbly, only to be cut off by Belle.

"It was my fault," Belle said, emotionless. "I led them to the stronghold." The words fell from her lips as if they were only words on a grocery list, not a revelation, a guilt-laced confession. She had seen the date on the report. She had known it was all her fault. This was just confirmation.

"You would never lead them there on purpose," Alfred soothed.

"They knew where we were before," Stig reassured. "It was only a matter of time."

Ella slid down the wall, knees curled to her chest. Belle would never say it. She would never, no matter what, stoop that low; but they both knew whose fault it really was. Ella had been the one who snuck out with Lilles, both determined to prove themselves to their elders. She had been the one to disregard the warnings, stubborn in her insistence that she was a fully capable member of the resistance. She had walked Lilles into that trap. By the time Belle and the other Resistance members found them, tied up and bloodied awaiting rescue, it was too late. Had it been just the small camp of S.P.A.C.E soldiers waiting for them, maybe the bloodshed would have been minimal, but the convoy of military personnel just a few kilometers from that camp laid in wait for the survivors to emerge. In all of the chaos, they hadn't noticed their followers. They tried to fight. But those who weren't gathered in cuffs met their fates on the cliff's edge that day.

There wasn't room for tears in the hollowness that haunted the cavities of her body. Instead, Ella floated above herself, looking down over her small, broken form, wishing she could sink into the knotted floorboards.

"I'm sorry," Stig reached out to pat Belle's hand but she turned away.

Her eyes glossed over the menagerie of knick knacks on the wall. Old paintings, crawling ivy, figurines of some movie characters all clung to the peeling white paint. A clock as old as time itself ticked obnoxiously above the front door. But she didn't see any of it. She could only see the invisible blood stains along the wall that she had created. She swallowed hard, knowing what she had to do to repent.

"I need to go to Kolasi," she murmured, not bothering to look at anyone.

"You're sure?" Alfred asked. "It's only..."

"I need to know if there's any survivors," Belle cut them off. A lie. What boiled inside her couldn't be explained away through words. It wasn't enough anymore. She needed to feel her fingers on the pulse of her enemies again.

"We'll do whatever we can to help you," Stig said earnestly. "I owe you my life."

"Fine. Then we'll leave in a few hours when the sun rises," Alfred sighed. "If you'll excuse me then, I'm gonna go back to bed. Feel free to sleep in the living room." Ze gestured to the small room on the right furnished with a single couch, an old t.v, and a small asla bed.

"Al!" Stig said sharply. "They're our guests!"

"And I'm tired! You know I need my six hours of sleep, and they already interrupted it!" Alfred sauntered off down the hall towards the only bedroom.

Stig turned towards the pair. "I'm sorry about zir. Ze gets grumpy when zir is sleepy." Do you need anything? I can stay up with you two, maybe cook you something?"

"We'll be fine," Belle said sharply. "What should I do with the car out front? I need to get rid of it."

"I can take care of it," the Saybrim nodded, then turned his attention to the girl still sitting on the floor. "Ella, are you alright?" There was no response. "Ella?"

Ella snapped out of her trance and gasped. She blinked a few times, realizing her mouth still tasted slightly of vomit. She swallowed hard, plastering a small smile on her face. "Yeah, yeah, I'm fine. Just tired."

"Well, I'll leave you two to get some sleep. There should be some blankets in the bin out there." Stig took a few steps to the front door and gave a sad smile to Belle. "I like to think the Resistance is still out there, waiting for you two to find them."

# Thirty-Two

# Happy Endings are for the Hopeful and the Heartless

Perri stepped from the bathroom in just shoes, refusing to let her feet touch the stained carpet. The warm summer breeze from the open window teased at her wet hair and bare shoulders. The water on her bare skin had become her ritual when the world became too much to bear. At least the dirt she could wash away.

She looked on as Najah and Cambrie sat on the bed, head on shoulders, arms entangled in each other. Despite everything they had uncovered at the ball, they weren't talking about plans to take down Triton's empire, or plans to move on from this place-even though they desperately needed to. The words on their lips were of regrets and reassurances. They were distractible, disoriented, and yet, Perri couldn't blame them. She too kept glancing at the front door.

Cambrie's eyes stared dully ahead, exhaustion seeping into their limbs. They couldn't stop their thoughts from bouncing around in their skull. They hadn't meant for this to happen. They hadn't wanted

Belle to see them like that. Despite everything, they hadn't wanted to hurt her. Maybe she deserved it though. But what if she got hurt? And Ella...she would easily get blown away in Belle's whirlwind. Had she realized that she wouldn't be returning to the very group she had been so adamant about being a part of? Or had she acted on impulse to save her sister from herself, only to later realize the consequences of her actions?

"They'll be okay," Najah whispered to Cambrie for the hundredth time-although every time she said them the words seemed to lose their potency. "We can look for them."

Najah let the last group conversation they had play out in her head. The Novulan. That's what they had called themselves. A squad of heroes hobbled together against all odds. Friends, perhaps, family, even. But in mere hours, she had helped tear them apart. It had been a mistake. She wasn't made for the happy endings that Cambrie deserved.

Najah untangled herself from Cambrie, trying to ignore their questioning gaze and the cold their absence left behind. She stared at the bags packed by the door-knowing what needed to come next, but not wanting to say it. Moving on made it permanent.

After a moment, Perri spoke up, her voice soft. She couldn't meet her friends' eyes as she curled up in a white sweater, pulling the sleeves over her palms. "We don't need them. We need to go, though."

Najah held up her palm and looked at Cambrie, who then turned slowly towards the assassin. The bags beneath their eyes seemingly got darker by the second. Their breathing was shallow, and any momentary joy they had felt earlier had fled.

"She's right. We have one goal and we've already deviated from it enough. We don't need them."

There was a silent consensus as they rearranged the room and grabbed their bags. The Novulan was down to three. But before they shut the door, Najah dragged her finger along the mirror, leaving her last bit of hope behind.

## Thirty-Three

# Am I Good Enough or Am I Unforgivable?

## CW: Self harm and suicidal ideation

The safehouse couldn't quite live up to its name with its paper thin windowless walls, wooden door, and rusted over lock. But crowded in between dozens of other identical houses, it was on a street too poor and busy to keep tabs on the revolving door of neighbors each month. While the roof might have been flimsy, it would provide shelter in the safety of people just trying to make it. Belle and Ella crossed the threshold, knowing better than to look in the corners of the room. The wooden floorboards were soft beneath their feet. A single dim light bulb illuminated their grim faces as they tried to ignore the rotting smell coming from the ancient fridge.

The boat ride over to Kolasi had taken five cramped hours with both women stuffed into the storage area beneath the deck, curled up in the wet darkness. When they had arrived at the decrepit dock that the Resistance had put up years ago, far from the border security, Stig and Alfred didn't dare to step foot in the country again. Instead, they recited instructions to the house, wished the pair luck, and bid them farewell. The afternoon sun hung heavy over the mountaintops as they arrived.

Ella's stomach twisted in on itself as she hurried about the place. She was starving, her mouth dry as the dessert. Her nose wrinkled as she caught a whiff of herself-hints of old vomit, ocean water, and sweat clung to her body.

"What's our plan?" Ella asked. She rummaged through her bag to find a snack, only to find the crushed remnants of an energy bar. "Go and find the others?"

"Yeah, right after we stock up on supplies," Belle muttered. "We left most of our shit behind. You should shower though. You smell horrendous."

Ella downed her energy bar in one bite. She funneled the crumbs into her mouth, and tossed the wrapper onto the table. When her search for her clean clothes proved fruitless, she huffed, grabbed an outfit of Perri's, and headed to the bathroom. She bit back a shriek as she saw a ridiculously large spider crawling on the shower wall.

Belle ran through the maps in her mind, going through every passageway again and again. She had seen the memo on Triton's desk and tucked it away from the others. He would be at Holia House tonight, Ahitophel's palace, coming with talks of trade negotiations.

Belle slumped down in her chair, knowing she was unforgivable. The starvation, and the coverage of her scars for those who desired her; the brands and the bloodshed for those who dreaded her; the cruelty endured and dreams destroyed for those dearest to her; and yet, it was never enough. She had done it all-watched the mutilation of her mind and legacy, and they would all find her acts unforgivable. Even this, her dreamed act of repentance, would leave them spitting on her headstone. So she would go and be unforgivable once more.

She hurried around the room, searching for anything that could keep her hands busy. She was afraid that if she stopped moving again and gave herself time to think, she would second guess herself.

As Ella returned from her shower in pants that dragged on the floor, she grimaced, rubbing her eyes.

"The water is really cold and it smells like eggs. Hurry up and take yours, so we can go get some actual food. I'm starving," the girl complained.

"I'll be quick," Belle said quietly. She turned away from her sister and hurried towards the bathroom, wanting to lock herself away before she changed her mind.

"Belle, you know I came with you to find the Resistance members and to make sure you stayed safe, but I want to go back to the others when we're done. You know that, right?"

"I know," Belle said sharply, still not looking towards Ella. "And you'll see them again."

As Ella hurriedly picked through the store's kiosk to find what she wanted, Belle couldn't help but notice the way the sun peeked through the bars on the windows, caressing her sister's face. Even with a large hood shadowing Ella's face, the small smile when she picked out a package of candy was unmistakable. She bounced on her toes as the kiosk dispensed her snacks and new clothes. She ran her fingers across the soft cotton of a pair of yellow pants before shoving them in her backpack. All of the tiniest details that made up the sun to Belle's moon nearly caused her to break down then and there.

Ella forced a smile as they left the store. The air had turned dark around them, but she still played up a laugh, still poked fun of her sister's clothes. If she pretended that she was good, perhaps she could fool everybody again. Perhaps she could erase the past. Maybe they wouldn't keep dying in front of her with every breath she took because for *once* she would be good enough.

The sun was delicious on her cheeks, the wind cool on Belle's face. Ella's laughter was a melody that the animals scurried towards as flowers bloomed in the cracks of the sidewalk. It was all painstakingly, simply beautiful. And it was over much too soon.

When they arrived at the safehouse, Belle couldn't focus. Her heart had taken the place of her brain, deafening and bloody behind her temples. She nearly gagged as she tried to collect her thoughts, words failing her. Her body was a landslide, unreliable and sagging under the weight of what she had to do. She wanted to give in, but she had to follow through with her mission. She had to leave the world a better place.

"Belle?" Ella asked as she munched on a pretzel. "Belle? You okay?" The girl waved her hand in front of her sister's face.

"What?" Belle shook her head. "Sorry."

"I asked if you knew how to find them."

"Who?"

"The rest of the Resistance? Ya know, the people I've been talking about this entire time? Have you seriously not been listening to me? Unbelievable." Ella stood and brushed her hands off on her pants. "Whatever. I'm gonna pee. Maybe when I'm done we can talk?"

Belle nodded, biting back everything she wanted to say. She watched as her sister crossed the threshold to the bathroom and shut the door, unaware of anything that was about to happen.

As soon as the door shut, Belle shoved a chair under the doorknob. She snatched up the communicator from the bag and dialed the other members' number. Two rings later and Cambrie picked up.

"Ella, are you okay?" Cambrie asked, voice panicked. "Where are you?"

"She'll be fine. Remember these addresses," Belle said shortly. "The first is to a friend's place to get you into Kolasi. The second is where she is."

"Belle? What's going on? Are you okay? I didn't mean-"

"Belle?" Ella called from the bathroom. "Who are you talking to?"

Belle began to give the addresses, voice cold. "Come and get her. Look after her. Make sure she's safe. I'll make sure Triton and Ahitophel never hurt anyone again."

"Goddess Belle what are you talking about? What are you doing? Please, don't be stupid! We'll be there by tonight! Ju-"

Belle hung up the communicator and tossed it onto the table. She slipped her gun and the remaining bullets into her pocket. She could have sworn her whole body trembled as she approached the bathroom door.

"Belle! The door is stuck! I can't get out! Who were you talking to?" The fear was evident in Ella's voice, something that Belle despised.

"I have to go." Her voice shook and there was a lump in her throat.

"Go where? Belle! Where are you going? Please, let me out! You don't have to do this!" Tears streamed down Ella's face as she pounded on the door.

"The others will be here for you tonight. I have to do this, I have to end this. I have to kill them. You'll be okay, I promise. Just stay here and wait for them. They'll keep you safe." Belle's voice broke as her control over her emotions dissipated. Tears coated her cheeks. "I love you."

"You're scaring me! Please! We can do this together! We can kill them together! I promise! Please Belle!" Ella pounded harder on the door so hard the wall shook. She slammed her entire body against it.

And Belle, without a single glance backwards, fled once more.

## Thirty-Four

# BOOTS TOO BIG TO FILL

## CW: Abduction

Ella had ignored the familiar feeling that settled in her gut earlier. She had written it off as stress or grief when she looked into her sister's eyes. But no. It was just a disguise to hide Belle's plotting. Of course she would run. It was the only thing she knew.

Ella slammed her weight against the door again, letting snot run down her face. How dare she? She couldn't just leave everytime it got hard. She couldn't act as if Ella were the weakest link, the biggest inconvenience, and then pull the same stunts over and over. She was the reckless one, the impulsive one, the selfish one. Belle was everything she claimed that Ella was. And Ella despised her for it.

Ella kicked at the door. Something cracked. Her fuel was her thoughts, anxiety giving her adrenaline. Her body would be bruised in the morning but she couldn't care. Another crack resounded as she flung herself against the door. She tried once more, only to hear something clattering to the floor. One more desperate kick and the door flew open, breaking the door bolt and splintering the chair on the other side.

Ella nearly tore the front door off its hinges in her hurry. It slammed behind her as she took off down the sidewalk. The world was a blur as she searched for the familiar bob of curls, or the flash of leather boots, a footprint left behind. But Belle had disappeared without a trace, and the streets held no hint of humanity. Only the howling gail kept Ella company as rain splattered onto her cheeks.

As she determined that her search was fruitless, Ella retraced her steps to the safehouse. Every possibility pounded against her skull as she tried to think. *Belle was going to kill them. Kill them. Kill Ahitophel and who? Triton? Where? It was a suicide mission.*

She approached the door, engrossed in her own memory. She would call Cambrie back and see if they knew anything. They had to know something. They had to have been the last call Belle made.

As Ella crossed into the house, a chill crept down her spine. She shook it off, her eyes latched on the communicator lying on the table. With a throbbing head, she redialed the number from the last call still lingering on the screen. Each second had her heart picking up its pace and her stomach flipping in knots. Finally, as Cambrie picked up, Perri shrieked in the background. An upbeat mashup of a song played.

"Don't show me that! That's still my dad! I can't believe people make those videos of him! Ew!"

"Shut up!" Cambrie shouted. "Belle? Ella?" Cambrie asked, their voice breathy. "Where are you? We're on our way!"

"Where's Ahitophel? She's going to kill him!"

"Yeah, I know. He and Triton are going to be speaking at some conference at Holia House tonight. Just wait there. We'll be there in six hours."

"It's gonna be too late," Ella whispered, not needing to do the math in her head. "She'll be dead by then. I have to go. Meet me there."

"Dammit Ella, if you go-"Cambrie hissed, but the line went quiet. The communicator shut off.

Her heart sank to her stomach as she realized she shouldn't have returned here. She really needed to stop ignoring her gut. The broken chair had been shoved to the side. Despite her stillness, the floorboards creaked. And now, here she was, her closest weapon in her backpack. With a swallow, she ran for her bag.

She dove for it as a Vitare strutted from the bathroom, a smirk on his face. She whipped out the blade and held it like she had been taught, knowing now was the time to put on the fight for her life.

"Thanks for the confession, girl," he said. He rolled his eyes as Ella readjusted her grip in her sweaty palms.

"Who are you? What do you want?" she shouted. She backed up closer towards the door but he followed. "Don't come any closer!

"Don't try and fight me girl." He held up his hand and the knife flew from her palm into his.

With that, Ella tried to run. But with another flourish of his hand, her muscles weakened. She tried to move an inch but found herself paralyzed. He spun her blade around in his fingers. He crept closer until his breath was hot on her face and she could smell the harsh hospital soap that clung to him. His tattoos were similar to the curves and swirls of a brain.

She tried to kick him, to spit in his face, to pee herself, become so utterly feral and disgusting he'd have to let her go. But all she could manage to do was stare up at him as his powers tightened around her body. He stopped spinning the blade between his fingertips and used it to lift up her chin.

"Poor, stupid, little, girl. You don't even know what you've done, do you?"

He traced her jugular with the tip, pressing ever so lightly on Ella's skin. She held her breath, her heart in overdrive. Any second now she swore she would drop dead from a heart attack.

"Now I know exactly where your friends are."

Her mouth went dry. The man just smirked and pulled the knife away from her throat, slipping it into his jacket pocket.

"Don't worry though, I'm under strict orders to leave them alone and bring you in alive."

He lifted two fingers upwards, causing her to float beside him. He looked at her critically.

"Although, maybe when they're done with you, you'll wish that I had killed you instead."

## Thirty-Five

# Dandelion Seeds Aren't Sun-Kissed Wishes

## CW: Suicidal ideation

Belle only bothered to wipe the blood from her skin because it could be the difference between success and failure. She wasn't delusional enough to think that the stains would actually disappear from her hands. Not that one more life was going to matter much. Still, as Belle bent down to take the Alcorium from the caterer, she closed the woman's eyelids and murmured a prayer over her body. Then Belle stripped the woman bare, feeling bile rise in her throat. The clothes were still warm as she slipped them on.

Rain slapped at her cheeks, the alleyway doing little to protect her from the storm. The setting sun cast a glow over her as she dumped the body behind a pile of garbage. She squinted against the glare, seeing nothing but the outline of the skyline and faded stars over the horizon. No one saw her as she double checked for the weapon pressed against her hip.

Belle's breath was jagged as she pressed the Alcorium into her skull just as Perri had taught her, easily overriding the systems. With a wince of pain, the piece was secured in her skull. The guest pass was already pulled up to the side, along with a show that had no doubt been the cause of the caterer's distraction. She took a few moments to acquaint herself with the device, closing out anything that proved unhelpful. Then, she brushed off her clothes and headed towards Holia House.

The world around her sparkled in new gemstone hues and the broken buildings she had previously passed buzzed with potential. Her steps matched the beat of the song that had begun to play in her ears. But, unlike the ring wanted, it did nothing to fix her racing thoughts.

Each block she walked was another moment she was condemning to the dream realm. Her desire to wear a silken wedding gown slipped away around block two, her wish to watch Ella grow fell through her fingers at block three, her longing for children left at block five. So by the time she managed to slip into the back door with the other bustling caterers, she had relinquished those dandelion seeded thoughts to the eastern winds.

Belle slid into the shadows of the canapé trays and moved along the map in her mind. Once out of the kitchen came a bathroom, which she slid into without once tripping the watchful eyes of the guards. As she stepped inside, a painting of Ahitophel in red robes and a golden crown surrounded by an army in white linens wielding blades stared down upon her.

Upon finding the room empty, Belle pulled the Alcorium from her head and dumped it into the toilet. Then, she traced her fingers along the frame of the painting. Her breath hitched as she found the latch promised to her and the hinges creaked. The darkness of a labyrinth was revealed. She took her last glance around, then entered and closed the painting behind her.

She counted her steps as her eyes adjusted. If she was silent, she could hear the words whispered on the other side of the walls. But as she reached her destination, she could hardly hear over the pounding in her head.

In this maze meant for secret lovers and rushed escapes, she was stopped by nothing but her own thoughts. She could still turn back. But there was no life for her if she had to return to one still ruled by men like them.

So when she heard the conference begin, she pushed open the door to her hiding spot in an alcove. A statue of a fish had swiveled open. It was too gaudy for her tastes. That didn't matter though. It would be redecorated in blood soon enough.

Her footsteps matched her heartbeat. To her delight, the guards posted at the entrance to the conference room were distracted by a reporter demanding access. She was acutely aware of the gun on her hip. She opened the door. A cool breeze hit her ankles. The stolen pants were too short. Triton and Ahitophel stood at a pedestal with practiced smiles. Cameras circled them. She ran. Yelling started from behind her. She grabbed the grip from her waistband. She took her aim. Reporters screamed. She never took her shot.

As her limbs froze and she found herself paralyzed, she watched the rulers be taken to safety. A Vitare moved her fingers in the air in front of her, which forced the gun to fly from Belle's hand. Her limbs snapped together. The guards swarmed her. Handcuffs were slapped on her wrists. They didn't bother with weapons. But she so wished that she had a barrel pressed to her head.

## Thirty-Six

# LOOK! IT'S A CAR! IT'S A PLANE! IT'S A STOLEN SHIP!

## Mentions of abduction

"Yeah, the neighborhood is used to people going in and out. A lot of the residents were allies to the Resistance, back then, before the massacre. They would offer up their homes and resources, which most folks couldn't really afford to do," Stig called down to the trio waiting under the boat's floor. "So Ella should be safe there. Are you sure that you don't need us there?"

Five hours. Five hours of non-stop chattering had Cambrie ready to bash their head on the sides of the boat. They knew that these people were only being friendly, but they needed to think through every scenario their companions could be walking into.

Najah had already gone over all the plans for Holia House and the Kolasi prison dozens of times while Perri slumbered in a ball. The waiting game did little to ease the odd tension between Cambrie and Najah, the women purposefully avoiding each others' gaze. So they sat with silence between them, wishing away the minutes.

Soon the boat landed and the trio hurried towards the city. Stig had told them multiple times the safehouse was along the way to Holia House, so they would make a pit stop there to ensure that Ella hadn't changed her mind and stayed.

They had all decided a rideshare, while risky, was unavoidable if they wanted to get to the safehouse in any decent amount of time. They all tried to avoid the cameras scattered throughout the driverless vehicle, but knew full well that their faces were already being put in some database somewhere. The midnight sky seemed to mock them; each passing star seemed to scream: *"You're too late!"*

Each was wrapped up in their own nerves as they pulled up to the safehouse. The darkness here seemed too dim, too relentless, even for the thief and assassin who had lived in the shadows.

The trio pushed open the unlocked door and it was immediately an all too telling story.

The emptiness paired with the broken chair, the discarded communicator, and scattered backpack gave them what they needed to know. Najah swallowed her discomfort, the scene intrinsic in her gut. She had seen this play out one too many times. But as she made her way through the room, her mind began to piece things together. There wasn't a drop of blood for someone who left a place so obviously disrupted. It was a message.

Cambrie walked around in a daze, tracing their hands over the dusty surfaces of countertops. They peered into the bathroom, picking up pieces of wood but not looking at them.

Perri however, hadn't even made it two steps past the threshold.

"Shit," Perri muttered. "Is she-?"

"No-" Najah began, but was cut off by Cambrie rushing across the room for Perri.

Cambrie lunged for Perri, grabbing her by the collar of her shirt. They shoved her into the doorframe, the door swinging back into the wall with a thud. "Don't you dare even think that!" they hissed.

Perri held up her hands, her eyes wide. "Okay! I'm sorry!"

Najah grabbed Cambrie with one hand and pulled them away. "Stop! We know she's not dead! Look!" She gestured around the room. "Someone wanted us to know she had been taken, but they didn't hurt her. Who would want that?"

"Triton or Ahitophel." Cambrie breathed.

"Right. They probably overheard something on the Alcoriums and tracked her here or something. Think about what we know. They're working together, and they have no problem swapping prisoners with each other. I would guess that Triton would want to deal with her on Inanis soil, where he's more comfortable and has a lot more power to do what he pleases."

Cambrie took a breath, thinking it through before nodding. "That makes sense. But what about Belle?"

"They would've known about her assassination attempt before, right? If they had time to send someone after Ella?" Perri asked. "So Belle wouldn't be able to take them out. They also wouldn't kill her on the spot. That's not how they ever planned on dealing with assassins. It's too public."

"More than likely someone caught wind of it before. It could've been possible after, but I can't see how in that chaos anyone would've been able to get to Ella before we did. So if I had to guess, they're planning on taking Belle to Inanis too. Where though?"

"The Egg? That's where they have the best interrogators, if they want more information on us," Cambrie muttered.

"That would make sense," Perri shrugged. "But are we really sure about all this? What if we're wrong?"

"I don't know. What other choice do we have?" Najah asked. "It's not like we can check the news to see if there were any assassination attempts."

"I guess, if this is our best chance," Perri said, lips pressed in a small line.

Cambrie nodded. "Let's go then."

Najah snatched up the backpack from the table and followed Perri outside As they got into the car and Cambrie slid into the "driver's seat."

"Where are we going?" They asked. "We can't exactly drive there."

"Here," Perri said as she plugged in the coordinates for Cambrie. "We're gonna fly."

"I'm sorry?"

"You heard me," Perri nodded. "It's the fastest way. Besides, don't you think we deserve a better ride than this?"

The others murmured their agreement as the car hurtled down the road. The music that blared pounded against their ribs. There were words they could have said to one another, but as each one pondered with weapons in laps, nothing felt appropriate. There wasn't a language worthy enough to carry the complicated messages. Small talk was too unimportant while anything else felt claustrophobic. A declaration of appreciation felt too inappropriate for the undertones of finality it held. So instead, as they pulled onto the dirt road that held an illuminated hangar, they muttered messages of good luck to each other. They just hoped they didn't live to regret the words they didn't say.

## Thirty-Seven

# Dis Wasn't the Hell I Was Promised

## CW: Torture/medical experimentation

It was a merciless process, for she had become the sacrificial lamb under the cruel bite of man. Ella's tongue was bloodied by her own teeth and she found herself blinded by a light brighter than the hell she was in. Stripped and bound naked for their calloused fingers they had suspended her above death's gentle grasp.

Some vampiric box drank her veins dry while another pumped ill begotten life back into her. Time was illusionary in the sterile white walled cave. It could have been hours, days, or months that the coats leered over her with metallic tools of massacre. They handled her as some misbehaved animal, their laughs as she screamed were seared into her mind. Although it could have been some hallucination, somewhere in the last shreds of her sanity she doubted that even her own mind could be this cruel.

When they had finished with their games, one of them wiped away the dried vomit from her neck and chest. She stared up into his eyes, vision blurry. She wanted to speak, beg him to set her free. But the seizures had made her mind slow and the cotton in her mouth weighed a thousand pounds.

So he set to work, never meeting her gaze. His gloved hands swabbed every inch of her without a word. Then, the soft whir of his machine began to pinprick her skin. She stared up at the lights, hoping if she stared hard enough, perhaps she would go blind and be rendered useless.

"She's not ready!" A voice called from the other room. "She hasn't gotten off the table yet! She's recovering! We haven't gotten her to testing! Ma'am that's-this is a new procedure-yes, but-" The man moved too far away to be heard, for which Ella was thankful. It was one less thing to contribute to her pulsing headache. But soon, he responded again, his voice was far calmer. "Yes ma'am. You don't want the marks?" A silence followed. "Okay, then we'll put in an Alcorium and send her with you." A Siren man strode into the room and spun his finger in a 'wrap it up' motion to the man beside her. "Of course ma'am. I am so sorry for arguing with you, I don't know what came over me."

The man's Alcorium was green as he stared at Ella. She shivered as he looked over her bare body with a clinician's gaze. Her right leg, arm, and shoulder had been tattooed with the signature golden ink. And while she couldn't see what symbols swirled on her body, her blood boiled within her with an almost comforting heat.

As the tattooist began to pack up his things, the Siren picked up an Alcorium from the steel tray beside Ella's bed. She could only hear the clanking of plastic on metal but she knew what was coming. A wet cold touched the left side of her head and alcohol filled her nose. She was nearly numb to the nauseating scent of it. But her stomach still lurched. Somewhere in her there was a thought to run. She yanked her arms against the restraints but it only caused the Siren to smile.

FAYE PEREZ

"Go ahead and try to fight it, but we both know this is what's best for you."

She was exhausted. Her limbs were steel beams that took all her focus to move. She kicked a leg against the restraint, only to find herself out of breath. The man clicked his tongue.

"Now, Ella, you're going to wear yourself out," the man said as he discarded the alcohol pad. His voice was slow. "Now, you're not getting the full treatment we normally give new Vitares," He leaned over so that Ella could see him. His mustache made him look like one of those cliched villains in cartoons. There was nothing behind his eyes. "But promise me you're going to be a good girl for your new handler. I know you can do it. You're strong now."

"Where's Belle?" Ella choked out, the words like magma in her throat.

"Oh don't worry," he said as he pressed the Alcorium to her head. "She'll be in your spot very soon."

## Thirty-Eight

# THE SHITTIEST SHIRT EVER

Irony is a cruel mistress. Belle sat handcuffed to the same ship she had hijacked a year previously, her butt going numb against the grated metal floor. She had been stripped of her shoes and socks, so her feet were freezing under the chilled air conditioning. Her thighs had been chained in between the grates as a punishment for her behavior. They had her arms above her head, attached to a bar just out of her reach. Every so often, a S.P.A.C.E soldier would pass by, taunting her like a caged animal with their freedom.

They watched her like predators stalking their prey. She was almost flattered by the sheer number of them stationed to guard her, although they all knew that if she could get her hands free, she could kill them all. There were five of them sitting with her, two more up front, and another dozen milling around outside, waiting for the go ahead to close up the ship. There were faces she recognized. One she had eaten every meal with, and remembered his penchant for fish; another she knew had struggled with his aim but had a photographic memory. Another she had only seen in passing. Still, no one bothered to acknowledge her.

It was an absolute joke that even after her arrest, no one had both-ered to put a bullet in her brain. When she first arrived, she had begged for it in every way but words. Her teeth had sunk into one guard's hand when he got too close, her feet knocking the wind from another. She spat in their faces. She had called out every nasty, degrading word in the book. But all it had earned her was a bloody nose from the fist of a Commander and a longer list of enemies.

But now, as time crept on, with a wiggling tooth and blood running down her throat, she couldn't help but feel the anxiety creep in. There was no prison big enough to hold her list of crimes now and they had been relatively careful to preserve her body. So, whatever was coming next had to be some fate she couldn't stomach imagining.

The whispers of the soldiers couldn't travel through the ship's black Graviminium walls, the metal impenetrable to both loose lips and missiles. So despite Belle's attempts to eavesdrop, she found herself lost as ever.

She rattled her handcuffs against the bar and banged her ankles on the floor until they went numb. The guard to her left rolled his eyes.

"Stop that," he said, holding his bandaged hand close to his chest.

"I have to take a shit," Belle said loudly.

"Not my problem," he said.

"It will be. I have the worst stomach issues and you're standing right there, aren't you? It's gonna be one hell of a shift if we all have to stay in a ship that smells like shit."

"You're bluffing. You're just gonna bite me again."

"Oh shut it, Cannes," the soldier to Belle's right said. "We're not supposed to talk with her, remember?"

"Oh what? You're scared of me? Imagine what the others would say."

But she received no response to her retort, so she hung her head backwards. She said a bloody prayer, begging the harsh Mythos her sister clung to to hear her just this once. If not for her, for the safety of Ella. Then when she opened her eyes, she let blood drip onto her feet.

"I was in your spot before. I was a soldier. I did it to feed my family. I don't blame you for being here. You and I both know it's basically the only way to survive. But they had me transporting slaves-children! I wouldn't do that. So I rescued them and I joined them-"

"Shut up!" The soldier on the left roared as he approached her. "You're a terrorist! You killed Hinley!"

"Cannes!"

But it was enough for Belle to wrap her calves around his and catch him off-balance. He tumbled to the ground. Then she shifted her hips upwards so that she suspended herself and bent her legs out of the chains. She stood as the soldier did, landing a solid kick to his mouth. His partner approached as he stumbled back, but shouting from outside caught them both off guard.

Belle wrapped her thighs around the soldier's throat as she rested on his shoulders. He pried at her legs, and the other man finally trained his gun on her. She grinned.

"Do it," She taunted. "And risk hitting your partner."

Smoke and rose creeped into her nose, and she pressed her tongue to her cheek. As the soldier beneath her slumped to the ground and the other pressed his finger to the trigger, the door to the ship swung open. A pair of hands yanked the man from the ship. Then, Perri stuck her head in.

"Hey there! You can't just go and assassinate people without me!"

## Thirty-Nine

# Get in Losers, We're Going to Commit More Felonies

"Hurry up, get up!" Perri shouted as Najah unlocked Belle's handcuffs. The assassin practically shoved the Human up towards the cockpit. "We don't have much time!"

"Where's Ella?" Belle cried. She fell into the pilot's seat, her stomach churning. Her fingers trembled as she hit the buttons ingrained in her muscle memory. The base had been no match for her companions. But she paid no mind to the carnage behind her. Instead, she desperately searched for her sister.

"Can you get anything?" Cambrie called out as they tossed the guards' bodies out of the airship. The mix of unconscious and dead rather ungracefully tumbled down the stairs to the cement below.

"Not from this one either!" Perri huffed as she let Cambrie take the last guard away. "I can get in their heads, but they know nothing."

"Where's Ella? I'm not leaving until someone tells me where she is!" Belle shouted, her heart in her throat. Ella couldn't be dead.

"Well we know she's in Inanis!" Cambrie replied as the stairs retracted into the ship and they shut the door.

Najah, with her hands bloodied, held one of the pilot's severed fingers out to Belle. Belle closed her eyes, trying to process everything that had happened within the past five minutes. Najah shook her head and held the finger to the fingerprint scanner on the dash.

"What?" Belle paused, letting shock run over her. She paused in her button clicking. "What do you mean?"

"Get this thing in the air then we can talk!" Perri shouted. "C'mon! They'll be sending in reinforcements! We're not gonna be any use to anyone if they catch us!"

"What's going on!" Belle shouted as she pushed a few more buttons. The plane began to move along the runway. She turned around to stare at her companions as the autopilot took over.

Cambrie took the seat beside Belle, elbows on their knees. "Ella called me after you did and said that she was going after you. Then, it was as if the line was cut, and when we got to the safehouse, there were signs that she had been kidnapped. We strongly think she's still alive though. All the signs were there. We're thinking she's at the Egg."

"Ella's at the Egg?" Dots spotted Belle's vision as the news rolled over her. Somewhere along the way, she had to have hit her head. It made no sense. She couldn't have gotten dragged there.

Perri stared at the floor as she heard Belle's voice break. All confirmation had pointed that Belle had been headed there too had they not found her ship still idling on the runway. She was still trying to reckon with that fact, to force it to make sense in the grand scheme of things. But she shook her head as her communicator rang against her thigh. Finn's number popped up against the screen.

"You have to come to the Manor now," he rasped into the receiver as soon as she accepted the call.

"What's going on? Do you know where Ella is?"

"Pythoness something is-" the line went dead as gunshots echoed in the distance.

"Go to the Manor!" Perri screeched.

"But Ella-" Belle began.

"Now! She's there! She has to be!"

Najah and Cambrie's faces had frozen as they overheard the gunshots, but Najah slowly nodded in agreement.

"Go," she whispered.

Belle shakily adjusted the ship's course, swallowing hard. She gasped for air, wondering if there would ever be a moment for her to breathe freely again.

"It has to be connected," Perri breathed. The space between her ribs ached with concern, not just for the Ella, but for her lover and her mother as well. She cradled her head in her hands.

Najah sank down beside her, placing a hand on her shoulder.

After a few moments, Perri rubbed her face. She couldn't sit in the anxiety anymore. She needed action. "So, how are we going to do this?"

She was met with silence and exhausted eyes.

Finally, Najah spoke up. "I don't know, but we're gonna fight like hell."

There was a murmur of agreement from the rest of them before Belle's shoulders sank and she spoke up.

"Look, I know that I've been a lot to deal with and what I did today was stupid. But I really do appreciate you coming and you all looking after Ella."

"This is what friends do, right?" Najah replied.

"Yeah, I'm pretty sure since Ella named us something cool now, you're kinda stuck with us," Perri smiled.

Cambrie gave a small smile. "Yeah, we need you."

"Would've been nice if you actually hit Triton though," Perri smirked. "Aren't you supposed to have a really good aim?"

"I didn't even get a single shot out," Belle groaned. "Speaking of which, I don't suppose you have-" Najah handed Belle a spare gun. It was heavy in the Human's palm. "Thanks."

Perri clutched the knife in her palm, the handle rubbing against her ring. It still sat heavy on her finger. It was supposed to be a symbol of love but it was more like a painful promise that if any of this went south, he would pay the price.

As they began their descent, they readied their weapons. In the night, they glinted like death itself. Cambrie touched Najah's hand, trying to convey their thoughts without saying them aloud. And for a moment, as Najah smiled back and squeezed their hand back, it seemed like she returned them.

"There's no room to park this without destroying the neighborhood unless we land on the lawn," Belle muttered.

"There's no one..." Perri whispered as she stared out the window. "There should be people down there."

"Just park it on the lawn. They're obviously waiting for us. Might as well make an entrance," Cambrie shrugged, voice higher pitched than normal.

"Where are the guards?" Najah asked as the ship began to hover over the Manor lawn.

"There are none," Perri responded, her breath catching in her chest.

As the ship touched down on the lawn, the Novulan readied themselves. And while it should have come as a relief that no one came running, they only felt the cold brush of a deadly omen.

"Where are they?" Perri asked, her voice frenzied. "Where are the guards? Where's Finn? My mom?"

"Where's Ella?" Belle cried.

Their feet pounded against the grass still slick with the summer rain as soon as the door opened. An unnatural heat coursed through the midnight air. Only the slap of the Inanis flag against the metal pole echoed in their eardrums.

Najah ran through a mental list of all of the security systems they should have set off, and with each one she listed, the tighter her chest became. The yard only seemed to double in length with each step she took, her body desperate for some clue.

That's when the stench hit her nose. It was faint at first, but unmistakable, and she only grew more sure as she ran closer. Absolute carnage came tumbling down the front steps. There was a reason no one had come running after all.

She doubled over as the smell forced itself on her tongue. She could practically taste the flesh, the blood, and it was vile. She vomited with enough force that she hoped the memory would abandon her mind along with the bile.

Belle's legs gave way as she saw the hall of bodies. Dozens of unidentifiable corpses lay charred, piled on top of each other as if they had clamored for an exit none of them had reached. Any one of these bodies could have been Ella.

"No! No!" she screamed as the shards of her glass heart fell apart and shattered yet again.

Cambrie fell to their knees beside her, grabbing her by the shoulders. "It's not her," they hissed. "Stop screaming, you're gonna give us away! Get up. Get up! Please, it's not her. He wouldn't bring her here to kill her like this."

They hauled Belle to her feet like a doll, fully supporting the Human against them. The adrenaline was doing wonders to numb their mind from these horrors. It would be filed away to be put on replay another day. But for now, they just had to find the source of the carnage.

Further down the hall, Najah realized, among obscene amounts of ash, were victims who hadn't been granted the mercy of an instantaneous death. Organs had been strewn across the floor, blood caked onto the wallpaper. A few bodies had been butchered without a care for the pain they endured. A face had been cut completely from someone's head like some sick halloween mask. There was no hunger, no desire in this slaughter, only brutality.

As Perri stood, a realization hit her. "Triton can't do this, wouldn't do this. He'd never ruin his house like this, would never kill his entire guard-especially not like this. He's not one to make messes." As if to emphasize her point, she stared up to where someone had been impaled on the chandelier above her, their blood dripping onto the floor.

Just then the slamming of a door reverberated through the halls and an all too familiar voice shouted which made everyone's blood run cold.

"Where is she?!"

"I don't know!"

The group flew towards the sound. Then, Perri's body went numb and she disappeared into thin air.

## Forty

# PRODIGAL SUN AND THE LAST SUPPER

The dining table stood forgotten, a testament to the better days. Remnants of table linens floated in the air like macabre confetti. A dismembered arm lay across a silver platter. Dark liquor bottles had shattered, causing the vice with a temptress' tongue to pool onto the mosaic tile, delicately admired no more. It wrapped around sodden ankles with a loving touch, shards of glass embedded into skin.

However, Perri had no time to take in the scenery as she had reappeared close to her father, who had the barrel of his gun pointed at her boyfriend's head.

Momentary confusion was replaced with abject horror as the ammo left the barrel. Finn fell to the floor in an unceremonial slump. But before Triton could take his quivering finger off the trigger, his face furrowed in a way that asked a thousand questions, a wave of energy rolled off Perri and sent him flying. She couldn't care. The screams that left her lips were that of a feral incomprehensible beast. She would be the one who would kill him.

"You killed him! You killed Anna!" The words resounded through-out the city itself as she stalked forward.

"What are you?" Triton muttered as he sat up and braced himself against the arched wall, trying to stand. He clutched his head as blood seeped through his fingertips. Then, he watched with horror as his daughter's bloodlust curled around the handle of a knife. "Please, I'm your-"

The room darkened. Perrianna Nextulus towered over her father and plunged her knife into his throat.

As he slumped back down to the floor with a gurgle, she followed his movement. He tried to grab the knife but Perri was much faster. She yanked the knife from his throat and plunged it into his heart. It took nothing to kill such a powerful man, but her sorrow and fury didn't dissipate through the blade. So she stabbed him again. And again.

His blood sprayed against her forehead as she buried the weapon into his chest once more. She had to feel something, anything, other than this. This had to fix everything. This had to make up for everyone she had lost.

The macabre display only ended when the others swarmed into the room, weapons readied for a battle that already finished. But the weight of a thousand unanswered questions still pressed against the gilded ceiling with enough force that it threatened to crumble. And from somewhere deep within the entrails of the Manor came crashing, rumbling-as if the place itself was a beast awoken.

"Where is she?" Belle shouted, her voice strained.

"We'll find her," Najah said. "But first-"

"What happened here?" Elisa Nextulus cut in, her voice still the soft and smooth honey it was before. "Perri?"

"Mom?" Perri dropped the knife, her body trembling. Her voice cracked as she stared at her bloodied hands. "Please. It's not what it looks like. He killed them. He killed Finn, he killed Anna. I had to. He was controlling everyone-"

"I know." And with that sentence the woman of glass let her edges crack and slice open the stunned minds of the others. "And I know right now you're hurting and you all want answers, but we should figure out what caused the damage outside."

"You knew?" Perri picked up the knife again, a flame reignited with her. Tears clouded her vision. "You fucking knew? Were you helping him? You were helping him, weren't you?" She was at her mother's throat in an instant. Blood filled her mouth as she bit her tongue in order to keep from digging the blade into delicate flesh. "Give me one reason why I shouldn't fucking kill you."

"I don't think she's-" Najah began, mind reeling back to that night at the ball.

"We still need to find Ella!" Belle cried. "Do you know anything about my sister?"

"Do you really think I would help him? I only just found out." Elisa said, brushing stray hair from Perri's face as she completely ignored Belle. "You're my daughter. Besides, the more I uncover about his plans, the more horrendous they are. He hired that assassin to kill you, you know. I never wanted to play any part in this. Please, believe me." It was her mother, *her mother,* standing before her. She wasn't capable of working with Triton. She couldn't be. She couldn't.

Perri's head swiveled from her mother to Najah and back to her mother, biting her lip. She recoiled from the woman before her, trying to make desperate sense of it all. "But you...your Alcorium...was it-?" Perri began. But she was cut off by the doors to the dining room swinging open.

If one were to look through cracked kaleidoscopic windows, perhaps they could see the resemblance of Ella beneath the emotionless golden tattooed husk of a girl. But as she stood there in the doorway all bruised and branded, there was little sign of the ray of sunshine. Except for, that is, interwoven in the tattoos along her arms.

As Ella walked into the room, she paid no mind as she passed by her friends still standing near the door, nor to her sister, or Triton's corpse against the wall. Instead, she left a trail of bloody footprints behind her as she began to approach Perri and Elisa.

"What did they do to you?" Belle cried before Ella could reach them. "Who did this?"

"Be careful-" Cambrie warned.

But it was already too late. Without even so much as a flicker of recognition, Ella stopped and reached her palm out towards her sister. The space about six feet to Belle's left flickered with a zap of electricity and the scent of burning foliage filled the air as a large flower arrangement burst into flames.

It all began clicking into place. It was never a monster that killed everyone here. It was never Triton. It was a new Vitare, unable to control her powers. It was Ella. Their Ella.

"What did they do to her?" Belle screamed, her voice already having reached a frenzied pitch. "Ella please! It's me! I'm your sister!"

Heartbreak suddenly painted life in the hue of a particularly cruel harlequin. As the dining chairs caught fire, Cambrie tackled Belle and held her close.

Najah used her vines to bind Ella's arms to her sides. Perri broke free from her mother's side and reached for the girl's hand. But it was as if she were touching molten lava. The pain was agonizing. She cradled her fingers to her chest, her vision spotting. The vines were already withering away when Perri grit her teeth and fell into Ella's mind.

As the Siren stood in the dark abyss, a chill crept up her spine. There were no waves of memories threatening to overtake her. Only solitary words hung in the highest corners like spiderwebs, creaking out murderous intent:

*Kill. Kill.*

The translucent threads that formed the loops of the *l*s were fragile, as if these thoughts weren't fully formed. Perri had never heard of anything like it. She reached out as if to grab them but the words only floated higher. She had been inside the mind of a Vitare once during her training, and knew neither they nor Najah were anything like this. No. This was beyond the mind of someone without emotion. It was someone without memory, without any conscious thought.

The dusty air threatened to choke Perri as she ran through the possibilities in that dim place. It couldn't be that Ella was a Vitare now. It had to be the Alcorium they used. If they could just remove the Alcorium then maybe...

Perri withdrew back into her own body and conveyed those instructions to the others who were simultaneously dodging attacks from Ella and trying not to let the room burn around them.

Najah wrapped her vines around the girl after making sure they were sufficiently coated in the most potent rose oil she could make. As Ella numbly stumbled to the ground, Perri dove after her and reached for the Alcorium hidden behind her braids. Perri shouted all the words she knew to release the device but they all began to feel like desperate prayers to forgotten deities. As she tried to slip her nails between plastic and skin, she realized it was as if the implant had been welded to the skull.

The iron chandelier creaked as the ceiling around them cracked. The vines around Ella shriveled away once more just as she got to her feet and dozens of metal objects came flying across the room.

Perri rolled out of the way as a particularly large fish statue nearly impaled her. Knives were pulled from waistbands. Cutlery was picked up from the floor. Even hardware was pulled off the door and made to join the growing atmosphere of objects swirling around Ella. Cambrie cried out as a trident from off the wall ripped through their leg. They cradled the injury, bone sticking out through the pierced flesh. Then, just for a moment, everything stopped spinning.

Ella waved her hands and everything flew away from her at breakneck speed. Everyone dove to the floor as the chandelier crashed into the center of the room. A dozen knives embedded themselves into the wall.

From the back of the room, Elisa screamed as a knife tore into her arm. Tearfully she cried out: "You're not going to be able to stop her! She killed all the guards!" She gripped her arm tight, keeping an eye on Ella as Perri made a beeline for her.

"Get out of here Mom! Get somewhere safe. I'll find you when this is all over, I promise," Perri said between gritted teeth.

"Come with me, please. You don't need them. You don't belong with them. If you come with me I'll..."

"No. I need to do this! Go!" As Perri turned, she was hit with Belle's look of utter dismay.

Belle had known deep down. It was only a matter of time. But, she could have sworn she saw Ella hesitate. Tears slid down her cheeks. She had felt the gun slip from her fingers into the magnetic field. So, Belle faced her sister. She didn't try to move. She didn't beg. For a moment, their eyes met.

Then Ella pulled the trigger.

# Acknowledgements

I grew up knowing nothing aside from the fact that I was destined to be an author. This book is every dream I have ever had. There are no words to describe the emotions that I feel writing this final page. However, I wouldn't have been able to accomplish this without a team of amazing people by my side.

First, to my parents. Thank you for nurturing my creativity and allowing me to find my spark. I don't know if I'll ever be able to repay you for investing in my early writing career by driving me to writing camp each summer and buying me every book I ever desired. Mom, thank you for teaching me that reading is the best form of magic. You were right. Thank you also for being my harshest writing critic. It only drove me to write better stories. Without you, this would have released long before it was ready. Dad, thank you for being my number one fan even at my worst times, and for counting coins at the kitchen table with me so I could fund this dream.

To my best friend and partner in crime, Olly, thank you. You watched this story blossom from individual Wattpad novellas to this, which truly, is impressive. You've brought this world to life with your gorgeous artwork so often. But most importantly, you've stood by me through the good times and the bad. I am the person I am today because of you. There is no one else I would ever want to ride this wave with me. I love you. P.S. thank you for your biology info-dumping and the knowledge of snail teeth.

To my editor and best friend, Elaina, thank you for the endless hours of work-but more importantly-love, you have infused into this book. Your never ending support and belief kept me going on all of those long nights. Thank you for always wanting to listen to more of my info-dump sessions, even when you didn't understand what I was talking about. I love you. Kachow.

To my writing buddy Odin, even though you can't read this, thanks for keeping me company through all of those writing sessions. I'm sorry I had to delete all of your very important contributions that came in the form of laying on my laptop. I promise I'll buy you all the treats. I love you stinky butt.

To my therapist, you really deserve more than a book acknowledgment. Thank you for believing in me and ensuring I could achieve this dream.

To you, the reader. Thank you for investing in the story I loved for so long. I hope that now that it's in your hands, it brought you as much joy as it brought me.

Finally, to my younger self, congratulations. You did it kid.

# ABOUT FAYE

Faye Perez (she/they) writes about speculative fiction novels about the heroes that are kept in the dark. She graduated with a B.A. in Sociology from the University of Michigan-Flint, which means they spend far too much time pondering about the state of the world. They're a sucker for queer love stories and putting together oddly specific playlists. When she isn't writing or spending too much time on TikTok, she's hanging out with her dog Odin. Fires in Their Wake is their debut novel.

Find her at www.fayeperez.com